Muna Shehadi's enthralling and evocative novels
have been richly praised:

'Her vivid characters walk right off the page and into your heart'
VICKI LEWIS THOMPSON

'I absolutely *adored* this beautiful book. Profoundly moving and very wise, this stunningly original and touching tale is one to savour and re-read . . . So very beautiful and thought provoking on so many levels, this is a must read for everyone, a wonderfully absorbing tale that I guarantee will make you think, question and change . . . An immersive delight of a book'
RENITA D'SILVA

'Very compelling . . . wonderfully heartfelt . . . The unravelling plotline tantalises the reader with its clever twists and turns – impossible to put down!'
SARAH STEELE

'Captivating right out of the gate. This unique and beautifully told tale, laced with mystery and secrets, will keep readers hooked . . . A deeply moving and insightful story that will stay with me for a long time'
ALISON RAGSDALE

'I loved the combination of mystery and love story – every time I put it down, I couldn't wait to get back to it. I really enjoyed Muna's writing style, too'
EMMA ROBINSON

'I was charmed by its feisty heroine who faces physical, intellectual and emotional challenges with such grace and fortitude. And the sensual descriptions of food were an extra treat!'
JULIE BROOKS

'A wonderful read with evocative descriptions and enough family secrets to create a gripping journey of discovery'
WOMAN

Muna Shehadi's lifelong love of reading inspired her to become a writer. Muna grew up in Princeton, New Jersey, and lives on the beautiful coast of Maine, which she couldn't resist featuring in her Fortune's Daughters trilogy. *The Paris Affair* is the first title in her Women of Consequence trilogy.

For more information, visit her website: **munashehadi.com**

By Muna Shehadi

Fortune's Daughters trilogy

The Summer Sister (*previously published as* Private Lies)
The Winter Sister (*previously published as* Hidden Truths)
The Spring Sister (*previously published as* Honest Secrets)

Standalone

The First Wife

Women of Consequence trilogy

The Paris Affair
The Jewel of Cairo

MUNA SHEHADI

THE JEWEL *of* CAIRO

Copyright © Muna Shehadi Sill 2025

The right of Muna Shehadi to be identified as the Author of the Work has been asserted by her in accordance with the Copyright, Designs and Patents Act 1988.

First published in 2025 by Headline Review
An imprint of Headline Publishing Group Limited

1

Apart from any use permitted under UK copyright law, this publication may only be reproduced, stored, or transmitted, in any form, or by any means, with prior permission in writing of the publishers or, in the case of reprographic production, in accordance with the terms of licences issued by the Copyright Licensing Agency.

All characters in this publication are fictitious and any resemblance to real persons, living or dead, is purely coincidental.

Cataloguing in Publication Data is available from the British Library

Trade Paperback ISBN 978 1 0354 0780 4

Typeset in Sabon by CC Book Production

Printed and bound in Great Britain by
Clays Ltd, Elcograf S.p.A.

Headline's policy is to use papers that are natural, renewable and recyclable products and made from wood grown in well-managed forests and other controlled sources. The logging and manufacturing processes are expected to conform to the environmental regulations of the country of origin.

HEADLINE PUBLISHING GROUP LIMITED
An Hachette UK Company
Carmelite House
50 Victoria Embankment
London EC4Y 0DZ

The authorised representative in the EEA is Hachette Ireland,
8 Castlecourt Centre, Dublin 15, D15 XTP3, Ireland
(email: info@hbgi.ie)

www.headline.co.uk
www.hachette.co.uk

To my father, Fadlou Shehadi,
for opening my eyes to so much of the world

Author's Note

Alma Phil was born in Moscow in 1888 to a family of jewelers. A talented artist, she was hired as a draftsman by the House of Fabergé in St Petersburg at the age of twenty. Her job there was to enter detailed drawings of the jewelry produced into a log book, along with material costs and hours. In her spare time she made entirely self-taught sketches of her own designs. Her uncle, master jeweler Albert Holmström, happened on those sketches and was so impressed he brought them to the attention of the sales department. Her pieces were put into immediate production.

Alma's career skyrocketed when a Fabergé client, Emmanuel Nobel, requested quick delivery of forty brooches of unique design, to be distributed to his dinner guests in their table napkins. Sitting by the window on a January day, Alma was inspired by frost formations on the glass to produce six intricate snowflake designs. These inspired a whole line of jewelry and eventually led to a commission for an Imperial egg, a gift from Tsar Nicholas II to his mother, the dowager empress. The Winter Egg, glowing white in Siberian rock crystal with zigzags of miniature diamond 'frost', opened to a springtime basket of wood anemones carved from white quartz.

The following year Alma received another royal commission, this time an egg for the tsar's wife. The Mosaic Egg was a colorful jeweled marvel inspired by the minuscule squares of Alma's mother-in-law's cross-stitch. Inside the egg, a medallion with the faces of the tsar and tsarina's five children painted in profile.

In 1917, the Russian Revolution forced the closure of the House of Fabergé and cut short Alma's promising career. She fled with her husband to Finland, where she taught German and art and inspired a new generation of devoted students, who had no idea of her former illustrious career until years after her death in 1976.

The jeweled blue 'lotus flower' egg in this book is my own fabrication.

THE JEWEL of CAIRO

Prologue

In July of 1915, Ibrahim Sayed, the immensely wealthy Cairo jeweler, contacts the House of Fabergé in St Petersburg, Russia, to commission a jeweled egg, one of those most famously associated with tsars Alexander III and Nicholas II. It is to be a tenth-anniversary present for his Greek wife, Cora. He requests that the egg be designed by Alma Pihl, the only female ever to have created one of the Imperial eggs. Ibrahim would like this egg to fit into a piece he already owns, a model of Apollo's chariot, commissioned from a young jeweler on the Greek island of Crete. The chariot's base holds a secret compartment in which he hid his wife's engagement ring when he proposed. He asks that the key to this hiding place be disguised in the egg's interior.

Fabergé agrees to the commission, and Alma designs an egg incorporating Egyptian elements with a shape and decorations to complement those of the chariot. A twist of the jeweled and enameled falcon top causes the egg to open like the petals of a lotus flower, revealing a tiny king and queen wearing enamel robes and the traditional crowns of the pharaohs. The queen holds a bouquet of ruby roses, the king an ornate scepter, cleverly made from the key to the carriage's hidden drawer.

When the egg arrives in Cairo in 1916, specially delivered by an emissary from the House of Fabergé, Ibrahim is delighted. On the anniversary day, he takes his wife out of the heat of Cairo to El Alamein on the Mediterranean shore for a feast he has arranged to be served in a private tent, flaps left open to catch the salty breeze. When the meal is nearly over, he retrieves the egg. For my queen, he says, bursting with excitement, and bows, handing over the little box. Cora chuckles and ruffles his hair affectionately, accusing him of flattery. When she opens the present, she is stunned and deeply touched by the egg's beauty, then teasingly says she doesn't deserve anything so extravagant and pretends to be cross with him. He can see she is enchanted, and that night they make love with more than their usual passion.

To the everlasting grief of his devoted wife, Ibrahim dies in 1934, at the age of fifty-three.

On her own deathbed decades later, Cora gives the egg and carriage to their son, Fadil, who has taken over the Sayed jewelry business with his wife, Leila. She also entrusts him with the secret of the hidden carriage compartment and its unique key.

To their sorrow, Fadil and Leila are able to conceive only one child, Sami, the light of his mother's life, the despair of his father's. Sami is charming, handsome, lazy, opportunistic and not above playing chameleon with his beliefs and values to get what he wants. Fadil often despairs about passing their shop on to a Sayed who doesn't value the family business.

However, in 1951, when Sami is a teenager, a member of the Egyptian royal family, the beautiful Princess Fawzia, comes into the shop to commission a necklace. Sami is smitten, and Fadil grudgingly allows him to try his hand at designing. Sami comes up with a sketch of such grace and beauty that a proud Fadil awards him the commission, relieved that his son has finally become a true Sayed.

The Jewel of Cairo

Tragically, in January of 1952, during the uprising against the British occupation and those who benefited from it, Fadil and Leila are killed trying to protect their shop from looters and arsonists. The exquisite diamond necklace, completed and awaiting delivery to Princess Fawzia, disappears, presumably stolen. At seventeen, Sami is forced to give up his life of pleasure and take over the business. He never learns the secret of the carriage.

∽ Chapter 1 ∾

Friday, April 9, 1976

Lilianne Maxwell strode briskly through the crowd in Cairo's Tahrir Square. For the month she'd been in Egypt, she'd been escorted everywhere by colleagues who insisted foreign women should not go out alone. Breakfast, lunch and dinner, mornings, afternoons, evenings, all were fair game for the invitations that poured in, from her father's friends in diplomatic or business circles, from higher-ups at the Cairo National Bank, from Egyptian government officials eager for American business involvement, even from the family across the hall in her apartment building.

Egyptian hospitality was legendary. But today, a glorious Friday afternoon with the city calling as loudly as her wanderlust, Lilianne had declined all invitations and succeeded in sneaking out, thrilled to be on her own.

The thrill hadn't lasted long. Lilianne's genes had stubbornly ignored her mother's Egyptian blood in favor of her father's Anglo-Saxon coloring – back in her mother's bloodline, an Abdallah must have married a Jorgensson. Tall and blonde, she attracted male attention everywhere she went, even when conservatively dressed in the beige linen suit she'd worn to work, even wearing dark glasses to avoid eye contact. Obviously non-native, she was also an immediate target for people persistently trying to sell jewelry and souvenirs.

Through Cairo's familiar chaos, she passed between the black stone lions guarding the entrance to the Qasr el Nil bridge. Car horns honked incessantly in the ubiquitous traffic as their drivers jockeyed and maneuvered for space, ignoring lanes, signs and signals in a series of constant near-misses that would terrify even a New York cab driver. A bus inched by, packed so full that the dozen or so men on its rear platform had to lean out to fit. As it passed, two more men ran to grab the offered hands that swung them up to find invisible footholds on board.

Ignoring the usual comments and come-ons from the predominantly male bus passengers, Lilianne continued on to the bridge, stopping halfway to gaze at the river, the lifeblood of the country. On arrival into Cairo, she had seen from her airplane window the Nile's fertile valley, resembling a narrow green stem through brown desert, eventually blooming into the delta that emptied into the Mediterranean. Here on the ground, the river was wide and glorious, conveying sailboats and barges past the apartments, palaces and hotels crowding its banks.

Half of Lilianne belonged here. Her mother, a native Cairene, had fled the city's tight embrace aged eighteen, for the relative freedom and openness of the US, a move that caused a complete break with her disapproving family. Somewhere in this crowded, remarkable sprawl lived strangers closely related by blood. Grandparents, uncles, cousins . . .

A man stopped next to her, complimenting her fair complexion in broken English. A small group of grinning teenagers blocked her escape route, proffering beads and statuary: 'Special price for you, beautiful lady.' Lilianne cut them off in fluent Arabic, pushed through and kept walking. Heartless, but there were so many needy and only one of her.

On the other side of the bridge lay Zamalek, an island dividing the Nile, home to embassies, stores, restaurants, gardens, sports fields and the Cairo Tower, a phallic upthrust decorated with lotus-flower lattice stonework, built in the 1950s by then-president Gamal Nasser as a symbol of Egyptian pride.

At the top, Lilianne was rewarded not only with a break from the harassment and crowds below, but with a breathtaking view of the city, bisected by the glittering river, sprawling toward the distant pyramids, its horizon spiked with minarets that five times a day sent out the *adhan*, or call to prayer. A fascinating mix of ancient, medieval and modern, fading into hazy eternity.

Her eyes drifted guiltily toward Shubra, where her mother, Dina Abdallah, had grown up. Lilianne hadn't yet told the Abdallahs she was in town. Her mother had made it sound as if once Lilianne contacted them, not a moment of her time would be her own. Not only that, they'd disapprove of everything she was and everything she'd done, and would try to change her.

Granted, Mom had a particular point of view, but since graduating from college, Lilianne had been fiercely independent, and the idea of becoming enmeshed in the sticky web of a family she barely knew did not appeal.

Yet now, looking out toward their neighborhood, she couldn't help wondering about her grandparents, Zahra and Braheem, about Mom's brothers, Khaled and Ramy, all of whom Lilianne had encountered only in black and white, reluctantly shared images from her mother's photo album. Over the past month, there had been times Lilianne felt she could sense her relatives, like phantom limbs, reminding her of what belonged to her but was not present.

She should call. If only she weren't so busy . . .

Back at street level, Lilianne strode through the Al Zohriya gardens, longing to slow down and savor the green spaces being enjoyed by Egyptian families escaping concrete and noise. But, like a shark, she needed to keep moving to avoid drowning in the sucking turbulence of men and peddlers.

Wearing her best 'don't-mess-with-me' expression, she passed the grounds of the Zamalek Sporting Club and headed toward the elegant Omar Khayyam Hotel, one of the oldest in the city, a palace built in 1869 by the reputedly wastrel leader of Egypt, the khedive Isma'il Pasha. The building beckoned as a respite from the overstimulation of the city, a place where Lilianne could sip a drink and be deliciously ignored.

The Khayyam was a fantasy in stone at the Nile's edge, a splendid mix of Arabic and European influences. Carved marble and latticed wood, hanging metal lanterns and crystal chandeliers, Oriental carpets and decorative ceilings, French Empire furniture and paintings, a style symptomatic of a country looking to define itself after decades of colonization.

Lilianne sank into a seat in the elegant bar room, breathing in the quiet, and ordered a Scotch and an *International Herald Tribune.* Along with the drink and paper, the waiter brought a dish of olives with a small bowl of *labneh* and the ubiquitous *baladi* bread, a thicker version of pita sold fresh daily at government-subsidized prices from donkey-drawn carts throughout the city's neighborhoods.

As she sipped her Scotch, tearing off pieces of *baladi* to scoop up the addictive combination of briny olives and creamy, tangy *labneh,* she skimmed the headlines. Fire in a Malaysian shopping complex, NFL draft starting in the US, a sunken cargo ship off the coast of Greece.

A throat-clearing made her glance over. Two tables away, a man expensively dressed in a tan linen suit with a white shirt and paisley silk tie was immersed in the sameissue of the *Tribune* she was reading. His thick hair was neatly combed, his skin a deep gold with the permanent five o'clock shadow of hair too dark to be invisible. Very handsome. Just as Lilianne was about to turn away, he met her gaze. She tensed, but he only smiled, nodded a greeting and went back to his reading.

Relieved, Lilianne finished the paper and her snack, paid her tab and wandered into the palm-tree-lined hotel courtyard, weighing the annoyance of further pestering if she ventured out again against the pleasures of discovering a new neighborhood.

As she stood undecided, the evening call to prayer – the *Maghrib* – filled the air, dominated by a nearby mosque, the sound overlapping with dozens of other prayer calls from mosques throughout the city, a mesmerizing cacophony that never failed to elicit in Lilianne an emotional response.

She leaned against a marble column, closed her eyes and let the hauntingly exotic tonality fill her. *Allah is great. I testify that there is no god but Allah. I testify that Muhammad is the messenger of Allah. Come to prayer. Come to salvation. Allah is great. There is no god but Allah.*

When the last echo faded, Lilianne roused herself and consulted her map, feeling, rather fancifully, as if the call had carried a message for her along with the faithful. She'd walk, even if she had to resort to combat.

'May I be of some assistance?' The words were pronounced in the perfectly enunciated English peculiar to foreign speakers.

Lilianne looked into the dark eyes of the man who'd been sitting near her in the bar. Had he followed her, or was this a coincidence?

'Thank you.' She smiled tightly. 'I'd like to explore Zamalek, but I'm not sure of the best route.'

'If you will permit, I'd be delighted to play guide and escort. Zamalek is safer than some of the city, but it can be difficult for women to walk alone in Cairo.'

'So I've noticed.'

'But you walk alone anyway.' His eyes crinkled in a grin. He wore the air of someone who knew he was attractive, though he stood at a respectful distance and his eye contact had none of the appraising 'how-do-I-get-in' quality of a predator. Lilianne guessed he was ten years older than her, which would put him around forty. 'Very brave.'

'Brave or foolish, often the same thing.'

'Forgive me for not introducing myself. I am Sami Sayed, third-generation owner of a jewelry shop on Brazil Street, here in Zamalek. We Sayeds are an old and respected Cairo family. My mother taught me good manners and respect for women. Both are at your service.' He clicked his heels and gave a slight bow, an old-fashioned gesture that charmed her.

Lilianne had been told about – and experienced – the extraordinary friendliness, hospitality and generosity of Egyptians toward friends and strangers alike. In New York City, a guy offering to show a woman around would be given a suspicious dismissal. The gesture here was more routine politeness. She folded her map, musing on the irony of having to be with someone in order to feel independent. 'Thank you, Mr Sayed. You're kind to offer.'

'It will be my pleasure.' He held out his hand. 'You must call me Sami.'

'Lilianne Maxwell.' She liked his handshake, firm and brief. 'You must call me Lilianne.'

'Lovely to meet you, Lilianne.' He extended his arm gracefully toward the street. '*Et fadaleh.*'

'Thank you.'

'Do you speak Arabic?'

'Some.' The lie came easily, her protective instinct at work. The less he knew about her the better. She'd studied Arabic since college, to honor the heritage her mother did her best to deny, and counted herself as decently fluent.

'What brings you to Cairo, Lilianne?'

'I'm here for work.'

'What kind of work do you do?'

'I'm a senior analyst for a US investment firm.' Her father's company, Maxwell Investments.

Sami's eyebrows nearly shot off the top of his forehead. 'Senior analyst! I'm impressed.'

If she were a man, he wouldn't have blinked. 'And you own a jewelry store.'

'Yes, I own the store, and the store owns me. I grew up in an apartment above it, as did my parents and their parents. We Sayeds can't stay away from the gems.'

A bitter note in his tone told her there was more he wasn't saying, but she stayed silent, walking toward the Nile under the 26 July Corridor bridge, where they encountered an elaborate brick residence. Sami told her it had been the home of Aisha Fahmy, sister of Ali Fahmy, who'd built the palace and lived in it until his murder in 1923 by his wife, a former Parisian courtesan. Scandal! Next to it, a magnificent neo-Gothic mansion built early in the century by a Frenchman, currently housing the Venezuelan Embassy. 'Many of the old palaces along the Nile are embassies now. They give our little island quite the panache.'

He took her elbow to cross the street, since doing so was a matter of stepping out into the never-ending line of cars and hoping you didn't get killed. Lilianne allowed his touch, but was pleased he released her when they reached safety on the opposite curb.

'You've never left Cairo? For school or maybe jewel-shopping?'

'I have gone in search of good stones and good deals, yes. But to live? If you asked my parents, they'd say you might as well ask Adam and Eve if they wanted to move from Eden.' He winked. 'I have great plans for someday, *inshallah* – God willing. I would like to travel more, not be so tied to the shop. For now, it's a good life, an honorable life at a good moment for our country. Ah, you must try this.'

He'd stopped at a cart selling charcoal-roasted sweet potatoes and bought one after haggling officiously with the man over the price, which seemed more than reasonable to Lilianne.

Sami handed her the steaming potato, stuck with two forks so they could share. The orange flesh was smoky, tender and sweet. 'You like this?'

'I like this.' She took a second bite to show her approval. 'Where would you go if you left here?'

'Ah, that's easy. Paris first. City of light and love.'

Lilianne stopped eating, struck by a pang of homesickness. She'd just spent two of the best years of her life in Paris, for the last several months surrounded by three people she'd become closer to than any she could remember. Connie Pappas, colorful flower-child – still in Paris, but knowing her hummingbird nature, not for long. Helen Kenyon, shy, sheltered Midwesterner who'd blossomed during her all-too-short time in France. She and Lilianne had parted bitterly over the handsome, brilliant photojournalist Gilles Aubert, whom Helen had fallen madly in love with, and he with her. What should have been a happy ending was ruined by Helen's cowardly decision to return to her farmer fiancé in Kansas. Connie had been philosophical. Lilianne had been furious. Watching Helen and Gilles together, the natural way they complemented each other, the joy they took in spending time together, had finally given Lilianne an inkling of what romantic love could be. Before that, the concept had seemed messy, complicated and unnecessary. 'I lived there before I came to Cairo.'

'I envy you.' Sami patted his heart. 'Such a beautiful place. So civilized. Everything Egypt should be but can't quite manage.'

'Why do you think that is?'

He shot her a look. 'Egyptians.'

They wandered on. With Sami next to her, Lilianne was finally able to look around more comfortably. Zamalek, like so much of Cairo, was a mixture, old and modern, rich and poor. All around, reminders of the ancient city, intricately carved entrance doors, some half open to reveal stone courtyards, some with enormous decorative lanterns hanging ready to light the entryway. Now and then a stray cat – the pigeons of Cairo – would skulk across their path.

And everywhere food! Souped-up cafés for diplomat lunches next to carts selling fruit or counter kitchens selling chips, falafel and fried dough balls soaked in syrup. Men dominated the streets, in groups or singly, but there were women as well, in groups or with men, nearly all in jeans or other Western clothing. Among them, a healthy scattering of foreigners, probably embassy personnel as well as tourists from all over the world, walking the same city Egyptians had been walking since thousands of years before Christ. A humbling thought.

Everywhere they were greeted as if they were old friends. Men joked with Sami, welcomed Lilianne to Egypt, to Cairo, shopkeepers handed her samples of whatever they were making, invited her to taste more, asked her how she liked their country and city. The street felt like a community she'd become part of simply by being there. This was exactly what she'd been after when she'd naïvely left the office that afternoon – some sense of the city outside of the carefully curated outings she'd been taken on since she arrived.

In between Sami's lessons on the history of Zamalek, first populated by royal palace workers, then gradually taken over and renovated by the wealthy, they ate food Sami insisted Lilianne try from what he assured her were the neighborhood's top spots. *Koshary*, Egypt's national dish, consisting of spiced rice, pasta and lentils doused with tomato sauce, topped with chickpeas and crisp fried onions, then laced with garlic vinegar for a superb mixture of tastes, temperatures and textures. *Ta'ameya*, Egyptian falafel, made with fava beans instead of chickpeas, tucked into *baladi* bread with tomato, pickles, cucumber, onions and parsley, under a blanket of creamy tahini sauce. Just as Lilianne's stomach was about to burst, Sami insisted she try *feteer meshaltet*, an Egyptian layered pastry known for its delicate, flaky texture and rich, buttery taste.

All with Egyptian dinner time only a few hours away. Lilianne was doubly glad she'd claimed tonight for herself.

'How do Egyptians keep from being overweight? I see people eating all day long.'

'That's easy. The rich stay thin to maintain their status, the middle class stay thin to appear rich, and the poor don't have enough to eat.'

Lilianne took the last bite of pastry her stomach could manage. 'There has to be more than that.'

'We have a healthy diet. Much more than Americans, who I think eat only hot dogs and French fries. You can see here and here, and there.' He pointed to two stalls and a cart, each loaded with melons and strawberries, banana-cluster chains dangling from the ceiling, oranges, grapes, dates and a few other fruits Lilianne didn't recognize. 'We eat vegetables and fresh fruit. Ah, the fruit! Wait until summer and autumn, when there will be three times the variety.'

'My mother jokes that in New York if you want to hear someone talk without stopping, ask an Arab cab driver where to get good grapes.'

'Ah yes?' Sami acknowledged the greeting of a man across the street. 'And how does your mother know this?'

'She's Egyptian.'

He stopped walking, eyes even wider than they'd been when Lilianne announced she was an investment banker.

'You are joking?' He pointed to her hair. 'Your father must be, what's the word . . . all white everywhere?'

'Albino? No.'

'Why didn't you tell me this before?'

'Because "Hi, I'm Lilianne, I'm half Egyptian" is a strange way to introduce myself?'

'Half Egyptian!' He slapped his thigh. 'Then we are brother and sister.'

She shrugged, smiling, glad she'd let him show her around. 'Could be.'

A black car with tinted windows slowed and stopped next to them on the narrow street. The back window rolled down to reveal a middle-aged man, prevented from sitting upright by an enormous stomach. His pudgy, freckle-spotted hand emerged from the car, followed by a thin, raspy voice. 'Sami Sayed.'

A character straight from an Egyptian Godfather movie.

Sami clasped the offered hand. 'Abraam Al-Kalib, *al salamu alaykum.*'

'*Wa alaykum al salam.* My friend has a necklace that needs repair. An old one, from her family.'

'I am honored. Please have her come by the store whenever it's convenient. For you and your friends I am always open.' Sami gave his slight bow, and made a move to withdraw his hand, but the man's fleshy fingers must have tightened, because he gave up the effort.

The car behind them honked its displeasure at being blocked.

Al-Kalib's enormous chauffeur got out, folded his massive arms and glared at its driver. The honking stopped.

And cut! That's a wrap. Good work, everyone!

'How's business, Sami?' Al-Kalib's eyes were shrewd and cold.

'Very good, *Alhamdulillah*.'

'Let's hope it stays that way, eh?'

Lilianne took in a quick breath. She was not imagining the threat in those quiet words.

Fascinating.

Sami blanched. 'Yes, yes, *inshallah*.'

The fingers released. The window rolled back up. The chauffeur unwrapped his arms from his manly chest, got into the car and moved on.

Lilianne glanced at Sami, who was straightening his cuff, looking mildly shaken. Was he in some kind of trouble? Mob trouble? Loan shark? Both? 'Who was that?'

His full lips were pinched. 'One of the most powerful men in Cairo.'

'He doesn't look like someone you'd want angry at you.'

'Who does? We cross here.' Sami casually stepped out in front of a car, which slowed without any sign of annoyance from the driver.

She followed his lead, both in crossing the street and dropping the subject of the man in the black car. 'People must be regularly run over here.'

'Not that regularly.' Sami approached a storefront gleaming with gold, and opened the heavy wooden door with his family name lavishly scripted across the interior glass panel. '*Ahlan wa sahlan*, welcome to Sayed's, jewelers to the common people, the middle class, the rich and the royal. Please come in.'

She walked in and nodded to a somber dark-skinned young man lolling behind the counter, who snapped to alarmed attention when he caught sight of her escort.

'Thank you for taking over while I was out, Youssef,' Sami said in Arabic. 'You may go back and finish your work.'

Youssef nodded and disappeared into the back of the shop.

'Your assistant?'

'A talented young man. I still do the design, but he's taken over a lot of the actual workmanship. My eyes aren't what they were when I was twenty. Neither is my patience.'

'Your shop is beautiful.' She wasn't flattering him. This was a far cry from the tourist stuff sold downtown, where shelves were crammed with gilt busts of King Tutankhamun and Queen Hatshepsut, gold bracelets hanging edge to edge, and dense mats of necklaces. The jewelry in Sami's store showed clear loyalty to Egypt, with a predominance of gold, the vibrant blue of lapis lazuli, green emeralds and opalescent pearls in the traditional symbols – ankhs, scarabs, lotus flowers, falcons and snakes. But these pieces had been brought into more modern times, graceful lines that only hinted at the original shapes, or asymmetrical takes on the ancient forms. A set of bracelets with unusual curves that formed a series of overlapping circles on the wearer's arm. A necklace dangling a lapis lazuli scarab whose gold legs extended and blended into a sinuous golden frame. A pin of multi-hued turquoise lotus flowers that tangled with each other in a glittery bouquet.

'Thank you. Many of the pieces are my own work.'

'I'm impressed.'

Sami leaned closer, conspiratorially, though they were alone in the shop. Lilianne was struck again by his clean-shaven good looks: deep-set, nearly black eyes with long lashes under neat brows, a fine high forehead and cheekbones, and a long, sharp-bridged nose. His aftershave was delicate and subtle, his clothes a perfect fit. A very attractive man.

True to her nature, she felt nothing. No interest, no chemistry, no sexual curiosity. Nothing. A shameful and tragic flaw she'd confessed only to one person, which had turned out to be one too many.

'I once designed a necklace for a princess of Egypt. Fawzia, daughter of King Fuad and Queen Nazli. The finest piece I ever created.' His eyes gleamed with pride. 'I was sixteen and fell madly in love with her the second she walked into our shop. I begged my father to allow me to submit a design. He indulged me by letting me try, but had no intention of choosing my work. I slaved for weeks. A lacework pattern of diamonds in the shape of the Egyptian collar necklace historically worn by royalty, scaled down for her beautiful neck. My father couldn't believe what I'd done, and I couldn't believe he chose it for Fawzia. The proudest moment of my life.'

'She must have loved it.'

'No, this is the tragedy.' He stepped back, his fine features clouding. 'She never saw it. The work had just been finished, then came the riots in 1952 against foreigners in Egypt and against our profligate king. The city was a disaster, our shop burned. Our safe, in the back of the store, was intact, but the necklace was gone. My father must have hidden it elsewhere, or tried to, but both he and my mother were killed in the violence, along with many others, and the necklace never resurfaced.'

'I'm sorry.' She was struck both by the senseless loss of the story and by the dry way Sami recited the words, as if he'd said them so many times they no longer held meaning.

'I haven't forgotten the sounds of those riots, the smell of the fires. The panic at age seventeen when my parents didn't come home and didn't come home . . . What was I to do? How was I to live? It was a terrible day. My parents were dead and I'd let down my princess. Poor boy!'

His mocking tone further surprised her. 'That *is* a terrible day. How did—'

'Life goes on, *Alhamdulillah*, thanks to God.' His eyes came abruptly back to life. 'One day I'll show you what I'm working on upstairs.'

'In your design studio?'

'The shop studio is in the back room there.' He gestured toward the door Youssef had disappeared through. 'Upstairs is my personal studio, in my apartment.'

'Ah.' Lilianne bent her head over a glass case to avoid commenting further. Where she came from, inviting a woman up to your apartment to see your jewels . . . She'd heard that one before.

Her eyes came to rest on a bracelet whose thick gold band parted to embrace a scarab holding two tiny diamonds between its front legs, its head blue from lapis, its body a deep red. On either side, two lotus flowers inlaid with turquoise bloomed from tiny lapis-striped vases.

Lilianne was not that keen on jewelry, rarely saw anything that appealed, but the little beetle had caught her fancy.

'What do you see?'

She pointed. 'That one.'

'Ah! A lady of discerning taste. That's one of my designs. You must try it.' Sami took a ring of keys out of his pocket, unlocked the case and handed her the bracelet.

Lilianne slipped it on. The metal was cool, the colors glowed against her skin, fairer than Sami's, but with the same olive tint.

'In our history, the scarab was associated with the sun god Khepri, a symbol of daily rebirth. The god was believed to roll the sun across the sky. Which is how these little beetles became important. You know what the scarab is also called?'

'No, what?' Lilianne looked up from the bracelet to find Sami's eyes glinting with amusement.

'Dung beetle. They roll their eggs into balls of dung, which they also eat in large quantities. So you see what we Egyptians hold sacred.'

Lilianne laughed, the feeling strange until she realized it had been a while since she'd done so out of more than politeness. 'I think it might go deeper than that.'

'Yes. I don't remember details.' His smile was sheepish and endearing. 'The symbol has thousands of years of precedent in Egypt, so I can't claim to have designed it, only added my own interpretation.'

'It's beautiful.'

He inclined his head. 'I'm honored. And I would be even more honored if you'd let me take you for a real Egyptian dinner tonight. Not the tourist places.'

'Dinner?!' Lilianne put a hand to her stomach. 'I ate enough on our walk here to last me until breakfast.'

'Ah, no.' He lifted a warning finger. 'While you're here, you must learn to eat like an Egyptian.'

Lilianne slid the bracelet off and laid it on the counter, weighing how to phrase her rejection. 'I'm afraid I have dinner plans. And you've already been so generous with your time.'

'It's been nothing but a pleasure.' He went behind the counter and rummaged in a drawer, coming up with a business card he handed to her. 'You're here for a while, though, yes?'

'Until I hear otherwise.' She examined his card, black and white script with a diamond nestled in the Y of his last name, pleased he wasn't pushing harder for her company.

'Come, I will find you a cab.' He walked outside with her toward the river and flagged a taxi within a few minutes. 'Where to?'

'Maadi.'

The driver nodded. Sami slipped him some money and said, in Arabic, 'Treat her like your own daughter or I will hear about it.'

'Thank you, Sami.' Lilianne offered her hand, pretending she hadn't understood his warning to the driver. 'For the escort, the food and showing me your shop. *Ma'a el salama.*'

'Goodbye.' He shook her hand with a big smile, his black eyes warm. '*Ashofak bokra, inshallah.* See you tomorrow.'

She nearly fell into the foreigner trap of correcting him. *Tomorrow?* But here, where time was ignored almost as often as traffic rules, the phrase meant more along the lines of 'hope to see you sometime'.

There was more to translate here than just Arabic.

After a traffic-clogged ride back to her spacious furnished apartment, provided by Maxwell Investments, Lilianne changed into jeans and a sweater, then poured herself a glass of water and went out onto her balcony overlooking the evocatively named Street 85, east of Mostafa Kamel Square. She was feeling oddly empty and restless. Curious, since she'd so been looking forward to her precious first night free of social obligation.

Her phone rang. She jumped up, telling herself it was undoubtedly a business call. But wouldn't it be wonderful if it was Connie calling from Paris with news that Gilles was safe, or even better, a call from Gilles himself? He'd been so gutted by Helen's rejection that despite Connie and Lilianne's pleadings, he'd requested a transfer to cover the raging civil war in Lebanon, practically a suicide wish. Lilianne had heard from him every few days over her first couple of weeks in Cairo, but nothing since. She told herself he was just busy, but the worry persisted.

Hearing his deep voice would go a long way toward lightening her mood tonight.

'Hello?' She crossed her fingers, waiting for the response.
'Lilianne Maxwell?'
Lilianne wrinkled her nose. Not familiar. 'Yes.'
'John Baker, US State Department. We met at the embassy last week.'

Uhh ... Her mind clicked through a mental Rolodex of recent contacts.

'Yes, I remember.' Vaguely. Dark suit, short hair ... That described half the people in the building. If she was right, John Baker was average height with handsome features, rigidly parted hair, perfect teeth, a brutal handshake and vaguely musty breath. A political officer, she thought. Not someone she'd been thrilled to meet, or someone she was thrilled to have interrupt her evening. 'How are you?'

'I'm doing fine, how about yourself?'

Herself was annoyed. 'What can I do for you?'

'Wondering if you'd have a minute to meet Monday morning?'

'Let me check.' Interesting. What would his division want with her? She dragged her day planner out of her briefcase, then flipped the pages until she landed on April 12. 'Ten o'clock?'

'That would be fine. I'll have you on the list for entry.'

'Okay ...' She turned, pulling the phone cord with her. 'Anything you can hint at? My family all right?'

'I'm sure they're fine.' He chuckled drily. 'Can't talk more now. See you Monday.'

Lilianne hung up the phone and stood frowning. 'Can't talk more now' could mean classified. Was he CIA?

During her master's program at Harvard, Lilianne had been recruited by the CIA, and participated in training at Camp Peary in Virginia, aka 'the farm'. She'd excelled, and at first thought she'd found a way to define her career. Then two things had happened. One, her father had had a mild heart attack, and had to cut back his duties at Maxwell Investments while he recovered, and two, Lilianne had begun to suspect she was too much of a loner to be all-in on teamwork, and she wasn't willing to be so thoroughly controlled in her career, told where to live, what to wear, whom she could be friends with. She also couldn't see any women at the top, which was where she wanted to be.

Maybe John Baker knew something about her investigation into Maxwell Investments' proposed partnership with the Cairo National Bank, though she had yet to find any red flags. She could think of nothing else that made logical sense.

But as she returned to the balcony to resume trying to enjoy her solitude in the cooling evening, the voice of intuition Lilianne had learned to trust over the years told her the Monday meeting would signal a turning point in her stay.

Chapter 2

Monday, April 12, 1976

Lilianne met John Baker in the lobby of the US Embassy. Downtown, not far from Tahrir Square, it was another former palace, ornate with turrets and decorative stonework, balconies and windows that arched to an elegant point.

She braced herself for the bone-crushing handshake. 'Hi, John. Good to see you.'

'Thanks for coming in. Any trouble finding us? Is it still beautiful outside? Supposed to get hotter later in the week. This way.'

She followed his breakneck pace, lips curved in amusement. Apparently she was not required to answer his questions. But yes, it was still a beautiful day, in the mid seventies, sunny and breezy, as it had been most every day. Lilianne had yet to experience Cairo's summer heat or one of the hellish sandstorms that blew in from the desert.

'How are you liking Cairo? I was overwhelmed at first, but love it now. Mind if we take the stairs? The elevators are slow here.' He marched briskly toward the dark wood of the lavish curving staircase. Lilianne followed, wondering if he ever let his friends and/or family respond, or if he just kept talking past them as well.

He tore down a tile-patterned hallway and stopped to open a

carved-wood door that led into a room that was similarly tiled and elegant. 'After you. Thanks for coming, have a seat.'

The decor in his office clashed horribly with the exotic ambience – modern business furniture, light wood, sharp angles, and chairs upholstered in baby-blue corduroy.

'So.' John sat behind the desk and folded his hands. 'Sami Sayed.'

Lilianne managed to keep the surprise off her face, and the dismay. John was CIA. She'd been followed yesterday. Or rather, Sami had been. He was either causing trouble or could lead to people who were. The man in the black car, maybe, Abraam Al-Kalib.

'Seems like a nice guy,' she said evenly. 'You're keeping an eye on him, I take it.'

'He's a person of interest, yes. You know the drill.'

Lilianne nodded, resisting the urge to shift in her chair. Yes, she did, and was glad that drill wasn't hers. Being at Maxwell Investments had its own difficulties – the boss was family, and her quick rise had caused some resentment – but her work was generally respected, especially after Paris, where she'd exasperated everyone by insisting something was off in the company Maxwell was targeting for acquisition. After weeks of stubborn digging, Lilianne had triumphantly uncovered irregular accounting practices that could have been a major problem if the deal had gone forward. Her looks and gender were still liabilities in a man's world, but that coup had gone a long way toward proving she'd earned her spot, and she hoped it would help when the time came to move further up the ladder.

John sat back, elbow on one of the armrests, chin on his hand, sizing her up. 'Seems like the two of you were pretty friendly yesterday.'

Lilianne did not like the way he said that. 'He offered to show me—'

'That will actually suit us fine.'

'I see.' She eyed him steadily, showing that even though she'd left the CIA, her training hadn't left her. She had a pretty good idea what would come next. Lilianne would agree to serve her country, of course, but it meant seeing Sami again and dealing with the consequences of forging a fake friendship. 'What do you need exactly?'

'Nothing big. Just spend time with him. Let us know if names or places come up that seem worth passing along.'

'What's the focus?'

'That's classified.'

She'd bet Al-Kalib. 'Anything you can tell me about Sami?'

John leaned forward, hands apart on the desk, another pose that came across like he practiced at home before deploying it in public. 'He's a small player, maybe a hustle or two on the side, but as far as we can tell, harmless. Jewelry store's been in the family for generations. Western-styled Egyptians, long-time wealth, tied to the old royal regimes.'

'Okay.' Points to Sami for honesty. 'You want to know who he hangs out with and what he says about them. Reports would go to you?'

'I'll give you the name of an officer. Send them in bank envelopes.'

'And the terms?' She didn't need the money, but she strongly believed that the higher the price tag, the more people and things were valued.

He named a low figure; Lilianne countered until they agreed on a price, then she tossed in the story of meeting Abraam Al-Kalib for free, satisfied when he looked pleased.

'Should I initiate the next contact with Sami?'

'Better if he finds you. He likes to hang out at the Cairo Cellar for a drink, plays tennis Tuesday and Thursday mornings at the Gezira club. We can get you a membership. You play?'

She nodded, remembering the hated childhood lessons at the Fairfield Country Club in Southport, her mother insisting she learn both tennis and golf. Without those skills, Lilianne would inevitably marry a worthless bum who'd never rise beyond a beggar's salary. That was how things worked in Dina's world.

As much as Lilianne hated to admit it, her skill at both games had come in handy.

They chatted a few minutes longer about logistics, then John escorted her out of the building and said goodbye with another finger-mangling handshake.

Lilianne strode away, inhaling the warm air, feeling as though she'd been dragged into an alternate universe. She'd come to Cairo to delve into the inner workings of a local bank and to reconnect with her heritage.

Now she'd also be working as a spy.

Chapter 3

Present day

Sophie Aubert sat in the snack-house pavilion at the Fairfield Country Club in Southport, Connecticut, having a late high-fat lunch with her BFF since first grade, Belinda Zimmerman, aka Beezy. Early-afternoon sun glinted off the children of extreme privilege splashing through the waves of the Long Island Sound. Behind them, over the fence, more happy splashing in the junior Olympic pool just outside the clubhouse cabana.

Sophie was not splashing happily; she was gritting her teeth under a fake smile, because bending boobs-forward over their table, bleached blonde hair accented by a wide pink headband, was Cathy Adamson, whom Sophie called the Catheter because she got right up into you and made you pissed.

'I wanted to make sure the cookies you agreed to make for the Pequot book sale volunteers will be—'

'You betcha, they'll be ready.' Out of the corner of her eye, Sophie saw Beezy smirk. 'You betcha' was the type of phrase Sophie used only when irritated. 'Ginger cardamom, lemon rosemary, Earl Grey chocolate and sesame chocolate-chip.'

'Oh.' A frown marred the ivory surface of Cathy's forehead. 'How unusual.'

'Yes.' Sophie was not thinking about the cookies. She was

thinking about the Incident, and had decided that the best way to stamp it so far into the ground it would never rise again was a direct attack disguised as sweetness. Always a winner if the balance was right.

'All the Pequot Library events are stellar. We're so lucky to have that place.' Cathy flashed a smile, teeth as straight and white as she was. 'Enjoy your lunch. And have a great rest of your—'

'One thing, Cathy.' Sophie grimaced as if she were terribly reluctant to go on, which she wasn't. 'I wanted you to know you were overheard at the Davises' party saying that since Peter divorced me I've gone downhill. I'm *sure* you didn't mean it the way it sounded.'

Cathy froze, turning headband-pink. 'I . . . I . . .'

'Don't even *think* about apologizing.' Sophie waved that *super*-silly thought away, bolstering her smile to keep it from turning feral. 'I know you were just worried about me and it came out wrong. But, well, I guess other people thought you were dissing me.'

A snort escaped Beezy, quickly disguised as a cough.

'So . . .' Sophie injected her expression with extra earnest warmth. 'I wanted to reassure you that I'm fine. It's just that divorce is hard. Even three years later.'

She let her voice crack with emotion. The Catheter, now the color of sunburn, took a step back from the table. 'I'm so sorry. But . . . yes, I've been worried about you.'

Sophie's turn to hide a snort. *Like hell.* Cathy worried only about Cathy.

'Thanks. That's sweet. But you don't need to, I'm fine. See you tomorrow!' She waved as if Cathy were already far away, which quickly became reality.

Sophie's smile disappeared. There was a group of women in

her small town, probably in every small town, who'd never left high school, emotionally speaking. Still in the same cliques, still trying to make themselves feel more important by putting other people down. It made Sophie tired. Most Southporters were gems, but as the saying went, the few bad apples should be thrown into the woods to be eaten by squirrels.

'That was the best smack-down I've seen in years.' Beezy's freckled face shone with admiration. 'You came out smelling like a rose. We all know what *she* smells like.'

'Politeness is an underrated weapon.' Sophie picked up her sandwich, wishing she could feel rose-smelling and triumphant, but the interaction had sapped her.

'I think the new you is fantastic,' Beezy said. 'Total change, leave the old behind. It's exactly what you needed.'

Sophie shrugged, scrubbing her hands through her hair, shorn from the thick, dark length she'd worn since girlhood into a funky cut with spilling-over bangs, short around the sides. She'd also double-pierced her ears and had a morning glory vine tattooed around her left ankle. Maybe not the most appropriate look to take on at forty-five, but after the divorce, she'd felt compelled to look as different from Sophie-married-to-Peter as she could.

Not in the rebellion-look plan were the twenty pounds she'd gained, but she didn't miss a thing about fretting over every calorie. 'You are a great friend.'

'I'm an honest friend.' Beezy tugged at a strand of her glossy blonde mane. 'I'd totally do it but I don't have the guts. And Jim would have a heart attack.'

'No reason for you to.' Sophie and Beezy had been joined at the hip since they met in first grade, when Beezy's family moved to Southport. They'd called themselves the Twin Negatives – Sophie dark, born on Crete and adopted to the US at five months old, Beezy a towhead of Scandinavian heritage. The only other person Sophie had been that close to was her imaginary friend Lulu, who appeared after Sophie's many pleas for a baby sister were rudely ignored.

'What's on your schedule this afternoon?' Beezy pushed back her crumb-sprinkled plate.

'I'm doing prep for a catering job at Ross and Angela's tonight, then going over to Willow Street to see Mom and Dad and finally meet their friend Helen. They're back as of late morning.'

'Oh, that's right! The big RV road trip from Kansas. After all those years hearing about their vacations together, it will be fun to meet Helen.'

'I loved those trips. I got to stay at your house and help drive your parents crazy.'

'Wasn't it great? I was bummed when they stopped.' Beezy bent to pick up her bag. 'I gotta run. Scotty has softball this afternoon so I must return to mom duty. By September I am so ready for the school year, I can't stand it.'

Sophie stood and pushed in her chair. Beezy's life was perfect. She had a romance-novel marriage, two smart, delightful children and a successful career as an interior designer. She was beautiful, funny and kind, and all of it came easily to her.

For a while Sophie's life had been that perfect too, except for not being able to have kids. Fertility specialists of course couldn't find a thing wrong with Peter. He had Olympic-athlete sperm in ginormous numbers. It was her. Of course it was her. Bad eggs, they theorized. Put 'em in a bowl of water and they'd float.

She and Beezy walked together to the parking lot, dodging wet, sandy kids and the parents trying to keep them under control.

'I keep meaning to ask, how's the blitz going?'

Uhh . . . Sophie had promised herself a focused effort this month to drum up more clients for her faltering personal chef business. In fact, she'd made herself tell Beezy about the marketing plan so it would be too humiliating to wuss out and not do it.

She hadn't done it. 'It's not going.'

'What? Why not?' Beezy stopped at her sunshine-yellow Mercedes coupe. 'People aren't responding?'

'I have yet to blitz.'

Beezy pout-frowned at her. 'Why?'

'I hate that part of the business. I just like the cooking.' She felt like a traitor to women's rights causes everywhere, but it was true.

'So quit. You've got alimony, your condo is paid for . . .'

'This business is my only remaining identity and source of pride. I chef, therefore I am.'

'No, no, no.' Beezy launched herself at Sophie with her trademark bear hug. 'Don't be that way. You have much to be proud of.'

Like . . . ?

'I know. I'm being dramatic.' Sophie relaxed her half of the hug, ashamed to admit that she didn't hate being financially dependent as much as the thought of what it would take to free herself from the handouts. 'See you tomorrow?'

'Tomorrow I'm playing tennis.' Beezy waggled her salon-shaped eyebrows. 'With Nanny and Booboo.'

'Say hi from me.' Sophie waved and got into her Prius, chuckling. Nanny and Booboo were grade-school nicknames for Nancy and Barb, good friends who'd once made the mistake of gloating over a lacrosse victory during PE. Sophie and Beezy had come up with the names at Beezy's house over a giant bowl of popcorn and collapsed into giggles so long and loud that Beezy's little brother had pounded on the door, ignoring the sign that said *Private Keep Out: Especially Brothers*, demanding to know what was so funny.

Sophie started the Prius – paid for by her parents, sigh – worried, not for the first time, that since the divorce, she'd been depending too much on Beezy for social and emotional support. Beezy had her own perfect life to live.

As she was about to pull out, her phone announced an incoming text.

It was from her mother: *We're back! Long lines at Stop & Shop, Gilles delayed at studio, Helen alone at home, ill, not answering texts, probably asleep, but are you free to check on her?*

Sophie texted back immediately. *Just leaving the club, be there in five.*

She drove past the golf course, inhabited by clusters of people who could afford the exorbitant entrance fees. On her left, picturesque views of sailboats and yachts moored in the long protected finger of the harbor.

Sophie's adoptive mother, Lilianne Maxwell, had been born here, as had her maternal grandfather, Franklin Maxwell, and on and on back to the seventeenth century, when Southport was still part of Fairfield. The village had changed over her lifetime, from a picturesque hamlet of quiet old-money wealth to a showy bastion of the entitled. Its beauty was intact, its charm undiminished – if you looked in the right directions – but increasingly, fantastic eighteenth- and nineteenth-century houses were being razed and replaced with soulless McMansions whose only purpose was to show off the wealth of their owners.

Peter, and his new improved wife, Lexy, had invested their combined gazillions into ten thousand square feet on two acres next to Long Island Sound. Five bedrooms, six bathrooms, pool, hot tub, tennis courts ... Every night from their second-floor master bedroom suite they could hear the sea.

Divorced Sophie lived in fifteen hundred square feet in Southport Woods Condominiums, a place her parents bought her after Peter wanted out of their marriage. Every night from *her* bedroom she could hear the I-95 traffic.

Not that she was in any place to complain about her parents' extraordinary generosity. Her bitterness came from losing the love of her life to a young, pretty, ambitious, successful and all-around ideal woman.

All things Sophie had tried so hard to be.

A few minutes later, she pulled into the driveway of the 1830 Victorian she grew up in on Willow Street. Arriving here, even after so many years, still felt like coming home, which in her current broody mood made her feel mildly pathetic. Forty-five years old and Mommy and Daddy's house still felt like her own.

She got out of the car, striding toward the side entrance along the row of hedges lining the driveway, where Lulu would wait for her every day after school, sometimes springing out to surprise her. That memory always made Sophie smile. She'd begged to be able to bring Lulu to school, but while Mom indulged her fantasy by setting a place for her imaginary friend at the dinner table, she'd put her foot down about school, saying Lulu would be much safer and happier at home.

Sophie mounted the steps of the side porch – no one used the front door except guests – and knocked quietly to be polite. When no one answered, she stepped inside.

'Hello? Helen?' She climbed the curving wooden staircase, glancing in at her old room, most of whose contents she'd stolen to furnish the new condo, including her childhood quilt, knick-knacks and posters. After growing up in this wonderful old house and living in an equally wonderful old house with Peter, she'd done as much as possible to cram her bland, antiseptic divorcée habitat with color and character.

Down the hall, the guest room door was open. She peeked cautiously inside. A couple of suitcases, twin beds still made. No Helen, but on one of the beds lay a large doll, nearly two feet long, head on the pillow as if she were taking a nap after her long journey. She was dressed in a stunning green gown with matching evening slippers on her tiny feet, and a fur cape with a jeweled brooch closure. Crowning her dark curls, a sparkling tiara. Her expression was one of such mournful beauty that Sophie immediately wanted to comfort her.

'Well, hello.' She lifted the doll into her arms, feeling a sense of déjà vu, as if she'd been around this remarkable creature before, long ago. She didn't see how that could be possible. 'What's your name? Do you belong to Helen?'

She touched the round pink cheeks, admiring the dark eyes and meticulously painted brows and lashes. The only flaw to such perfection was the hair, which sloped crookedly to one side of her smooth forehead. Impossible that the creator of such a gorgeous creature would have made a mistake like that. Sophie's guess was that the doll had been exposed to dampness or heat that had slipped her wig. The fix would probably not be much harder than loosening and resticking. A quick look and gentle tug showed that the glue was indeed fragile.

Sophie was dying to straighten it. Crooked drove her crazy. Back during the so-good days of their marriage, Peter would teasingly knock pictures and rugs askew in their house to see how quickly she noticed and put them right.

Very quickly.

Back downstairs, still cradling the doll, she found the famous Helen – who else could it be? – stretched out asleep on the couch in the living room under a mound of blankets, in spite of the room's temperature being over seventy.

Sophie seated the doll on a chair and pulled out her phone to text her parents. *Helen asleep, all well.*

'Lilianne?'

The weak croak made Sophie's head jerk up; she crossed to the couch to introduce herself. 'Sorry if I woke you.'

Helen's blue eyes widened, and she gasped. 'Connie! Connie! My God. What are you doing here? How did you get here?'

Oops. Sophie knelt to show her face more clearly. 'I'm Sophie. Gilles and Lilianne's daughter. Sophie.'

Helen continued to gape, obviously trying to fit pieces together. Her cheeks were flushed, eyes bright. From the nap, or fever? Sophie was tempted to touch her forehead to check, but . . . boundaries.

'No, no. Of course. Connie isn't . . . Oh, but you take after her. You really do.' A tear rolled down her unnaturally rosy cheek. 'Dear Connie.'

This was extremely weird. 'Who is Connie?'

'She's . . . We were friends in Paris. I thought . . . Oh no. Oh dear.' Helen blinked a few times, then passed her hand over her eyes and lay still.

Sophie stiffened. Was it time to panic? Because she was close enough that she could do a bang-up job. 'Helen?'

She was about to nudge her when Helen uncovered her eyes. 'I'm so sorry. I just made a terrible mistake.'

'No, no. It's all good. Not a problem.' Sophie spoke soothingly, still worried that Helen was not well. Mistaking her for someone else was at worst embarrassing. 'You must have been dreaming. How are you feeling?'

'Better.' Helen pushed off the blankets, slowly swung her legs off the couch, then pulled herself up to sitting, Sophie ready to help if she wavered. She was of slender build, but tall, like Sophie's mom, dressed casually in blue cotton pants and a blue and white striped top. The hand reaching for her glasses on the coffee table was steady. 'I had a good nap.'

'Mom is stuck at the supermarket. Dad's at his studio. I'm sure they'll be back soon. They asked me to check on you.'

'They shouldn't have bothered you. I'm fine.' She put on the glasses and studied Sophie's face anxiously. Helen was beautiful, must have been a stunner in her youth. 'Sophie. Of course. Please ignore what I . . . As you said, I must have been dreaming. I made a mistake.'

'It's no big deal.' Sophie got to her feet, surprised that Helen's error had so unsettled her. Maybe she was a perfectionist, like Lilianne. 'Can I get you anything? Water? Something to eat?'

'No, no, thank you.' Helen smoothed her gray bob and looked around. 'This is such a lovely house. I spent so much time imagining what it might look like.'

'I've spent that much time imagining what *you* look like.' Sophie sat opposite her. 'When did you all get back?'

'Not long ago. Or, actually, I have no idea what time it is.' Helen looked perplexed. 'Your parents never showed you pictures of me? Or of our trips? Or of all of us in Paris?'

'Not that I remember.' Her parents shared nearly nothing of themselves. 'It's almost three.'

'Ah. I'm a little out of it still. I had surgery a while ago for a broken hip, back home in Kansas. Your parents showed up last month in the world's largest RV, total surprise, and scooped me up to come visit. On the way I got sick, somewhere around DC. It was probably too soon for me to travel, but we had so much fun. Your mom and dad have taken such good care of me.'

'They're good at that. I loved being sick when I was a kid.' Sophie got up to bring the doll over to Helen. 'I found this beautiful lady up in your room. I hope it's okay that I brought her down. I'd love to know more about her. I feel like I've seen her before.'

'Ah.' Helen relaxed back on the couch, gazing affectionately at the doll. 'That's Sarah. Sarah Bernhardt, one of your mother's and my closest friends. She's very old and, we found out, very valuable and totally unique. There's not another one like her. A friend gave her to me in Paris, then I left her with your mother when I came back to the US. I imagine Lilianne wouldn't have brought Sarah out to play with you often because of her value, but that's probably why she looks familiar. Isn't she lovely?'

'A work of art.' Sophie gestured to the doll's forehead. 'Except for the crooked hair.'

'Yes, that is strange.' Helen lovingly stroked the dark curls. 'I don't remember that in Paris, but it was crooked when Lilianne and Gilles brought her back to me in Kansas several years ago.'

'The glue must have loosened in heat or humidity, then stuck again.' Sophie hesitated, itching to mend the doll, not sure of her right. 'I'm pretty good at crafty things . . .'

'And a good cook. Lilianne and Gilles brag about you.'

'They absolutely should.' Sophie smiled, loving Helen's giggle, though she doubted her parents had been bragging. A high-powered corporate lawyer and a renowned photographer had little to boast about with their housewife-turned-leech child. 'I don't think it would be a complicated fix. If you trust me, I can investigate.'

'Well.' Helen frowned briefly. 'I'd love to see her back to her old self. If you promise she won't come to any harm, then yes. Thank you.'

'You're welcome, and I promise.'

The side door opened, followed by careful masculine footsteps on the entranceway tile. Sophie laid Sarah down on a chair, excused herself and half ran toward the sound. 'Dad? That you?'

'Sophilu!' Gilles grabbed her in a hug, using the combined nickname for her and Lulu he'd invented when she was a kid. He seemed unusually animated.

'Welcome home!' She hugged him back. 'So glad you guys are back safely. I loved all the pictures you sent.'

'It was a great trip, but good to be back.' His eyes went toward the living room. 'How is she?'

'She's fine.' Helen's voice was strong. 'Come see for yourself.'

Gilles let out a loud laugh and strode into the living room. Sophie followed, mildly taken aback. Her quiet, careful father seemed to be shooting off energy. Had he had good news at the studio?

'You look much better.' Her dad was standing over their guest, hands on his hips, grinning for all he was worth. Helen must have been quite sick. 'You had us worried. You had *me* worried. Lilianne knew you'd be okay.'

'Lilianne knows all. You should listen to her.' Helen beamed at him, then coughed, hand to her throat. 'I hate to ask, but could I have that glass of water now, Sophie? I'm awfully dry.'

'No problem.' Sophie went into the large sunlit kitchen, where she filled a glass with filtered water from the refrigerator door dispenser, absently admiring the colors thrown by the crystal hanging in the window. She'd bought that for her mother in seventh grade, thinking it was the most precious and magical thing she'd ever seen. A diamond that shot out rainbows! Mom had faked immense pleasure, bless her, and hung it there, and as far as Sophie knew, it hadn't moved.

She carried the glass back toward the living room, then stopped abruptly in the doorway. Her father was leaning down, hand cupping Helen's cheek, gazing at her as if he'd just kissed her and couldn't wait to do it again.

What the *heck*?

'Here I am! Back from the kitchen! With the water!' She expected them to jump guiltily.

They didn't. Sophie made herself move into the room and held out the glass to Helen, looking back and forth between them. Her mother and father's marriage was hardly passionate – think separate bedrooms – but she couldn't imagine her father going at it with one of their closest friends.

'Thank you.' Helen reached for the water. 'I think that fever wrung all the moisture out of me. I'm parched.'

They seemed comfortable and cheerful together. Sophie must have imagined more into the gesture than was there. But it had sure looked like imminent nookie to her.

The side door was flung open. 'I'm home. Finally.'

'Mom!' Sophie went to greet her. Lilianne was staggering in under the weight of four loaded shopping bags, two over her shoulders and two dangling from her hands, which didn't stop Sophie from hugging her warmly. 'Welcome home! Let me help you.'

'Thanks.' Lilianne handed over the dangling bags and shrugged those on her shoulders down to replace them. 'Everyone in Southport is shopping right now. Saturday afternoons are the pits.'

'I'll unpack these.' Sophie carried the bags into the kitchen. 'You go be with Dad and Helen.'

'They don't need me.'

Sophie whipped around to study her mother, who was placidly removing Persian cucumbers and bunched radishes from one of her well-used cloth bags. 'What did you mean by that?'

'Just what I said.' Lilianne put the vegetables into the

refrigerator's crisper. 'There are things to do in here, and they're fine on their own.'

'Right. Right.' Sophie was still suspicious. 'It just sounded weird.'

'Okay.' Lilianne pulled two heads of lettuce out of the bag and put them in the sink. She looked older, and tired. It was so hard to imagine her mother slowing down. Lilianne Maxwell was an indomitable force of nature. 'Can you stay for dinner?'

'Nope. I have to leave . . .' Sophie glanced at her watch, 'ugh, pretty soon. I'm catering a dinner party tonight.'

'Tomorrow night then? I think we're having ham.'

'Love to, thanks, Mom.'

They finished unpacking the groceries and went into the living room, where Helen and Gilles were sitting close together but at least this time not looking as if they were dying to make out. If anything was going on, Mom the All-Seeing would have picked up on it, Helen would be out on her ass, and the conversation in the kitchen would have gone very differently.

'Look who's here.' Lilianne bent over the doll, touching her round cheek. 'What a surprise you were to unpack earlier, Sarah.'

'My granddaughter, Teresa, snuck Sarah onto the RV before we left Kansas,' Helen told Sophie. 'She wanted her to be with me on my birthday. It's part of a long tradition.'

'When is your birthday?'

'Wednesday! July fifteenth. Coming up so soon.' Gilles pointed to Sophie. 'I'm seeing cake in our future. Think you can make one?'

'Happy to.' Her baking was another of the delicious reasons her weight had blossomed. Totally worth it. 'I'll have Sarah fixed up by then, so she'll be looking her best.'

'What do you mean?' Lilianne asked. 'She's just been fixed up. At the doll shop in Kansas.'

'Sophie offered to straighten her hair,' Helen said. 'I still can't—'

'No. No, no.' Lilianne dismissed the unthinkable by snatching Sarah up. 'Even the doll shop didn't dare try. She's worth half a million dollars, too valuable for anyone but a professional to touch.'

Sophie felt herself shrinking. Mom didn't mean to, she never meant to, but . . .

'Nonsense.' Helen looked squarely at Lilianne and held out her hands for the doll. 'We promised to enjoy Sarah in spite of her value. I don't like her hair being on wonky and I'm sure she doesn't either. Sophie promised to be careful and to bail at the first sign of trouble.'

Wow. Sophie watched her mother with fascination. Very rare that anyone went up against Mom so directly. Even Dad chose his moments.

Incredibly, after a few tense seconds, Mom's face softened. She handed Sarah back. 'Helen, you're right. She deserves to look her old self.'

Sophie's jaw dropped. Figuratively. Since when had Lilianne Maxwell been the willow and someone else the oak? Helen must be a regular Amazon warrior when she was healthy.

'Thank you for offering, Sophie.' Helen held out the doll.

'You're welcome.' Sophie stepped forward to take Sarah, feeling her mother's doubt behind her. 'I need to run, sorry. Should I take her with me now?'

'Of course.' Helen smiled. 'She'll be a beautiful birthday present restored to her original splendor, thank you.'

Sophie hugged her parents and left with the doll carefully swaddled and laid into a stiff plastic bag by a worried Lilianne, while Sophie worried even harder about how long her mom's fussing was taking.

Luckily, she had just enough time to get prepped and set up in Angela and Ross's enormous kitchen before the guests arrived. The dinner came off perfectly: a bay scallop starter with citrus, almonds and fresh watercress, followed by roasted loin lamb chops with garlic and rosemary, next to a side of black barley and broccoli rabe with golden raisins and pine nuts. Dessert was a Pavlova, marshmallowy meringues topped with assorted ripe berries and vanilla whipped cream.

By the time Sophie had cleaned up and returned home, it was nearly midnight. Pumped by her success and an abiding hatred of early mornings, she still had plenty of energy, so she plopped her equipment down in the tiny kitchen to unpack later, and brought Sarah into her condo's second bedroom, which she used as a craft room.

Several minutes of online research confirmed her hunch. Long-ago dollmakers used glues that deteriorated over time, so Sarah's hair should be fairly easy to remove and reposition. Sophie unpacked her gently and laid her on a towel, aiming a bright desk light at the doll's head. 'Don't worry, you'll only be in surgery a short time. Recovery will be complete as soon as the glue dries.'

Starting at Sarah's temple, she pulled carefully but firmly, delighted when the cloth the hair had been sewn onto lifted fairly easily away from the ceramic. Using a sharp blade to convince sticking bits to give, she proceeded cautiously, barely breathing, sweating from the tension, wishing her mother hadn't dropped how much Sarah was worth.

Slowly, surely, the hollow head was revealed, its inside stuffed with white cotton cloth. Centimeter by centimeter, Sophie proceeded, finally lifting off the entire wig intact, gasping out her relief. Woohoo! She hadn't ruined half a million dollars!

All that was left was to carefully wipe away traces of glue

from the skull with warm water, then reglue the wig. Assuming she could get that on straight, her mother would have nothing to criticize.

In the midst of her nearly complete triumph, she got up from the table clumsily, foot catching, making her stagger against the table. The cotton tumbled from Sarah's head and landed with a thud on the towel under the doll's body.

Sophie blinked.

Thud?

The bundle was heavier than she'd expected, something hard and round inside. 'Got rocks for brains, Sarah?'

She unwrapped the cloth, which turned out to be a handkerchief, and gasped, then stared, unmoving except for an occasional blink.

Unthinkable.

Impossible.

She sat down with a thump.

In her hands was the most exquisite jeweled egg she'd ever seen. Its cerulean-blue sides were divided into strips, like the closed petals of a flower, each petal decorated with lacy gold and rows of impossibly tiny, perfect pearls. At the top, the petal points came together under a miniature glittering falcon, its spread wings curving upward.

Sophie sat gaping. Who had last seen this? Where had it come from? When and why had it made its way into Sarah's hollow head? How long had it been in hiding? When was the last time anyone used a handkerchief?

She traced a path down a row of miniature pearls, then up the smooth, gleaming blue enamel until she reached the tiny hawk. The egg's petals curved so perfectly together. Did they open?

Impulsively, she gave the falcon a gentle tug. Then a push. Then a twist.

The blue petals bloomed outward, revealing two miniature figures inside, a royal couple robed in blue and green, sitting on yellow enameled cushions, their upswept gold crowns bearing tiny cobras, reminiscent of the pharaohs of ancient Egypt. The king held a jeweled scepter, the queen a bouquet of roses – tiny rubies on miniature green enameled stems. The quality and detail of the workmanship were mind-blowing.

A word flashed into Sophie's mind, making her gasp before she could censor it as absurdly impossible.

Fabergé.

Chapter 4

Wednesday, April 14, 1976

'I've checked all financials back to 1973, all vendor contracts, compensation, capital expenditures, all incorporation documents, licensing, et cetera. The records aren't always perfectly organized, and sometimes they take forever to show up, but I haven't found anything off. I'll go over human resource issues, legal issues, projections and so on next. I'm feeling good about this one.'

Franklin Maxwell, Lilianne's father, chuckled. 'After what you put us through in Paris, I'm willing to trust your instinct.'

Lilianne grinned wryly. 'Been lucky so far.'

'More than luck. You have my nose.'

'Literally.' She pictured her long-nosed father affectionately, sitting behind the massive cherry desk in his Upper West Side office, emperor of his domain. He loved their Southport home as well, but there he was constantly being pulled into service by Dina's insatiable appetite for activity, both social and physical. 'How's Mom?'

'Clam-happy in Florida. Probably out on the tennis court right now. She loves it down in the swamps. In fact, reason I called . . . You know she's been wanting me to take early retirement and move there full-time?'

Lilianne could only think of one word to describe how her father would feel about that. 'Yuck.'

'I admit, she got me thinking about it.'

'Really?' Lilianne couldn't imagine her father either retiring early or living in Florida full-time. He was too much like her, happiest when he was working, making things happen in the world. It was Mom who loved the do-nothing luxury of a country-club setting. She'd found it in Dad's hometown of Southport on Connecticut's Gold Coast, but had been spending more and more time at their condo in Naples, on the west coast of Florida. 'And . . . ?'

He cleared his throat. 'There's the matter of my health.'

Lilianne's adrenaline charged forward while she kept her voice calm. 'Bad?'

'Not bad. Warning signs. Dr Reynolds wants me to slow down.'

'Slow down or halt?' Her mind was racing. How could Mom or Dr Reynolds think that cutting Franklin Maxwell off from everything he'd built and lived for would be anything but a disaster?

'He said slow down, but I'm calling a halt, Lilianne. I don't want to be a half-assed member of my own company. I'm either in or I'm out.'

'So you're thinking about a permanent move to Florida?' The idea was ridiculous. Ludicrous! Franklin Maxwell, lifelong New Englander, in the land of palm trees, golf and Mickey Mouse?

'Packers and movers come next week.'

'Next *week*!' She couldn't believe what she was hearing. He and her mother had made a decision of this magnitude and hadn't said a word until now? 'But . . . so you'll sell Willow Street?'

She couldn't imagine it. The rambling Victorian had been in the family for generations. Lilianne adored that house.

The Jewel of Cairo

'I was hoping you'd want it.'

'Wow.' She got up and started pacing the nicely appointed office Cairo International had made available to her in the Nasr City district of the capital. On the large desk sat a plate of bananas, guava, strawberries and dates, all in season and at perfect ripeness, more than she could eat. More than three people could eat.

Step, step, step, step, to the fullest reach of the phone cord, and turn. A view of the modern building across the street.

Did she want to settle in Southport? She hadn't thought that far ahead. Owning a house, having a permanent address and all the responsibilities that went with it made no sense in a job that took her all over the world for long stretches of time. It seemed so . . . staid and domestic.

Step, step, step, step, turn. A view of filing cabinets, a conference table and chairs.

Selling that house meant giving up part of her family's past, cutting her off from the hometown she loved. Instinctively, Lilianne wanted to say don't sell, she'd take it. But if that gorgeous house would sit empty most of the year . . . another family should have it.

A flare of angry denial at the thought of anyone else in the Maxwell homestead almost made her speak up, but she couldn't make such an important decision based on emotion alone. 'I might want it. Not now, but . . . I don't know.'

'You don't have to decide today. We've been talking about this move for years. It's only come to do or die in the last week.'

'I never thought you'd do it.' She couldn't help feeling a little disappointed. Franklin Maxwell selling out for development living!

'I'm sixty-five, with a bad heart, and I've been told that if I stay with the current grind, I'm a good candidate for another heart attack or a stroke. Florida doesn't look bad compared to that hell.'

'Florida *is* hell.'

He laughed. 'Moving will make your mom happy. It might surprise me and make me happy too. It'll definitely make me live longer.'

'I'm all for that.' She turned from filing cabinet to window, trying to process this. Who would run Maxwell Investments without Franklin Maxwell? His next in command, Kane Keith? Brilliant but misogynistic, a man who resented Lilianne's rise. She could not work for him. And she was still too young and inexperienced to take over the reins herself.

Lilianne pushed taut fingers against her forehead. She'd convinced herself that being the boss's daughter didn't make a bit of difference. Yet Dad hadn't even left the company and she already felt orphaned.

'Other than that, you doing okay? Need anything?'

Lilianne grinned through her distress. The same questions he asked, with love, every time they spoke. 'Fine, Dad, thanks.'

'Have you been in touch with your grandparents?'

She felt like a child caught with undone homework. 'Not yet. I keep going back and forth. What do you think?'

Her dad's pause meant he was deciding what to say. 'Hard for me to advise, Lil. I've never met them. Your mother has her perspective on the situation. I imagine they do too.'

'She thinks they're smothering, they think she's wild?'

'Could be, I don't know. If you're curious and want to meet them, it couldn't hurt. Dina would certainly understand. But if you're unsure, you should call and talk it over with her.'

'I know what she'd say. I got . . .' Dramatic pause. 'A letter.'

Dad's deep chuckle filled the line. 'Ah. A letter. Then you *know* what she thinks.'

The Jewel of Cairo

'I certainly do.' Dina Maxwell, fiercely loving and fiercely opinionated, loved the phone except when she had something significant to say. Those communications always took place on paper. There had been other letters, most of which hurt, one of which Lilianne had burned. In them it was always made clear that Lilianne's beliefs and her choices were wrong.

Mother and daughter were opposites. While Dina leaned toward both the luxurious and the domestic, Lilianne was ambitious and practical. Where Mom loved decorating, shopping and throwing big parties, Lilianne was happiest engaged in political and financial matters, reading, and seeing friends in small groups. Where Mom traveled in style – top destinations, best hotels and restaurants – Lilianne explored on her own, hoping to stumble over local favorites. Dina became docile and flirtatious around men, while Lilianne expected to be treated as an equal.

The biggest obstacle to their closeness was built when Lilianne approached dating age and it became apparent that her mother's great dream was for her to marry well and have multiple children, like the larger family she came from, and the one that she and Franklin weren't able to have for reasons hinted at but never explained.

After years of prevaricating, Lilianne had realized that keeping her secret was becoming more painful and damaging than letting it out. She'd lost her nerve several times, but finally managed it on a summer evening a few months before her sixteenth birthday, when she and Dina were alone, arranging flowers cut from the enormous garden into vases to distribute throughout the house. Looking back now, it was easy to see that most of the small amount of time they were together – Lilianne was practically raised by nannies – was spent doing things her mother enjoyed.

Dina had settled a crimson dahlia among white roses, and this provided the perfect opening for a comment about how happy it made her to think of Lilianne someday arranging flowers from her own garden with her own daughter.

Lilianne, turned instantly to ice, had screwed up all the courage her fifteen-year-old self could manage, and in a voice squeaky with fear had told Dina that she had no sexual or romantic feelings for guys – or girls; that she never had the crushes her peers did, and that the thought of kissing and . . . the rest of it . . . was disgusting. Marriage would never happen for her.

Dina had given her a series of looks: shock, suspicion, skepticism. Then, in spite of Lilianne's insistence, had pronounced that impossible. Over the next year or two, she'd dragged Lilianne to doctors, who brushed the problem off as low libido, then to psychiatrists, who prescribed antidepressants that left her lethargic, dry-mouthed and constipated. Still not 'cured', Lilianne had submitted to another round of doctors and psychiatrists, in New York City this time, becoming increasingly oppressed by her rage and shame. It was being made all too clear by the best of the best that the point of being alive was to make young copies of oneself. Absent that drive, Lilianne was therefore not fully human. Worse, she was letting down her family, her community and her species.

Other than that . . .

Finally, a compassionate New York therapist told her that along with one per cent of the population, she fit the Kinsey Report's definition of category X, essentially the wastebin of humanity, people who didn't have the decency to fit any reasonable slot.

Equal parts dismayed and relieved, Lilianne had put a stop to the visits and tests and told her mother she had a freak for a daughter and she might as well get used to it. She'd gone back up to her room, the little-used fantastic three-story dollhouse her Maxwell grandparents had given her still in the corner, the doll family – with multiple doll children that Mr and Mrs Doll had enjoyed making, the way people were *supposed to* – forever having dinner around their cherry dining table, under their tiny crystal chandelier that lit with the flip of a minuscule switch on the wall. On her bookcase, mysteries, literary classics and a smattering of Gothics, jump ropes, yo-yos, her softball mitt, stacks of jigsaw puzzles and weathered board games with crushed corners. On the wall, a bulletin board with pictures of her closest friends, ones she regularly lied to about crushes and being constantly curious about what 'it' was like.

She'd closed the door with more force than necessary, clenched her fists, squeezed her eyes shut and taken a solemn oath standing in the middle of her blue flowered rug with the burned patch from her and Cindy Tregoe's first and last attempt at smoking cigarettes. No matter what happened, anywhere, anytime, cross her heart and hope to die, she, Lilianne Maxwell, would never, *ever* tell anyone her secret again. It would stay hidden and die with her. And – cross her heart one more time – she'd spend the rest of her life working to become the most successful woman she could in all ways except those that women of her generation were supposed to.

Then she'd burst into tears for the rest of the afternoon.

Whether Lilianne's father had been told his daughter was abnormal was never clear. During Lilianne's childhood, their relationship had been affectionate but, with his work preoccupation and long commute, distant. These days it was mostly about business, because that was who her father was, though it had brought them closer, so she was grateful.

Still buzzing with adrenaline over Dad's retirement bombshell,

Lilianne ended the call and picked up her purse. She'd done as much work as she could – still waiting for this report and those numbers and that statistic – and she needed to brush off the impact of her father's news, get over to the Sayed jewelry store and start her other job.

She'd waited a few days so as not to appear too eager to see Sami again, and had decided the best approach, rather than to 'bump into him' as John Baker suggested, was to show up at his shop claiming she couldn't stop thinking about the scarab bracelet and had to have it. Even better, she could charge the cost of the bracelet to the CIA and have a lovely souvenir from Uncle Sam.

The cab ride, somewhere around seven miles, took nearly an hour, of which Lilianne felt every cranky second. She'd need to greet Sami calmly to gain his trust, let slip nothing that reflected her mood or her mission. Luckily, hiding was something she'd practiced nearly all her life.

Outside Sayed's, she took a moment to reset, then pushed inside. Sami's handsome face lit up as she entered the shop, causing her a moment of guilt that she firmly shoved away. If Sami was party to something illegal, he deserved to be found out. If not, their association wouldn't cause him any trouble. He waved a brief welcome, then turned back to a well-dressed matronly woman bending over a glittering necklace. As he listened, the woman pointed out where the necklace needed repair and cleaning, jabbing her finger at the piece as if Sami had been responsible for its wear. Was this Black Car Man's friend? Her presence could be the perfect launching point for discussion later. If Sami would talk.

Meanwhile, Lilianne wandered the store, glad for the delay so she could further reorganize her frazzled interior and focus on what she was here to do.

Finally, Sami bowed the woman out of his shop, closed the

door and turned to Lilianne with a wide smile. '*Marhaba*, hello, Lilianne.'

'Hi, Sami.' She pointed to the counter she'd lingered over on her previous visit. 'I came for the bracelet. I can't stop thinking about it.'

'Ah, yes. *Youssef!*'

His assistant appeared in the doorway as if he'd been waiting for the chance. '*Anna hanna.*' Here I am.

'Mariam Hamada has brought us another piece for repair.' Sami picked up the necklace in both hands, as if he were cradling a baby. 'Can you put it in the safe? I'm helping this lovely lady with a bracelet.'

Lilianne watched as Youssef reached for the necklace. For a second before Sami relinquished the diamond- and emerald-jammed piece to his assistant, he gave it a look Lilianne would have liked to call admiration or wonderment, but which she could only describe as hot lust, as if his aura of polished civility concealed a bestial interior.

Startling.

'Now. The bracelet for my new friend.' He unlocked and opened the case, throwing a look over his shoulder toward the door Youssef had disappeared through. 'You're the third person today who has been interested in this one. It won't be here long.'

Uh-huh. Lilianne slipped it on. 'It's beautiful.'

'Then you must have it.'

'How much is it?'

'Consider it my gift.'

'*La, shukran*, no, thank you, impossible.'

'I insist.'

This game was played all over the country. Anything admired must be offered up immediately, a gift it was well known should not be accepted. 'It's too much, Sami.'

'You would be doing me a great honor by accepting.'

'I'd be cheating you.'

'Allow me this chance to please you.'

Lilianne couldn't contain her grin. 'Some of your customs I just do not understand.'

Sami threw back his head and laughed. 'It's our way. You might as well ask the Nile to stop flowing.'

'It's a lovely and generous offer, thank you. But I will pay.'

He inclined his head in defeat, as they both knew he would. 'Shall I wrap it for you, or would you like to wear it?'

'Wrap it, please. If I wear it, I might have to give it to someone.'

'Yes, you might.' He took the bracelet over to the register, still smiling. 'Now, I must ask if you've been for a sail in a *felucca*.'

'I've seen the boats, but no, not yet.'

'Are you free now? I will take you.'

She hesitated, as if extending the afternoon with him wasn't exactly what she'd been hoping for. 'As long as it's an invitation between friends.'

He scoffed. 'You Americans and your bluntness. I would simply like you to enjoy my city – your city too, the city of your Egyptian half.'

'Thank you, Sami.' She slipped the package into her leather Dior bag, pleased to have the bracelet as a souvenir of this trip, and pleased to have set her terms early to avoid misunderstanding.

'Youssef can take over the shop. If we go right away, we'll see the sunset, a little after six o'clock. You will love it.'

'I'm sure I will.' She smiled blandly, hoping he'd be willing to talk about politics, people he knew, Black Car Guy, anything that might give her an insight into whatever the CIA was looking for.

Youssef was summoned, the reins handed over. Sami and Lilianne took a cab to Opera Square, at the other end of Zamalek, where the Qasr el Nil Bridge Lilianne had crossed the previous Friday ended – or began, depending on one's perspective. Feluccas, traditional wooden sailboats, bobbed in the water, some looking as if they'd been around since the time of the pharaohs. A few of the captains wore *galabyas*, the traditional loose white garments reminiscent of nightgowns, whose light color reflected the sun's heat and whose lack of confinement allowed in breezes. The sun was on its way down, the winds were light, the temperature around eighty, warmer than it had been so far that month as it headed inexorably toward the searing heat of summer.

Sami bargained with the captain of the boat he chose, a *galabya*-wearing man with a white turban that set off his dark skin, his handsome face marred by premature wrinkles, most likely from malnutrition. For all the country's rich history, the poverty there was shockingly widespread.

Up close, the boat was larger than it appeared in the middle of the river, probably big enough for ten people. Lilianne settled next to Sami on the padded bench near the bow and watched the captain hoist the sail, then push off using a long red and white pole. The sails caught the breeze, the boat picked up speed and the sounds of honking traffic receded into the swish and gurgle of the hull through water. Lilianne found herself gratefully shedding the tension she'd been carrying. Around them the city felt both more modern and more ancient, glass glinting on high-rises, palm trees and minarets outlined against a sky gathering itself for twilight.

She relaxed against the railing. If she had to be a spy while she was here, at least she'd landed a pretty cushy assignment. 'This is wonderful, Sami.'

He beamed with pride. 'There is no better way to see Cairo. Except from the top of the pyramids.'

'From the top?' When Lilianne went, there had been guards everywhere. Definitely no climbing. 'I thought it wasn't allowed.'

'Anything is possible if you know the right people and are willing to pay. I can get you anything you want. Hashish, someone to fix your drain, Skippy Peanut Butter ... I know everyone in Zamalek.'

Definitely a cushy assignment.

'Look there. And there. And there.' Sami pointed out various spots in the cityscape. 'Cranes and construction. Is this good? Yes, it's good. Jobs and tourism and investment in Egypt. Is this bad? Yes. The city is changing, the population is exploding, people flocking here for jobs, more than our infrastructure can handle. Under Nasser, the poor were happy. Under Sadat, the rich are happy. But nothing has changed for either one.'

'Which side are you on?' Lilianne asked the question playfully, examining the skyline as if his answer couldn't matter less.

'I don't want my country run by royalty, I don't want it run by foreigners, I don't want it run by Islamic fanatics. I want it run by Egyptians! But I am a realist. Egyptians are not good at running things. This is what happens when a colonial force bullies citizens into its own structures and customs then withdraws. Corruption moves into the vacuum, opportunism moves in, poverty results from greed. Who's going to fix that? The people who benefit don't want it fixed. The poor don't have the means or the power. So it's how things are.'

'Do most of your friends feel the same way?'

'Most of my friends welcome Sadat's changes, yes. Most are businessmen, like me. But Sadat promises openness from one side of his mouth and orders protesters crushed from the other. We worry about the rise of the Muslim Brotherhood, whose members are skillful at recruiting the most vulnerable and the most idealistic. They don't like Sadat. The rest of us are tired of change. We went from a selfish king to British rule, to socialism under Nasser, now a return to Western-leaning government. The people are ping-pong balls batted between opposing forces. We want to be able to live, to enjoy our families and our food and our beautiful city, and to feel Egyptian.

'Look there.' He pointed to an enormous building under construction. 'A Hilton hotel that will forever change the skyline. And you are here to bring your American banking. We welcome the money, but it's not Egyptian money, not an Egyptian hotel. In the end, no one is satisfied. What can you do? Change is inevitable.'

Lilianne nodded, tucking away what John Baker might find useful. 'What do you think the next change will be?'

'There are rumbles . . .'

She felt a prickle of apprehension and had to work not to lean forward eagerly. *Yes? Yes? What kind of rumbles?*

Sami gestured heavenward. 'But only God knows for sure. Now. I have talked too much. You must tell me about your home and your family, Lilianne. Do you have brothers and sisters?'

She allowed him to change the subject. 'I'm an only child.'

'Cousins, then, aunts, uncles?'

Lilianne put on a face of polite regret. 'Most of them live across the country. In California.'

'And on the Egyptian side?'

She shrugged, guilt springing into action. 'Unfortunately, I never met them.'

'I'm sorry to hear that.' Sami's dark eyes softened into sympathy. 'Everyone should have a big family. My parents wanted more children, but none came. Friends of my parents were like family after my mother and father died, but they moved out of Cairo, down to Faiyum, which suits me. I can go see them whenever I wish, but they don't bother me.'

'From what I've encountered, that doesn't sound like a very Egyptian attitude.'

Sami winked charmingly. 'I have many Western traits. Tell me about your parents.'

'My father owns the investment bank where I work.' At least for now. Lilianne still hadn't adjusted to the idea of Dad anywhere but in his New York office. 'My mother stayed home.'

He raised his brows. 'Stayed home?'

'No office job. She was a wife and mother.'

He nodded politely, but Lilianne could practically hear him thinking the Arabic equivalent of 'well, duh'. Women had made some strides here, gaining the right to vote under Nasser, but most still held very traditional roles.

'Which of your parents is Egyptian?'

'My mother.'

'Her family name?'

'Abdallah.'

'That doesn't narrow it down much. Now you, Lilianne . . .' He patted her knee paternally. 'Do you have a man in your life?'

She had despised that question for over a decade, and didn't think she'd stop anytime soon. Her brain sped through possible answers as she chided herself for not anticipating that he'd ask. Her agent training called for telling the truth as much as possible to avoid lies that might trip her up later, but it was tempting to invent a boyfriend, both to make herself seem unavailable and to avoid the inevitable surprise at her single status.

What? No boyfriend? But you're so pretty!

She thought of Gilles, somewhere in Lebanon and, she hoped, safe. 'There is a man who is special to me.'

'Ah.' Sami nodded once and lapsed into silence. Subject closed, though something lingered unsaid.

They sailed on, the gentle breeze making their journey slow but steady, passing other feluccas, pleasure boats and a motorized barge loaded with shipping containers en route to the city. The sun headed toward the horizon, bringing houses, buildings and minarets into dark relief. Color filled the sky: yellow, orange, rust, and the underside of a single cloud in pink. As the captain turned the boat around, the evening call to prayer added echoing melodies to the glorious sight. *God is great. There is only one God . . .*

Lilianne watched and listened with a full heart, willing her sense memory to cement the experience. It was easy just then to believe what Connie maintained, that your collective heritage lived in your heart and soul, not just in your blood. Lilianne thought of her grandparents, her uncles and cousins, out there somewhere, hearing the same call.

'Even I am moved, after so many years,' Sami said softly. 'This is when it becomes impossible to think of leaving Cairo.'

'But you want to?'

'I am bored. Losing my parents meant I inherited a life of heavy responsibility at a young age. I want to see the world, and I want to live well in it.' He flung out his arms, then brought his hands to his heart. 'When I am too old to keep playing, I'll come back home to die.'

Their sailboat rocked in the wake of a passing motorboat. Lilianne made sure she looked relaxed and unconcerned as she prepared her next line of questioning. 'I hope you don't mind me asking, but I'm curious about the man in the black car. Abraam . . . something. What he said about hoping your business kept going well. The way he said it . . .'

Sami turned away from her, looking over toward the shore. 'He is a powerful man. Half the city is in his pocket.'

'Oh. He's not going to cause you trouble, is he?' Said with her best naïve-worry voice.

'Not if I've left the country.' Sami laughed uncomfortably. 'That's a joke.'

Lilianne doubted it. 'So . . . do you do business with him?'

'Jewelry business only.' He spoke too quickly.

'What makes him so powerful?'

'You are curious about him.' Sami was looking at her a little too closely, complexion fading with the light toward dusk.

'He reminds me of every mob movie I've ever seen.' She giggled for good measure. 'So theatrical.'

Sami relaxed, as she'd hoped he would. 'He has money, therefore power. He manipulates, he corrupts, he does favors. If people do what he wants, they succeed.'

'If they don't, they're in trouble?' She wondered if Sami was already in trouble, or merely headed for it. 'Tell me about your childhood.'

She listened, as they sailed, to stories of his athletic and academic prowess, his penchant for mischief, and the infinite ways he drove his traditional parents crazy with his disobedience and rebellion.

In turn, Lilianne painted a rosy picture of her childhood in Connecticut, leaving out the loneliness, the succession of nannies supposed to substitute for parents, the struggles with her 'difference', her attempts to fit into an adolescent student population motivated by social cues she didn't understand.

As the boat neared the dock, the dusty, honking chaos of the city closed around them, a jarring let-down from the magical trip.

'Thank you, Sami.' She let him help her out of the boat. 'That was a treat.'

'There are peaceful places in Cairo if you know where to find them.' He took her arm and stepped them out into traffic to cross Opera Square. 'Now I will take you back to the shop to show you my special project. Safiya will be there to chaperone if you are worried about your virtue.'

'Safiya?' Girlfriend? Wife? Lilianne was admittedly relieved.

'My housekeeper. She is from a small village in the south, near Aswan. I pay her fairly, she eats well, does light work and can send money back to her family. Very common to have help in the house here.'

Lilianne nodded, amused that he seemed compelled to explain the custom. Did he think she'd disapprove? Lilianne's mother rarely mentioned details of her upbringing in Cairo, but the Abdallah family had Nailah, who'd helped cook, clean and raise Dina and her two brothers. Nailah was one of the few people Dina didn't speak of with scorn in the rare times she'd talked about her homeland.

They took another cab back to the jewelry shop – walking would probably have been faster – greeted the silent Youssef and climbed the stairs to the second floor.

The living room of Sami's apartment was a riot of color, wall-to-wall with carpets, with more hanging on the walls. Brass tables provided a rich golden accent, and green plants flourished in sun streaming through the curtained windows. The effect was plush and exotic, with velvet cushions on the couch and an ancient globe on top of a two-tiered stand. Open next to the window on a table flanked by two chairs was a backgammon board, with intricate mosaic inlays of different-colored woods accented with mother-of-pearl, ready for play at a moment's notice. A white Persian cat entered the room to investigate, followed by a reed-thin woman with dark skin and open features. She wore a *hijab*, covering her hair and setting off her gaunt, stony face, and a mid-calf black dress with a white apron, like a French maid.

'Ah, Safiya, we'll have tea in my studio.'

The housekeeper nodded, glancing at Lilianne, who smiled, hoping to communicate friendliness. Safiya turned and left the room.

'Now.' Sami rubbed his hands and led Lilianne toward the back of the apartment, removing keys from the pocket of his linen trousers, which he used to unlock a thick door. 'Here is where the real Sayed magic happens.'

His studio was spare, an abrupt contrast to the color and richness of the main living space. An office chair, tables, machines and tools neatly arranged on metal trays. Against one wall, a large wooden cabinet that Sami produced another key to unlock.

'This is something you will not find anywhere else.' His excitement was palpable. He opened one of the doors and drew out a black velvet case, whose lid opened to reveal a necklace so astoundingly intricate that Lilianne couldn't hold back a gasp of wonder. If a lace collar could be tatted from diamonds, she was looking at it.

Sami picked it up to better display its glory, and she noticed the piece wasn't quite finished. A handful – possibly literally – of diamonds was missing along one edge.

'This is my prize. A copy of the necklace that disappeared during the riots.'

A frisson of excitement. 'The one you designed for the princess.'

'Princess Fawzia, yes. I'm making it again, slowly, slowly. Only the most perfect diamonds. They don't come along that often.' He turned it back and forth to catch the light, sending sparkling rainbow dots throughout the studio. 'Always I'm searching. My sources know where they can send the stones when they come across them. Bit by bit I am reconstructing it. Not much more to go.'

'Is the princess still alive?'

'Oh yes.' He pointed toward the window. 'She lives here in Zamalek.'

'So you'll finally be able to give it to her.' The fairy-tale symmetry of this gesture was making even practical Lilianne a little starry-eyed.

'No.' Sami gently laid the necklace back into its case. 'I am a romantic, but also a realist. If I sell this piece, and another family heirloom I'll show you in a moment, I will be set for life. I can get out of Egypt and go wherever I please, do whatever I please.'

Lilianne murmured approval she didn't feel. Poor Fawzia!

'Let me show you the other piece, commissioned from one of the greatest jewelry houses of all time by my grandfather, Ibrahim Sayed, in 1915 as a gift to his wife for their tenth wedding anniversary.' He put the necklace case in the cabinet and withdrew a black metal box. 'You will never hold one of these again, I guarantee you.'

Unlocking the box, he pulled out a purple satin padded bag. Inside the shining folds rested a miniature golden carriage, like something Cinderella would ride in, except that in place of the usual body, the designer had substituted a jeweled egg in lustrous blue enamel, comprised of what looked like folded petals, with tiny pearls and diamonds highlighting its sides and a spread-winged falcon on top. It was exquisite – miniature and perfect. Lilianne guessed at once, yet hardly dared say the word.

Fabergé.

Chapter 5

Safiya stood in Sami's kitchen, stiff and silent, waiting for the water on the stove to boil. This blonde woman was more beautiful than any of them. *Inshallah*, maybe this one would stay, be enough for Sami, so he'd leave Safiya alone. So far she'd been lucky not to be carrying his child. If she went back home to her husband with another man's baby, he or his family members would certainly kill her. It had already happened not far from where she lived, a girl Safiya had known only by sight.

But in her home village, Nagaa ad Disah, there were no jobs. Nowhere she could make enough to help her parents and her sons. Her husband, Menes, hadn't been able to work since his illness. He'd become weaker and weaker, until he could no longer object to Safiya and his parents dragging him to a doctor in Aswan. Tiny worms that lived in the river, they were told, that burrowed into human skin and laid eggs, eventually causing bad sickness. The treatment had killed the worms, but the cost to Menes's body was terrible. Safiya had heard that the best jobs were not in Aswan, much closer to her home, but in Cairo. So though it killed her every day to be so far from her two young sons, she'd come to the big city, so much bigger than she'd ever imagined, and taken this job with Sami, who'd seemed so gentle and refined and generous – until it became apparent he didn't need her only to cook and clean.

What choice did she have? Poor people could not choose. She submitted to his demands in the home and his demands in the bedroom and told herself that it could be worse, all while trying to control the forces tearing her apart. The pain of missing her sons, and the pain of her hatred for Sami Sayed and all arrogant foreign-raised men who thought they were better than other Egyptians, and who saw women not as humans but as toys for their pleasure. Allah – may he be praised and exalted – would certainly punish Sami in heaven, but – seeking His forgiveness – Safiya would love to find a way to add her own punishment while he was still here on earth.

The water boiled. Safiya poured it over Assam tea leaves, left it for five full minutes so it would be strong, the way he liked it, with milk, the way he'd learned from the English, instead of drinking mint tea or hibiscus or coffee like a true Egyptian. While it steeped, she took out an ornately engraved silver platter and arranged on it dried figs, dates and apricots, too many for two people, but it would be disrespectful not to offer too much. On another platter, fresh bananas, and on a third, smaller plate, *basbousa* – Sami could barely go two days without his favorite sweet cake. She'd made this one with coconut and hazelnuts, a favorite of her elder son, Amon, whose seventh birthday had been yesterday.

Pain compressed her heart until she felt it would stop beating. How desperately she missed him and his little brother, Bebti. Their arms around her squeezing tight, their heads nestled on her shoulder, the soft cheeks she couldn't stop kissing. Growing up without their mother!

Safiya's parents sent news now and then, thanking her for the cash, describing her sons' growth, updating her on Menes's health. Both illiterate, they went to one of Safiya's brothers, or to a scribe in the village, and dictated their news. The first time a letter arrived, Sami had brandished it, offering to read it aloud. Safiya nearly told him where he could put his superior attitude. Her uncle had taught her, and her cousins and her brothers, to read and write. But a strong instinct told her to hide her pride and offer thanks instead.

Only later, after catching Sami switching diamonds, did it occur to her that the stupider he thought she was, the less he'd hide from her. So she gladly let him read news of her parents' simple village lives, the hard days in the sugar cane fields, the riches from their garden, the antics and accomplishments of her children and the health and happiness of her brothers, cousins and their families. Sometimes, if Sami was in a good mood, she'd ask him to reread the letter, as if she hadn't been able to take it all in the first time, so she could savor every word again.

When he was finished, she'd dictate her own letter back home, responding to the news, asking more and more questions about her sons, telling lies about her work being good, her boss generous and the city magnificent.

How she missed her quiet village, perched amid palm trees on rocky ledges overlooking the Nile. Twice a year, before Eid al-Fitr and Eid al-Adha, Sami allowed her ten days to visit her family. Precious, precious days. She'd sit on the southward train brimming with light and energy; ten days later on the northward train hunched and weighted with dread and grief.

After those absences, Sami was always at his most rough and impatient.

But she had a weapon against him for when the right moment arose. While bringing in food or clearing dishes from his studio, she'd caught glimpses and eventually pieced together how he was building the new necklace he was now bragging about to

The Jewel of Cairo

the blonde woman. He'd remove diamonds from precious pieces that came in for repair, and replace them with stones of lesser value. Because he was fastidious in all things, he kept careful notes about each substitution. Three years she'd been there and watched this happen. He must be confident the owners would never notice.

Someday, when she no longer needed Sami Sayed, she'd find a way to use this against him. When good luck came, even the blind mended broken watches.

Safiya picked up the heavy brass tray with the tea, the food and the silverware, and carried it toward Sami's studio, where the blonde woman was laughing.

Please let her be the one.

Chapter 6

Present day

That night, Sophie discovered something she'd never imagined she'd know: it was hard to sleep after discovering a Fabergé egg, with no apparent owner, that was worth many millions of dollars.

Frantic googling had frustrated her with lack of details, but one photograph and description confirmed her initial hunch. Commissioned in 1915 by a Cairo jeweler, Ibrahim Sayed, the egg was the last the Fabergé house made for a private client before the Bolsheviks nationalized the famous jewelry company. The most recent owner, Sami Sayed, grandson of Ibrahim, was deceased, with no living relations Sophie could discover. The egg was listed as lost.

Not anymore.

The last 'lost' Fabergé to resurface, the third of the so-called Imperial eggs, had been acquired in 2009 from a Midwestern flea market by a man with no clue what he'd bought. Years later, he'd stumbled over the truth and contacted a dealer. The egg sold to a private collector for an amount estimated to be in the tens of millions.

Tens of millions.

Sophie had practically hyperventilated. This egg, not being

Imperial, would probably be worth less, but when the amounts got that high, it hardly seemed to matter.

After another hour fretting at the computer, she told herself to stop obsessing and go to bed. Quite obediently, she did go to bed, but did not stop obsessing.

Toss, turn, toss, turn.

Assuming this was the lost original and not a 'Fauxbergé', a term she'd just learned, how did the egg get into the doll? Had someone stolen it from Sami Sayed? Mom had been in Cairo decades ago, but she couldn't have any idea about the egg or she wouldn't have let Sophie near Sarah's hair. Why hadn't whoever had hid it come back to retrieve it? Sophie couldn't imagine anyone wanting such a precious thing to disappear forever.

Did anyone else on the planet know where the egg had been for so long?

Sophie was certainly the only person who knew it had been rediscovered now.

Toss, turn, toss, turn. On half of the turns, though none of the tosses, Sophie could make out the egg glinting on her desk, carefully surrounded by balled-up socks to keep it from rolling off.

Hopelessly enthralled, she threw off her covers, approached the treasure and, for a long, unabashedly greedy moment, let herself imagine this extraordinary piece belonging to her. No more pressure to work. She could buy her own rambling old house in Southport and live on the income from the rest, plus whatever she'd eventually inherit from her parents. Once again life would be easy, enviable, luxurious, like the life she'd led with Peter, like the life he was living with Lexy.

She got back into bed, ashamed of her covetous fantasy. Finding the egg certainly didn't make it hers. Would there be a search for Sayed heirs? If none were alive, who had legal right to the egg? Cairo? Russia? Whoever owned Sarah? Who *did* own Sarah? Helen? Lilianne?

She forced herself to take deep, lingering breaths in an attempt to slow her hammering heart and frantic mind. This was nothing she could solve now or by herself. The egg had been missing for decades. Nothing had to happen tonight.

Tomorrow she'd tell her parents and Helen over dinner, and together they'd figure out what to do.

After the late-night excitement, and a series of dreams in which she dropped and shattered the Fabergé, lost it, and fed it to a crocodile in the zoo, waking up the next morning should have been its usual torture. There was not an alarm, no matter how soft or gentle, that didn't make Sophie want to smash it and go back to sleep. That morning, however, her eyes shot open and she leapt out of bed. Was the egg still on her desk?

It was, blue, shimmering and precious, absurdly out of place surrounded by socks decorated with sushi, lobsters and the phrase 'Duchess of Sassytown'.

She couldn't leave it out like that all day. The best hiding place she could think of was nestling the treasure into the doubled cups of one of her bras and covering it with a favorite pink-and-orange-striped pair of panties.

Sophie was pretty sure no other Fabergé ever had it that good.

After breakfasting on a slice of home-made pecan sour-cream coffee cake, she contemplated the day ahead, taking it as a given that no matter what she planned to accomplish, she'd be distracted by the fact that several million dollars' worth of jewelry had taken up residence in her underwear drawer.

As for the much less exciting part of her life, there was what she should do, and what she was more likely to do. She should gear up for her marketing blitz. Social media posts, telephone calls, stuffing mailboxes ... but her personal chef business was doing just well enough, with three regular clients plus an occasional special event, so spending time on self-promotion she hated and was bad at seemed unnecessary.

Deep down? She didn't want to be much more successful. Success meant long hours and stress. Success was what her ex and her parents pushed her to achieve, and what she felt she *should* want but couldn't quite.

Today she'd deliver the cookies to the Pequot Library event and plan a week of menus for the Stoddards on Harbor Road, the Helversons on Taintor and the Danas on Westway, ending with dinner at her parents' and the news of her discovery.

The day got off to a busy start when her phone rang. Patty Helverson and her family were Sophie's oldest and most loyal clients. Four kids, one mother-in-law plus two parents equaled seven people with big appetites, cha-ching.

'Hi, Patty, I was just settling down to work on your next week of meals.' Tiny lie. 'How's it going?'

'Sophie, it's not good. I'm sorry, I have bad news. Steve got laid off.'

'Oh no.' Sophie's stomach tightened. 'I am so sorry to hear that.'

Patty had no idea how sorry.

'We're having to cut expenses.'

'Yes, sure, of course. So ... rice and beans this week?' She tried for humor, knowing it was useless. Her biggest source of income was about to get the ax.

'I wish it was that easy. We're going to have to take a pause. I'm miserable not only because I'll have to start cooking again, but because we really wanted to support you.'

'Aw, thank you.' She'd been primed to hear 'because your

meals are so delicious', but okay. Support was good.

'I'll put out the word to see if anyone's looking. I did just hear that Janice Davis's youngest, Kate, is getting married. She'll need a caterer. I know you did her sister's wedding.'

Sophie brightened. A big wedding would help. 'Thank you. It's been a real pleasure. I hope Steve finds a new job soon.'

'Thanks, Sophie. I feel terrible abandoning you.'

'Oh no, no, things are fine. I'm doing great.' Well. She certainly wouldn't starve, because she had rich parents and a rich ex-husband who'd gotten her started in this damn business.

She'd fallen in love with Peter in high school, freshman to his junior. He was tall, self-assured, athletic, golden-boy handsome; Brad Pitt combined with Michael Jordan and Warren Buffett. Sophie grieved when he went to college, and for the next four years still got a shiver when she glimpsed him back in town. A year or so after her graduation from the University of Connecticut, they'd found themselves at the same summer party and talked for a long while, during which time Sophie kept expecting him to go in search of someone hotter, prettier, more popular, astonished that he stayed, more astonished when he asked her out, flabbergasted when he kept asking, and flat-out gobsmacked when he proposed.

Peter was everything she'd ever dreamed of in a husband, and Sophie had never worked at anything as hard as she'd worked at being his wife. She made sure their house was perfectly decorated, made sure they gave fantastic parties, made sure he had the drinks and food he liked, attractively garnished, graciously served. She'd learned golf so they could play it together, played tennis with his friends, made sure she was in bikini shape year round, and that their sex life was varied and exciting. She volunteered at the Pequot Library, at Trinity Church, at Project Hope. She was busy, productive, and so happy . . .

The Jewel of Cairo

Until the awfulness of being unable to conceive visited their Eden, followed by Peter's eventual insistence that they give up trying. He became moody and irritable, which Sophie naïvely attributed to their shared disappointment, and had insisted that if they weren't going to have kids, Sophie should start a food-related business to grow into her own brand, which she could look toward expanding nationally.

It had sounded so exciting and doable when he believed in her that strongly. So she'd started this personal chef business, bankrolled by Peter, and found a few clients, mostly friends doing her a favor. She enjoyed the cooking, but hated the feeling that sink or swim rode solely on her shoulders.

Still, she'd kept at it, thinking she could earn back the respect and love of her husband, who seemed to be working harder, later, more weekends.

Yeah, no.

Peter had sat her down one evening and told her gently – like gently inserting hot skewers under her skin – that he'd married her for the support she could give him, but that more and more he'd come to want a marriage of equals.

Ah.

Not only that, he'd fallen in love with an equal woman, and Equal Woman had fallen in love with him. He was terribly sorry, but he wanted a divorce. And oh, by the way, wasn't it good after all that they'd stopped trying to have the children Sophie craved? Easier to disentangle with just the two of them.

Oh yes, Peter! So good that the one thing she'd wanted in her life as much as she'd wanted him had also not worked, and thanks for pointing that out.

To her credit, she hadn't told him to go screw himself. Instead, she'd said, I hope Lexy makes you happy, and then hired the most bad-ass sharky lawyer her mother could find.

That part she would change if she could. Bad-ass sharky lawyers don't leave one feeling good about anything, though her mother was still cackling over how Sophie had benefited financially.

In any case, aside from her total emotional collapse, she'd gotten through it.

She scurried around the kitchen packing up the cookies for the book sale volunteers, only sneaking one, then decided that because she didn't really need to go to the library until later, she deserved to sit in her living room feeling sorry for herself and watching *Four Weddings and a Funeral*, which she loved, because . . . Hugh Grant.

Why hadn't she married *him*? She'd have been so much happier.

After the movie and another cookie, she loaded her car and drove to Pequot Library. Built in the late nineteenth century, it was more like a stone castle than a library, with archways, and high-ceilinged rooms bursting with elaborate woodwork. The annual book sale brought people from all over the world, lured by the promise of finding a rare or long-treasured volume among the thousands donated. Like looking for a needle in a haystack. Or a Fabergé egg in a doll's head.

Today the place was crawling with volunteers preparing for the onslaught, vast tents set up under which dozens of tables bore enormous numbers of books, CDs, LPs, DVDs and much other stuff. The most expensive volumes were housed in the library's auditorium and reading room.

She found Cathy 'the Catheter' inside, flushed and frantic. 'Cookies. Thank you. Put them . . . oh God, anywhere that's not covered by anything else.'

'Sure. Have you seen Janice? I heard Kate is getting married.'

'I think in the reading room.'

'Thanks.' Sophie sashayed off with a wave, trying to look as if landing this wedding didn't matter, and trying not to think about having to admit her business had failed, and having to watch people pretend sympathy while thinking, *Without Peter she's nothing.*

The reading room was one of Sophie's favorites, long wooden tables set up under low lamps hanging from the high ceiling. A fireplace at one end hosted comfy leather chairs; at the other, large leaded-glass windows provided light and views. She found Janice sorting through a box of contributed volumes, and congratulated her on the engagement of her youngest with the happiest smile she could manage.

Janice thanked her, pushing back her expertly cut salt-and-pepper bob.

'Will you be needing a caterer again?' Sophie asked.

'Oh.' Janice's sharp features fell into dismay, then impatience. 'Yes. About that. We're hiring from New York this time. Kate's fiancé is big money. This wedding is going to be huge. For the food, we thought we should have . . .'

Sophie waited, then decided to rescue Janice from having to finish the sentence with *something better than your dinky operation.* 'A larger company.'

'Yes, exactly.' Huge relief. 'You know, his whole family will be there, Hamptons vacationers, pied-à-terre in the city, the whole bit.'

'Of course.' She kept her smile warm. 'You want to impress them.'

Janice laughed uncomfortably and put down the books she was holding. 'Sounds shallow when you put it like that.'

Sounds shallow when you put it like anything.

Sophie checked herself. Tragic truth: at Kate's sister's

wedding, Sophie had scorched a tray of lobster puffs. Brides deserved everything perfect, as did their mothers. Sophie would exit quietly. 'Please congratulate Kate for me.'

'I will!' Janice had already ducked her head back into her box of books.

This called for another cookie. Mom would say it was too close to dinner time, so Sophie would have two.

Rotten day. She missed Lulu, who always made her feel better, listened so carefully to all her problems and reacted exactly the way Sophie needed her to. It sucked to outgrow friends, even those that were imaginary.

Maybe she'd go shopping.

At six p.m. sharp, she was at 14 Willow Street bearing a gift of a small bouquet of pink and purple flowers in a blue vase from Fairfield Florist, and a carefully swaddled Sarah, perfect symmetry restored to her hair and a Fabergéctomy performed on her head.

'Knock knock!' She stepped inside, inhaling the applewood-smoke aroma of roasting ham.

Her parents and Helen were out on the sun porch, glassed in during the winter, screened in during the summer, relaxing in the white wicker furniture with navy cushions that fit the space perfectly in style and size but was spectacularly uncomfortable. On the smudge-free glass-topped wicker coffee table, a bowl of nuts and a platter of smoked salmon and crackers, with dill, capers and lemon for garnish.

'Well,' Sophie said brightly, then realized her head was so full of Fabergé eggs that every other subject had deserted her. 'Hello, everyone.'

'Oh, pretty flowers, aren't you sweet.' Lilianne pointed to the bar. 'We're having G&Ts, help yourself.'

'Thanks.' Sophie got a seltzer with lime and sat opposite her father and Helen, wedged together on the loveseat. She took a quick sip, then reached into her bag. 'I brought someone with me.'

'Sarah!' Helen clapped her hands. 'She looks marvelous!'

'You did a wonderful job, sweetheart.' Lilianne and Gilles both beamed, making Sophie pathetically pleased at their approval.

But Sarah *did* look wonderful, her lovely forehead unobscured, tiara-topped hair in its usual dark, curling splendor.

'What a treat to have her back to perfect.' Helen reached for the doll. 'Thank you for being brave enough.'

'Or stupid enough.' Sophie loaded a cracker with sour cream, salmon and everything else. *Should she tell them now?*

'How was your day?' her dad asked.

'Bad.' Sophie made a face. 'I lost the Helversons. Steve got laid off.'

Her father's look of concern made her feel she'd already failed. 'They were your best clients.'

'I'm aware.' She popped the rest of the salmon into her mouth. 'It'll be fine.'

'What are you planning to do?' Lilianne was undoubtedly opening a mental spreadsheet. 'I can ask around at the club. Someone will—'

'I'd rather do this myself.' Total lie. She'd rather cash in the Fabergé, move to Tahiti and hire a hunky Swede to cater to her every need. 'I have some marketing plans ready to go.'

Her mother eyed her dubiously. Sophie didn't blame her. 'Marketing plans' out of her mouth sounded like as much bull as it was.

'Before you came in, we were reminiscing about Paris.'

Sophie turned gratefully to Helen, her savior for changing the subject. 'Which trip?'

'The first one.' Helen and Sophie's dad exchanged fairly goopy smiles. Sophie stole a look at her mother, but Lilianne had on the same goopy smile, so it must be okay. 'When I was fresh out of college, a kid really. That's where I met your mother and Gilles.'

'Really?' Sophie frowned, trying to remember if she'd ever asked where her mother had met Helen. 'Somehow I thought you and Mom had gone to college together.'

'Oh no.' Helen shook her head. 'Your mom was Wellesley, I was Kansas State. That Paris trip was my first abroad, a dream come true. I was lucky enough to bump into your mother and Connie early in my stay.'

'Connie.' Sophie reached for more salmon. 'Is she the friend I look like?'

It was difficult to describe the quality of silence that followed. Helen nearly jumped out of her skin. Her father stared in alarm. Even Lilianne looked taken aback, which never happened.

'What do you mean, Soph?' Gilles spoke cautiously, trying too hard to act casual.

'I'm afraid that was me.' Helen put her glass down, looking miserable. 'I was napping yesterday when you were both out. I woke up to Sophie. She looked so much like Connie, I thought it was her. I'm sorry.'

'So . . .' Sophie looked back and forth between the three stunned-silent adults. 'Is it *bad* that I look like Connie? Is she hideous?'

'Oh no, no. Connie was beautiful.' Lilianne smiled. Strained smile. 'Now that I look, I can see there might be a slight resemblance, maybe more in certain lights. Dark hair. That's about it, though. I think the ham has rested long enough, and the potatoes should be done. Let's eat.'

She shot to her feet, followed by Gilles, who helped Helen stand.

Sophie wasn't ready to move. 'Where is Connie now?'

'She died. Really tragic.' Her father linked arms with Helen. 'May I escort you to dinner, Ms Foster?'

'Yes.' Helen still looked miserable. 'Of course.'

'How young?' Sophie's heart was thumping. She had a hunch about this being important, and not only because everyone was trying so hard to make her think it wasn't. Helen's waking words had come back, in a different context: *you take after her* . . . 'What year did Connie die?'

'I don't remember.' Lilianne turned. 'Sophie, can you come dress the salad?'

'Was it 1978?' Sophie stood, raising her voice. 'The year I was adopted?'

No one seemed to want to answer that.

'Because as you no doubt remember, my birth mother died when I was a baby. Coincidence?'

Lilianne froze in the doorway, staring at Gilles. Helen froze on Gilles's arm, staring at Lilianne.

Gilles at least had the decency to stare at Sophie. 'Not a coincidence. Connie was your birth mother.'

'*Gilles.*' Lilianne took a step toward him, as if she could somehow catch his words and hide them before Sophie heard.

All of Sophie's muscles gave out at once. She sat with a whoosh of cushion and a creak of wicker. 'A friend of yours. A *friend of yours* was my birth mother.'

'Yes.'

'Why the hell didn't you tell me you knew her?' Her voice came out high and shrill. 'You could have told me everything. Everything about her. You *knew*.'

'It's complicated.'

'We thought it was best.'

Her parents spoke at the same time.

'What's complicated about "Our friend Connie is your mother. She died and we adopted you"?'

Her parents exchanged glances.

'This is all my fault,' Helen said.

'It's not your fault.' Lilianne reached consolingly toward her.

'I'm sorry, Sophilu.' Her dad's face reflected his anguish. 'This wasn't up to us. We made a promise.'

Sophie laughed in disbelief. 'Who would have more of a say in my adoption than you? Who deserved to know more than I did? What—'

'Stop.' Lilianne struck her best power-lawyer pose, arms folded, features severe. At forty-five, Sophie was still tempted to run to her room and slam the door. 'We can go around in circles for the next two hours with us saying we can't talk about it and you insisting we can, or we can sit down and have a nice dinner together. You choose.'

'Who was my father?' Sophie ignored her mother and spoke directly to Gilles.

'Also dead.' His handsome features radiated genuine regret. 'I'm sorry.'

'Same time as my mother?'

He shook his head. 'Earlier. We don't know the circumstances. I believe it was . . . violent.'

This was in*sane*. Sophie had craved this information her entire life. Now it turned out the people closest to her had always been capable of supplying it, but they hadn't and still wouldn't, for reasons they couldn't tell her.

If only she could reach into her parents' heads as easily as she'd been able to reach into Sarah's. But she knew that look on her mother's face. And she knew her father wouldn't betray his wife.

'Well.' She took a beat to force a smile. 'That's a boatload of dead parents. Dinner sounds like a good idea, Mom, thank you.'

The Jewel of Cairo

After a pause during which everyone, including Sophie, seemed unsure if she really meant what she'd said, her parents and Helen moved into the dining room, Helen on her father's arm, Lilianne with her usual brisk purpose. Sophie followed them, madly calculating how she could trick someone into letting slip more details during dinner, her announcement about the Fabergé on hold in the face of something less important to the world but so much more important to her.

The ham was delicious, served with baked sweet potatoes and her mother's signature creamed spinach. Conversation was stilted at first, but Sophie made a point of playing cheerful and chatty, asking questions about the trio's road trip, then about Helen's ranch in Kansas and her granddaughter, Teresa. Gradually, she hoped skillfully, she could turn the conversation back to Paris.

During the break after salad and before dessert, she decided to strike. 'What was Connie like?'

Helen looked to Lilianne. 'May I answer that?'

Brittle smile. 'I don't see why not.'

'She was marvelous.' Helen's blue eyes softened into affection behind her lenses. 'Colorful. A bit of a flower child, but in the best way. Full of joy and love and optimism and energy, very conscious of spreading all those things to everyone she met. She was a collector of friends, interested in everything. She brightened whatever room she was in.'

Sophie ate up every word. Her birth mother! 'What did she look like?'

'Beautiful.' Gilles's smile was wistful. 'She had dimples like yours, and your dark, thick hair. She wasn't tall, and she was curvy, also like you. She and her family were from a village on Crete. Her parents emigrated to Vermont – is that right, Lilianne?'

Lilianne was tight-lipped, staring hard at Gilles, telegraphing, *Stop Talking* so intensely it was nearly audible. 'Yes.'

'What was her last name?' Sophie directed the question to Helen, in case she hadn't seen Lilianne's glare. 'Connie what?'

'Connie . . .' Helen glanced at Lilianne. 'Huh. Isn't that odd? It was there earlier, now *whoosh*, gone. Senior brain moment. Connie . . . Kappas? Packus?'

Sophie had to hand it to her. She was good.

'I'll get dessert.' Lilianne stood and picked up the ham platter. 'Help clear, Sophie?'

'Sure.' Sophie rose, playing her cooperative-child role as obviously as possible, and stacked the rest of the plates to bring into the kitchen. *Connie* and *Vermont* weren't much to go on. Crete could help, but only slightly.

In the kitchen, her mother turned. 'I know what you're doing.'

'I know you know, but what am I?' Sophie sang. 'Can't blame a girl for trying.'

Lilianne's face softened into laughter. 'You are so much like her.'

'Tell me more?' Sophie put on her best pleading face. Effective with Dad, and very occasionally with her mother.

'I don't know what I can add to what Helen already—'

'Please, Mom.'

Lilianne bowed her head and sighed, then looked back up. 'Connie was into everything. But she got bored quickly and moved on, always wanting new excitement. She spent whatever money she made, didn't save or worry about her future.'

Sophie stopped scraping plates, not wanting to miss a word. This was sounding familiar.

'She was intuitive, could often tell what people around her were feeling and sense whether they were going in the right direction. Then she'd jump in with encouragement or warnings.

Very direct. No sugar-coating. But with such humor. She was hilarious.'

Sophie wanted her to go on all evening. Apparently many of her own traits, those that had felt like major flaws in this house of directed overachievers, had come from her mother. The news made her feel like singing and like crying. For the first time, she felt she was getting permission to be herself.

'Her parents were old-world strict and Connie was rebellious. I think her childhood was difficult, probably for the whole family. She wasn't close to her parents or her sister. She made it through a year of college, recognized it wasn't for her and spent her life traveling abroad, seeing as much as she could, doing as much as she could. She had endless energy. Classes, sightseeing, clubbing, men—'

'Whoa.' Sophie recoiled in faux-horror, needing either to break the mood or collapse. 'She clubbed men?'

Lilianne snorted and reached into the cupboard. 'Collected them. Sometimes only for an hour, sometimes more, but she loved them. In great quantities.'

'Oh.' That didn't sound anything like Sophie. She'd been faithful as a dog during her marriage and celibate during her post-divorce PTSD. 'What else?'

'Hmm.' Her mother frowned, holding a bar of high-end chocolate. 'She did have a dark side, Sophie. She was a partier, a drinker, and I think on Crete she got into trouble with some other substances. I don't know details, but some of her letters seemed written under the influence and pretty strange. Not when she was pregnant with you, though. She wrote when you were on the way saying how happy she was, and sounded completely clear.'

'Do you still have the letters?' Sophie couldn't be more eager to meet this woman, see her writing, hear her voice, touch something she'd touched. 'Any pictures?'

'Somewhere . . .' Lilianne gestured vaguely toward the second floor, not volunteering to run up and find them, either now or in the future.

With a jolt, it occurred to Sophie that beyond this promise not to reveal her parentage, it was also possible Lilianne was finding it difficult to share motherhood with another woman. Sophie wouldn't insist. For now.

'Thank you for telling me, Mom.'

Lilianne turned from arranging chocolate in a shallow china bowl. 'I know this is hard on you. Believe me, your father and I did not want it to happen this way.'

'I believe you.' Sophie gave her a long hug, wrapping her arms around her mother's slender waist and squeezing good and hard, the best, most loving hug she could manage.

Lilianne hugged her back, swallowing a few times, breathing a little strangely. 'Your mother was a rare and wonderful human being, Soph. I loved her, and I love that she lives on in you. I wish I could have shared all this with you growing up.'

Sophie raised her face to kiss her mom's cheek. If she hadn't believed her before, she did now. The regret, the sadness in the voice so rarely affected by either.

'Thanks, Mom. I love you.'

Lilianne nodded, clearing her throat.

Did it make Sophie a horrible person to be glad her mother had cracked a little? It happened so seldom. For Sophie to crack emotionally, she just needed to be awake.

She extracted herself from the hug. 'I'll get the dessert plates.'

After dessert, Sophie helped with the dishes, then kissed her parents, hugged Helen goodbye and rushed back to her condo, where, after checking to see that the Fabergé was still safe in her underwear, she plunked herself at her desk, too impatient even to get her good-night-sweet-dreams bowl of ice cream. Mint chocolate chip this week.

'C'mon, Google, be my friend.' She opened a browser window and started typing. *Connie. Vermont. Crete.* Not much, but it was all she had to go on.

Search, scroll, search, scroll . . . nothing but dead ends.

Another try.

Constance. Vermont. Crete.

Search, scroll, search, scroll . . . more dead ends.

Constance. Vermont. Greece.

Search, scroll, search . . .

She gasped. Too easy. An obituary from a Vermont paper, the *Barre Montpelier Times Argus* from 2005 for Phyllis Corson, née Pappas, owner of Asphalia House in Rutland, a sanctuary for women in recovery from addiction. Phyllis's parents, Eleni and Georgios Pappas, had emigrated from Greece in 1939. They started Asphalia after the death of their daughter, Constance Pappas, in 1978.

Sophie could hardly breathe. Constance Pappas. Her mother.

Constance's sister, Phyllis, had taken over Asphalia House in 2000 after Eleni's death.

Sophie sat staring, half laughing, half crying, then it hit her like a ton of bricks. Eleni and Georgios Pappas were her *grandparents*. Phyllis Corson was her *aunt*.

All dead. Of course. Being related to Sophie must be fatal.

The obit went on . . . high school, college, this, that, lovely woman, asset to the community . . .

Sophie's mouth dropped open. She blinked at the screen. Blinked some more.

Phyllis was survived by her husband, Clyde, four children and five grandchildren.

Ka-boom!

Just like that, somewhere in Vermont, lonely only child Sophie had cousins, nieces, nephews and an uncle. With luck, her cursed self hadn't made any of them drop dead in the intervening years.

She smacked her hand on her desk and jumped up. She didn't care who had promised what to whom. After a lifetime denied any knowledge of her origins, the chance to learn about them was even more compelling than figuring out what to do with a Fabergé egg that wasn't hers.

No matter how much her parents objected, as soon as she could get away, Sophie was going up to Vermont to meet her birth family.

Chapter 7

Saturday, May 1, 1976

Lilianne closed E. M. Forster's *Passage to India*, a novel she'd pulled from the shelves of her apartment and spent hours with that morning and into the afternoon. A day reading in bed, what a guilty pleasure. She couldn't remember the last time she'd indulged. In Paris, there were always expeditions with roommates Connie and Helen, plus Gilles and whomever Connie was dating that week. Any reading Lilianne did had been work-related – ledgers, balance sheets, contracts.

She'd been swept into the shared rooming situation by Connie's enthusiasm for gathering people around her. The resulting drama with Helen and Gilles had sucked her further in, a fate she'd always prided herself on avoiding. Let others tangle and angst over loving or not loving; she'd soar freely above it all, one of her abnormality's silver linings. Coming to Cairo on her own had been a relief. Today's indulgence reminded her of the importance of making sure she kept carving out time for herself.

The job at the bank was still going well, though the Egyptian concept of time was a perpetual challenge to Lilianne's love of efficiency. Reports were cheerfully promised 'tomorrow' until she was ready to shriek. However, when the requested records did appear, they were all squeaky clean. She was betting Cairo National Bank would be an excellent investment opportunity for Maxwell in what promised to be the economic center of the Arab world.

It still felt surreal to be thinking of her future at Maxwell Investments without her father involved. Where would she go next? Maybe back to the US? She missed her hometown of Southport, missed the independence and freedoms she'd always taken for granted in the Western world. Cairo and Egypt still fascinated, but being the obvious outsider was taking its toll. Would she stay working for Maxwell? If Kane the Jerk took charge, probably not. Lilianne would have the same chance of advancement as an eight-year-old.

In the meantime, there was Sami. A week after their float down the Nile, the two of them had visited the Khan el-Khalili, a market area of the city that had been around since the fourteenth century. They'd ambled through narrow streets choked with color, shops selling jewelry, antiques, copperwork, spices, rugs, lamps, leather goods, souvenirs – everything. They'd ended the afternoon sitting outside, sipping coffee served on brass tray tables at El-Fishawy Café, run by descendants of the El-Fishawy family since 1797, Sami fending off the usual vendors with sharp Arabic Lilianne had to pretend she didn't understand. 'Mosquitoes,' he had told her. 'No matter how many you swat, more keep coming.'

Now, a week later, she should take him up on his offer to climb to the top of the The Great Pyramid at Giza, but she was finding it hard to be enthusiastic about the underhanded nature of their friendship. What little she'd learned of him had been dutifully passed along to John Baker, but she was increasingly feeling as if there wasn't much else to dig up. Sami's views on politics were typical, and he was too smart to let slip anything valuable. Beyond that, he was charming, personable and easy company, though she sensed something dark under his glib surface. Personally, she worried he was misinterpreting her continued interest in spending time together.

Dragging her wandering thoughts out of bed, she showered and pulled on shorts and a T-shirt, looking ahead to the rest of the empty afternoon. This would be the perfect day to call her grandparents.

Instant claustrophobia sent her searching for excuses not to.

Her phone rang. Lilianne turned to stare, as if it would announce who was calling so she could decide whether to answer.

Thoughts of Gilles made her decision for her. Good news from him or about him would put a lot of worrying to rest. 'Hello?'

'Could this be the dynamic, beautiful and spiritually pure Lilianne Maxwell?'

Lilianne let out a shout of laughter. 'Connie! How perfect to hear from you. I've been thinking about you today.'

'Yes, your karma was calling me.'

She rolled her eyes over a grin. 'Any word from Gilles?'

'Crap, no. I was hoping you had some.'

Lilianne's hope deflated. 'Nothing for way too long.'

'I tell myself no news is good news, but I'm starting to have a hard time believing it.'

'I'm sure he's fine.' A pause while they were both horribly afraid he wasn't. 'Are you in the rue Pierre Nicole apartment? I miss that clanky elevator.'

'Why no, I'm not, my love. I'm somewhere very far away from the apartment. In fact, I am in a very, very ancient country.'

'You made it to Greece!' Lilianne grinned widely. 'Are you on Crete? Have you found your grandparents' village?'

'Not Crete. I'm at the apartment of my new delicious friend, Sean, in Maadi, Cairo, home of pharaohs and falafel. "Street 15 near Mustafa Kamel Square", Sean says.'

'Oh!' Lilianne suppressed a jolt of dismay she shouldn't be feeling. 'You're right around the corner from me!'

'Far out! I'll come see you right away. Can I?'

'Of course you can.' Her stomach twisted. 'Who is Sean?'

'Guy I met on the plane. Some kind of foreign service dude from England. Cute to the max.'

Lilianne shook her head. Connie's ability to land men was legendary. Either she was open to more types of people than the norm, or she simply didn't care who showed interest. 'Come on over. How long are you here?'

'As long as I feel it, baby.'

That could be long.

Lilianne rattled off her address, ashamed of her hesitance. Seeing Connie would be a day-brightener. The woman could brighten a total eclipse.

After a quick glance around to make sure her place was in order, Lilianne headed for the ground floor, summer sandals clattering down the stairs, and through the front doors into the hot afternoon sunshine. There she waited, pacing, until a familiar figure turned the corner of her tree-lined block, wearing a peasant blouse embroidered with multicolored thread, and a long scarlet skirt. Her dark braid curled over one shoulder, a gaudy paisley canvas bag hanging off the other; hot-pink flip-flops lit up her feet. In this country of conservative dress, Connie was a startling sight, like a scarlet macaw strolling a lava field.

The second Lilianne saw her, sheer joy replaced her hesitation. She hurried along the dusty road, sending a feral cat scampering.

The Jewel of Cairo

Connie dropped her bag and wrapped her arms around Lilianne, the top of her dark head resting at chin height. Lilianne had to breathe deeply to keep from tearing up. How could she have thought she wouldn't be overjoyed to see her friend?

'I want to know everything you've been doing here, what you've seen, who you've met.' Connie pulled back from their hug. 'Fill me in on the vibe! This city is such a head trip!'

'Come up, come upstairs to my place. We'll have a drink on my balcony and talk about everything.'

'Thank you, my love! I'm running on fumes. Woke up two weeks ago and thought, "Enough Paris. Lilianne needs me."' Connie flashed her irresistible dimpled smile. 'It took me a while to extract myself from the city and the apartment, and I worked about a thousand hours to afford the ticket, but here I am.'

'I'm thrilled.'

'I am too! What adventures we'll have.' She threw out her arms. 'I want to learn belly dancing and ride a camel. For a start. Then I want to be kissed near the pyramids – not by you – and recite poems to the Sphinx.'

Lilianne smiled indulgently, wondering how to break it to her irrepressible friend that Cairo, like Paris, was a city of wonders, but not one a woman could dive into with the kind of abandon Connie favored.

They chatted madly down the sidewalk, into her building and up the stairs to the second floor. Lilianne pushed open the door to her comfortable apartment, which turned lifeless next to Connie's swirling color. 'Welcome to my groovy pad.'

'Thank you, my darling. It is indeed a groovy pad! It needs a disgusting orange couch like the one we had in Paris, but it will do fine!' Connie looked around and pointed at the two bedroom doors in turn. 'Which will be mine?'

Lilianne went cold. One thing to have a new playmate in the

city, quite another to take on a roommate who'd eliminate the only place she could enjoy her solitude.

Connie whirled around in the silence. 'I'm awful! You didn't invite me, I just assumed after we had so much fun in *la belle France*. So uncool! Bogus, in fact. Never mind!'

'No, no . . . Of course I want you here.' Lilianne almost made it sound convincing. 'I was just surprised.'

Connie put her hands on her hips and advanced sternly. 'Think it over. If you're miserable with me here, then I'll be miserable, and the whole spiritual energy of my visit will flush down the crapper. I'm sure Sean will let me stay with him.'

Lilianne took a breath, thinking of the fun they'd had in Paris with Helen – and Gilles; the nights sharing wine and conversations ranging from philosophy to food to history to gossip. The way they'd pulled delicious dinners out of whatever they found at the markets. The way Lilianne had felt like an integral part of a close group of friends for the first time in her life, and loved it, at least until the drama started.

She looked her friend in the eye. 'I was in a solitary mood when you showed up. Of course I want you to stay here. There's plenty of room, and I would love it.'

'No bullshit?'

'None.'

'Thank you, my sweet. I should have let you know sooner that I was coming, but I so love surprises. Speaking of . . .' She took the canvas bag off her shoulder and bent over it. 'I brought someone with me.'

Lilianne clapped her hands as a large, beautiful doll emerged from the garish cloth. 'Sarah! Our best friend. It's so good to see her.'

Sarah Bernhardt had been a gift from Madame Laurent, the French professor Helen had worked for in Paris. Helen, Connie and Lilianne had treated the doll as another roommate, consulting her on important matters and including her as a special guest at parties and birthday celebrations. Silly but harmless. Seeing her dark curls and green gown, her diamond jewelry and fur cape brought on a flood of nostalgic affection.

'The rest of my stuff is at Sean's, but I wanted to make sure I brought Sarah with me right away.' Connie held out the doll. 'She has missed you terribly.'

'I missed her too.' Lilianne took Sarah into her arms and stroked the soft fur, looking around the apartment for a suitably important spot. 'Where should we put her?'

Connie pointed decisively to the top shelf of a bookcase in a corner of the room. 'Up there. She can look down on all of us.'

'As Her Highness should.' Lilianne replaced an olive-green vase with the doll, leaning her carefully against the wall so she wouldn't be in danger of tumbling off.

'Madame Sarah, how beautiful you look.' Connie curtseyed gracefully, then her rapturous expression clouded. 'Oh hell, Lilianne. I miss Helen.'

So do I. They stared mournfully at the doll Helen had brought into their lives then left behind when she bolted miserably home to the US, having smashed Gilles's heart.

'Come, we'll get something to drink.' Lilianne led the way to the apartment's modern, serviceable kitchen – about twice the size of the microscopic one they'd shared on rue Pierre Nicole – still trying to fathom how having Connie here would change her stay in Egypt. 'Are you hungry?'

'No, no, Sean fed me. I'm happy until dinner.'

'You're happy all the time.' Lilianne opened the refrigerator and pulled out a pitcher of lemonade. There were juice bars all over Cairo in which you could get delicious fresh juices squeezed for you on the spot: orange, guava, mango, strawberry, apricot, sugar cane ... But the Egyptian way of making lemonade was her favorite, sold in every coffeehouse. She'd copied the recipe after watching carefully as whole lemons were blended with sugar, water and fresh mint.

Connie flitted around the kitchen, examining and touching everything in reach – the bowl of mangos and persimmons on the yellow counter, the dark-wood cabinets, the electric stove Lilianne had to learn her way around after so many years cooking with gas, the noisy refrigerator. 'Lemonade? What's in it?'

'Lemons.' Lilianne poured two glasses and added ice.

'Got any vodka?'

'Nope. Come outside.'

'Yes, yes.' Connie's face was glowing. 'I want to see everything. Are you going to paint the walls? Raspberry red? Lemon yellow? Orange orange?'

'I don't know how much longer I'll be here.'

Connie followed Lilianne out onto the small balcony. 'Well, you have to stay at least as long as it takes for me to check out the city. Sean told me about a disco on a houseboat on the river. Want to go tonight?'

'I thought you said you were running on fumes.' Lilianne sat, rattled by the idea of a night of loud music and dancing after so many relatively peaceful outings, and gestured to the chair next to her.

'When has that ever stopped me?' Connie glugged down some lemonade. 'That is delicious. Even better if it had vodka in it.'

'Sorry.' Lilianne was relieved she didn't stock it. Connie tended to overdo, though she held it well. 'Can't stand the stuff.'

Connie gave an exaggerated sigh. 'I'll last until cocktail hour, I suppose. So, tell me everything, Lil! What have you been doing? Who have you been seeing? How do you like it here? Met any friends? Not as good as me, of course.'

'No, not as good as you. Impossible.' Lilianne thought of Sami. Not a friend, though she was fond of him. More like an assignment. 'It's impossible not to be social here. I've been invited everywhere every day since I landed, and I'm only exaggerating a little.'

'By work people? That doesn't count.' Connie made a face. 'They're boring bankers.'

'Ahem.'

'You're the not-boring kind, my love, of course.' She leaned back and rested her magenta flip-flops on the railing. 'And your grandparents? What are they like? I can't wait to meet them.'

Lilianne pursed her lips.

Connie's feet hit the cement floor with a rubbery smack. 'Oh no! Did they not want to see you? I'm so sorry.'

'No. No. It's just I haven't . . . I've been busy, and . . .'

Connie let her mouth hang open. 'You are kidding me. You've been here since what, mid March? Two and a half *months*, and you haven't contacted your own family?'

Lilianne stared, hoping to cow her into silence, then remembered this was Connie. Connie didn't cow. Nor was she ever silent. 'I'll call them soon.'

'What's the real reason?' Connie's brown eyes narrowed. 'Are you chicken?'

'Mom said that once they knew I was here they'd take over my life.'

'Oh! Oh yes, I see now, I understand.' Connie's features relaxed; she nodded vigorously. 'You're *totally* chicken.'

'I'm not chick—'

'Then what, you forgot how to say no if they invite you too often?' Connie scoffed at that one. 'Name the last person you let walk all over you, Lilianne Maxwell. In fact, name *any* person you've *ever* allowed to walk all over you.'

Lilianne looked down into her lemonade, pressing her lips together. Then she blew out an involuntary but credible imitation of a snorting horse. 'Okay, maybe I'm a little chicken. But, Your Smugness, it is a complicated situation. Mom said they'll do nothing but criticize my life.'

'Hmm.' Connie was staring at her suspiciously. 'I don't know what people are like in Egypt, but if they're anything like the Greeks, which I suspect they are, family is everything. You could be Jacqueline the Ripper, but if you're related, they'll be thrilled to see you and want to feed you more than you can eat.'

'I know, I know.' Lilianne stood abruptly and peered down into the street. She loved her mother and father, but considering her history with nannies, it would be a stretch to say family was everything to her.

'Getting that first call over with is the hard part.' Connie stood too and put her hand on Lilianne's arm, squeezing it hard. 'But it will be worth it. I promise.'

'Maybe.'

'New subject.' Connie dropped her hand. 'What do we do about Gilles?'

Lilianne pictured the handsome Frenchman, his dark eyes and full mouth, his killer smile and his keen intelligence, his sensitivity and his passion. She couldn't bear to think of him immersed in the savage stupidity of war, even if he carried a camera instead of a gun. 'The worst couldn't have happened or we'd see it in the papers.'

'But there's a lot of awful that isn't the worst.' Connie's sunny face had clouded, a rare expression for her. 'I called Agence France-Presse before I left, but they wouldn't tell me anything, even after a double dose of Connie Pappas charm. I even called Gilles's parents, but they're off traveling. Or so their butler said. *Beaucoup* bucks in that family, *mon Dieu*.'

The Jewel of Cairo

Lilianne sipped lemonade, necessary for her dry throat. 'I have to think he'll be in touch when he can. The war sounds hellish. Not the greatest inspiration for writing cute postcards.'

'I guess not.'

Silence again, while they both tried not to think inevitable thoughts.

'I did hear from Helen.'

'Oh? How's she doing?' Lilianne tried to keep her voice light, even knowing she couldn't fool Connie.

'Seems cheerful enough. Lots of farm details, corn plans and such. She and Kevin are getting married in June. The nineteenth.'

'Stupid girl.'

Connie sent Lilianne a pointed look. 'She chose. She'll make it work.'

'I know, you're right. Did she ... mention me? Or Gilles?' She wished it didn't matter so much. This was exactly the type of emotional entanglement she scorned. No one should have such power over her feelings from halfway around the world.

'Nope,' Connie announced cheerfully. 'She did not. You are all stubborn idiots. However, I know in my heart, deep down where it counts, that this will pass and you'll be together again. The day you and I found her, I felt in my place of sure truth that we'd be lifelong soulmates, so it's only a matter of time. One of you will crack.'

Lilianne laughed. It was nearly impossible to be miserable around Connie.

'You're thinner, Lil.' Connie scrutinized her. 'I'm thinking you haven't been so happy here.'

'I've been great.' She was surprised her most intuitive friend could get that one wrong. 'Work is much calmer here, and the culture is fascinating.'

'You're lonely.'

'I'm not, actually. I've had plenty of—'

'I plan to cheer you up.' Connie put her empty lemonade glass on the wobbly metal table. 'First, we're going shopping, because you need to stock something a lot stronger than lemonade. Second, we're going dancing tonight with Sean and his friend.'

'I don't really feel like—'

'Third.' Connie held up a finger to ward off more interruption. Lilianne obediently lapsed into silence, hiding a groan. Was it possible to kick her best friend out this soon after she'd said Connie could stay? 'Tomorrow, when you're at your most hung-over and exhausted, and therefore most weak-willed, I'm going to come at you with the telephone. Because all you need to get out of your funk . . .'

'*What* funk?'

'. . . is me, of course, and large doses of your Egyptian family.'

Chapter 8

Thursday, May 13, 1976

Lilianne stood on Al Khamraway Street, in the Shubra district, staring up at her grandparents' building. She hadn't really planned to come here today, but after lunch, with requested work documents still MIA, she'd decided to explore a new neighborhood, and found herself in a taxi headed toward this one.

Right. Just happened to find herself on her way to this spot without any idea how it happened.

Connie had been working on her during the past activity-crammed week and a half she'd been Lilianne's roommate again. Disco dancing, camel rides, belly-dancing lessons, shopping sprees, all had acted like a recharge, making Lilianne feel she'd been going through the motions before her friend arrived. Sean was a nice guy, rail-thin with shaggy blond hair, who seemed no more right for Connie than any of the others, but she never seemed to care. He brought along a few friends on some outings, and Connie picked up a stray companion here and there as she always did.

Being reconnected with her adventurous spirit must have had something to do with Lilianne being here today, fantastically nervous, even though she hadn't called and could just as easily stand here for a few minutes then walk away.

She took in details of the three-story cream stone building: wrought-iron balconies, stone scrolls and flowers carved around the windows, arched niches decorating its sides. Ideally, her grandmother would look out the window, see a tall blonde in Western business dress looking nothing like any Abdallah had ever looked, and think, 'Oh, that must be my granddaughter, I'll go down and see her.'

How did someone willing to spy for the government, who'd coolly fended off furious executives, horny men and one knife-wielding mugger, quake at the idea of seeing her own relatives?

A woman opened one of the second-floor windows and shook out a towel. Lilianne watched the dust motes dance down, swirling in sunlight, then swallowed in shadow. The woman caught sight of her. Lilianne offered a smile, heart pounding. *Are you my grandmother? Do you recognize something in me?*

The head disappeared. The window closed.

This was stupid.

She stepped into the street and crossed over to the building's front door on shaky legs. Peering at the names of the apartment residents, she forced her finger to press the buzzer next to *Abdallah* before what little nerve she had deserted her.

There. Lilianne could fire a weapon, disarm an opponent, sniff out corruption *and* press a buzzer.

She waited, heart still racing, cheeks flushed, not just from the heat.

No response.

She waited longer, experiencing annoying doorbell indecision. Keep waiting? Ring again and risk being obnoxious? Decide no one was home and leave?

'*Alo?*' An older-sounding woman.

'Good afternoon. Is this Zahra?' Her grandmother's name felt more foreign on her tongue than the Arabic

'Who is there?'

Deep breath. 'Her granddaughter. From—'

'Aida?' The doubt was evident.

'Lilianne Maxwell. From the United States. Dina's daughter.' She waited, holding her breath.

An exclamation of surprise, then the intercom went dead.

Lilianne looked around, not knowing what to do. Sweat made its way down the middle of her back. Hot today, in the upper eighties, and only May. Summers in Egypt were supposed to be brutal.

She snorted. When in doubt, talk about the weather, even when talking to oneself.

The intercom crackled again, then the same woman's voice. 'She is coming.'

'Zahra is?'

No response. Sweating harder, Lilianne drew herself up tall, reminding herself that she was strong, capable and brave, and that no one could have power over her unless she allowed them to.

The door was flung open to reveal a plump woman in a blue-and-white-striped dress, hair dyed jet black, lips painted pink, features so much like Dina's would be in another few decades that Lilianne started, utterly disoriented.

'Ah, I'm sorry.' The woman spoke in careful English, eager expression dimming as she looked around and behind Lilianne. 'I am looking for someone.'

'Zahra Abdallah?'

'Yes?'

'I'm Lilianne. Dina's daughter.'

'Lilianne! But . . .' Her dark eyes widened; she gestured indignantly toward Lilianne's head. 'Blonde?'

Lilianne shrugged and switched to Arabic. 'My American father's fault.'

'*Ya lahwi!*' Her grandmother covered her mouth, eyes filling with tears. 'I didn't believe Nailah, I had to come see for myself. Who is this person saying she's my granddaughter? I thought she was losing her mind. I still can't believe it. Come, come here.'

She took Lilianne's shoulders and kissed her on both cheeks, then held her at arm's length to study her fully. 'Welcome, *habibti, inti*. Why didn't you let us know you were visiting? How long are you in Cairo? When did you arrive? Come in, come up, we'll have coffee. You must stay to dinner. Braheem will be home. I'll call your uncles. We'll have a party. Where are you staying, what hotel? You must come stay with us. Are you alone or—'

'Yes, alone.' Lilianne followed her up the stairs amid the barrage of questions. 'No, no party. Not today.'

'What does this mean, no party? We are Egyptians, we celebrate everything. Nailah! Put on the coffee!'

The apartment was cool, comfortable and attractively furnished, living room floors smothered in Oriental rugs, leaving barely a glimpse of the rust-colored tile underneath. Plants added a fresh green note, and large windows provided a view of the city and the spires of the nearby Al Khazindar mosque.

A woman who must be Nailah shuffled in, face deeply etched with wrinkles, wearing a black sweater, skirt and stockings. Her eyes were full of tears as she clasped Lilianne's face in her hands, crooning Arabic endearments. 'I raised your mother. Dina! I loved her as if she were my own daughter. She broke our hearts when she left. All of them, broken like glass—'

'Coffee, Nailah. Dinner tonight for the whole family.'

'I'm sorry.' Lilianne's reaction was instinctive. This was too much already. 'I can't stay for dinner.'

'Yes, yes.' Zahra nodded vigorously. 'You must, you must.'

The Jewel of Cairo

Lilianne held up her palms to indicate helplessness. 'I have an engagement already.'

'This weekend, then. Saturday. We'll have dinner, all the Abdallahs. You can meet your uncles and their children, and my great-grandchild, Dalia. Praise God we have you with us!'

Lilianne's stomach clenched. She hated being the center of attention except in a work environment. But she couldn't pop in and out of her family's life without getting to know any of them. She'd known that when she showed up. She'd known that when she *resisted* showing up.

'Now. Sit, sit.' Zahra gestured emphatically to an overstuffed cream chair 'You must tell me everything. Coffee, Nailah! She just made some, why is she so slow?'

Still weeping, Nailah emerged from what must have been the kitchen with an engraved silver tray laden with the traditional long-handled beaker-shaped coffee pot and china cups, plus a bowl of blushing apricots and a plate heaped with date-filled cookies. She put the bounty down on the brass table in the center of the living room and stood shaking her clasped hands toward Lilianne, who smiled and inclined her head, hoping that was a sufficiently gracious response to the gesture.

'*Yallah*, Nailah,' Zahra said. 'Call Braheem and tell him his granddaughter is here.'

'Yes, yes, God be praised.' The old woman shuffled off, sniffling and wiping her eyes.

'So you see something of what your mother did to us.' Zahra's smile was tight. 'Sugar?'

'A little.'

Zahra poured the thick brew, stirred in some sugar with a miniature silver spoon and offered the cup in its tiny saucer.

Lilianne took it, weighing her words. 'I'm sure Mom leaving was hard for everyone, but—'

'Hard! I nearly died of the grief. My only daughter. Such a headstrong girl.' Zahra passed over the plate of apricots, then the cookies, even though both were easily within Lilianne's reach. 'Eat! Eat! You're too thin. We should have more to offer you. Nailah is getting old. I can call her if you need—'

'No, this is plenty. More than enough. Thank you.' Lilianne felt compelled to defend her mother. 'Mom wanted a life in the US and thought—'

'Wanted? It was all she talked about. "I need to get out of here." Insisting we speak English so she could practice. You'd think she grew up in a pigsty the way she talked about our life.' Zahra clucked her tongue. 'This all started after she met my sister. Sabra married a rich Jordanian and moved to his home. Every time she came to visit, it was all Paris this and London that and New York City and San Francisco. Your mother could not get enough. There was no stopping her.'

'She's a determined woman.'

'That is God's truth.' Zahra stirred a spoonful of sugar into her own cup. 'And you, *hayati*, are you like her?'

Lilianne sipped her typically Egyptian coffee. Thick and bitter with just a touch of sweetness. 'I'm more like my father. Even-tempered. Quiet. But yes, also determined.'

'Your mother was not quiet. She never stopped talking. I barely got a word in when she was around. How is the coffee? Is it too strong? More sugar?'

'It's perfect.' Lilianne couldn't imagine where her mother got her need to talk so much . . .

'How long have you been in Cairo?'

Lilianne hesitated, then dared the truth and the expected firestorm result. 'Since March.'

'March? March?! You didn't call us since *March*?!'

'No.' She looked her grandmother straight in the eye. 'I wasn't ready.'

Zahra looked surprised, then lifted her chin, regarding Lilianne speculatively. 'Tell me what brings you to Cairo. A long trip? Your husband's job?'

'My own job. I work for Maxwell Investments, my father's company. I'm here to—'

'Investments.' Zahra put down her cup and folded her hands in her lap. 'In my day, banking was not a job for a woman. My granddaughter Aida, Khaled's oldest, is studying to be a doctor in London. The world is changing.'

Lilianne took a bite of cookie to avoid answering further. The pastry was buttery and crumbly, the filling silky and sweet. 'Oh, these are good.'

'Nailah has a gift for *ara'eesh*. And many other things. Now tell me, Lilianne, *habibti*, I have so many questions. Are you married? You have a boyfriend?'

Lilianne shook her head, the familiar dread-knot forming in her chest. She washed down the last sweet bite with another sip of bitter. 'No to both.'

Zahra frowned and waggled a long finger. 'You'll need a man to protect you, to watch out for you and spoil you. Being alone is no good. Not for a woman, not for a man either. It's not in our nature.'

Lilianne looked down into her cup, where the thick grounds had made a pattern along the sides in grainy black and white. She was fifteen again, facing her mother with her awful secret. *No, no, Lilianne, you're just young. Everyone needs someone, it's human nature. You'll change when you meet the right person.*

'The right person will make all the difference. You'll see.'

Lilianne smiled, braver than at fifteen, and wiser, used to this response. It still hurt. 'Maybe that's it.'

'Aha.' Zahra put down her cup and slapped her hands on her thighs. 'I know a man for you. He's the son of—'

'No.' Lilianne kept her smile on. 'No. Thank you, but no.'

Zahra's expression changed into one that was so familiar Lilianne again experienced a wave of disorientation. Head tilted, dark brows down, full mouth slightly puckered. Skepticism, exactly the way her mother showed it.

'Then what for the rest of your life alone, Lilianne? What purpose without a husband, without children? Your work?' She made a distinctly Arabic scoffing sound, also familiar, though Dina had only rarely used her native language. 'That is not a purpose. That is not a life.'

Lilianne gulped the rest of her coffee and put down the cup, fighting the urge to fling angry words at her grandmother. She'd expected this exact lecture, and had prepared herself. She could not react like a child. 'I appreciate your concern, but how I live my life is up to me.'

A pause during which Zahra's black brows climbed the lined grid of her forehead. Then a smile spread her mouth, and her eyes grew softer, wistful, then shiny with tears. 'So there you are. Dina, my lost child. Hair blonde now, accent and clothes American, born to a different generation, but you are my child. And I will not lose you the way I lost her.' She lifted her hands. 'I have learned my lesson. Your life is yours to live, *hayati, inti*. Ignore an old woman's old-fashioned ideas.'

'Thank you, Teta.' Lilianne used the Arabic word for grandmother for the first time, and was gratified to see Zahra brighten.

'Ah, here he is. More coffee, Nailah!' The front door had opened to admit Lilianne's grandfather, a short, stout man with blunt features who greeted her warmly. He sat on the couch next to his wife and regarded Lilianne through square black glasses.

'So you see.' Zahra gestured across at her. 'We have Dina's child here.'

'How could I miss it?' He also spoke in Arabic, eyes twinkling. 'She looks just like the rest of the family.'

Lilianne blinked.

'Tall.' He put a measuring hand way above his head. 'Thin.' He patted his bulging belly. 'And blonde.' He pointed to what was left of his midnight-black head of hair. 'An Abdallah through and through.'

'She's a banker, Braheem. Working for her father's investment company. A woman in a man's world.' Zahra spoke with a trace of unexpected pride.

'Good for you.' Braheem took the news in stride. 'And lucky men.'

'No husband, no boyfriend.'

'Ah.' He folded his arms, grinning at Lilianne. 'Saving yourself a lot of pain, eh?'

'Oh!' Zahra smacked him teasingly. 'You. And she's been here since *March* and didn't call us.'

'Welcome, Lilianne, *ahlan wa sahlan*. It is good to meet you. We miss your mother every day.'

'Thank you.' She smiled, relieved that her grandfather wasn't jumping to put her or her choices through any kind of test. Unfortunately that also meant he didn't have much to say.

For the next hour, she tried her best, asking questions about his rug business, which he answered, then asking questions about his children, which Zahra answered, then answering their questions about what Egyptian foods she'd had so far, so her grandmother would know what to tell Nailah to prepare on Saturday when the clan gathered to celebrate the return of this substitute for the daughter, sister, cousin and aunt they'd lost.

After that, they resorted to what Lilianne had seen of Cairo, and what the weather was like, and that they hoped she wouldn't have to live through any sandstorms because she hadn't seen hell until a bad one blew in.

Through it all, as Lilianne talked and smiled, she was fighting deep unease. Why had she come here? These were total strangers, born to a very different culture. What had she expected? That she'd feel some magical instant connection that would fill a hole in her life she'd never known she had? Had she thought meeting them would help her feel more at home in this country? Feel part of an idea of family she'd never really missed?

She didn't belong here, and never truly would. Blood didn't matter. She should have trusted her instinct and kept to herself.

Lilianne stayed until bolting wouldn't feel rude, then announced with appropriate regret that she had to leave, and prepared herself for the inevitable and nearly endless protests over her impending departure, another rite she'd been through at every Egyptian home she'd visited.

After the cheek-kissing and the agonizingly slow progress to the apartment's front door, Braheem gestured to the exit, indicating she should precede him. '*Et fadaleh*. I'll see you out.'

Lilianne groaned silently and stepped onto the landing.

Like Zahra, Braheem ignored the elevator and turned to the staircase, then surprised her by breaking into fluent English. 'I try to walk when I can. It's good for the heart.'

'True.' She followed him down the spiral flights, wrung dry of chatter ideas, no longer caring if there was awkward silence.

At the building's front door, he turned, blocking her quick exit. 'Lilianne.'

Thwarted. So close. 'Yes, Jiddu.'

'I want you to understand something.' He took off his glasses, held them up to the light and polished them with a shirt tail. 'Our daughter Dina was a family member for eighteen years.

Then one day she was gone. It took us many, many months to understand that she wasn't coming back, and many more to understand that she would no longer speak to us, and many, many years after that to accept it.

'Now, today, here you are. It will take time for you to find your place in this family, and it will take time for us to fit you in as well.' He put the glasses back on and took her hands in his warm, large ones, forcing her to meet his eyes. 'I hope you will give us that time.'

Lilianne opened her mouth, at a loss how to answer such a beautiful, heartfelt plea, while Braheem seemed perfectly content to stand there, holding her hands and gazing at her, patiently waiting for her response. She had to force herself not to fidget.

'Yes, yes, of course.' Her voice came out too high, and she could read the disappointment in his eyes.

Braheem dropped her hands, pulled a business card and a pen out of his jacket pocket, wrote a number on the back of the card and held it out. 'Call when you want to see us. We love your mother very much. All of us. Her brothers, her mother, me . . . Please tell her.'

Lilianne nodded, all she could manage, then took the card and escaped out the front door into the heat of the afternoon.

Chapter 9

Present day

'Happy birthday!' Sophie placed the cake she'd made in front of Helen in her parents' dimmed dining room. 'Chocolate strawberry cream. I hope you and Sarah like it.'

'Sarah will eat anything with chocolate.' Helen looked lovely, no longer pale or gaunt, glowing in the candlelight. 'Thank you, Sophie, this is gorgeous.'

'Make a wish and blow.' Sophie stood by, reading to pluck out the candles before they dripped wax. She was admittedly impatient for the meal to be over, though of course . . . cake. After the festivities, she was going to make her big announcement: that she was leaving for Vermont on Saturday for two weeks to visit her birth family. The news about the Fabergé egg could wait until she was back. One life-changing uproar at a time.

She'd had trouble booking a place to stay in Vermont on such short notice. Her first choice had been a beautifully furnished guest cottage with gorgeous views, but it was only available by the month, and Sophie didn't have a month. Even two weeks was pushing it with her clients. So she'd settled on a room in someone's house – ugh – in Rutland, hoping it would offer at least some privacy, double-hoping she'd be spending most of her time in the bosom of her family, surrounded by constant rejoicing.

Helen pursed her lips and blew, annihilating the ten flames. Gilles, Lilianne and Sophie cheered.

'What did you wish for?' Gilles asked.

'Can't tell you.' She gave him a flirtatious grin, which he returned.

It had not escaped Sophie's notice that her father seemed happier than she'd ever seen him since Ms Helen Foster had been around. The weirdest part was that Mom seemed fine with their ... special bond, whatever it was. But okay, not Sophie's business. She guessed.

The cake *was* gorgeous, if she did say so herself, and delicious. Rich chocolate with ganache, strawberries and whipped cream between the layers. Sarah got a tiny ceremonial slice, which she gazed over with mournful beauty until Gilles ate it as his second helping.

They'd had champagne before the meal, but with the cake her dad poured Armagnac, a swanky brandy from southwestern France. Everyone was in a happy mood, laughing and telling stories, so Sophie waited until the energy at the table lagged and yawns started appearing, so as not to cut short Helen's celebration. Then it was time.

'I have some exciting news.'

Her father tilted his head. 'Ten more clients?'

'Uh, no.'

'Five?' Lilianne said hopefully.

Sophie sighed. It would be nice if her parents found joy in things unrelated to her business. 'I found members of my birth family. In Vermont.'

She hadn't expected cheers, but the silence was unnerving.

'Four cousins and an uncle. Clyde, my uncle, was married to

Connie's sister Phyllis, who unfortunately died of breast cancer in 2005. My cousins are Donny, Fred, Naomi and – get this, Mom – Lily Anne. Did Connie's sister know you?'

Mom shook her head emphatically. 'Phyllis and Connie weren't close.'

'Well.' Sophie prepared to dive in further. 'I've decided to drive up to Vermont and spend—'

'No.' Her mom looked panicked.

'Let her finish, Lilianne,' Helen said. 'Go on, Sophie.'

'I'm going up this weekend.' She tried not to look like a defiant adolescent, though she felt like one. 'For two weeks.'

'Do they know you're coming?'

'Not yet.' Sophie glanced warily at her mother. 'I thought it would be better if—'

'No. This is—'

'Lilianne.' Gilles gave her his I'll-handle-this look, which he didn't pull out often. 'I expected this. I've been thinking it over. We can't stop you, Sophilu. You're not three years old. Not that we had much luck stopping you even back then.'

A wan smile on Lilianne's face gave Sophie hope.

'We've told you about our promise, which I know is unsatisfying to you, and frustrating for us. But . . .' he shrugged in his French way, lips pursed, '*we* made that promise. Not you.'

Her hope balloon rose higher.

'Have you thought about what showing up might do to *them*?' Lilianne leaned forward for emphasis. 'How your sudden appearance might affect your cousins and their father?'

No, Sophie hadn't. She'd seen the whole thing as a joyous Hallmark movie reunion starring herself.

Oops. 'What kind of problems would I cause?'

Her mother and father looked at each other.

Sophie rolled her eyes. 'Let me guess. You can't tell me. You promised.'

'It seems silly now, Lilianne.' Her father spoke gently, hand on top of his wife's. 'The person we promised isn't around anymore.'

Which could mean Connie, or Phyllis. Maybe they'd promised Connie not to tell her family she'd had a baby.

'I won't break a solemn promise.' Lilianne bunched her mouth in disapproval. 'If you go, Sophie, and there are consequences, they'll be on you.'

'Okay.' Sophie lifted her hands in a shrug. 'But it's hard to feel threatened when I have no idea what those consequences could be.'

'Fair point.'

'The birthday girl has something to say.' Helen smiled warmly at Sophie, and in spite of the fact that she seemed to want to have sex with Sophie's father, Sophie felt a surge of affection. 'I set this whole kerfuffle in motion, for which I'm sorry. But I'd like to jump in with what I think dear Connie would say.'

'Oh yes, please.' Sophie was all ears.

'She would have told you that finding out about her family meant the universe was pointing you in that direction. She'd say there was something in Vermont that you need in your life right now, and that this is a sign you should go.'

Lilianne made a sound halfway between a scoff and a sob. 'She did love that stuff.'

'I always thought she was a little off when she talked like that, but she really did believe it.' Helen shrugged. 'Who am I to argue with karma and fate and what the universe says?'

They all laughed, mostly to relieve tension and because Helen was adorable.

'Thank you, Helen.' Sophie looked to her parents. 'How's

this? I won't announce who I am right away. My cousin Lily Anne runs a sober house that her grandmother – or I guess *my* grandmother – started. I thought I'd begin by meeting her, and if she doesn't need a cousin in her life or if we hate each other, I'll ditch the genealogy search and slink away anonymously. Good compromise?'

Her mother looked distressed. Her father nodded, but his jaw was tight. 'Works for me. Lilianne?'

'I . . . guess it's fine. As your dad said, you're entitled to this. And we trust you . . .'

Implicit end to that sentence: *pretty much.*

'Thank you.' Sophie relaxed her shoulders and gulped the rest of her Armagnac, needing the jolt. Her father's flinch told her she'd just shot back about forty dollars' worth.

Oops. Her parents loved her, no doubt about that, but there had been so many times over the years when she felt as if she could never learn all their rules, never make the right choices, never be quite the child they deserved. Maybe she'd find herself more at home with her own blood, maybe she wouldn't. But now that she knew she wouldn't be breaking her parents' hearts, Sophie was itching to get going.

Back at her condo, she made sure her shopping list and bags were ready for an early-morning trip to Stop & Shop. She'd have to prepare two weeks' worth of meals for her clients before she left, which would make the next few days totally insane.

She undressed for bed, then took a long, thrilling moment to ogle the Fabergé, sparkling fantastically in her dresser, not sure what to do about it while she was away. Her condo had never been broken into, but of course if she left the egg here, burglars would swarm the place as soon as she drove away. She could get a safety deposit box, but the idea of having her treasure stuffed away in dark metal bothered her.

Ideally Sophie would bring the egg with her to Vermont, but there would be other residents where she was staying who might snoop. So . . . hide it back in Sarah's head? Stash it somewhere in her parents' house? Ask Beezy to look after a mysterious package? No answer came that would satisfy her.

She didn't sleep well and was up early, still undecided. Maybe Connie's all-knowing universe would show her the way.

After a hurried shower and breakfast, she pulled on loose cotton pants and a top and stepped into her Teva sandals.

Stop & Shop wasn't too crowded on a Thursday morning, so she was able to fill her cart without feeling like she was running an obstacle course of bodies. At the meat section, she was contemplating sirloin tips when a woman reached in front of her for tenderloin.

'Excuse me. Oh, hey, Sophie!'

Lexy. Peter's perfect wife. Looking perfectly perfect in a mini sundress that showed off her long, evenly tanned legs, and arms with serious muscle definition.

'Hi, Lexy.' Sophie stretched up the corners of her mouth, showing teeth, since smiling naturally was beyond her, wondering why Lexy was at the supermarket instead of at her high-powered job that was better than anything Sophie could ever do.

'It's good to see you.'

Really? Sophie couldn't say the same. Seeing Lexy hurt. 'Thanks. How've you been?'

'Good. I'm taking the day off. The long weekend, actually. We're going down to DC to visit my folks.'

'Oh, nice.' Sophie had nothing to say to this person, and really hated that Lexy was being warm and friendly and didn't seem uncomfortable – though what would she have to feel uncomfortable about? She'd won on all counts. 'I'm off to Vermont for a couple of weeks.'

Lexy's eyes lit. 'I love Vermont. Where are you staying?'

'Outside of—'

'Lexy! Hey, just wanted to say congratulations!'

Sophie turned to see Franny Faber, one of the most odious people on the planet. Not that Sophie was judging.

Franny put her hand on Lexy's abdomen. 'How are you feeling, Mama?'

Sophie's blood ran cold. The passes-for-a-smile refused to hang on no matter how hard she tried to prop it up. She wanted to die. A baby. Lexy was having a baby. Pregnant. Probably on the first try.

'I feel okay.' Now Lexy did look uncomfortable. She must know from Peter that Sophie couldn't conceive, maybe also how desperately she'd wanted to. 'How are *you* doing?'

'I hear Peter is *thrilled*.' Franny gave Sophie a smug look that said, *neener neener. . .*

Well, no. She didn't. But it felt that way, so deep was Sophie's misery.

A baby. Peter's baby. A baby that thrilled him, when he'd put an abrupt end to trying with Sophie. After all they'd been through, he'd suddenly become unsure whether he wanted to be a father. Sophie had blamed herself, thinking her fixation on children might have been part of why he checked out of their marriage.

This time he'd apparently jumped in with both balls blazing.

She wanted to throw up.

'We're both happy. Good to see you, Sophie. Take care.' Lexy took Franny's elbow and directed her toward produce, while Sophie's muscles refused to function. She watched as Lexy, the happy mommy-to-be, ditched Franny by the tomatoes and hurried back.

'Sophie.' Her forehead was furrowed with anxiety. She still looked stunning. 'This is absolutely not how I wanted you to find out. I wanted you to hear it from me or from Peter. I don't even know how Franny knew. Probably my blabbermouth mother. I'm so sorry.'

'Thank you.' Sophie sounded like an old woman being held underwater. Part of her wished she were.

The worst part was that it would be hard to continue hating Lexy because she'd just been friendly, gracious, and protective of Sophie's feelings.

Too bad she hadn't thought to do that when deciding to be Peter's mistress.

Lexy went on to do the rest of her shopping. Sophie stood at the meat counter for a really long time. Long enough for people to start giving her strange looks.

She didn't care. The pain was heavy, paralyzing. Peter was going to be a father with this other person, after he hadn't wanted to be one with Sophie. After he'd been so relieved when they split up that they'd never managed to conceive.

For the next half-hour, Sophie went back through the store, returning every item from her cart. Back went the pasta, the pastrami, the peas. Back went the cheese, cherries and Cheetos, the apricots, anchovies and adzuki. She was not spending any more time and energy on the good people of Southport.

As soon as she got home, she would call her clients to announce she was closing her farcical excuse for a business. Then she'd cancel the two-week reservation for the icky room in the weirdo woman's home and book the pretty little guest house for an entire month. At least.

As soon as she could pack and disentangle, she was getting the hell out of Connecticut until she could bear to come back.

Chapter 10

The drive to Bridgewater Corners, Vermont, was a little over three and a half hours. Sophie left a hot and humid Connecticut after lunch on Friday, sweaty, cranky and humiliated, with a multimillion-dollar antique in her suitcase that she'd been too rushed and upset to deal with properly.

Canceling her personal chef clients had been easy. Extremely easy. WTF easy. She knew there were plenty of other options nowadays, cheaper than what she provided. Plenty of companies offering customizable meals by mail, plenty of decent ready-made food in the supermarkets, an abundance of high-end takeout options.

But *Sure, okay, thanks for letting us know!* took her aback. Really? Not even a meek protest? She hadn't brought even a little extra deliciousness and brightness into their lives that they'd miss?

It had taken her a quarter-box of Kleenex to find a bright side, but she had found it, by God. Her clients had made it easier to disappear. Easier to go on this journey of discovery without guilt, and without letting anyone down.

There.

After an utterly crap sleep, Sophie had done her best to leave the mortification behind her on the road, enjoying the steady cooling as she traveled north into the green mountain state, which, not coincidentally, was full of green mountains – beautiful, peaceful ones – rushing streams and puffy-clouded skies. Yes, her life was in ruins again, but she was on an adventure all by herself, the first time she could remember traveling solo. All her traveling as a child was done *en famille*, and there had been a lot of it. She and Peter had also traveled quite a bit, and she'd been looking forward to a child they could spoil in the same way.

She eased her foot back on the accelerator. This was a forward-looking trip. She didn't want to spend it, or any more of her life, being bitter and jealous.

GPS relieved her of the tedium of I-91, directing her to smaller roads, trading speed and monotony for towns and interest. She opened the window and found to her great pleasure that it was safe to breathe real air, though if air-conditioning didn't exist, she'd have moved to Newfoundland by now.

She followed Route 12, delightfully named Skunk Farm Road, up to Route 4, which headed west through Woodstock, a town of enchanting cuteness that quickly became overwhelming cuteness, then downright nauseating cuteness, except for the covered bridge just past town that made her think of *The Bridges of Madison County*.

Vermont definitely rated high on the adorable scale; small towns with historic houses, quaint brick-fronted downtowns, barns and horse paddocks all sitting comfortably where they were built, none at war with the landscape. Few newer houses, no sense of people trying to outdo each other with trappings of wealth. She built herself a delightful fantasy of hard-working craftspeople and farmers, horse people and artists, writers and bakers and . . . yeah, probably plenty of corporate types too, but it was her fantasy, so she could think what she wanted.

Bridgewater Corners, Vermont, built along the Ottauquechee River, did not turn out to be the adorable village she'd hoped for, rather an assortment of buildings along Route 4: an inn, a pizza place, an old mill, a fire station and a community center. Still, at least it felt real. Real and small and maybe a little tired. However, it held the only available lodging within a reasonable distance of Rutland, so . . . home sweet home.

Sophie turned onto Bridgewater Creek Road, hoping the cottage had been available because it required a longer stay and was in the middle of nowhere, and not because it was haunted or looked nothing like the pictures.

Owen Briggs, whom she'd dubbed Owen the Owner, had given no parking instructions, but there were three buildings on the property – a large house in need of painting, and two smaller buildings, ditto. One of those looked like a barn, the other probably a converted garage, which she recognized from the online photos as her home for the next month.

Well.

She pulled up close to the cottage, feeling shaky and uncertain for the first time on this big adventure. Usually she stayed in charming boutique hotels in large cities around plenty of other people. Here she'd be on her own.

Not for long! She had family to get to know. Her fondest hope was that Lily Anne could use a volunteer at Asphalia. Places like that were always dying for free help, and Sophie had plenty to offer.

She emerged from her Prius into the warm, clear air of the afternoon, inhaling clean nature smells – earth, forest, mown grass, a soupçon of horse manure. From her trunk, she took out her suitcases, hurriedly repacked yesterday for this longer stay.

The clunk of the closing trunk was loud in the silence. Hell, the creaks and pops of her car's cooling engine were loud. A

The Jewel of Cairo

crow burst into view, cawing, and nearly gave her a heart attack. Southport was quiet, but this place took peace to a new level.

Feet crunching on gravel, she approached the cottage, feeling like a trespasser, wondering if Owen the Owner was in the main house, peering at her through his window.

Keys would be in the door, he'd told her. Apparently not a big crime risk around here, which made her feel a bit better about her hurried decision to keep the Fabergé egg with her. She felt fiercely protective of both the jewel and its secrets. So exquisite. So perfect. To have and to hold until conscience and common sense did them part. In the meantime, she intended to do more research while she was here, to see if she could uncover anything more about the egg's fascinating history.

She found the key dangling from the lock and turned the handle, beset by an attack of nerves. This place was miles from anything and anywhere.

No whining! She was fine. Worst case, she'd pay the full month and slink home.

Just the idea of going back after she'd bolted so impulsively made her all the more determined to stay. The only people who knew she'd ditched her business were Beezy and her now-ex-clients. Even her parents didn't realize yet how long she planned to be gone.

The cottage door swung open and Sophie let out an *ohh* of approval. The interior looked exactly like the website photos, which was perfect, because they'd been gorgeous. The furniture was mostly in a Shaker style and of remarkable quality. In the middle of the room stood a coffee table with tapered legs, four sleek stone inserts making an attractive grid of its top. A rocking chair had been placed by the wood stove, at once graceful and sturdy, begging to be sat in. Nearby, a sofa with scrolled arms and moss-green upholstery. Even the little table and chairs in the open kitchen were masterpieces of balance and detail, the cabinets simple but made with equal care.

Up the creaky, uneven stairs to the only bedroom, where the workmanship of the graceful queen-bed headboard made her gasp. Spanning the top of its gentle curve flew a flock of tiny mallard ducks, perfectly formed from inlaid colored bits of metal.

Someone around here was really into wood.

She put away her clothes in the charming dresser – even the backs of its drawers were solid, smooth and perfectly fitted.

Someone around here was into wood *and* had money. What a gift to discover such luxury in the most unlikely place.

Having unpacked, the Fabergé egg assuming its rightful place among her underwear, Sophie went back downstairs, uneasy again in the silence and solitude. Nearly six p.m., time to think about searching for a supermarket.

Her best bet turned out to be a little market she must have passed on the way, the Bridgewater Corners Country Store, which would have basic groceries to tide her over. When she visited her cousin's place in Rutland, she could shop in that city.

On her way out, she checked the cottage's refrigerator, which contained small bottles of orange juice and milk. On the counter, a Keurig coffee maker with a large supply of pods, and an attractively arranged bowl of granola and chocolate bars plus bags of nuts and dried fruit. In the cabinets, mini boxes of cereal and a few basics: olive oil, vinegar, thyme, rosemary and oregano, and salt and pepper. Nice touches.

The Bridgewater Corners Country Store turned out to be a little bit of this and that: a large menu of freshly made sandwiches, a decent selection of beer and snack foods, Vermont products, and maple soft-serve ice cream that looked so delicious Sophie ate a cone in the store while waiting for her pastrami Reuben. A list of breakfast sandwiches also tempted her, so she ordered one to reheat in the morning, promising herself she'd buy nothing but vegetables at the supermarket the next day.

Back at the little cottage, she ate the smoky, juicy, cheesy sandwich, listening to the wind in the trees and the summer sounds of birds and crickets, feeling a little light-headed from the drive, and a little lonely.

The sound of a truck made her tense expectantly. Owen the Owner? They'd exchanged emails, hers chatty, his terse. She hoped he'd be a pleasant neighbor for the next month. Maybe he'd be close to her age and they could be friends.

The truck motor quieted. Should she go out and say hello? Or respect his privacy in his own home?

She decided it was better to catch him outside for their first meeting instead of having to knock, or make him come over here to welcome her, so she rushed from the house before he went inside his, looking forward to having someone to talk to.

Owen turned out to be stocky, average height, wearing dirty jeans and a navy T-shirt. Between the long, low brim of his Red Sox baseball cap and a bushy beard that swallowed practically his entire face, it was hard to gauge what he looked like beyond blue eyes and curly hair. He kicked his truck door closed with his lace-up boot, arms full of grocery bags.

'Owen?' She approached, smiling, hoping his dour look would lift after she attacked him with friendliness. 'I'm Sophie, your tenant for the month. Need help with those bags?'

'I got 'em.' He held them without straining, about six bags, probably weighing a lot.

'Oh, okay. Good.' She waited for him to welcome her, then when it became apparent he had no such plans, she dived in again. 'It's good to be here. Your state is so beautiful. I had a smooth drive up from Connecticut. Nice to be away from the crowds.'

Sort of.

He nodded.

'Anything I should know about the place? It's a really cute cottage, and the furniture is amazing. Where'd you get it?'

His expression – what she could see of it – stayed as still as his body. 'It's what I do.'

'*You?*' She couldn't take in that this unkempt, taciturn man was such a remarkable artist. Which was stupid, she supposed. Not all artists had to have pink hair and piercings and talk about intentionality and how they didn't create the work, the work created *them*. 'You made that? All of it?'

He shifted. 'Yup.'

'Wow. They're beautiful pieces. You're very talented.'

He didn't react. Cousin Lily Anne better be really fun to be around, because Owen was not looking promising.

'How long have you been a woodworker … artist, craftsman …whatever?'

'Most of my life.'

'Wow again.' She studied him at leisure, easy to do with his eyes fixed on a spot that wasn't her. She'd put his age close to fifty. His brows were a little wild, and his equally wild hair reached to his shoulders. Nice eyes, though. He'd probably be pleasant-looking enough if he knew how to smile. 'Where do you work?'

He jerked his head toward the barn.

'Where do you sell from? Where's your shop?'

He gave her a look as if she were simple. 'Online.'

Apparently she *had* been simple. 'Are you a lifelong Vermonter or a—'

'Yup.'

The Jewel of Cairo

She couldn't help it, she giggled.

He frowned.

'Sorry. You have to understand, this is a thrill for me. I'm finally meeting one of those Vermonters I've heard about all my life who don't talk.'

He looked toward the trees, then back. 'And you're one of those tourist people I bump into all summer long who don't stop.'

She laughed at that, glad to see a glimmer of humor around the edges of his deadpan. 'You sure you don't want help with those bags?'

'I'm sure.'

'You want me to be quiet and go into the cottage, don't you?'

One bushy brow rose, a micro-inch. 'Could be.'

'Gosh, well, unfortunately I've just decided to tell you the story of my entire life, starting with the day I was born, leaving out not a *single second*.'

That got a grin, a friendly one, showing mildly crooked teeth that were a nice normal color, not the fluorescent-bulb white people didn't seem to realize made them look like aliens. 'Maybe some other time.'

'Okay, I'll leave you alone.' She half turned back toward the cottage, then stopped. 'If I need anything, should I text, call or barge into your house without knocking?'

His mouth twisted wryly. 'Texting is good.'

'Thanks. Nice to meet you, Owen. See you soon.' She gave a cheerful wave and went back to the cottage, imagining him still standing there with eighty pounds of groceries dragging down his arms, wondering what the hell he'd done to be punished by her renting from him.

The thought tickled her more than anything had all day. Poor Owen. She wouldn't keep torturing him, of course, except it had been fun, and he hadn't seemed to mind that much.

Back inside, she opened a beer, because she was forty-five and all alone, without a job or purpose of any kind outside of this Vermont mission, and it seemed the sensible thing to do. Then she texted her parents and Beezy that she'd arrived and that everything was many-exclamation-points fabulous and exciting.

After that, she listened to music on her phone and looked through an issue of *Food & Wine* magazine she'd brought with her.

Before long, it started getting dark, and it felt like the world was closing in on her little lighted house, and she had to read the recipes in the magazine in great detail because it was hard not to start imagining the mysterious expanses of forest around her and what might prowl in them, possibly dangerous animals

She locked the door, pulled the shades, turned up her music, finished the beer and the magazine, thought about calling Beezy, then decided that bothering her on a Friday night, her date night with Jim, just because Sophie had the heebie-jeebies would be crossing the too-pathetic line.

Going to bed early this first night was a good idea. Tomorrow would be tiring.

The flock-of-ducks bed was comfortable as well as beautiful, plus there was a ceiling fan to keep air circulating, and an A/C unit in the window in case of hot nights. She lay down, settled herself into her sleep position – on her side, one leg bent, one arm under the pillow – and waited for dreamland.

Instead of oblivion came a gradual creeping panic that she might have made a stupid mistake coming up here.

A noise sounded outside, a high, cascading note, like the whinny of a psychotic horse.

Sophie shot up in bed, breathing hard, telling herself it was not a psychotic horse, it was . . . the *ghost* of a psychotic horse.

The sound came again. Some kind of owl? She scrambled

for her phone, turned on her Merlin bird ID app and held the phone out the window to record the song for identification until her arm ached.

Nothing.

Fine. Whatever. She lay back down, assumed her sleep position again.

Immediately the call returned. Sophie shot up, grabbed her phone. Opened the app and . . .

Silence.

Little bastard.

Heart pounding, she slipped out of bed, went to her dresser and pulled out the Fabergé egg. Just the sight cheered and calmed her. How the upturned wings of the falcon atop the egg were subtly striped in blue and green, like rows of infinitesimal feathers. How the tip of the king's scepter had a series of tiny ridges and indentations, maybe representing an ancient language or art form lost on Sophie. How the rubies making up the rose bouquet in the queen's lap were echoed in the eyes of the cobras encircling her and her husband's crowns. So minuscule, so perfect. It was hard not to fantasize about keeping the egg a secret, hers to enjoy forever, even knowing that was selfish and ridiculous.

What had Ibrahim Sayed's wife, Cora, felt receiving such a miracle for an anniversary gift? Was her husband a scoundrel who placated his neglected spouse with a constant stream of baubles? Or was this a gift commemorating ten years of devotion and happiness? From a king to his beloved queen, the most precious thing he could imagine, made uniquely for her.

This was Sophie's fantasy, so the latter became truth.

She cupped the cool metal in her hand, forming a picture of the Egyptian jeweler who had commissioned this piece way back early in the last century. Tall, she decided, dark, of course, and very handsome, with a wonderful big mustache. She imagined his excitement and impatience for his slender, lovely wife to see the gift he'd ordered many, many months earlier and anticipated for that long. Cora, expecting maybe a necklace, a bracelet or a ring, would have opened the box of spectacular wooden mosaic – or perhaps a bag of brilliantly embroidered silk – and seen this stunning piece. Over the next awed minutes, she would have slowly come to realize what her husband had done, and the enormity of what this gift meant. So much time, so much planning. So much love.

Sophie laid the egg gently back into her drawer. Sliding into bed, she decided that crying for a while wouldn't be such a bad idea, because her life was a mess, and because who wouldn't want to inspire that depth of love? Whether it involved Fabergé or not was beside the point. As long as it was given with that much adoration, Sophie would be happy with a pair of socks.

Crying released some tension and made her feel more relaxed. Drowsy, even. Outside, it stayed quiet, which, while not as scary as hearing the owl or zombie predator, still made her uneasy.

Tomorrow she'd go to Rutland, to Asphalia House, and meet Lily Anne. They'd become friends, and when Sophie felt it was safe to let her know they were cousins – she still wasn't sure why her parents thought this would be so dangerous – Lily Anne would be absolutely delighted.

Tonight would be her limit on anxiety and self-pity. Tomorrow everything would be better.

Chapter 11

Thursday, May 13, 1976

By the time Lilianne got home from the visit with her grandparents, sweaty and annoyed by heat, noise, dust and traffic, she just wanted to strip off her confining suit – how did Egyptian women survive the summers wearing so many clothes? – and jump into shorts, a tank top and an Olympic-sized gin and tonic, and too bad if it wasn't five o'clock yet.

Ten minutes after a refreshing shower, grateful for the apartment's central air-conditioning, she was settled on the living room sofa with *The Egyptian Gazette*, her drink and her complicated feelings about the encounter with her grandparents when Connie barged into the apartment wearing a lemon-yellow sundress with a magenta shawl covering her bare shoulders.

'It is a massive drag to be female in this city.'

'Really?' Lilianne turned a page, suppressing a smile. Two weeks earlier, she would have bristled at the disruption of her solitude. But having Connie's sunshiny energy around when she was this worked up would probably be the best cure. 'If *only* someone had warned you.'

Connie planted fists on her hips with considerable force. 'I am allowed to complain if I— Oh my heaven, is that a gin and tonic?'

'Help yourself.' Lilianne jerked a thumb toward the kitchen, not surprised when Connie made a beeline for it.

'For one thing,' Connie's voice drifted out with bottle-clanking noises, 'there aren't women in the cafés. I mean ... women don't drink here? Even coffee?'

'They drink coffee at home with each other and alcohol out with other people, friends or husbands.'

'And second, because I am a woman drinking alone, apparently that means I am available for every man who walks by.'

'Wait, aren't you? What changed?' Lilianne smirked, waiting for the reaction.

Connie made a sound of mock-rage and appeared around the door jamb with an ice cube, which she lobbed at Lilianne. 'Here. To help you chill.'

Lilianne caught it and lobbed it back. 'I'm not the one who's all worked up.'

Not exactly true.

'Anyway,' Connie came back into the room, clutching a large glass Lilianne would bet held a stronger drink than hers, and sank to the floor, crossing her legs. 'The city is totally radical, if only because it's the first place that's ever made me wish I were a man. Everywhere else, it's only been when I've needed to pee and there were no toilets around.'

'Guys get all the luck.' Lilianne turned another page, pretending to read calmly.

'What's wrong?'

'Wrong?' She looked over at Connie, trying to hide her surprise, though by now she should know her friend's intuition was freakily accurate. 'What makes you think anything's—'

'Your vibe is off. Your aura is disturrrbed. Sarah thinks so too. See the sad look on her face?' Connie gestured up to where the doll leaned regally on her bookcase dressed in her emerald finery, and swallowed an inch of her drink in a gulp. 'You can tell or not, up to you.'

Lilianne shut the newspaper and drew her knees to her chest. 'Well, Sarah. I visited my grandparents today.'

'Hey, good for you! I'm proud of you. So . . . ?' Another big swallow and a sympathetic look. 'It didn't go well?'

'It was fine. Nice people. But it was weird. Like they were thrilled to see me because we're family, except we're total strangers. Nothing to talk about.'

'Let us an-a-lyze.' Connie dragged out the word. 'What did you want from the visit? What karma did you expect that you didn't get?'

'I don't know.' Lilianne hugged her arms around her bare knees, hating feeling confused and vulnerable. 'They asked all the questions Mom said they'd ask: why didn't I call sooner, why am I not married, why am I a banker instead of a wife or a schoolteacher or librarian.'

'Yeah, I've been meaning to ask that too.'

Lilianne made a face at her. 'Then they insisted on having everyone over to meet me on Saturday.'

'*Everyone?*' Connie opened her eyes and mouth extra wide. 'How big is their apartment?'

Lilianne sent her a look of disgust. 'I might have to be busy.'

'Nope.' Connie's features snapped back to normal. 'You won't be busy. You're going to go, and you're going to have some awkward moments and some bad moments and some dull moments, and then you'll also have good moments and emotional moments and warm gooey moments, and I bet at least one fantastic mind-bending moment.'

'Yeah, when I get to leave.' Lilianne swung her feet to the floor to cope with another surge of irritation, hating the whiny poor-me tone that had crept into her voice. 'So here's a question for you. Why do I get shoved out to embrace my family and you get to ignore yours?'

'Ah.' Connie pointed to her half-empty glass. 'For this answer I need a refresher. I sweated out half my water content in the heat. Surprised I'm not shriveled.'

Lilianne watched her scurry to the kitchen, frowning. Connie's life and habits were none of her business, but they were sometimes hard to watch.

A minute later, Connie returned with her full-to the brim glass. 'Now. I believe the question on the floor was, why do I get off the hook on spending family time and you don't?'

'That was the question, yes.'

Connie sat on the floor next to the couch and put her drink on the coffee table near Lilianne's legs. 'To start, my parents and grandparents love me, but they don't really jibe with my groove. I'm too loud, too weird, and too ... me. My sister, Phyllis, loves me, but I was always getting into trouble and she was always having to bail me out, or cover my ass, or deal with problems I'd created.

'Plus Mom and Dad and my *yeya* and *pappou* had to spend all their energy trying to change me into what they wanted, while Phyllis is perfect in every way, therefore easy for them to ignore.' Connie's voice was even, calm, without a trace of bitterness. 'So family time to me means my sister being resentful and Mom and Dad treating me like I'm toxic waste from Planet Strange. Major downer.'

'Ouch. I'm sorry.' No wonder Connie became a wanderer. Lilianne wouldn't count her own busy parents as deeply involved in her life, but she knew they loved her, and they were always there to run to if she needed them.

'You think I drink a lot now? I go all out after I visit them in Vermont.' Connie raised her glass. 'It's my spirit-cleansing ritual.'

'Sounds more like pain medication.'

She lowered the glass. 'Maybe that too.'

'So you never go home.'

Connie's dimpled smile grew lopsided. 'Nope. I never do.'

Lilianne stayed quiet. Saying she was sorry wasn't what Connie needed. Sympathy would only push her into insisting she was fine.

'You know,' Connie tilted her head, 'we're a lot alike, you and I. Sarah agrees.'

'What?' It was the last thing Lilianne expected her to say. 'We're complete opposites.'

'Nope. Very similar. We both stay on the move, don't form permanent connections, carry around a lot of childhood pain and—'

'My childhood was idyllic.' She felt weirdly panicky. 'Country-club living on Connecticut's Gold Coast. What's painful about that?'

Connie smiled a slow, knowing smile. 'Maybe you'll tell me. Or you can tell Sarah if it's easier.'

'Tell you *what*?' Lilianne stood abruptly, legs propelling her up as if they had minds of their own. Then she stood there awkwardly, because there wasn't anywhere she needed to go, except away from this line of questioning. 'There's nothing to tell. I love my parents, I travel because it's my job, I have plenty of friends. You and Helen and Gilles probably closer than any of them. And Sarah, of course.'

'Then how come I know virtually nothing about you except the basic facts? Where you grew up, what you do for a living – though I don't understand any of it – what you like to eat, the movies and books you find stimulating . . .'

Lilianne sat back down.

'Let me tell you what happened to me today.' Connie shrugged off her shawl and tossed it onto the beige couch, where it landed in a hot-pink heap. 'I was exploring an old neighborhood near the Khan el-Khalili, or however you say it, which was so amazing and so cool, like going back farther in time than I've ever gone, surrounded by every color and smell I've ever encountered. But I got thirsty and wanted to sit quietly with a glass o' something. Then I notice there are no women anywhere having drinks alone.

'And I remembered what you said, and realized there would be nowhere to be invisible and observe.' She lifted a lecturing finger. 'Let me tell you, if Connie Pappas gets to the point where she's tired of being the center of attention, it's bad.'

'Very bad.' Lilianne wasn't sure where this was going, and it made her nervous.

'So just when I'm about to give up, I feel a hand on my shoulder, and this absolutely beautiful woman, out shopping with her mother, takes pity and invites me into her home for a lemonade. I follow her to this tiny apartment, where she not only gives me lemonade but teaches me how to make this divine coconut yogurt cake called *basbousa*, which you and I absolutely have to make.'

'Sure.' Lilianne moved impatiently. How did cake connect to her?

'The point is, my darling, within an hour and a half I knew more about this woman and her family than I've found out about you in the last two years.'

Boom.

Lilianne raised her eyebrows, trying to project calm surprise, finding it harder than usual to hide her hurt. 'Therefore we are opposites. You're open. I'm closed. I rest my case.'

'Jury's still out.'

She caught herself about to stand up again. 'Look, I don't go on and on about myself, but I'm not hiding anything. Ask me whatever you want.'

'Okay. I will.' Connie thought for a moment, tapping her chin. 'Here's one to start with. Why don't you ever date? Men, women, whatever your thing is?'

Lilianne felt her face go stony. She dropped her eyes from Connie's wide dark ones. The one question she couldn't answer. The question she'd been running from since adolescence. To stave off rumors and curiosity, she'd gone on dates, in high school and college, when asked, when set up. For all she knew, the miracle could still happen, she might just be a late, late, late, late bloomer.

She wasn't. So she'd started dragging out all the tired excuses: it didn't work out. He's not for me. No chemistry. Not interested. Too busy for a relationship. Not ready.

Silence hung until Lilianne cleared her throat. This was too dark a secret to share, even with Sarah. 'Fair question. I haven't ever met anyone I want to be with.'

'Okay.' Connie nodded her acceptance. 'But I'm curious, have you ever just gone out with someone anyway? Just to feel close? I mean, you don't have to be me, but plenty of times I sleep with guys I don't have feelings for, just because I like the excitement, the fantasy, the warm body . . .'

Lilianne flashed to the drunken night in high school when she'd made out with Jed Powers in the vain hope that she'd feel something, anything. But his hot hands crawling over her body, his tongue leaving slug trails on her skin had produced only bewildered feelings of revulsion followed by the most inconvenient need to giggle. *This* was what all the fuss was about? This comically slobbery heaving and groaning was what her girlfriends spent all their time plotting and planning and fantasizing and swooning over?

She couldn't believe it. What was wrong with everyone?

But of course that wasn't the question. What was wrong with *her*?

'Yes, I have. But I don't . . . It's not . . . satisfying.'

'Well. Lilianne Maxwell, woman of a thousand mysteries, how about that. You're the wait-for-Mr-Right type.' Connie spoke with the admiration peculiar to discovering a rare species. 'I never would have pegged you as old-fashioned, but I love it. In fact, Sarah and I adore that about you.'

Lilianne couldn't meet her eyes, so she forced a smile up at Sarah. 'Thanks.'

'You know, any way you want to live is cool. I'm glad you told me. I hadn't been able to figure you out. Helen though you were in love with Gilles.'

Lilianne's smile turned natural. Gilles was about as close as she'd ever come, though her body still refused to crave anything from him but his company. He'd had her pose for his camera more than once, over her objections, and she'd been amazed and intrigued by how he saw her, by the mystery and sensuality his camera had found in her ordinary face and body. 'I do love Gilles. I love him a lot. I also love you and I love Helen.'

Connie nodded thoughtfully. 'Okay. I think I dig it. One more question, though. The big one.'

Lilianne worked to keep looking pleasant, wanting to grab at her skin to avoid more of it being peeled away. 'Sure.'

'Am I right that you'd give me everything you own if I stop talking about this now?'

'*Yes.*' The word surfed out on a rush of breath. 'Everything. Take it. Please.'

Connie's dimples deepened into her laugh. She got to her

knees and waddled over to the sofa. 'Lilianne Maxwell, you are a beautiful, beautiful person.'

Lilianne made a sound of scorn, grinning her affection for this sweet mess of a woman.

'Hug time!' Connie opened her arms.

Lilianne leaned toward her, torn by her relief at having kept her secret safe, and guilt that she'd half lied to such a sweet, trusting person.

'What's that, Sarah?' Connie cupped her ear toward the doll. 'Yes, I agree. Good news, Lilianne. Sarah has decreed that your interrogation is over.'

Lilianne raised her gin and tonic. 'I'll drink to that.'

The phone rang. Connie scrambled to answer. 'Hello? . . . No. No. This is Connie Pappas . . . What? . . . *What?* I'm sorry, do I know you? . . . Yes, she's here, but . . . What did you say?'

Peculiar. Lilianne got off the couch and crossed to the phone. 'For me?'

Connie nodded and held up a 'wait' hand. '*Who* is this?'

The answer must have shocked her, because she gasped and turned abruptly, covering the receiver with her hand, face as pale as it had been rosy before.

'Oh my God, Lilianne, I didn't recognize his voice at all. It's Gilles. He's asking for you. He sounds absolutely terrible.'

Chapter 12

As soon as Lilianne put down the phone from talking to Gilles, she picked it up again and started dialing. This was where she thrived, in the world of crises and their solutions.

'What are you doing?' Connie had abandoned her drink and was sitting on the sofa, hands clasped between her knees, absolutely still. For once. 'Who are you calling?'

'My dad. I need help to go get him.'

'To get your dad?

'No, Gilles. He's in Paris. I don't think he's talked to anyone in weeks.'

Connie looked more distressed than Lilianne had ever seen her. 'Where will you take him?'

'I'll bring him here. He shouldn't be alone.'

'*Here* here?' She gestured around her head. 'Like your place? Where will he stay?'

'We'll figure it out.' Lilianne spoke impatiently, annoyed because she hadn't thought that far ahead. Adrenaline had her focusing only on the need to rescue. 'You can bunk with me, or I can see if one of the corporate apartments at the bank can be rented out. Something will work.'

Connie's mouth formed an 'oh', but no sound came out.

No answer in Connecticut. Thursday; maybe Dad was in Florida for a long weekend. She dialed, hoping to catch him.

Her mother picked up. 'Lilianne! What's happened?.'

'I'm fine. Is Dad there this weekend?'

'He's in the bathroom. 'What's happened? Tell me.'

Lilianne took pity on her mother's anxiety. 'A friend in Paris is recovering from an illness and needs help. I'm going to bring him here, but I need to check with—'

'What illness? Is he contagious?'

'No, Mom.'

'Why you? Doesn't he have friends or family there? I don't understand.' Dina gasped hopefully. 'Is this someone you ... care for?'

Breath for patience. 'He's a friend. You *know* that.'

'Right, yes.' Her disappointment was evident. 'So why isn't someone there helping him?'

'I get the impression he doesn't want to impose.' Actually, Gilles had said he couldn't bear anyone seeing him in such bad shape, even his family. Then he'd thought of her, and knew she was what he needed.

Lilianne had nearly cried.

'So you'll nurse this guy back to health?'

'That's the plan.'

'How will you manage that with all your work?'

'That's what I want to talk to Dad about.'

'Well.' Her mother chuckled. 'I'm proud of you, Lily Bud. You're putting a person ahead of your work. Taking responsibility for someone else's happiness. Like a grown-up.'

Lilianne struggled to parse that one. She was thirty-one years old with a master's degree from Harvard; a senior analyst with an international company, a world traveler who had repeatedly built a good life in a series of foreign countries; she was spying for the CIA . . .

How did wanting to take care of a man make her suddenly grown up? 'What was I before?'

'You've always been . . . Well, it seems like a new you.'

Always been what, Mom? Selfish? Immature? Not quite right? 'I went to see Teta and Jiddu this afternoon.'

Silence that went on long enough to make Lilianne ashamed of wanting payback.

'I wondered if you would.' Her mother's voice sank and flattened. 'How was the visit?'

'Pleasant, given that we don't know each other.' Lilianne softened her tone, wishing she'd approached this differently. 'They miss you. So does Nailah.'

'Nailah, *ya Allah*.' Dina's words thickened. 'And . . . they're all well?'

'Yes, Mom. They're in great shape. I'll be meeting the rest of the family on Saturday. Your brothers and their wives and children.'

'Oh, nice.' Her mother's voice cracked. 'Here's your father.'

'Mom, wait . . .' Too late. She heard her mother murmuring to her dad and the crackle of the phone being passed.

'Hi, Lilianne. Your mom gave me the gist. You've turned Florence Nightingale all of a sudden?'

'Something like that. I'll stay on top of things at work. I'm waiting for some last reports, but I doubt I'll find anything that will cause problems. Meanwhile, I wanted to know if it would be okay to use Marge to make travel plans. I'll try to fly out in the morning, back Monday, with a better idea of what I'll be able to do after that.'

'Yes, absolutely. But you're sure you want to take on responsibility like this? There's no one in Paris who can help him? I don't know what shape he's in, but with all you have on your plate, I hate to see you saddled with—'

Lilianne smiled at the interruption of her mother's scolding voice, no doubt instructing her husband not to interfere. 'I'll be okay, Dad. If it's beyond me, I can get him help here. Thank you.'

She put down the phone, then picked it up again, adrenaline flowing. As much as she wished this wasn't happening, and for all her worry about Gilles's sanity, it was some relief to be able to stop the angsty introspection and do something she could understand and control.

'What now?' Connie asked.

'I'm calling the European agent Dad's company uses, to book a flight to Paris. Want to come with me? My treat.'

'Uh . . . what's wrong with him?'

Lilianne examined Connie's stony face. This wasn't the reaction she'd expected from her friend. 'Not sure, but I think it's like shell shock.'

'But he wasn't in combat. He was just taking pictures.' Connie seemed completely lost.

'I know, I know. But it probably doesn't matter whether you're holding a gun or a camera, you're still in the mess. We'll help him. It'll be okay.' Her call connected to the slim, unflappable Marge Atkeson, able to book – and often rebook – complicated reservations without blinking. 'Marge, it's Lilianne, glad I caught you. Sorry to be calling this late, but I need to go to Paris in the morning.'

'Sure thing. How many traveling?'

'Two people?' She looked at Connie, who shook her head vigorously. 'Make that one person, earliest you got. Returning Monday, two people. First class if they have it.'

'Gotcha. I'll call you back.'

Lilianne thanked her and ended the call. 'Connie, are you okay? You didn't want to come with me? See Gilles? You could cheer him up much better than I could.'

'I don't think I can deal with that much negative karma.' Connie laughed uncomfortably, not smiling. 'I'm afraid I'd—'

The phone rang. Lilianne held up a sympathetic wait-a-sec finger and grabbed the still-warm receiver. 'Hello?'

'Lilianne? John Baker.'

Oh no. Her upper lip curled. 'Hi, John.'

'How's tricks? All settled in? Enjoying your afternoon? I wonder if you could come see me tomorrow morning.'

Lilianne made a face. 'I'm in the middle of making emergency plans to fly to Paris in the morning, back Monday. Can it wait?'

'How early is your flight?'

She'd expected that. His type wanted what they wanted when they wanted it. 'I'll know in about ten minutes.'

'Stop by on your way to the airport. This'll be quick. I can be here any time.'

'Okay. I'll let you know.' Lilianne hung up and turned back to Connie. 'I was—'

The phone rang again. She shrugged apologetically and picked up the receiver. Maybe she should just glue it to her ear. 'Hello?'

'It's Marge, I've got a flight at ten forty-five tomorrow morning; two people returning Monday at five thirty p.m. First class all around. Would that work?'

'Perfect.' Lilianne jotted the information down in her calendar.

'I'll have the tickets sent by courier to your place asap.'

'Thanks, Marge! You're a peach. I owe you.'

'Couple extra days of vacation would be just the thing.'

Lilianne grinned. 'I'll talk to Dad.'

She hung up and picked up the receiver again, eliciting a huff of disbelief from Connie.

'One more.' She paged through her calendar until she found John Baker's number, arranged to meet him at seven a.m., then put the phone down, intending that it would stay there while she got to the bottom of Connie's strange reaction. 'There. Now tell me— Oh crap.'

'Now what?'

'My grandparents. I was supposed to go there for dinner Saturday.' She retrieved Braheem's card, remembering her grandfather's neatly manicured hands jotting down his number. 'Last call. I promise.'

She dialed, and waited impatiently for an answer.

'Nailah?' She switched to Arabic. 'It's Lilianne. Is Zahra there?'

'Lilianne! How are you? We haven't stopped talking about your visit. What a miracle.'

Lilianne closed her eyes and forced a mental reset. She might be in US business mode, but the Abdallah household wouldn't be. 'Thank you. It was so nice to meet you, Nailah. I just spoke to my mom, to Dina. She sends love.'

'Ah!' The cry was anguished. 'What I wouldn't give to see my baby girl before I die.'

Lilianne pressed her lips together, feeling an unexpected emotional tug over the old woman's pain. Nailah had been a second mother to Dina. 'I hope that will happen. Maybe my coming here and seeing you will change her mind. *Inshallah*. Is Zahra there?'

'*Aiwa*. I'll get her.'

Lilianne stood patiently – mostly – waiting for her grandmother to get on the line, picturing her walking through the apartment to take the receiver from Nailah's hands.

'Lilianne, *habibti*, how are you?'

'I'm doing well. But I'm afraid I won't be able to join you on Saturday after all.'

'Ah.' Said after an inhale that sounded as if she'd been mortally wounded. 'Braheem told me that was the last we'd see of you, but I said no, no, we are family, she'll be back.'

'Let me explain.' Lilianne felt so terrible she found herself almost eager to see her grandparents again, if only to prove that Zahra's faith in her was not unfounded. 'I have to go to France for the weekend. I just found out that a friend there is suffering from an . . . illness, and needs my help.'

'Ah. I see.' Zahra clearly thought she was making excuses. Lilianne didn't blame her. 'I'm sorry to hear she's not doing well.'

'He's been in Lebanon. In the war.' She braced herself for the inevitable speculation about their relationship.

'*Ya Allah*,' Zahra gasped. 'Wounded?'

'Only in his mind.' She didn't know the Arabic word for shell shock. 'He's a photographer for Agence-Presse. A friend from when I lived in Paris. He's all alone and—'

'Alone? No family?'

'Not nearby.' A lie. He had a brother and parents who would undoubtedly drop everything and come to Paris if they knew, but Gilles refused to contact them or allow Lilianne to. 'I'm going to bring him here so I can take care of him.'

The words sounded ridiculous even to her. Why tear a man away from his country and family and bring him somewhere utterly foreign?

It was all she could think to do. She braced herself for her grandmother's judgment and contrarian advice.

'*Ya haraam*.' Poor man. 'You'll be the best thing for him. If you need help, I can come, or send Nailah . . .'

'Thank you, I'll be fine.' Maybe. 'I'm sorry to cancel this late. You were so kind to invite the whole family to meet me.'

'No, no, this is nothing. Your family isn't going anywhere. You will come next Saturday and bring your friend. We'll have the party at our jasmine farm, near Shubra Beloula, in the Delta. At noon, so we don't tire him. It's very beautiful and very peaceful. Braheem can pick you up and drive you. Very easy. You can spend the whole weekend with us if you like. If you have to go back to work and your friend is comfortable with us, he can stay as long as he wants.'

Lilianne determinedly swallowed the tears clogging her throat, feeling her body releasing some of its tension. Not for a second had Zahra questioned what she felt she needed to do, nor had she questioned her ability to do it. Until this moment Lilianne hadn't realized how desperately she needed both those votes of confidence. 'Thank you, Teta. This is so generous of you. I don't know what shape he'll be in.'

'We are used to people who are ... struggling. One of my friend's sons ... Well, your friend won't bother us. If you need a rest before Saturday, call us.'

Once again Lilianne was astonished by the generosity and empathy of the Egyptian people. She couldn't imagine leaping to welcome someone with serious mental problems into her home.

The irony of the thought hit her with a shock. Welcoming someone with serious mental problems into her home was exactly what she was doing.

Even if Zahra's offer came only from a sense of cultural duty, it felt like a hand extended to pull Lilianne from quicksand. 'Thank you, Teta. I am so grateful.'

'It's nothing, Lilianne, *habibti*. Nothing! You are family.'

Lilianne said goodbye, replaced the receiver more calmly

than she'd picked it up and turned apologetically. 'That's it. I'm finished.'

Connie giggled forlornly. 'Lilianne Maxwell, executive in action.'

'It's what I do.' She crossed to her friend and sat next to her. 'Okay, Connie. Your turn. What's going on? Why didn't you want to come with me to get Gilles?'

Connie looked down at her hands, still clasped between knees draped in bright yellow folds. 'I'm not good at nursing people. Sickness makes me panic. I wouldn't know what to say to him.'

Lilianne put a hand on her slumped shoulder, wishing Connie hadn't just outlined her own fears. 'It's *Gilles*.'

'It wasn't, though. It was like he was possessed by someone else, someone I don't know at all. It scared me.' Connie screwed up her face, managing to look both contrite and adorable. 'I'm not a nurturing person.'

'Of course you are. You take care of all of us. You and Sarah.' Lilianne rubbed Connie's back, her dread returning. As Dina Maxwell had been about to point out, Lilianne wasn't a nurturing person either. She was a manager, an organizer, gifted at delving into institutions to inspect their innards for flaws. Now, in the panic rush of her need to help a friend, possessing zero medical or psychiatric experience that might benefit him, she'd taken charge of a man with complicated problems that could take months or years to resolve if they were even resolvable.

But after hearing Gilles's dull, weak voice saying he no longer had anything to look forward to, that suicide was constantly on his mind and that Lilianne was the only person he trusted to help him, there was nothing she could do but try.

The Jewel of Cairo

Friday, May 14, 1976

John Baker met Lilianne promptly at seven, and by the time they made it up to his office, he had asked several questions about the nature of her trip to Paris that, as usual, she never got the chance to answer. Under the circumstances, this was fine by her.

'Please, sit, sit. I'll make this brief. I know you have to run.' He sat behind his desk, hands clasped, index fingers together, pointing toward her – one of his Important Man poses. 'The work with Sami is good, your reports were what we needed. We're going to wind down your role there, but we need one more thing.'

'Okay.' Her relief at being set free was short-lived. She didn't like the wary look on John Baker's face.

'We'd like you to put a listening device in Sami's apartment.'

Even Lilianne was surprised at that, though she managed not to show it. 'When?'

'Soon as possible.'

'Not my specialty.'

'We'll show you what to do. You'll manage.' He opened a drawer and pulled out a device about the size of a pack of gum. 'The SRT-91. Fairly new, couple of years ago, very good item. Masks with dirty pulsing. Very hard to detect, even by people who think they know how to find these little bastards.'

'Right.' She was getting irritated. At John because he was taking it for granted she'd jump at a task that was beyond what they'd originally agreed to, and at herself because she knew he was right.

'You'll be planting that with a Knowles BA-1501 mike, this baby right here. We'll take care of the listening end.' He gave her brief instructions on how to work with the device, where best to hide it and how to use the fast-working adhesive.

'Okay.' Lilianne leaned forward as if she were about to leave. 'That all?'

'That's all.'

She stood and gestured to the SRT-whatever lying on his desk. 'Could you have everything delivered to my apartment Monday afternoon, when I'm back? I don't expect to be searched on this trip, but I'd rather not have it with me.'

'Absolutely.' John placed his hands on his desk and pushed himself up. 'I'll walk you out.'

Two steps stepped into the hallway, she locked eyes with an enormous man coming toward her. Lilianne worked to keep the surprise off her face, and had the impression he was doing the same. She hadn't seen him for long, but she'd bet her life this was the driver of the black car, the guy who'd stopped indignant honking – and traffic – with his glare while his mob boss, Al-Kalib, intimidated poor Sami.

They exchanged impassive nods and he continued silently down the hall. Lilianne resisted the urge to turn and watch him go.

How interesting. Was he at the embassy on a diplomatic errand? Or was he working for the CIA and reporting on his boss?

She knew better than to ask. But if Al-Kalib's driver was working for the US, Sami was in less danger than he thought. Unless he was in more trouble than Lilianne knew.

♾ **Chapter 13** ♾

Present day

Sophie: *Hey, Mom, I'm going to meet Cousin Lily Anne today.*
Lilianne: *Okay.*
Sophie: *Don't worry, not telling her yet, remember?*
Lilianne: *I remember.*
Sophie: *Love you.*
Lilianne: *♥*

Sophie took one last look in the bathroom mirror to check her appearance before she left for Asphalia House, and smiled experimentally, wondering if her cousin would have the dimples Sophie had inherited from Connie, or if that trait belonged only to Connie's side of the family.

She wrinkled her nose, still getting used to the idea of Connie as her mother. So far the woman was more concept than person, even after seeing pictures Lilianne had grudgingly pulled out, and reading the very few letters Mom had received – mostly postcards with a scrawled line or two, a couple written when Connie was clearly high out of her mind. Maybe with time, Sophie could pull her closer, flesh her out, make her more real than the colorful ball of joy displayed in the photos. She hoped to. Maybe someone else in Vermont had known Connie when she lived here as a girl. Maybe Lily Anne's father, Uncle Clyde, had heard stories from Phyllis about her wilder younger sister.

One last look to make sure her nose and teeth weren't harboring anything uncouth, and she decided this was as good as her middle-aged, slightly overweight self could get.

Downstairs, she opened the cottage door to the morning air. After taking a while to settle in last night, she'd slept deeply, straight through until nearly nine. The mountain air would be good for her, she could see, though she already missed the ocean.

Owen the Owner's truck was parked in front of his house. Maybe he was at work in his barn workshop? She was tempted to pester him to see what he was working on, but this morning belonged to trying to meet her cousin. Sophie had thought of calling first, the more sensible approach, but she didn't want to make a formal appointment. By keeping her promise to her parents and not announcing who she was, she hoped this first meeting would be calm and low-key.

Jittery but excited, she got into her Prius, set her GPS to Asphalia's address on Church Street and backtracked to Route 4, continuing west for half an hour through forested hills, past a couple of closed ski resorts – Killington and Pico Mountain – and down into Rutland. Following Google's most efficient route meant that in the city she mostly saw ugly outskirts and pleasant residential neighborhoods. Later, when she did her grocery shopping, she could explore downtown.

From Crescent, she turned right onto Church, going old-lady slowly as she peered around for her target, passing several houses and an apartment building before she found what she was looking for. A pretty two-story white house with an open porch that had four pots of spilling-over purple and pink flowers hanging from its ceiling. Peaceful and inviting. No outward sign of the struggles inside, of women on the journey of clawing their lives back from the brink.

Heart thudding nearly audibly, Sophie parked and got out of the car, smoothing the outfit she'd chosen after going through pretty much everything she'd brought. Not too expensive, not too cheap. Not too fancy, not too casual. She'd settled on a pair of teal cotton/linen pants cuffed mid calf, and a boxy waist-length white linen shirt with three-quarter sleeves. On her feet, white sandals. On her wrist, a bangle that matched the color of her pants, ditto her simple ball earrings plus extra silver hoops she wore every day because they'd been gifts from Beezy to celebrate her double piercing. Nothing she could do about the expensive haircut, but with luck she looked like someone eager to work, and not the monied Connecticut dilettante she actually was.

There was always hope.

Up to the house on nervous legs. The front door was locked, but she pressed the bell and waited. This close, she noticed the subtle and gracefully scripted sign next to the door: *Welcome to Asphalia House.*

She hoped she would be.

Footsteps sounded, then the door opened to her cousin. No mistaking it. Dark hair, dark eyes slightly close together, long nose, dark brows, a dead ringer for her picture on the Asphalia House website, except a bunch of years older, close to Sophie's age.

'Lily Anne Corson?' Sophie sounded pipsqueaky ridiculous.

'How can I help you?' Lily Anne's lips spread in a practiced smile that showed . . .

Dimples. Exactly like Sophie's.

Sophie's mouth went dry, everything she had planned to say

bolted from her brain. This was the first person she'd ever met who looked like her. Never in a million years would she have guessed how much it mattered. She adored her parents, and had no complaints about how she'd been raised other than those any kid had. Lilianne and Gilles would always be her family.

But this person. This person was alive and well and shared her DNA.

Tears came into her eyes; her throat swelled and choked off the chance of words even if she could remember any.

'Come in. Come in.' Lily Anne stepped down and took Sophie's arm. 'Come inside, we'll talk.'

Sophie tried to thank her and came out with a soggy croak instead.

Her cousin led her into the house's narrow, featureless entryway and took a right into a small room with a battered couch, metal desk, gray filing cabinet and gray metal bookcase. The walls were bare; on the floor, dirty tan carpet worn nearly threadbare in spots. Sophie would guess there weren't a lot of funds for decorating, let alone remodeling, but she couldn't imagine the dreariness would help bolster anyone's spirits.

Lily Anne pointed her to the lumpy brown couch. 'Have a seat, take some breaths. Tissues are right next to you.'

'I'm so sorry.' Sophie wiped her eyes and blew her nose. 'I did not expect that.'

'You're not the first. All feelings are okay here.'

'Thanks.' She swallowed, sniffed, crumpled the tissue, and made a fantastic three-pointer into the wastebasket across the room.

'Nice.' Lily Anne's smile was quick, but Sophie could see strain in her face. 'Tell me where you are and what you need. All the beds here are full right now, but there are other places in town or out a little farther that—'

'Oh!' Sophie let out a ha-ha of embarrassed laughter. 'Sorry, I'm not an addict. Well, no, I'm not sorry that I'm not. But I'm not. Just emotional.'

'Okay.' Lily Anne kept her pleasant face on, and it occurred to Sophie that saying you weren't an addict was a classic addict line, and that she'd also sounded like a complete idiot. 'What brings you to Asphalia House, then?'

'I want to help, to volunteer here.' Sophie gestured impatiently, annoyed at herself for letting Lily Anne's steady brown gaze rattle her. 'Seems like the perfect thing to ask after making the worst possible first impression.'

'Not the worst. And thank you for wanting to help.' Lily Anne folded her hands in her lap, looking as if she had nothing to do but sit and talk to Sophie, while her foot tapped a steady beat on the depressing carpet. 'Unfortunately, we don't work with volunteers and we're fully staffed right now.'

'Oh.' Sophie's shoulders slumped. This hadn't occurred to her. She'd thought all non-profits were desperate for hands. They certainly seemed to be around Southport. 'Not even . . . I don't know, cleaning toilets?'

'Our residents do their own cleaning.'

Sophie dug out her résumé and handed it over. 'Cooking? I'm a personal chef.'

Lily Anne's eyes showed brief interest, but she gave the résumé a polite scan and put it back on her desk. 'Are you from Rutland?'

'No, I'm visiting. From Connecticut. For a month.' Sophie grabbed at the bits of her planned introduction creeping sheepishly back into her brain after their panicked flight. Tell Lily Anne enough so that her revelation made sense when it came, but not so much as to reveal their connection immediately. 'I'm on a personal journey. I've always known I'm adopted, but I just found out who my birth mother was, and that she had family in Rutland. I'm going to try to get to know them while I'm here.'

'Oh.' Lily Anne's gaze had sharpened. 'A month, you said.'

'Yes.'

Her eyes went back to the resumé. 'Looks like you've had private clients for the past six years, and catered weddings and special events.'

'Yup. That's me.' Her cousin's poise and reserve were intimidating. She reminded Sophie of Lilianne.

'What are your Southport clients doing while you're here for the month?' Lily Anne's voice was kind, but the implication was clear.

Coping fine. Sophie searched for the best answer, not wanting to admit she'd run out on them. 'They were fine with me taking this trip. All very friendly dealings.'

'Okay.' Lily Anne looked over Sophie's credentials again. 'I employ a cook who does our week-night dinners, Sunday through Thursday, and helps the residents prepare their own breakfasts and lunches. Her family is in Norway, her niece just had a baby and she's been asking for time off to go see them.'

Sophie tried very hard not to snap to attention. Another sign from Connie's universe.

'It's pretty extraordinary, actually, that you showed up just now with exactly that much time to give.' Lily Anne looked expectant, as if Sophie could provide some explanation.

She couldn't. 'This might work out then?'

'I'd have to think it through.' Lily Anne pointed to the resumé. 'I see you have references.'

'Yes.' Sophie was sparking with excitement, even knowing Lily Anne still might give her the thumbs-down. At least she had hope now. She felt like bouncing up and down in her chair. 'Feel free to call any of them.'

Obviously.

'Right.' Lily Anne gave a bright this-interview-is-over smile. 'Well. Thanks for—'

'Are you from Rutland?' Sophie wasn't ready to let this meeting end. Selfish, because Lily Anne looked tired and probably had a million other things to do today . . . and every day.

'No.' Her hands were tense, elbows flexed, ready to push herself up. 'I grew up in Strafford, Vermont, close to New Hampshire. My grandparents started this place.'

'I read that.' Sophie beamed. 'In honor of your aunt Constance.' What a total thrill to say Connie's name to Connie's niece.

Lily Anne's pleasant expression darkened. She shoved herself to standing. 'I'll tell you what. Give me a day to think this over. I'll call you tomorrow if it seems like we might talk further. Okay?'

'Sure. Yes, thank you.' Sophie got up, wanting to linger, wanting to talk further *now*, wanting to ask a million questions, about Lily Anne's brothers and her sister, about her dad and her late mother, wishing she could drag her to a bar and get a couple of drinks in to crack her professional shell.

Lily Anne escorted her back down the drab hallway, this time filled with the sound of female voices coming from the back of the house, and promised to be in touch one way or the other the next day, then Sophie was out on Asphalia House's front step, hearing the door close and lock behind her with a finality she hoped wasn't an omen.

So.

That had taken all of fifteen minutes. Not that she'd expected to stay all morning, but . . . What now? She decided to take a short driving tour of Rutland's downtown, which had equal measures of charm and decay. Alongside public artworks, cute shops and restaurants were too many empty storefronts, and several of the people on the sidewalk were pushing shopping carts full of their belongings or behaving as if they should be headed for Asphalia House themselves.

Perhaps Rutland had seen better days. She hoped better days were ahead of it as well. Maybe it was a town that took getting to know alongside someone who lived there. Right then she was inspired only to find a supermarket and get out, maybe spend the afternoon making cookies, or a pot of turkey chili, or a salmon salad, or all three. She could take cookies to Owen the Owner. He'd like that, wouldn't he? Everyone liked home-made cookies.

At the supermarket, she loaded up on more than she needed, being used to shopping for several families at once. Always a fun challenge to figure out what to make and freeze out of leftovers, and she'd be here a month so no harm done.

Back at the cottage, she hauled in her loot and called Beezy to gab while she was figuring out a system for putting things away. Beezy wanted to know everything that had happened, so Sophie brought her up to speed on the basics of the drive, her living situation with the Great Reticent Bearded One and the visit that morning with Lily Anne, which was all that had happened since she'd left the day before.

'I like the sound of this Owen. Mr Strong and Silent. After all the cerebral Wall Street types around here, a guy who works with his hands could be super sexy.'

'Uh . . .' Sophie wrinkled her nose. 'I would not say he's super sexy. Too much beard.'

'Not even sorta sexy?'

'Maybe in-dire-straits sexy.'

Beezy gave her fabulous giggle. 'I would think you're in a dire straits by now, girl. How long has it been?'

'Can't hear you.' Sophie made a few static noises, opening

a cabinet to load in cans of beans and tomatoes. 'Something's messing up the line.'

'Okay, okay, but don't rule him out. You always ignore the nice guys.'

'What?' Sophie put in a can of black-eyed peas. 'When have I ignored a nice guy?'

'When Phil Jensen asked you out. When Ned Smith asked you out. When Jordan San—'

'Oh come on. Phil was high school! And they were dorks! Super-nice dorks, but ... I mean, would *you* have slept with any of them?'

'Of *course* I ... Yeah, no. Not any of them.'

'Case closed.'

'I tried, I tried. So what's next with Lily Anne? What about the other cousins? Have you found them?'

'Only their names online. If Lily Anne doesn't hire me tomorrow, I'll have to blurt out who I am and ask about them. If she does hire me, I can wait until it feels more natural. Maybe it never will, but instinct says that's what I should do.' Instinct and her parents acting as if something in this situation would set off a nuclear device if handled badly.

'It's very cool! Like a Netflix miniseries. Plotting and planning, intrigue and infamy ...'

'Ha.' Sophie tried to imagine Beezy's reaction if she knew about the Fabergé egg – the only secret she had ever kept from her best friend. Hiding it felt terrible, like she was cheating. But for reasons she still didn't understand, her instinct was shouting loudly to keep the discovery to herself.

'All you need to finish the drama is a wild fling.'

'Yeah ...' Sophie shoved a folded paper bag into an empty one for reuse. 'Who knows, maybe there's a Mr Fantastic out there in the Green Mountains.'

'Oh God. What if you fall in love and become a back-to-the-lander who gives up showering and the Internet and wears furs from animals you shot yourself?'

'That will definitely happen.' Sophie snorted. 'So what's going on back home? I'm sure I've missed tons since yesterday afternoon.'

'Ah, you know, the Southport usual. Pequot Book fair ramping up. Kids' sports, pickleball, parties on yachts. This town has become really weird.'

'It *has* changed.' Sophie closed an overhead cabinet now stocked with flour, sugar and other baking supplies. It felt good to lay in stores. In case of hurricane or tornado or volcanic eruption. 'I forgot to tell you, I saw Lexy right before I left.'

Beezy gasped. 'No. Was it awful?'

'The worst. Not only is she pregnant with the spawn of Peter—'

A louder, longer gasp. 'No! Oh no! Soph! I'm so sorry. That must have sucked.'

'There's worse.' Sophie paused, grateful for Beezy's unfailing support. 'She was super *nice* to me. I can't even hate her now.'

'Oh yes you can. You go right on hating. You can do it. I believe in you.'

'Aw, thanks, Beez.' She folded the last grocery bag and crammed it in with the others. 'That's sweet of you.'

'Seriously, though, that's good. Maybe you're finally over him.'

'Finally? *Finally?* I've been over him since I found out he was cheating. Years of over.'

'*Really?*'

Sophie made a face. 'Mostly over. Getting there.'

'Here's what you need to do.'

'Is this new advice? Or the same advice you've been giving me since the divorce?'

The Jewel of Cairo

'I'm ignoring that. You're out of the Southport bubble; go have fun. Give Owen-who-works-with-his-hands a second look. Go to a bar and be available. Have a fling. Fall in love. Get laid, for God's sake.'

'Mm, yeah, don't think I'd do that for His sake.'

'Just do it, then. You need to get back on that bicycle, or whatever the metaphor is. *Crap*, I have to go, I'm late. I'm having lunch with Chloe to hear all about her and Rick's new condo in Phoenix.'

'Have fun!' Sophie hung up the phone, glowing from her bestie's familiar chatter, only to encounter the unnatural quiet of the cottage.

Face it, she was never going to be Nature Girl.

Happily, she'd soon blasted the unnatural quiet out of existence by playing Talking Heads' live album *Stop Making Sense*. Impossible to listen to sitting down, and just the thing for dancing cookie-baking.

She cut a stick of butter into slices and put it on a plate to soften while she gathered the rest of her ingredients. Flour, sugar, salt, baking soda, egg, oatmeal, walnuts, chocolate chips. By the time the album was over, she had her last batch in the oven, and gorgeously browned and crisp cookies piled up on the cottage's one cooling rack. One! How could any decent person survive such deprivation? 'Cooling rack' took place of honor at the top of next week's shopping list.

Kitchen back to sparkling, cookies smelling like chocolate-butter-walnut heaven, she piled a dozen cooled from an early batch onto one of the house's chipped plates. Chipped, but Wedgwood, so quite expensive at some point. Probably a hand-me-down from Owen's mom, or his mother-in-law if he was married, or some deceased aunt who set her own rabbit traps and smoked cigars but loved to set a proper table.

Outside, cooler than the oven-heated cottage but warming into a proper summer afternoon, a nice breeze fluttered her hair and clothing. She made her way over to the barn-like structure between the house and the cottage, set back against the trees.

Closer to the barn, she could hear the roar-whine of a sander, familiar from shop class and the occasional projects her father did around the house. Gilles was a man good with his hands, even though he'd been a philosophy major in college – which shouldn't rule out being DIY-savvy, but seemed to. The best use of his hands, of course, was to point and aim a camera.

When he and Mom had come to the States to get married, he'd been working as a photojournalist in France, but here his art photographs had started gaining attention. He still showed his work occasionally in New York galleries, but he'd cut back as the years mounted, not because of his age, but because he felt he'd run out of things to say, artistically speaking.

Sophie herself had never had anything to say artistically speaking, but she was incredibly proud of him and his work.

Though now that she thought about it, she wasn't sure she'd ever told him so. Her parents rarely initiated or encouraged exchanges about their own lives. Maybe when she went back, she could change that.

At the barn now, she waited for a break in the sanding noise to knock on the door. 'Cookie delivery!'

Silence.

She grinned, imagining his horror at her intrusion. 'Free cookies! No strings attached!'

A human-sized door cut into the enormous ones that would let tractors in and out creaked open, and there was her work-with-his-hands temporary landlord in overalls and a grimy gray shirt, beard doing its bushy thing, safety glasses pushed on top of his head, which, due to lack of baseball cap, she could see was also covered with a ton of curling hair.

'Hi.' She held up the plate. 'I made you cookies in exchange for a quick peek inside. Would that be okay?'

'Uh . . .' Owen rubbed his temple.

'That sounded like "yes" to me. Was it?'

He rolled his eyes with amused annoyance. 'Sure, come in.'

'Thanks.' She walked curiously into the large space. His workshop took up one side, neatly organized with various saws and drills, shelves with power and hand tools, and a couple of large workbenches. The other half was stacked with logs and boards waiting to be used, plus the usual garage stuff – lawn-mower, snow blower, rakes, etc. The smell was fantastic: wood, sawdust and a slight burning from the friction of sanding and cutting. 'What a great place. Have a cookie.'

He pulled off a glove to take one, and Sophie snuck a look at his hands, trying to imagine them on her skin.

Nope. Sorry, Beezy.

'What are you working on now, that table?' She watched him take his first bite, his straggly eyebrows lifting. 'Good?'

'Good.' He took another bite. 'Thanks.'

'Plenty where that came from.' She approached the table-in-progress. 'Tell me about this piece. If you have time. I don't want to be a pain.'

'This piece.' He followed her over and stood looking down at it. 'Commissioned by a family from Woodstock. Mahogany frame with a top of green Vermont slate.'

'Like the one in the cottage. I didn't realize that was slate, or that it was local. So pretty.'

He nodded.

'Do most people know what they want, or do they see other pieces you've done and ask for something similar?'

'Both.'

'Do you lie in bed at night and think about furniture, or do you get your inspiration from things you see around you.'

'Yes.'

'Another cookie?' She held out the plate, pleased when he took a second. 'That's about all my questions for this afternoon. Got any for me before I leave you alone?'

'One.' He looked at her gravely. 'What are you doing here?'

Sophie cocked her head. 'In your workshop, or in Vermont?'

'Vermont.'

'You probably wouldn't believe me.'

'Probably.'

She laughed. 'Fair enough. I've always known I'm adopted, but I found out recently that my birth mother was one of my mom's best friends. She died when I was about five months old. Hit by a car in Crete. In Greece.'

'I know where Crete is.'

Oops. He looked exasperated. She didn't blame him. 'I'm—'

'King Minos, the Minotaur, Homer's *Odyssey*, El Greco, the Ottoman invasion . . .'

'Yes, that's the one. My grandparents emigrated from Crete to Vermont in the late 1930s. They had two daughters, my birth mother and her sister, Phyllis. Phyllis's daughter runs Asphalia House in Rutland. Have another cookie?'

He picked two off the plate and offered her one, which she took.

'Thank you. So anyway, I went to see Lily Anne, my cousin, this morning to see if I could help out while I'm here, though I haven't yet mentioned that we're related. Seemed a lot to dump on her right off the bat.' She bit into the cookie, watching Owen carefully to make sure she didn't overstay. So far he seemed interested.

The Jewel of Cairo

'How is that a lot to dump on her?'

'Oh, well. I mean, wouldn't you think it was weird if a stranger showed up and said, "Hi, I'm your cousin"?'

'Yup.' He scratched his beard. 'But it would be a lot weirder if the stranger who showed up was my cousin and she didn't tell me.'

'Oh.' Sophie lost interest in her cookie, which pretty much never happened. 'Maybe I'm just chicken, then.'

'Sounds like it.'

'Hmm.' The cookie became interesting again, so she rewarded it with a big bite while she thought that over. 'I'm an only child, so I'm not used to being related to people. It was like winning the lottery to find out I have all these cousins around. But yes, also a little scary. What about you, do you come from a big family?'

'Two brothers.'

'What do they do?'

'Lawyer in New York, surgeon in New Jersey.'

She tried not to look surprised. What a terrible snob she was turning out to be. 'Where did you grow up? What did your parents do? Any of them woodworkers?'

He finished the cookie. 'Scarsdale. Wall Street, math teacher.'

Scarsdale! Well. Southport had nothing on that town.

'Are you married?' She felt herself about to blush, which was stupid. Why was it impossible to ask a guy if he was married without seeming like you were interested in applying for the job?

'Yes.' He barked the word, looking down at the table again.

She was glad she hadn't listened to Beezy and come in hoping to seduce him. 'What does Mrs Owen do?'

'Pediatrician. She's at her mom's now.' He was still talking to the table. 'My mother-in-law had surgery and she's helping out.'

'Oh, that's nice that they're close. And a doctor, good for her. Except for cake and cookies, I am phenomenally unaccomplished.'

The table released him from its spell, enabling him to look straight at her again with his blue eyes and nice nose adrift in that sea of hair. 'Do you have good friends? Have you loved and been loved? Read good books, eaten good food, drunk good wine? Made people happy?'

Sophie wasn't sure what to do with this eloquent side of him, though she liked what he was saying. 'Yes . . . ?'

'Then what more do you want to accomplish?'

She pretended to consider the question. He might have a point, but it wasn't one that would hold up in her world. 'Nobel Prize would be nice.'

Owen walked back to his workbench in disgust, which was just right.

She turned to watch him and popped the last of her cookie into her mouth. 'Do you have children?'

'Fifteen.'

She nearly choked. 'You have *fifteen* children?'

'All fifteen have PhDs, two have Pulitzers, one a MacArthur "Genius Grant" and two Booker Prizes.'

Sophie followed him to the side of the room. 'How much of that is true?'

'None. I don't have kids. I thought that sounded more interesting.'

'You were right. Since you're not going to ask me, I'll tell you that I was married but he found someone better.' Her voice grew thick, which was annoying. By now she should be able to talk about her divorce without grief. 'I don't have kids either.'

'Sorry.'

'I was too, about the kids. As for my ex, I think I'm better off without him.' She scoffed. 'No, I *know* I'm better off without him.'

He gave her a glance that just might have held sympathy. 'Yeah, you don't want to be stuck with someone who's not into you.'

'Nope.' She put the plate of cookies down next to him on the workbench and stepped toward the door, wishing he'd said something like *Peter was a fool to let you go.* Unlikely, since she hadn't mentioned Peter's name, plus not true. 'Thanks for letting me bother you.'

'Thanks for the cookies.'

That time he was supposed to say, *No, no, you're not bothering me at all.*

She grinned, partly in farewell, partly because she apparently had developed strong ideas about how poor Owen should behave.

At least she kept them to herself.

Outside, she walked toward her cottage, wondering how to spend the next couple of hours. This trip would be good for her, she could tell already. In Southport she'd become too enmeshed in her business and everyone else's. It was healthy to have time to be bored, because it made a person stretch to find new activities and passions.

Like brooding.

The problem with boredom was that Sophie was an extrovert, daughter of two introverts whom she undoubtedly exhausted. Peter had been an extrovert, like her, their collective energy increased and enriched by interactions with other people. When they'd met again after she'd graduated, it had been like the scene from the original *West Side Story* movie, where Maria and Tony met at the gym and the whole world blurred and quieted around them, leaving only the couple in sharp focus.

She didn't realize for many more years that the reason Peter had singled her out that night was because she was attractive *enough*, poised *enough* and accomplished *enough*, but would never overshadow his own energy or accomplishments. She was malleable, eager to please and so crazy about him, so besotted with the idea of landing the biggest and most undeserved fish in the sea, that she never got in his way, nor did she ever stop to figure out her own life and what she needed.

Ah, youth.

Now that she was at this new crossroad, she had a decision to make. She could either bake and cook her way through the rest of her life, then die poignantly alone, or do some digging and thinking and sorting of herself, and possibly still die poignantly alone. But this month in Vermont, finding out more about the family she came from, might help her discover more about herself. She had no idea how, but it seemed promising.

Already she felt different up here. Freer, less burdened by realities. More open to possibilities. Maybe on Connie's home turf she'd feel permission to be more like her. Maybe honoring and trusting her feelings about keeping the Fabergé egg secret was part of that. Maybe the universe had some lesson to pass along through the egg while it was in Sophie's possession.

Something to think about.

Back in the cottage, heating up along with the afternoon, Sophie decided that instead of staring at her phone, she'd pick a nearby town to explore, and revel in its Vermontness.

Google convinced her to return to Woodstock, because there was a daily glass-blowing demonstration advertised at one of the restaurants. She could also shop for pottery and about a billion other things she didn't need. Along with baking and cooking, she was a champion shopper.

Maybe not the introspection she should be doing, but at least it would kill the afternoon.

A few hours later, she came back with a stunning hand-painted 24-karat gold Christmas ornament for her parents – Christmas in July! – and for herself a graceful pottery bowl with light blue fish swimming around its outside. For Helen she'd nixed the bottle of maple syrup with sparkles in it – because . . . why? – and instead bought Vermont honey and a jar of beeswax salve from local bees that pegged itself as a cure-all for hard-working hands. Given that Helen owned a ranch, her hands had to be the hardest-working of any Sophie knew, except maybe Owen's.

Afterward, she'd gone into a furniture store, where she hadn't seen anything she liked nearly as much as Owen's work, and an art gallery. By that time she'd overloaded on crowds and overpriced luxury items, which showed what kind of complicated and emotional morning she'd had, because generally both those were candy to her.

As successful as her errands had been, Owen's words kept running through her head. *It would be a lot weirder if the stranger was my cousin and didn't tell me.* After trying the scenario out with her and Lily Anne's roles reversed, she had to say she agreed with him, and wasn't quite clear on what her parents' problem had been. In fact, the more she thought about it, the more she decided their reaction hadn't made sense at all. Why shouldn't she tell Lily Anne? In fact, why hadn't she picked up the phone as soon as she found out and told her cousins and their father the happy news over the phone? She could have arrived to warm hugs and a party instead of a weird job interview.

Back at the cottage, she turned on the A/C, kicked off her sandals and relaxed with a giant glass of water, drumming her fingers on the arm of one of the Owen chairs, wondering if she should have stayed in Woodstock for dinner after all. Eating a salad alone at home wasn't terribly entertaining. Maybe she could teach herself to juggle with the Fabergé egg and some chef knives.

Her phone rang. She jumped and grabbed it from the coffee table. *Corson, Lily Anne.*

Fingers crossed.

'Hi, Lily Anne! Happy afternoon!'

'Thanks ...' Lily Anne sounded the teeniest bit taken aback. Maybe Sophie should tone down the enthusiasm. 'I was wondering if you could drop by Asphalia House tomorrow afternoon. Is four o'clock okay?'

'Yes. Sure.' She made herself sound nonchalant. 'See you then. Thank you.'

'Right. Bye.'

A meeting on a Sunday. It had to be good news, right? One of her birth mother's universe signs telling her that everything she'd come here to do would work out for the best? Because there was no point in Lily Anne making Sophie come in just to say she wasn't going to hire her.

Either way, there was no longer any point in waiting to tell her they were family.

Chapter 14

Saturday, May 15, 1976

Lilianne stepped into the elevator of Gilles's building on avenue de Wagram, not far from the rue de Courcelles, which boasted a toy-sized view of the Arc de Triomphe at its southern end. As was typical of the architect Haussmann's style, which defined the city, the ground floor was reserved for commercial use, in this case a branch of Crédit Agricole, with apartments above, each room with its own balcony, excepting the fifth floor, whose balcony ran the full width of the building.

It was odd being back in the City of Light, so beautiful and so familiar. Yet the contrast with Cairo made it seem movie-set perfect, like it had been put together by an obsessive-compulsive. Welcoming smiles and friendly chatter were also absent in her dealings with people. At the same time, what joy to walk down a street and not be ogled and harassed at every turn.

She pressed five and watched the elevator doors close with a melodramatic sense of doom. She'd had to ring Gilles's buzzer three times before he answered with a low '*Oui?*' then buzzed her up without further comment.

No, she hadn't imagined him miraculously regaining his old self overnight, nor did she think he would have jumped up and down with joy at her arrival. But she had not expected such a cold reception. Had he changed his mind about wanting her there?

Too bad. She'd made the trip. Her plane had been two hours late, and she'd had to wait another hour for her suitcase because of a stuck hold door. Having been up at five to get to her meeting with John Baker at seven, no matter what happened after she got off this elevator and walked into Gilles's apartment, this would be one hell of a long day.

The elevator opened; Lilianne found Gilles's door and knocked, taken aback when it swung open. Either he wasn't locking himself in or he refused to come to the door to greet her.

This was weird. And ominous.

She stepped through the door, and was about to call out a cheerful hello when the smell hit in a rank wave. Rotting garbage, unwashed body, stale alcohol, possibly worse. In front of her, the typical narrow corridor with a herringbone-patterned wooden floor off which rooms branched, those on the left with views of the street, those on the right overlooking the building's interior courtyard.

Lilianne waited a few seconds until she could control her shock, then closed the door behind her. 'Gilles?'

Another few steps and she saw him, in a living room strewn with discarded clothing, dirty plates and bowls of decaying food. The windows were closed, blinds drawn, the smell unbearable. Gilles, her startlingly handsome, athletic, sensitive, intellectual friend, was slumped on the couch, staring down at his skinny legs protruding from a loose pair of boxers. On his shrunken torso, a food-stained undershirt.

'Hi.' She kept her voice gentle, hid her revulsion as she walked toward him, fighting shock and nausea. 'I guess I don't need to ask how you're doing.'

He made a small sound she hoped was a laugh. 'I guess that's obvious.' His voice was the same as on the phone, a hoarse, hollow shadow of its former rich depth and vigor.

'I'm sorry it got this bad for you.'

'Me too.'

'Have you seen a doctor? A psychiatrist?' She went around the room, lifting blinds, opening windows to the fresh outside air.

'He said I didn't engage in combat so I'll get over this quickly. A couple of weeks at most.'

Lilianne turned from the window. Gilles hadn't moved. 'When was that?'

'A month and a half ago.'

'Well. You only have negative four weeks to go and you'll be back to normal.' She was picking up pieces of clothing – pants, shorts, shirts, underwear – flinging them into a pile, desperate for order while she tried to figure out what else she could do for him.

'I'm sorry you had to come to clean up my ... messes. So sorry.' He raised his head halfway, extraordinary features obscured behind an ungroomed beard, greasy hair hanging limply, cheeks gaunt, a haunted, feral creature.

'I don't mind.'

He dropped his head again, and it hit her why he hadn't come to the door, why he hadn't answered her greeting, why he didn't meet her eyes. Lilianne understood shame. She should have recognized that stink earlier – worse than anything in the apartment.

Spurred by equal parts tenderness and determination, she went over to kneel in front of him, one hand on each bony knee, willing him to look at her. 'You have nothing to be ashamed of. You are a good man who took two hard blows. Like any injury, you need time to heal. If it's okay with you, I'll bring you back to Cairo with me. I will help you, and you will get better.'

His dull, haunted eyes met hers briefly, and she smiled, even as tears came into her eyes and her heart felt full to breaking.

'I smell terrible,'

'Yes.'

'And the apartment.'

'Worse.' She wanted to touch his face, a spot on his sunken cheek not covered by hair. 'But at least those are easy fixes.'

The air was already improving from the breeze coming through the windows. Lilianne stood and began stacking filthy plates. 'I'm curious. If you don't mind answering. Why did you call me?'

'I can't . . . My friends here, my family . . . it's too much pain for them. They'll cry and fuss, and be angry at me for going to Lebanon. I knew you'd come and do what needed to be done. No crying, no punishing.'

She understood. Call Lilianne, the cold, strong rock-woman. She'll do your dishes and your laundry, and demand nothing in return. 'But do they know you're all right? Connie and I were worried sick when we didn't hear from you for so long. I can't imagine what your family's going through.'

'My parents are traveling. My brother is busy.'

'Friends, then.' She picked up a bowl with a science project's worth of mold inside. 'I can call them and—'

'Helen.'

Lilianne jerked her head toward him. 'What about her?'

His head was back down, pulling his shoulders forward, as if its weight was too much for him to support. 'Have you . . . heard from her?'

'No.' She kept her voice gentle. 'But Connie has.'

'Is she marrying him? Kevin?' The words were wrenched out of his throat.

Lilianne clutched the stack of plates, wanting to hurl them

out the window and listen to the satisfying smash on the street. Wanting to spirit Helen here and show her what she'd done to this proud, remarkable man. 'Next month, Connie said. The nineteenth.'

His frame folded farther inward. A tear dropped onto the couch between his legs. Then another.

'Come, Gilles.' She put the plates down. 'Let's get you cleaned up. A shower first, then shave that beard before people think you're Karl Marx.'

'I can't.'

'Of course you can. Come . . . let me help.'

It took a while, but eventually she was able to coax him onto his feet and down the hall, shocked at how heavily he leaned on her and how slowly he moved. Only a few months ago he'd been the epitome of masculine, muscled grace.

While he showered, she did a quick clean-up of the apartment, tossing garbage and an alarming number of empty wine and liquor bottles. That done, she soaked the crusted dishes in the sink to wash later, one ear out for any sounds from the bathroom that might mean Gilles needed her, trying to concentrate on what she could do for him right now so the past and future wouldn't overwhelm him.

After an absurdly long time, he joined her in the kitchen, clean-shaven, looking more like himself and also more ill and frighteningly skeletal. How long since he'd had a decent meal?

'There you are.' Lilianne smiled, heart pounding painfully. 'Feel better?'

He shrugged. 'Cleaner.'

'Sit.' She pointed to a stool she'd set on the tile floor. 'I'll cut your hair. You look like a wild man.'

'Where were you trained?' He spoke clumsily, as if he were

discovering speech again, but she was encouraged by the glimmer of humor.

'École d'Incompétence.' She brandished a pair of scissors, found in his studio. 'Every cut comes with a guarantee: you'll have a style unlike anyone else in the city.'

She did an okay job. At least he looked less like a mountain man and more like the city sophisticate he was. She'd planned to bring him food shopping with her, but his pace was so slow she worried the errands would exhaust him. His kitchen cabinets were bare, and the refrigerator held only bottles of white wine, three eggs and a few rock-hard ends of cheese. She hated to leave him, even for an hour, but the man had to eat.

'I'm going to get groceries. What have you been eating?'

'Not enough.'

'Drinking?'

'Too much.'

'Let's reverse that.' She picked up a shopping bag she'd found earlier and put by the front door. 'I stole your keys. I'll be back in an hour.'

'Lilianne.'

She turned back to find him regarding her with warmth in his eyes that reminded her of his real self and gave her some hope. 'Yes, Gilles.'

'Thank you. Again. I had no right to invade your life like this.'

'You had every right.' She smiled, allowing their eye contact to go on too long just for the joy of seeing that light brightening his eyes. When it seemed someone had to say something or the moment would turn ludicrous, she turned with a wave and let herself out of the apartment.

Groceries were available in any Parisian neighborhood, and this one was no exception. She had to do some walking and asking, but she found what she'd need for the evening meal and breakfast the next day.

Back in the apartment, she found Gilles at the living room window, staring down at the street. He turned when she came in – an improvement over her first entrance.

'Hungry?'

He shook his head.

'You need to eat.'

'I know.'

'Come.' She led the way into the kitchen, where Gilles set the table – so slowly! – and she laid out her purchases. A quiche and a salad of grated carrots, plus the ubiquitous baguette, cut in thinner slices than she might otherwise offer. She sensed too much food would be as bad to start with as too little.

They drank from a bottle of wine that Lilianne made sure stayed on her side of the table, doled out stingily, though Gilles didn't seem upset by the small amount.

While they ate – neither of them could manage much – she kept up a slow-moving stream of talk about life in Cairo, about Connie, about Sami, and her visit with her grandparents. When she sensed he was becoming restless and impatient, she gave him silence.

By the time the meal was over, dishes washed and dried, including those that had mounted up before her visit, Lilianne was nearly as drained and exhausted as Gilles.

However, there was no way she'd let him sleep on sheets that were probably as disgusting as he'd been when she walked in, so while he finished drying the dishes and wiping down the counters, she found his bedroom – remarkably neat – and the linen closet and whipped a new set of sheets onto the bed, bundling the old ones for the laundry – though burning them might be a better option.

To her great relief, the bed in the guest room was already made up.

She said goodnight and closed the door to her room, amused at her urge to go into his and see him tucked safely in. Apparently she did have some nurturing genes lying around. She'd have to be careful not to use them all up.

The trick would be not to look too far ahead. She'd bring Gilles to Cairo and help him through the worst, though what he needed was not a big bustling city of dust and heat, but somewhere cool, peaceful and green, a world of nature with life in evidence everywhere he looked. She'd also need to find a way to convince him he needed to let his family know he'd left Lebanon and was safe.

Eventually exhaustion overcame her worry and the strangeness of her surroundings, and she slid into sleep, only to be awoken by hoarse shouts of terror that had her running to Gilles's room before she was fully awake.

He was still in bed, yelling and flailing against an invisible enemy.

'Gilles, it's Lilianne. Wake up. You're dreaming. You're safe. You're safe with me.'

His bloodshot eyes opened wider than she'd thought possible; he stared rigidly at the ceiling, breath coming too fast.

She laid a hand on his shoulder, hoping the touch was soothing. 'Nightmare?'

'They come. They come all the time.'

'Who does?'

He looked at her in surprise. 'The nightmares.'

She snorted and sat down on the edge of his bed. 'That stinks. You get to suffer all day and all night too.'

'Very generous.' He moved restlessly, his limbs swishing across soft, clean cotton. 'I was working well in the Lebanon.

The Jewel of Cairo

Functioning well, in spite of the fear and the violence. But it became harder to get the shots. Harder to show up every day. Harder to get out of bed. Then it became impossible. I came back here thinking once I was out of that hell I would recover.'

'Not so easy.'

'I started to think dying was the only answer.'

'I'm glad you called me. We'll find a way out.' She thought again of where he could be most at peace. Cairo was too active, dusty, dirty. He needed somewhere tranquil, uncomplicated, with quiet routines and no surprises.

Southport. The name jumped into her head along with a thrill of adrenaline. Perfect. She'd just been talking to her father about accepting his offer of the house, which was big enough that Gilles could set up a studio when he felt like taking up his camera again. They'd be blocks from Long Island Sound and Southport's charming harbor, its beaches, islands and nearby woodlands.

As long as Gilles didn't mind leaving family, friends, country and everything he'd known since birth . . . Would a big change jar him into worse shape or offer him a fresh new start?

'In Paris, there is such beauty, elegance and good manners that you can pretend people are kind and good and civilization is worthy of them.' He spoke haltingly, one arm across his eyes. 'Of course there is terrible bureaucracy here, and hate and snobbishness and a lot of dog shit on the sidewalks, but you can choose to ignore all that. Every day you can choose to ignore all that, and pretend being alive and human is the best way to live, and that you deserve it.

'In war, there is nowhere to look away, no way to ignore the horror. The ugliness is so much uglier, and there's no time or place to pretend that humans are kind and dignified and civilized. All you see, every day, is proof of their cruelty and their bestiality and you start to believe that's the truth of life and of mankind.' His voice broke. He swallowed several times before he could continue. 'Once you've seen that, you can't go back to believing anything else.

'That's what made me want to die. Because death made perfect sense. If I had become part of the ugliness, then the world should be rid of me and my inability to be human the way I believe I should be.'

Lilianne took in a sharp breath, understanding the emotions if not the despair. 'There are different ways of being human, Gilles. This isn't one-size-fits-all.'

'I have nothing to contribute any more. I can't work. I can't love. I am useless.'

'You're not . . .' Lilianne stopped herself. Contradicting him wouldn't help. Telling him he had many joys ahead of him once he healed wouldn't work either. Not if he didn't believe it. Not if the future he saw contained only this ghastly present. 'If I became seriously ill for a time, would you tell me I was useless and that the world would be better off without me?'

He looked at her gravely. 'Of course.'

She laughed at his answer, pleased to see his dark expression lightening. 'Well okay, then.'

'You must be exhausted, Lilianne.'

That was an understatement. 'Can you sleep?

'I will eventually.'

'I'll stay a little longer.' She sat next to him, trying to remember back to when she was a little girl with nightmares. What had her parents done?

She remembered her mother singing to her in Arabic when they accidentally left a favorite stuffed animal in a hotel.

Lilianne wasn't going to sing, in Arabic or otherwise.

Another memory, of her nanny, Colleen, sitting by her bed,

stroking her hair until she relaxed enough to go back to sleep. She looked at Gilles's haunted face, feeling awkward and self-conscious, trying to frame the question in her head. *Is it okay if I touch you?*

She couldn't make herself say the words. Instead, she tentatively reached out to smooth the hair she'd just cut, to trace with a gentle finger the dark lines of his brows, his broad forehead, the slope of his nose, the curve of his now-smooth cheeks. 'This okay?'

'Yes. It's good.'

'I'm glad.' She kept up the stroking until his breathing settled back into sleep, then she got up and tiptoed back to her own room, ready to let fatigue reclaim her.

Instead, she lay awake most of the night, her brain spinning. Now that she was no longer in an adrenaline-fueled rescue rush, the worries crept in. Some war veterans were never able to return to normal life. She'd taken on Gilles as her responsibility. If she couldn't help him, would she have to throw him back, like an adopted rescue dog that proved too much? Or would her life be forever tied to his misery and dysfunction?

She tried to shake off those thoughts, to picture instead a rosier future, one in which she wafted him to Southport in a shimmering bubble and healed him with her magic wand. He'd return to Paris, able to resume his career and his life, meet another wonderful woman and have the family he'd envisioned having with Helen.

But the dark thoughts kept at her, shadows underneath the sunny fantasy surface, like sharks that had spotted their prey. Lilianne would do her best. She had the resources and would make the time, but she couldn't lie to herself. There was a good possibility that instead of being able to lift Gilles out of his suffering, her efforts would drag both of them down.

Chapter 15

Present day

Sophie: *Looks like I'll get a job cooking at Asphalia House! I'm going to tell Lily Anne today that we're related.*
Lilianne: *Already? So soon? Do you think that's wise?*
Sophie: *Definitely.*
Lilianne: *I hope you're right.*
Sophie: *I am. Love you.*
Lilianne: ♥

Sophie lowered herself gingerly onto the creaky couch in Lily Anne's office, smiling too hard. Her cousin looked worn out, eyes puffy and shadowed, voice husky. Not that Sophie's smile could help after what must have been a rough night, but it felt worth trying. She didn't want her big news to exhaust Lily Anne further. 'Thank you for having me back.'

'I spoke with your references. They were all very positive. Though apparently you left abruptly on this trip?'

'I'd just found out about my birth family, as I told you, and wanted to meet them.' Sophie thought that was enough explanation, but Lily Anne was waiting for her to go on. 'Should I say something else? That was the truth.'

'Sorry, no, I didn't doubt that. I'm wondering if you left your clients in a bind.'

'Oh, I see. No, this is Southport, no one's going to starve.'

Lily Anne did not look amused.

Oops. But Sophie didn't want to talk about her clients, she wanted to fix her mistake of the day before: not telling Lily Anne that they were cousins. 'I only had two clients. Three for a while, but one had just dropped me after her husband lost his job. The other two were friends who were fine managing on their own.'

'Two clients.'

Sophie wrinkled her nose. 'I'm a better cook than entrepreneur.'

Lily Anne's phone rang. She glanced over, but made no move to answer. 'As I told you yesterday, our cook, Annika, has been asking for a long vacation to see family in Norway. Normally we don't—'

'Can I stop you there?' Sophie needed to do this now. 'Sorry, but I have something important to say.'

Lily Anne looked surprised, then annoyed, in a *now*-what? way, then concerned in an is-she-a-flake? way. Sophie didn't blame her. 'I told you I came here looking for my family. That was true. But I did leave out one ... detail.'

'Okay.' Lily Anne waited, hands gripping each other in her lap.

'The detail is ... *you* are my family. You and your sister and your brothers. Your dad is my uncle.' She'd expected Lily Anne's silence, and her stunned expression, but still hurried on in near-panic. 'I found out last week. My birth mother was Connie Pappas.'

'Connie.' Lily Anne's pale face grew paler. 'Connie didn't have children.'

'Well ... obviously she did. Because ...' Sophie spread her hands, ta-daaa, 'me.'

The phone rang again. Lily Anne didn't even glance at it this time. Sophie's chair creaked as she fidgeted.

'Sorry.' Lily Anne rubbed her wide forehead, so much like Sophie's. 'I'm having a little trouble with this.'

'I did too. After all these years, suddenly I find out I have living family. And then I find out you're all of a few hours away from where I've lived my whole life.'

'How . . .' Lily Anne looked exasperated. 'Why didn't you know all this sooner?'

'My parents didn't . . .' Sophie searched for a way to make this sound more credible than it was. 'I found out by accident. One of my mom and Connie's oldest friends was visiting my parents. She was ill, and when she woke up, she was confused and sleepy and mistook me for Connie. I do look a lot like her. Anyway, it all unraveled from there.'

More forehead-rubbing, through which Sophie waited patiently. 'Why did your parents keep this from you?'

Sophie wrinkled her nose. She dreaded this part. 'That's where the real weirdness comes in. They promised someone that they wouldn't tell me.'

Lily Anne scowled. 'Oh, come on. Who'd not want you to know?'

'I have no idea. I can't imagine a scenario that would justify that much secrecy.'

Lily Anne hardly seemed to hear her. 'Why didn't *my* mother know? She and Connie were sisters. Not close, but not *that* far apart. If Mom knew, I'm sure she would have told us. So why didn't she?'

'Maybe Connie thought Phyllis would disapprove that she had a kid when she was unmarried?'

'No.' Lily Anne was adamant. 'Mom wasn't *that* prudish.

Given what she told me about Connie, I don't even think it would have surprised her.'

The cousins stared at each other, Lily Anne suspicious, Sophie praying she didn't reject the story out of hand. 'I've been struggling with this too. My parents were completely open about my adoption, so why leave out the part that my birth mother was one of their best friends?'

Lily Anne's eyes narrowed. Sophie could practically see her brain spinning through the scenario, looking for something that would make sense. Hers had been doing the same for days. 'After Connie died, wouldn't the authorities have looked to us as next of kin? We're not hard to find.'

Sophie gave a helpless shrug. 'Add it to the doesn't-make-sense list. Maybe Connie knew she was dying and said she wanted my parents to raise me? I don't know how that works legally, and I don't know why she wouldn't have wanted her own family to raise me. Or maybe the authorities did contact your family and your mom didn't want me.' She was surprised how hard that was to say.

More silence, which Sophie struggled not to fill, while Lily Anne contemplated the ugly carpet.

'You're sure about all this?'

'All I'm sure of is that your aunt Connie was my mother. I've seen her picture. Short, dark, always smiling, kind of hippy-ish.' Lily Anne was nodding at the description. 'My parents would have no reason to make up my parentage. They're extremely sane and brutally honest. Except for whatever they're withholding for whatever annoyingly mysterious reason.'

Lily Anne folded her arms. 'Why didn't you tell me this yesterday? And why are you trying to get a *job* here?'

Oops. Sophie should have talked to Owen sooner. He was right.

'I should have told you yesterday. But . . .' She took a breath. 'Two reasons. One, the story is so strange, I was afraid to. Two, I didn't know how you'd react, and I had this goofy idea that if you got to know and trust me first, it would be easier on both of us. Which probably only makes sense if you're me.'

Lily Anne still looked unconvinced. 'I can sort of see that.'

'I'm an only child, single, and I can't have children. Most of my parents' relatives are in Egypt and France. I won't mind if you and your siblings don't become my best friends, but I do want the chance to have . . .' She had to swallow, thinking of Peter and of Connie, and of how things could have been different. 'To have family. Blood relations. The reason I fell apart yesterday when you opened the door was because you're the first person I've ever seen in the flesh who shares my DNA. It was a big deal.'

Lily Anne stared down at her desk. She cleared her throat. Cleared it again. 'So . . . obviously, this is unexpected.'

'It was for me too.'

'It would have been . . . I wish you'd called me before you came up so I could have gotten used to the idea.'

'I should have. I had this fantasy that we'd get to be friends. Then, when I told you, there'd be a festival. You know, face-painting, cotton candy, snow cones . . .' Sophie's misery over how badly she'd handled this softened when her cousin's mouth lifted in half a smile. 'I do that, unfortunately. Play stuff out in my head, where the scenarios always happen perfectly, then rush to stage them in real life. It seldom works.'

Lily Anne was full-out smiling now. 'I'm the opposite.'

'Proof we're related.' Sophie gave a goofy thumbs-up. Lily Anne laughed. Tense laughter, but Sophie would take it. 'We do have the same face shape, dimples and good Greek noses.'

'True.' Lily Anne touched hers ruefully, healthier color returning to her face. 'What a weird day. I was up half the night with a desperate resident and an equally desperate caller, and now I have a cousin I didn't know existed. Unless you're trying to scam me.'

Sophie looked pointedly around the shabby office. 'Out of what?'

Lily Anne shrugged. *'Touché.'*

'Do you have pictures of your family here?' Sophie could barely contain her eagerness. 'Any of them?'

'Just my mom. I guess she's your aunt Phyllis.' Lily Anne picked up the picture of a salt-and-pepper brunette on her desk and handed it over. 'I see the rest frequently enough not to keep photos around.'

Sophie stared rapturously at the picture. Her mom's sister. Her aunt, though Phyllis looked nothing like either Sophie or Lily Anne. She was fairer, smaller-nosed, thinner-lipped, Greek genes in shorter supply. 'I'm sorry you lost her so young.'

'Thanks. It was rough. She fought for four years.'

'Where do your brothers and sisters live? And your dad?' Sophie handed back the picture. 'Close by, I hope?'

'They're all in Vermont. Close depends on your perspective. My sister Naomi lives in Cornith Corners, near the New Hampshire border, not far from Strafford, where we grew up. She married young and has four kids she home-schools. Her husband is a dairy farmer. My oldest brother, Jeffrey, died in his twenties.' Her face turned stony with pain.

Sophie gasped. 'Oh, I'm so sorry.'

'Thanks. It sucked. Fred and Donny both live in Strafford. They're also farmers.' Lily Anne gave a wry smile. 'Pot farmers.'

'Contributing to the well-being of humanity.'

She put her mom's photo back on the desk. 'Yeah, it's a little hard for me to see it that way, but we don't get much in the way of marijuana problems at Asphalia House, so . . .'

'So let the good times roll.'

That didn't go over well. Sophie would take note: drug jokes not funny. 'Your dad? My uncle Clyde?'

'Dad is retired from selling.' Lily Anne made a wry face. 'Alcohol.'

'Oof.' Sophie winced. 'That's a tough one.'

'He raised five of us on that salary. It is what it is. But yeah, it's not something I brag about here. He lives in Strafford too.'

'So they're all there. How far is it?'

'A little over an hour.'

'Oh.' Sophie couldn't help being disappointed. There went the fantasy of her family spending a lot of time together over the next month. 'So you're the outlier.'

'I'm . . .' Lily Anne stared down at her lap. 'I guess I am.'

'What were you going to say?'

She looked up, surprised. 'Are you always this direct?'

'Yes.'

Again that dimpled smile, like looking in the mirror at the wrong face. 'I imagined I'd be living a lot farther away from Strafford than this.'

'Really?' Sophie hoped she'd elaborate. A window into her cousin's mind. 'Like where?'

'Just . . . somewhere else.' Lily Anne looked at her watch. 'Speaking of somewhere else, that's where I have to be in about fifteen minutes. Why don't I introduce you to Annika, and you can start learning the ropes.'

Window closed. Sophie would have to find a time to get Lily Anne away from work and more able to talk. 'So I'm hired?'

'Of course.' Lily Anne got to her feet. 'You're *family*.'

Sophie cracked up. 'A little nepotism to brighten my day.'

'Annika has already bought her Norway tickets. Some last-minute deal. Can you start Tuesday so she can have a couple of days to pack and get ready?'

'I can.' She followed her cousin – her cousin! – out of the office, across the tired foyer and into the kitchen, which was a decent size but dingy, ancient appliances dented and scratched, and in appalling disarray. Pots and pans – clean – were stacked on nearly every surface except an island it would be nearly impossible for more than one cook to maneuver around. One cabinet had lost a hinge and the door hung at a drunken angle. The linoleum badly needed replacing, the dishtowels bleaching and the pantry reorganizing.

Sophie itched to get started.

The cook, Annika, was a plump middle-aged woman with a warm smile and the pleasant, empty eyes of someone who'd either checked out a long time ago or had never checked in. Watching her over the next hour made Sophie twitchy with impatience. Annika moved and spoke at a Zen pace, good for stress levels, bad for accomplishing anything quickly. She was making a pasta salad from a recipe that seemed to be ensuring flavor was not allowed to interfere. Cauliflower – delicious! But how white and unappetizing against an equally white background. White cheddar, mayonnaise, flecks of dried parsley, a pinch of mustard powder, wow.

Sophie could make a difference here.

That cheered her up. Even if she never got close to Lily Anne, and even if she had to travel an hour to meet the rest of her family, who might not be interested in meeting her, this quest would not be in vain as far as this kitchen was concerned.

She'd be expected to prepare dinner Sunday through Thursday nights. Another part-time cook took over on the weekends. She'd also need to make sure ingredients were available for the women to prepare their own breakfasts and lunches, based on shopping lists they provided every week. Annika had explained that for many residents, Asphalia House was their first experience – or first in a long while – with regular healthy meals. There was no way to ensure they continued good habits after they left, but at least many commented on how much better and stronger they felt eating well. A good incentive.

The blandness of the pasta salad was explained when Annika introduced Sophie to the menu bible, a thick three-hole binder with stained, worn pages. Three hundred and sixty-five days of dinner, with recipes and weekly shopping lists. The scrapbooky tome had apparently been put together by Lily Anne's grandmother, Eleni, probably fifty years earlier. It was full of sensible, nutritious and balanced meals, and empty of spice and imagination. The idea of being tied to cooking from it day after day, year after year made Sophie feel more claustrophobic than the clutter in the kitchen.

At a quarter to six, fifteen minutes before the residents' scheduled dinnertime, Annika having entrusted Sophie with tasks that required zero skill, a young woman launched herself into the kitchen. She was probably in her late twenties, big-boned with extra pounds, hot-pink hair shaved on one side of her head, a piercing in her nose and several in her ears, tattoos around her neck and down her arms. Damp hair and a powdery smell indicated she'd just showered. 'I'm starving. Who are you?'

'Sophie.' She smiled into the young face, which wasn't hostile but wasn't friendly either. 'Who are you?'

'Lizzie Borden.' She struck a star pose. 'Named Elizabeth at birth, but I like the shock value.'

'It's good and shocking.'

'What's for dinner, Annie?' Lizzie Borden was dressed in short pink shorts that matched her hair, chunky black lace-up boots and a lime-green shirt. On her face, pink cat's-eye glasses with rhinestones on the corners.

Blinding. Fantastic.

'Pasta salad.' Annika was salting and stirring.

'Need help?'

Annika looked wearily over to Sophie. 'She says that every day, and every day I say no, I got this. You'd think she'd learn.'

Sophie shrugged, refusing to get into the middle. She didn't see why Lizzie couldn't help if she wanted to.

'So what's your deal?' Lizzie looked her up and down. 'Where'd you come from?'

'Connecticut.' Sophie picked up the next in a pile of peeled carrots it was her job to cut into sticks.

'Oh, Con-*NEC*-ti-cut. I thought I smelled privilege.' Lizzie fanned in front of her nose 'Born with a silver spoon?'

'Oh no. God no. Not me.' Sophie split a carrot in half. '*Platinum*. Please.'

A snort of unwilling laughter. 'Got a trust fund?'

'Doesn't everyone?' She didn't, but it was fun playing up what Lizzie wanted her to be.

'So what are you doing here? Are you an addict? Let me guess.' Index finger under her chin as she pondered. 'Can't stop shopping at Tiffany's?'

'I'm taking over the kitchen for a month while Annika goes on vacation.'

'Can you cook?'

'Not me!' Sophie gave a ditzy giggle. 'But I'll figure something out.'

'She's kidding, Lizzie.' Annika hoisted the bowl of salad. 'She's a personal chef.'

'Oh, a *personal chef* from *Connecticut* cooking for addicts. How kind of you to bless us with your—'

'Go sit with the others, Lizzie.' Annika spoke patiently but with a hint of iron in her tone. 'We'll bring out your food.'

'I will.' Lizzie stole a carrot and crunched noisily. 'I suppose by helping us less fortunates, you'll have something new to brag about to your Ivy League crowd when you—'

'Go, Lizzie,' Annika ordered.

'I'm gone. Lovely to make your acquaintance, Princess Sophie.' Lizzie gave her a narrow-eyed stare and clomped off.

Sophie put the last of the carrots on the platter and reached for the tub of store-bought hummus to empty into a bowl. 'What's her deal?'

'You get all kinds here.' Annika gave the salad a final stir. The wet noise announced overcooked pasta. 'Some want to hide, some want to be noticed. Lizzie wants to be noticed.'

'You don't want her to help in here?'

Annika scowled. 'I don't like people in my kitchen.'

'Good reason.' Sophie might not mind, though. It would be a good test of whether Lizzie really wanted to help or was just trying to annoy Annika. She picked up the bowl of hummus and the plate of carrots. Bananas, and brownies made from a boxed mix – *ick* – sat waiting for dessert.

The dining room was a good size, with an art deco chandelier hanging from the ceiling and crown molding around the top of the cream-colored walls. The elegance stopped there. The same stained tan carpet in Lily Anne's office was underfoot here, too, and the only wall decoration was a couple of inspirational posters with visible creases from rough handling and previous folds. *Mindset Is Everything*, and *Yes, Yes, I Can*, with cartoon flowers on one and photos of carefully diverse smiling teens on the other.

Around the bare scuffed dining table waited seven women with an age range of a couple of decades, two with tear-stained faces, two sitting quietly, two chatting, Lizzie fiddling with her silverware. Seeing them gathered, it was hard not to focus on

The Jewel of Cairo

the combined weight of their dark experiences and the scope of their battles, behind and ahead.

Not for the first time, Sophie was grateful for her upbringing, and the minuscule-in-comparison issues she complained about. Mom was distant, Dad disengaged, neither passionate with the other. Now she added deep gratitude that the genes of Connie's addiction hadn't been passed down to her. Nor would they be to any children. A blessing, however painful.

Annika plopped the bowl of pasta salad on the table and retreated toward the kitchen. Sophie set down the carrots, unwilling to follow just yet. She wanted to do more than remain invisible behind the stove.

'Hello, ladies.' She put the hummus next to the carrots. 'I'm Sophie. I'll be filling in for Annika for a few weeks. Lizzie I already met. What are the rest of your names?'

The chatting ones were May and Emily. The weepy ones were Dee and Lori, the silent ones were Cindi and Barb, and the latecomer, arriving in a cleavage-first top, was Betsy.

Lizzie pointed to Sophie. 'Bet you're dying to ask what we're in here for.'

'I'd rather know what kind of food you like. Anything you want to try while I'm here? Something you miss from home?'

Lizzie laughed rudely and reached for the pasta. 'What home?'

'Oh, get over yourself.' Betsy had a turned-up nose, wire glasses and a thicket of blonde hair. 'You were born into one.'

'That was hostile, Betsy.' May, the most put together of the bunch, had fine features, eyes set close, sharp nose and pointed chin, and wore a yellow sundress decorated with butterflies.

'Sorry, Lizzie.' Betsy did not look or sound sorry.

Lizzie thumped the bowl of salad in front of her, having helped herself. 'I've had worse.'

Sophie tried again. 'I was serious about asking what kind of food—'

'Are you still here?' Lizzie demanded.

'Nope. I'm in the kitchen with Annika. You're talking to yourself.'

Lizzie rolled her eyes and shoved in a mouthful.

'We're not really focused on food here,' Lori said. She was dark, plump and vulnerable-looking, eyes shadowed with fatigue and grief.

'Right.' Sophie felt stupid for asking. 'I'll just do my thing, then.'

'What *is* your thing?' Lizzie asked. 'Counting diamonds? Scolding servants?'

'What's going on?' Lily Anne walked into the room, the question posed to Sophie. 'Is there a problem?'

'Big problem,' Lizzie said.

'No problem.' Sophie sent Lizzie a good-natured glare. 'Just getting to know the women I'll be feeding.'

'Lizzie?' Lily Anne spoke quietly. 'Did you feel there was a problem?'

Sophie laughed. 'She was kidding.'

'I'm asking Lizzie.'

Sophie narrowed her eyes at her cousin. Was she serious?

'She touched my body inappropriately,' Lizzie whined.

Sophie let out a snort. 'Give me a break.'

The look Lily Anne gave her would have frozen water.

'Oh, come on.' Sophie let out a laugh of disbelief. 'She's *kidding*.'

The women at the table watched, some amused, some horrified.

Lily Anne sighed. 'Did anyone else see—'

The Jewel of Cairo

'No, of *course* not.' Betsy rolled her eyes and shoved Lizzie's shoulder. 'She's just having her freak version of a good time.'

'You speak truth,' May said. The others nodded their agreement.

'Come on back to my office, Sophie.' Lily Anne smiled a gentle smile.

'Ooh, you're in trou-ble!' Lizzie taunted.

'Happy to.' Sophie stuck her tongue out at Lizzie and followed her cousin out of the dining room, hearing the giggles behind her, not blaming them at all. This was ridiculous.

In her office, Lily Anne closed the door and perched on the edge of her desk, gesturing Sophie to sit, which she didn't feel like doing. 'So, it might take you a while to get used to the vibe around here.'

'I didn't touch her.'

'Of course you didn't.'

'Then why did you pretend to take her seriously?'

'It's a boy-who-cried-wolf thing. Lizzie's only been here a couple of weeks. She's hurting. She's angry. I'm still working out the best way to reach her. It's a process. Not everyone will click with me. Sometimes the solution for an individual comes from one of the other residents or a member of staff. Sometimes she'll get there herself. Some of them we lose.' Lily Anne looked older suddenly, as if the weight of the need around her had sucked out her youth. 'Those are the hardest parts of the job.'

Sophie ached with compassion, wanting to hug her cousin, knowing it would be inappropriate. 'Do you ever feel like you can't handle all this?'

'Oh God, yes.' Lily Anne laughed bitterly. 'Just about every day, and I've been here for two decades.'

'Why do you stay?'

'There are enough victories to make it worthwhile. We're

doing a lot of good. It's not a job you do for fun, though there are wonderful moments. Watching the way the women support each other and the way they grow and change while they're here can be a joy.'

Sophie listened, thinking that in comparison to this earnest, hard-working, selfless woman, she'd been drifting along the surface of her life on a pool float with bottomless snacks, drinks and home theater. 'It must be odd for you to work here given that my birth mother was an addict.'

Lily Anne's features tightened. 'It's complicated. My grandparents ... *our* grandparents ... always felt they hadn't done enough to help Connie. Starting this place after she died was a way to take care of her retroactively. In the other camp, my mother felt the family had done too much, let Connie off the hook too many times, too early, and not made her face the consequences. But Mom loved her parents, and she respected their vision for this place and their need to keep it as an independent family business, so she took it on after they were no longer able.'

'And you? You said you never imagined yourself still in Vermont.'

'Right.' Lily Anne spoke curtly. 'You have a good memory. I ... There are reasons this job made sense for me too.'

Like what?

Sophie didn't understand why people were so afraid to communicate. All humans waded through crap at some point in their life, some deeper than others. Especially in a place like Asphalia House, where people were emerging from their worst and most vulnerable moments, why the shame? Maybe Lily Anne had been here for other people so long she'd lost the ability to unburden herself. Maybe she'd never been able to.

Sophie did not have that problem.

'Anyway, since you're only here a month, I won't go into

details, but I'd say when you interact with the residents, assume they've been through the worst thing you can imagine, because a lot of them have.'

'You mean . . .' Sophie kept her features earnest, 'like having your credit card turned down at Saks because Daddy forgot to pay the bill?'

For the first time since Sophie had met her, Lily Anne laughed properly. Color flooded her face, making her dark eyes pop. She looked like a different person, younger, freer, happier.

And it occurred to Sophie that the flaky Connie-theory Helen had put forth at her birthday dinner might have been only half right. The universe could have called Sophie to Vermont because of something she needed. But she was starting to wonder if it had also called her here for something other people did.

Chapter 16

Thursday, May 20, 1976

Lilianne sat in her apartment's living room, knees hugged to her chest, staring morosely out the window at the orange-yellow daylight, listening to bits of grit pelting the windows, as she'd been listening for three days that seemed like a week. The sandstorm had hit at dawn on Tuesday, the day after she'd landed back in Cairo with Gilles, and it was every bit the nightmare residents had warned it would be. Nearly impossible to go outside with sand stinging every bit of exposed skin and invading any unprotected crevice or orifice. Breathing . . . forget it.

The only thing to do was stay indoors and bear the hellish dim light, the roar of wind and the scraping of sand. They were running low on everything. Lilianne's breakfast had been cheese and crackers, because she couldn't bear to go out and she couldn't bear to leave Gilles.

Having him in the house had taken her over. Even when he was asleep, her ear was on alert, worrying that every noise could signify an approaching outburst or another bout of despair. She was more exhausted than she ever remembered being.

Some years back, she'd received a letter from her college friend Matti, a new mother at the time, who said that after she and her husband arrived home from the hospital with their

The Jewel of Cairo

infant son, they kept expecting someone to come get him so they could have a break. And where was the little being's instruction manual anyway?

Lilianne was beginning to understand. She'd never felt so out of her depth in her life.

Connie had been so freaked out by the change in their suave, confident friend that she'd withdrawn almost entirely, fetching and carrying as Lilianne asked her to but unable to take being around Gilles for more than a minute or two, staring helplessly as if she expected him to lose it any second, which made them all so edgy that Gilles had snapped at her several times, making her paranoia worse. Finally, yesterday evening, she'd announced she was going to Sean's because she missed him so badly.

As much as Connie had been more burden than help in some ways, her departure had made Lilianne feel terrifyingly alone.

The storm could not have been worse timing. Paris had been difficult, but helping Gilles clean up and begin eating properly again, being able to rescue him from the surroundings he'd been floundering in had filled Lilianne with a deep sense of purpose. She could and would return him to eventual health.

The trip from Paris to Cairo had been awful. Gilles had packed a few clothes, but refused to bring books, notebooks or even his cameras. Finished with those, he'd said. Finished with the human race and its evil. Lilianne had clucked sympathetically, then behind his back stuffed as much of his camera equipment into her own case as she could fit, not able to imagine him without it.

They'd taken a cab to the airport, Lilianne looking forward to having a nap during the flight.

No.

Gilles had become agitated, refusing to sit even when it was required that he stay seated. He'd been combative and rude to the stewardess when she wouldn't bring him drinks fast enough, and had refused any attempt Lilianne made to comfort him. She'd never been so glad to get off a plane in her life.

Until they climbed into the taxi, its ancient air-conditioning barely making a dent in the heat. Traffic had been horrendous, as usual. Gilles had thrashed with the misery of a caged beast, then finally, after the driver threatened to throw them out, held his head and rocked forward and back, moaning and cursing.

This had been step one of Lilianne's cure. Step two? Confine him to a small apartment with two women, one freaked out and one without a concrete plan, then unleash the power of hell outside.

One thing was clear. Sandstorm or not, Cairo was no long-term solution. The easiest would be to take him to Connecticut, to Southport. With Mom and Dad in Florida, she and Gilles would have her childhood home to themselves, where peaceful surroundings, simple routines and a place not already fraught with memories of either war or Helen might help him recover faster.

This morning she'd called her father, who'd been his predictably efficient, problem-solving self. Lilianne shouldn't worry about work. Her assistant could take over what now looked to be a matter of rubber-stamping the due diligence for Cairo National Bank. She should feel free to go and help her 'friend'.

She had a feeling the majority of people they encountered would assume Gilles was her 'friend'. Let them think what they wanted. There were worse things she could be accused of than friendship.

At the American Embassy and the French Embassy, she'd had long, complicated discussions about how to bring Gilles to the US as soon as possible for an undetermined amount of time. Eventually a French officer had jokingly suggested that the best way to allow him to live in the US past the six-month tourist visa period was to marry him.

Yeah, good idea. A passionate, sexual man, torn apart by tragedies, still grieving the love of his life, would lunge at the chance to marry a cold, sexless spinster.

The conversations had been discouraging; the amount of time necessary to procure a visa was longer than she'd wanted to wait. Which left unofficial channels, aka John Baker.

All this and she still hadn't found the right time to ask Gilles if he'd consider coming home with her to recover. She'd told herself there was no point asking if the logistics proved impossible, that she was paving the way to make his decision as simple as possible.

But she was also worried he'd say no and return to Paris, out of her reach, continuing his downward spiral toward filth and starvation. His parents would find him when they returned from wherever they were, Lilianne could make sure of that. But – she might as well admit this – she wanted to be his savior. She wanted to be the one who restored him to his charming, dynamic self. Was this ego? She wouldn't have thought she was the type for that, especially involving something so important as a friend's mental health. Maybe she just cared a lot about him, maybe more than she knew.

In any case, Gilles was an adult, and even an impaired adult could make and stand by his own decisions. Given that Lilianne hoped they could leave soon, even as soon as the following week, she couldn't put off asking him. If he was in the right mood, she'd try today.

A gust of wind brought a loud spatter of sand, the thick, rusty air making the city seem aglow with fire, or mysteriously transported to an alien planet. If Lilianne closed her eyes, she could imagine the sound into snow or sleet crystals hitting the windows of her bedroom in Southport, driven by a fresh wintry wind off Long Island Sound, turning the world clean white. She kept her eyes shut, holding onto that world for as long as her mind would bear the illusion.

The phone rang. Lilianne pounced to answer before the ringing woke Gilles.

'How are you liking our Egyptian weather?'

'Sami.' She put a hand to her temple. The SRT-91 listening device had been delivered Monday after she and Gilles got back. Another thing she'd have to do before she went back to the US. 'It's an experience.'

'It's hell,' he said cheerfully. 'Do you need anything? I am ordering food for myself and will happily have some delivered to you as my gift. You will say no, no, it's not necessary, because you are an independent American, but it would be my pleasure. I feel I must apologize for my country's behavior. A little food will help . . . how do you say it, tide you? And keep you from having to go out into the inferno. I need only your address.'

A little food was undoubtedly Egyptian for enough groceries for eight people for a week. But how tempting. 'I can't let you do this, Sami.'

'It's nothing, nothing! Your first storm and it's a bad one. Your address, if I may? The shopkeeper is waiting for my order and I have a driver lined up who will bring it.'

She was too tired to dance the rest of the dance. 'Sami, this is so kind of you.'

'Such a small thing. If you insist, you can repay me by allowing me to take you to the pyramids on Saturday morning. Early, early, before the sun, before they are officially open. I have promised to get you to the top. It's an experience like nothing else.'

Saturday morning. They were supposed to drive up to the

The Jewel of Cairo

Abdallah farm with her grandparents Friday night for the party Saturday. Lilianne put a hand to her stomach, the unsettled feeling having nothing to do with her meager breakfast. She had to do this. If she could get out of Egypt early next week, this was probably the only chance she'd have to gain access to Sami's apartment in order to plant the bug. She'd have to throw herself on her grandparents' mercy and force another change on their party in her honor, to which she'd show up tense over Gilles's possible bad behavior and exhausted from having gotten up that day well before dawn.

She was also going to have to bring Connie with her to distract Sami while she did her dirty work. 'I have a friend staying with me. She'd love to go too if it's not too much to ask.'

'For you, nothing is too much to ask! Your friend is welcome. We will climb and then come back to my place for a big breakfast to make up for the exercise.'

Sami had fallen into her trap before she could even set it. 'That sounds perfect.'

'It's a date. I will have groceries delivered now.'

Lilianne thanked him profusely and hung up feeling like a wrung-out mildewy sponge. This conscience stuff was a pesky annoyance. During training for the CIA, she'd thrived on the role-playing exercises they'd been given, matching wits on a barstool with another agent playing his own role by trying to trip her up. She'd stayed cool, able to chat and smile naturally while calculating which questions would be of value but not too pointed, not too personal, making sure she gave nothing away in a gesture or careless word. She'd aced the test and been so sure she'd found her calling.

For the first time, she could see another reason why she'd been wise to step away from being a full-time agent, one that had nothing to do with either her father's health at the time, being a loner or the organization lacking a clear pathway for women to attain higher positions. Betraying people who trusted you was not a pleasant experience. Sami for one but also Connie would have no sense of Lilianne's true errand. Underhanded, all of it.

She growled – quietly so she didn't wake Gilles – and paced the living room. Her grandparents had been nothing but generous. She'd avoided them for months, already made them postpone the party once, was planning to change it again ... then she'd abruptly leave the country, just as her mother had.

Her pacing continued, growing more frantic as the minutes ticked down to the inevitable waking of her patient.

And then it hit her. The perfect idea. A way to pay back her grandparents in the long run that would delight them, she hoped, and make up for all her sins here. Back in the US, once Gilles had himself on steady ground, she'd pay for Zahra, Braheem and Nailah to visit, and make sure her mother was around. Christmas, maybe? Some occasion that would bring Mom to Southport.

Nailah answered on the second ring and passed Lilianne joyfully to Zahra, whose warm greeting, to Lilianne's surprise, was both familiar and comforting. 'Everything is ready for the party this weekend. The storm will stop tonight. I hope you are managing. So crazy, these storms. I should have called to check on you. I'm still not used to having my grandchild right here! You have everything you need? Enough food? How is your poor friend?'

'We have plenty.' Or they would as soon as Sami's generous delivery showed up. 'My friend is having a difficult time, as expected, but he's better than the way I found him in Paris.'

'You'll bring him this weekend? The farm will be good for him after all the traffic and dust. And my Lord God, this awful sand. Our beautiful city must seem like hell on earth.'

'I'm afraid it does. Which is why I need to ask a favor ...' Even with the comfort of knowing she'd make it up to them, she felt like a brat asking for more changes, and a worse one when her grandmother immediately accepted and understood her fib that Gilles needed another evening here. On top of that, no matter how many times Lilianne tried to insist they'd take a cab, Zahra insisted harder that Braheem would drive all the way back to Cairo to pick them up Saturday morning.

By the time she hung up, Lilianne was nearly weeping with gratitude.

Half an hour later, Gilles still miraculously asleep, the apartment buzzer rang, and bag after bag of prepared meals, salads, fruits, juices and wines were brought up to fill the kitchen, lifting Lilianne's spirits further and at least giving her something to do putting them away.

When the last grocery item was shoved into the packed refrigerator, she heard Gilles's door opening – he'd taken Connie's bedroom, and Connie and Lilianne took turns between Lilianne's room and the couch. She strode toward the living room on high alert. What kind of mood would he be in? Would he be able to discuss moving to Connecticut? Would *she* be able to discuss moving to Connecticut?

First step: to make sure she looked relaxed and smiling when she rounded the corner. 'Good nap?'

'Fine.' He rubbed his eyes, dark hair tousled, wearing a wrinkled T-shirt and jeans that hung on him, his feet bare.

'Hungry?'

He shook his head. Lilianne still wasn't sure how strongly to urge on him the food he needed. Maybe the weekend would help. It was impossible to escape an Egyptian household without being stuffed silly.

'We have tons of new food. A friend—'

'I'm not hungry. Can you move Sarah?' He pointed to her in her place of honor on the bookcase. 'I can't stand looking at her. She reminds me of Helen, of Paris, of everything . . .'

'Okay.' Lilianne brought Sarah down and took her to her bedroom, where she laid her on the bed. 'Looks like it might be a rough day, Sarah. I'm taking you out of harm's way.'

Back in the living room, she found Gilles on the couch, head in his hands. She suppressed a sigh of exasperation. *Patience, patience.* Her least dependable quality.

And yet she'd surprised herself with her patience and relative competence so far, guessing often enough what Gilles needed to do or feel or hear to get him through the next day, or hour, or minute. Her one phone conversation with a local doctor – embassy connections again – had been next to no help about specifics. Every case was different, every man and every experience was different. She could try this, try that, but Gilles's best hopes were stability and time.

That she could do. As soon as she could humanly arrange it. As long as he consented.

Gilles flung his hand toward the angry orange light coming through the window. 'Any idea when this crap will be over?'

'Tonight. All done. You'll wake up tomorrow and be able to go outside.' She spoke soothingly. 'I'll take you to see the Nile. We can go sailing. Whatever you'd like to do.'

He stayed looking at his feet, lips pursed. 'I'd like to see the Nile.'

That was a good sign at least. She decided to take the risk, in spite of his uncertain mood, because 'uncertain mood' seemed to be where he was stuck, at least for the foreseeable future.

'We need to talk about something.' She sat next to him, pleased when he raised his head. 'I'd like to work on getting you out of here. Out of Egypt.'

His forehead wrinkled like a bewildered child's. 'Where would I go?'

'Both of us, I mean, out of Egypt.' Her heart ached. The Gilles she knew was a man of decisive action, jumping at a moment's notice to cover this story or that no matter what town or how far away, up for whatever activity their group had planned, or full of his own suggestions. 'If that's okay.'

'Yes. It's fine.' His forehead smoothed. 'I don't do well on my own.'

'Not yet.' So far, so good. 'Do you remember me talking about my hometown?'

'You mentioned the name once or twice.' He sent her a look containing a pale glimmer of his former humor. 'While I think I knew every detail of every house in Connie's. And most of Helen's . . .'

'Oh.' Maybe she hadn't talked about it much when he was around. Or maybe not at all. 'Well, Southport is a small town on Long Island Sound, the coast of Connecticut. Very picturesque. Very quiet.'

The gusting wind hurled more sand against the windows, making Gilles flinch. 'Quiet sounds good.'

She swallowed hard, found herself flicking at a loose thread on the couch. 'I wondered if it might be a nice change for you.'

'Southport? In the US? That's a big change.' He looked at the window again, at the rusty opaqueness of the air. 'That noise is horrible. Even more horrible after three days.'

'There's noise in Southport too. Birds and ocean waves, wind in the trees . . .'

His mouth looked as if it were trying to remember how to smile. 'Those are not bad sounds.'

'It might be a good place for you to heal.'

He looked at her as if she were joking. 'You think I'll be able to heal.'

Lilianne held his gaze, wanting to comfort him, not sure her touch would be welcome. 'Men have healed from war for as long as there have been men and wars. There's no reason why you can't get better.'

'I don't like it here.' He hunched over like an old man.

'No.' She dared a squeeze of his hand. 'I shouldn't have—'

'And I don't want to go back to Paris. Paris is full of Helen. Full of the life I had and the new life I thought I was going to have.' He leaned his elbows on his knees, rested his forehead on his hands, as if that many words at once had exhausted him. 'No more Paris.'

'A new start in a new place might help you. My parents are moving to Florida, and our house is empty. It's plenty big. We won't be on top . . .' She wanted to laugh. They definitely wouldn't be on top of each other. 'We won't be in each other's way. New York is an hour away, and—'

'For how long?' His head stayed down, but he did turn it to look at her. Her optimism peeked cautiously around the corner. At least he was thinking it over.

'Whatever you want or need. A tourist visa will give you six months. You can stay until you feel well enough to leave, or you can apply to stay permanently if you . . . if it works out.'

She was not going to bring up the joke about marriage.

Another pause. Lilianne waited, outwardly patient, remembering his former quickness, his agile mind, cheerful disposition and philosophical brain, willing them all to return, for his sake and hers.

'You can pick up and leave here?'

'My job is nearly done. My assistant can easily take over the rest.'

'When would we go?' Gilles had gone still, as if his entire body's attention was trained on this idea. 'A visa takes time. Months. The French push bureaucracy to its maximum inefficiency.'

'I have friends in high places. If you agree, we can leave fairly soon, I would guess. A six-month visa would give you plenty of time to decide what you want and where you want to settle.'

'I don't care where I go. It doesn't matter.' He dropped his head again. 'The question is whether you can stand me that long.'

Lilianne couldn't see into the future. They were both feeling their way through this, one day at a time. He felt useless. She felt helpless. They both needed time to understand how this would work, whether it would work. But one thing she was sure of. She put her hand on his forearm and held it firmly. 'I want you around. Even if you're no fun. If I change my mind, I'll just put you out with the garbage and it's all taken care of. Very nice trash collectors in Southport.'

He managed a half-smile. 'How will you be able to do your big-city bank work in this little town?'

'That won't be a problem.' Not entirely true. She'd still need to figure out her role at Maxwell Investments – or outside of Maxwell – with her father winding down his role as boss. She'd need to be around Gilles until he was okay on his own for extended periods. Maybe this was what Connie would call a sign from the universe that her life needed to change. 'I'll take a few months off.'

'I can't imagine that.' He looked directly at her, first time in a while, as if he suddenly realized she was more than a voice next to him.

Lilianne laughed uncertainly. He'd become more alert, more alive, more like his old self. 'What?'

'I'm remembering taking your picture once, in that little apartment on Pierre Nicole.'

'You took it more than once.'

'But this one time . . . I was behind you with my camera, in the living room, on that disgusting orange couch. We were all together after dinner, you, Helen, me, Connie and . . . whoever Connie's guy was then, laughing and teasing. I don't remember about what. You got up suddenly and headed toward your room, first to call it a night as always.'

'I'm sure I had work to do.' She sounded defensive.

'I'm sure you did.' He mimed holding a camera. 'I followed you a few steps and called to you. You turned around and I took your picture.' He was staring at Lilianne, but not seeing her, back in their shared apartment where he and Helen had fallen in love. The memories seemed to have normalized his speech, smoothed his tortured face, straightened his posture. Was it Helen? Or remembering his last carefree time before anguish and the war had smothered his trust and optimism? Was it remembering his camera put to use in happier times? 'That was the first time I felt I'd come close to capturing you.' His eyes focused, his gaze sharpened, becoming invasive.

Lilianne caught her breath, unable to look away from that dark, dark stare. Did he feel that . . . whatever it was, energy or connection? Or was she the only one caught?

'First time, and the last. Over as soon as you realized what I'd done.' He turned away, rubbed his unshaven chin with a sandpapery sound. 'I wonder where that picture went.'

'I didn't see it.' A lie. She'd seen it later in a manila envelope of pictures he'd brought to share, and had been tempted to grab it out and tear it up.

The mood in the room that night had been high, fueled by wine, by Gilles and Helen's love, by Connie and her flame's boisterous singing and raucous innuendo. Not the first time the group had shared that delicious intimacy, made sloppy and joyful by alcohol and the late hour. Lilianne had stopped drinking after one glass, mindful of the early morning ahead of her, and work she still had to do. Sitting in the midst of her closest friends, she'd been overcome by the chilling aloneness of being a non-participant in the human race's most ancient and cherished rituals of flirting and coupling off, a familiar emotion that hadn't attacked her like that in many years.

She remembered standing abruptly, saying goodnight, striding out of the warm, crowded living room; remembered Gilles's voice calling her with urgent concern, startling her, then her big mistake – turning to him before she'd composed herself, encountering the extra surprise of his lens, and then the certainty that she'd been exposed, violated. Gilles had shifted the camera to one side, and they'd shared the same intense gaze they'd shared just now, his searching, hers confused and vulnerable. He'd moved the camera to shoot again, but this time Lilianne had been prepared. Turning her back, she'd gone into her room, closed the door and sunk onto her bed, trying to control the feeling that she'd been breached.

'Okay then.' Gilles's words took a moment to register, yanking her back to Cairo. 'I'll come with you.'

Okay then. Her heart sped, her color threatened to rise. She had to work to stay cool. 'One condition . . . you tell your family where you are, where you're going and why.'

He scowled, leaning back, letting his legs sprawl. 'Okay.'

She suppressed a sudden nervous laugh. 'You're sure about this?'

'Yes. *Yes.* I said okay.'

'You did.' She stood briskly, triumphant and a little terrified.

What if she was wrong? What if she was only adding to his misery?

One step at a time. She was following her instinct that Southport would help Gilles more than any other solution available to her. Her instinct couldn't claim medical expertise, but it was all she had for now. As she knew well from her girlhood tours of Mom-ordered doctor visits, there was no shortage of medical and psychological help available to him in Connecticut and New York.

'I'll get the visa sorted out and we'll take it from there.'

Gilles lay back on the couch, staring at the ceiling, then covered his eyes with his hands. Lilianne went into the kitchen, made up a plate of bread, cheese and fruit with a glass of mango juice, and brought it in before leaving him to his demons and his grief, as she'd had to leave him more than once, unable yet to relieve either.

Then she went into her bedroom and picked up the phone to call John Baker.

Chapter 17

Present day

Beezy: *Miss you horribly. How's Cousin?*
Sophie: *Warming up. What's doing in Southposh?*
Beezy: *Book fair a smashing success. Peggy Dotson tripped after a drunk-sail and broke her kneecap. Jonah Swenson made a grab at Trixie while she was waitressing at the country club. Half his age! Old fart. Tell me more about Vermont.*
Sophie: *There's a resident here named Lizzie Borden.*
Beezy: *As in 'took an ax and gave her mother forty whacks'?*
Sophie: *Wouldn't surprise me. She's terrifying.*
Beezy: *Be careful! I want you back.*
Sophie: ♥

Monday, the day after Sophie's hiring and initiation into the Asphalia House kitchen, she employed one of her greatest skills. She shopped. Recklessly. At Rutland Appliances, she bought a six-burner range with two ovens and a hood, and a thirty-cubic-foot refrigerator with side-by-side doors over a bottom freezer, and paid a crap-ton of money to have them delivered and installed on Thursday that week. At Steiger Supply she bought all new pots and pans, cookie sheets with silicone liners, measuring cups and spoons, mixing bowl sets, a KitchenAid mixer and a Vitamix blender, plus a four-slot toaster and a countertop smart oven. She bought bright tablecloths, placemats and napkins, dinnerware sets and flatware, and decorative vases filled with silk bouquets. At Phoenix Books, she bought photography prints and paintings by local artists to brighten up a few walls.

Asphalia House would never be the same.

Next: meal planning. After a delicious lunch at the bright yellow Sandwich Shoppe on Merchants Row downtown, she drove to the Hannaford supermarket on the town's outskirts. If she could fit groceries into her loaded car, she'd like to get started on some ideas for the week. Her first night, tomorrow, the menu in the food bible was chicken salad, carrot sticks and rolls. The salad recipe contained chicken, mayonnaise, celery, onion, parsley and salt.

Not even pepper!

What a wide and wonderful chicken salad world was being ignored. A favorite recipe came to mind, which involved ginger and scallions, tahini, soy, sesame seeds and Szechuan peppercorns. Subtle and fantastic. Worth finding an Asian grocery store for the peppercorns. A quick search showed the nearest Asian grocery was over an hour away.

Oops. Another idea, then. A version with Middle Eastern flavors, za'atar and lemon, a yoghurt garlic dressing, with chickpeas, mint, tomato and cucumber. Her mouth watered just thinking about it. If she couldn't find za'atar locally, she could fudge it with thyme, oregano, sesame and sumac. If she could find sumac.

The rest of the week's recipes were equally dull, but oh, what could be done with hamburgers! Top them with slices of tomato, fresh mozzarella and torn basil leaves for a Caprese

The Jewel of Cairo

burger. Rescue dull turkey meatloaf with thyme, mustard and Worcestershire sauce. Supplant jarred sauce with roasted cherry tomatoes and add garlicky zucchini and goat cheese to a dull ziti bake.

The Rutland Area Food Co-op, to which she was directed by a helpful clerk at Hannaford, had sumac *and* za'atar, and she bought enough of the other ingredients for a trial run at home, which she'd remake Tuesday at the house and serve with homemade buttery wholewheat rolls, followed by a big pan of chocolate chip apricot bars for dessert.

Car practically scraping the ground, she drove back to Owen's little cottage in high spirits, imagining the improvement in Asphalia House's dreary atmosphere. She had plenty of time before the appliance deliveries to scrub and organize the kitchen. Ideally she'd love a fresh coat of paint, but . . . she only had a month. Maybe she could enlist the help of a resident or two? The work could count toward their chore requirement. She'd have to check with Lily Anne.

Tonight she planned to spend time with the local Facebook marketplace to see if she could find inexpensive area rugs and anything else that would help cheer up the surroundings. She had no doubt her cousin was running a terrific place that helped a lot of women, but the space was enough to make anyone miserable, and these women already had a head start on misery.

She pulled up to the cottage, noting Owen's truck. She was excited about experimenting with variations, not deviating too much from the food bible at first, but at least adding flavor to see how it went over. Maybe, if he was willing, Owen could try a dish or two along the way and see if he thought she'd be stirring the pot too much.

Or maybe that was just an excuse to talk to someone. She'd been alone all day, and he amused her. For all his grouchiness, she got the feeling she amused him too. There was worse to do than be amused together. He must be lonely without his wife, and Sophie was also out of her element. She could call her parents or Beezy for company, but Beezy was busy, and Sophie didn't feel like sharing her new connection with Lily Anne on the phone to her parents while it still felt so tenuous and complicated.

The Mediterranean chicken salad came together easily, and tasted heavenly. At least she thought so. Another opinion would help.

She brought the bowl and a spoon over to the barn, where she knocked and announced herself.

'C'mon in.' His flat, unenthusiastic tone made her smile.

'Hi, Owen.'

He lifted his head from sanding a board, then eyed the bowl in her hand. 'What's that?'

'A dish I'd like an opinion on. How's your day going?'

'Fine.' He wiped his hands on a rag. He was wearing jeans again, and a dark gray T-shirt. He'd look well in brighter colors. Jewel tones. Teal and red and royal blue. And no beard or mustache. And a good haircut.

Of course she would never tell him she thought so.

'How was yours?'

'Great, actually. My cousin gave me the cooking job for the month. I followed your advice and told her we were related.'

'How'd that go?'

Sophie wrinkled her noise. 'Point goes to you. I should have told her sooner. Anyway, it didn't nuke our chances of being friends, though she's cautious.'

He grunted. She'd take that as *I'm very glad you two got off on the right foot.*

'So at Asphalia House they have this huge book of recipes,

all the meals, every day all year long, and most of them are pretty bland. Like Tuesday is chicken salad, made pretty much the way chicken salad should be made.' She paused for effect. 'If you're boring.'

A quarter-grin at that. 'I take it you're not boring.'

'I try not to be.' She held up the bowl. 'So your job is to tell me if my version is delicious and will rock their world, or if it's too radical a departure from mayonnaise and salt.'

He tossed the rag on his workbench. 'How am I supposed to know?'

'Maybe you won't. But at least you get to try something delicious.'

Brief smile, nearly half his mouth that time. If she could get him to laugh as freely as her cousin had the day before, she'd get a point, and then they'd be even.

'I'll need to wash my hands.' He held them up. They were large hands, clean-looking, at least to her. Sawdust wasn't dirty. Maybe he'd been dabbling in some colorless chemical finish.

'No, no, don't bother.' She dug up a spoonful containing all the ingredients and walked it over to him, curious to see whether he'd let her feed him or would play manly man and insist on taking over the spoon himself. 'Delicious? Or showing off?'

He took the food off the spoon she held for him and chewed thoughtfully. 'Delicious.'

'Yes?'

'And showing off.'

'Hmm.' She glanced down at the bowl. 'I like to look at it this way. Food has more power than people give it credit for. If you eat the same things prepared the same way all the time, that's hours of your life spent not paying attention. Ignored hours only bring you closer to death. New flavors, new combinations, new cultures, they bring new awareness – of the time you're at the table, of the wider world, of other people's experiences. The women at Asphalia have tough, important work to do, and I think they could use a little time each day to focus outside themselves.'

He was really smiling then, which lit and softened his face. He did have pretty eyes. 'Your heart is in the right place.'

'But still showing off.' She shrugged. 'So be it. I mean I could tone it down, just do a speck of curry powder and chopped grapes, but . . . why not go all out at once, show them who I am and deal with the consequences?'

'I would guess that's your life's philosophy.' He stood, hands on his hips, looking at her as if she delighted him, which was brand new after all the scowling.

'Does your wife cook?'

Owen's face shut down. He dropped his gaze to his feet. 'Yeah, she . . . We share the kitchen.'

Oops. Something not right in that marriage. Maybe 'taking care of her mother' was code for 'needing time apart'. Poor Owen.

'That's nice. I did all the cooking for my ex. And the cleaning. And the entertaining. And the errands.'

He looked disgusted. 'What did he do?'

'Made money.' She decided that if Owen was indeed going through a rough marital patch, he might like her company as much as she'd like his. 'Do you want to share this with me for dinner, or are you already planning something?'

Owen tugged on his icky beard. 'I have food. I make one big pot of whatever on Sundays and eat it all week.'

'No.' She put a hand to her chest, inhaling sharply. 'Hours closer to death every night.'

His mouth twisted. 'It's easier. I'm tired at night, and don't always feel like cooking. If it's already made, I don't have to think about what I'm in the mood for, and how long it will take, and whether I have the ingredients.'

'Fair enough.' She held up the salad. 'Share tonight?'

He pursed his lips in a way that made her think he was going to whistle. 'Okay.'

'My place or yours?' She wanted the words back immediately, and rushed to displace them. 'You don't have an unoaked Chardonnay hanging around, do you?'

'I do, actually. I'll bring it over.' He picked up his sanding block. 'Give me a few minutes to tidy up here and shower.'

'Sure.' She was pleased he knew about wine, and a little surprised, which meant she was being a snob again, judging him because he lived out here in the sticks where you had to travel an hour to get Szechuan peppercorns. Shame on her.

She took her salad back to the cottage and set the beautifully proportioned Owen-made table for two, glad she'd bought some rolls from a downtown bakery unimaginatively called The Bakery. She still had plenty of chocolate chip cookies, and a couple of the rock-hard peaches she'd bought on her first shopping trip here had ripened nicely. She and Owen would be dining in style. Kind of nice to have a friend like him while she was here. No risk, no attraction, no mess. As long as he felt the same, which he seemed to. She hoped.

He showed up an hour later, wine in hand, bushy hair damp from the shower, beard trimmed so he looked less like a mountain man and more like a normal guy with a bushy beard who needed a haircut. His eyes seemed larger in his face, and she could even detect good cheekbones and the lines of a nice jaw.

She still hated beards.

'Wow, you look great, Owen.'

'Thanks.' He handed her the wine. 'I'd gotten a little scruffy.'

He could say that again. She opened the wine and poured them each a glass, then clinked with him. 'Cheers.'

'Cheers. Thank you for inviting me to share.'

'You're welcome.'

They took sips of the wine and made appreciative noises, then Sophie joined him at the table, and for several awful seconds everything changed, because they were sitting opposite each other instead of chatting standing up, and neither of them seemed to know what to do with this reorganization of their friendship.

Luckily, one of Sophie's superpowers, learned from years hosting friends, plus Peter's clients and colleagues, was the ability to blabber whatever was in her head to avoid awkward silences, even if it made her sound like a ditz. 'Did you always want to work with wood?'

'Yes. Did you always want to cook professionally?'

'Nope.' She served him a big helping of chicken salad. 'That was my ex-husband's idea.'

He gave her a look that made her wince.

'I know, I know, you think I'm a trad wife doormat.' She served herself a lesser helping.

He picked up his fork. 'What did *you* want to do?'

Sophie made a sound of exasperation. 'Well, that's the thing. Nothing really. Nothing I enjoy has ever grabbed me for long. I majored in English, then I got married and did a lot of volunteer work and other wifely things. I tried to get pregnant, but that didn't work, which was hard, so when Peter suggested the chef thing, it seemed like I might have found my niche. But I'd actually found someone else's niche. The pressure made me enjoy cooking less, and too much of the job turned out to be scrambling for new clients, and I stunk at that. It made me horribly anxious. Do you have to? Scramble, I mean?'

'At first.' He forked up a bite. 'Not anymore.'

'Your reputation puts you in high demand.'

He shrugged while chewing, which she'd take as a yes.

'Well my reputation sure didn't do that for me. And frankly, more clients meant more work. Maybe I'm just lazy, but I don't think life should be all about making more money. Peter did, so I was a disappointment. I'm pretty sure he suggested I start a business so he could respect me more. Have a roll.' She passed him the basket, pleased when he took two.

'Your husband sounds like a real type.'

'A type-A type, yes. Investment banker, really good at his job. I respected that.' She wished she could make Peter the villain of their story as easily as Owen could. But she really hadn't applied herself to the business. Or much of anything in life except being Mrs Peter.

'Will you take up your clients again when you go back?'

'Uhh . . .' Sophie put down her fork and picked up her wine again. She thought of the Fabergé egg and the independence that amount of money would give her from alimony and parental handouts, along with relief from the guilt of not pulling her own weight financially, and confidence that she could make her own decisions, rule her own destiny on her own two feet. All fantasy, since the egg didn't belong to her, but it was a fantasy she was guiltily attached to, even if it made her more like the woman Lizzie so enjoyed mocking. 'I made a clean break when I left. Would I start up again? No? Maybe? I don't know.'

'That sounds like a solid plan.'

She giggled, liking the way he ate, slowly, with relish. 'Mindfully' she supposed would be the right word, even though she was getting heartily sick of people using it. But that was how food should be approached.

'My birth mother traveled her whole life, one country to the next. Maybe I inherited my scatteredness from her.'

He lifted his gaze from his plate. His eyes were really quite attractively blue. 'Does that life appeal to you?'

'No.' She sighed. 'It sounds lonely. I'm a homebody. Did you go to college?'

He clearly disapproved of the question.

'Well don't bristle, not everyone does.'

'Yes.'

'What did you major in?'

'American studies.' He took a sip of wine. She liked the way he did that too, as if the fluid was too precious to be gulped. 'Dad was rah-rah US military, Stars and Stripes forever, et cetera. Mom stayed home. That's my story.'

Sophie shook her head adamantly, finishing a mouthful of chicken salad. 'That's not a story, that's a list of facts.'

He sighed, but good-naturedly. 'Okay. How about . . . after college, I didn't want to join the navy like my dad or pursue a high-powered career like my brothers because being part of an organizational chart, military or corporate, being told where to go, what to wear, having to account for my hours and productivity every day . . . not for me. I'm not a team player.'

He said the words with a contempt that made Sophie hide a cringe. She was the consummate team player.

'I did love working with wood, so I apprenticed myself to a furniture maker in Bradford for several years, learned enough to start my own business, and here I am.' He peered at her over another forkful of dinner. 'That enough of a story?'

'Almost. You forgot something.'

'What, you want more than that?'

'Your wife? When did you meet, how did you . . .?'

'Oh.' His face fell. The forkful stayed loaded on the fork.

Sophie frowned. 'I'm thinking this is a topic to avoid?'

'Please. Though I should . . .' He shifted in his chair. 'Yes. Please. For now.'

'Done.' Brief silence while she wondered what he meant by *for now*.

'What's all that stuff in your car?' He gestured toward the front. 'Are you planning to redecorate my house?'

'No. Asphalia House. New pots and pans, toaster and blender, plus little things to brighten up the place, like art on the walls and tablecloths and new—'

'I thought you were cooking. They asked you to do all that too?'

'No, no, this was on my initiative. The place needs a facelift. It's drab and depressing.'

'Hmm.' He frowned. 'That's . . . hmm.'

'That's "hmm"? How "hmm"?'

'If you came to work in my barn, threw out half my stuff and put in new, I'd be pissed.'

'Oh.' She reframed her idea from his point of view. 'Even if the stuff was better and cleaner . . . you wouldn't like the improvement?'

'Nope.'

'Why not?'

'Because it's my place, and I didn't have a say in it.'

'Oh.' She pressed her lips together, thinking that over. 'Maybe I should introduce things slowly.'

'Maybe. Or maybe I'm wrong. You don't have to listen to me.'

Sophie looked down at her food, which seemed to have grown into way too much for her stomach to handle. 'No, you're probably right. My fatal flaw is that I get all enthusiastic about an idea and go after it, then I stop to think about it, realize it's stupid and hate myself.'

He lifted his glass. 'Nice little process.'

'It's served me faithfully all my life.' She sighed, then shook off her dismay. 'What's your fatal flaw?'

'I don't like people.'

'Oh, very nice. Maybe you're around the wrong types.'

'People are the same everywhere.'

She offered him more wine, but he covered his glass. 'I haven't been everywhere so I can't know for sure, but I suspect that is self-protective bull-poop.'

'Maybe.' He grinned at her. 'Thanks for inviting me over. I'm having a good time.'

She grinned back and set the bottle back down. 'Are you surprised?'

'No. And yes.'

'Why did you come over if you thought eating with me would be awful?'

'At first I thought I'd pegged your type. Then I decided I might have made a mistake, which I had.'

'What type did you peg first?'

'East Coast sophisticate coming to Vermont to find a mountain man.'

'No, really? That's a thing?' She queasily remembered Beezy drooling over Owen being a guy who worked with his hands.

'It's a thing.'

'Does it go both ways? Men coming here to seduce pretty milkmaids or whatever the equivalent would be?'

Owen looked appalled. *Milkmaids?*'

Sophie shrugged. 'That's what came into my head. Reframe as you like.'

'All men try to seduce women, so no that's not a thing particular to Vermont.'

'So . . . did you come over because you thought I was going to try to seduce you or because you thought I wouldn't?'

'Wouldn't.'

'Well that's good.' She slumped in exaggerated relief. 'I'm not into seducing married men. Nothing in that but sleaze and heartbreak.'

Unless you were Lexy and got a ring and a baby instead.

'I came because I sensed you wanted company.'

'You were right. I have nothing interesting to say to me and I get bored. I invited you because I sensed you wanted company as well. Despite hating people.'

'You were right.'

And then they were smiling at each other, and it was time to change the subject. 'How did your work go today? Do you ever have days when it doesn't go well?'

'Sure. Who doesn't?'

'What happens on those days?'

'Either I can't think of a design idea or I'm distracted and make a stupid mistake.' He gestured around him. 'Everything in this house was a stupid mistake.'

'This house?' She twisted to peer at various pieces of furniture. 'It looks perfect to me.'

'Not perfect enough to sell. Most of these were learning pieces. Experiments.'

Sophie gasped and jumped up from the table. 'I just had a fantastic idea.'

His mouth twisted in amusement, a gesture that was becoming familiar. 'I bet you're going to tell me what it is.'

'You should do a woodworking demonstration for the Asphalia residents. They can come here for a field trip.'

'I don't really—'

'It would be so cool, Owen. They'd love it.'

'Not my thing.'

She narrowed her eyes. 'Not even if I pay you?'

'You think everything can go your way with enough money?'

'Oh yes, everything. Except my marriage. There was plenty there and it didn't help.' She brought over the peaches and cookies. 'Seriously, though, the women would find it fascinating. A bright afternoon in their tough lives. They'd be so grateful. And who knows? Maybe one or two will want to sign on as apprentices and you'll have secured their futures.'

He chose a peach from the bowl she offered. 'I'll think about it.'

'Are you saying that to shut me up?'

'Yes.'

She grinned. 'I'll suggest the idea to Lily Anne.'

Owen made a noise of exasperation. 'I think you are very wrong when you say you're not good at anything.'

'Oh?' She sat back down and picked up a peach, inhaling its sweet fragrance. 'What am I good at? Getting my own way?'

'Innovating, planning, organizing and executing.'

'Thank you, Owen. That's very kind.' She hadn't thought about that as her skill set, and liked the sound of it.

What she had been thinking about, though, for the past half-hour, was that not only did she feel different here in Vermont, but she was having a nicer time sitting in this little cottage in the woods with a mountain man she barely knew than she had in a long time, including in her beloved hometown surrounded by her wonderful family and her friends.

Chapter 18

Saturday, May 22, 1976

Lilianne woke at 4.23 a.m. to the sound of *Fajr*, the day's first call to prayer. She stretched to shut off her alarm, set for 4.30, and lay blinking at the dim ceiling. Saturday. Pyramids. Bug-planting at Sami's. Party at her grandparents' farm.

A long day.

She gave herself another precious thirty seconds before throwing off her blankets. It had been her night on the couch while Connie slept comfortably in Lilianne's bedroom with Sarah for company.

At least the noisy storm had finally subsided Thursday night. Yesterday, Gilles and Lilianne had gone for a walk in their lovely, newly quiet residential neighborhood, admiring the lush gardens and occasional villas. She hadn't wanted to risk traffic or peddlers upsetting him, though she would have loved to show him downtown Cairo and the Nile. Five days in Egypt and he hadn't seen a thing. They'd strolled amicably through the tree-lined sand-scoured roads to Street 9, where Lilianne pointed out the shops she frequented, keeping the tour as low-key as possible. To her delight, Gilles seemed fine, interested in his surroundings, tickled by the ubiquitous stray cats. He wasn't speaking much, but she didn't care. This boded well for the visit with her grandparents.

She'd returned to the apartment more optimistic than she'd been in days to find Connie back from Sean's and much more comfortable around Gilles's new, more human form. They'd had a decently cheerful dinner, during which Gilles had been more or less engaged.

Lilianne felt much better about leaving him alone this morning – he'd be asleep for at least a few hours of their absence – and they could keep breakfast at Sami's short with some excuse or other. *Hey, just bugged your apartment, gotta run.*

She used the bathroom, then groped her way into her bedroom. 'Connie.'

'No.'

'Time to get up.'

'No.'

'The only chance you'll get in your life to climb the Great Pyramid.'

'Too early.'

'Hey.' Lilianne yanked the covers off her protesting friend. 'Where's my adventurer?'

'Sleeping.'

'It'll be fantastic.'

Twenty minutes later, they were both ready, having dressed and eaten quick bites of bread, yoghurt and fresh apricots to keep them going until Sami fed them breakfast. Lilianne had wrapped the listening device carefully in a bandanna surreptitiously borrowed from Connie's suitcase, and stuffed it into her pants pocket, where it burned a nervous hole in her conscience and her gut.

A taxi brought them to the address Sami had given them, where he waited in the near darkness with two men and four horses. Lilianne introduced Connie, feeling more uncomfortable around him than she ever had. On paper, the assignment was simple. The reality was nothing but unpleasant.

'Nice to meet you, Sami.' Connie dimpled a smile and pointed to the horses. 'Are they going up the pyramid with us?'

'They will get you to the base. It's too far to walk.'

She turned to Lilianne. 'Do you know how to start one of those things?'

Lilianne feigned surprise, punchy from fatigue and the pressures ahead of her. 'You mean you didn't learn to ride at an expensive overnight camp up there in the sticks of Vermont?'

Connie snorted. 'Not in the family budget.'

'You are afraid?' Sami grinned at her. 'They are very gentle, I'm sure.'

'How sure?'

He laughed, and asked the men in Arabic if the horses were vicious killers, leading to emphatic denials.

The taller one pointed out the largest horse to Connie. 'No bad. Very nice.'

Connie wrinkled her nose. 'I can do "very nice". I guess.'

The men distributed the horses. Sami and Lilianne swung up on theirs. Connie got help from the tall man, who couldn't stop grinning. She obviously amused him, ready for her pyramid climb in orange and black checkered pants and red tennis shoes, the bright red sleeves of her top contrasting sharply with the horse's dark mane, a thick multicolored shawl over her head and tucked into her waistband. Despite the hot days, the desert turned chilly at night.

The horses made the trip easily, led by the guide, and they were soon at the base of the magnificent Great Pyramid, peering up its stony sides into the faint glow of the coming dawn.

'Four hundred and fifty-five feet up. Four thousand five hundred years old,' Sami said.

'Fantastic,' Lilianne murmured. 'Built so perfectly, all by hand. It's hard to fathom.'

'Pyramids are filled with magical energy, did you know that?' Connie stretched out her hands toward the stone. 'I can totally feel the power. Can't you?'

'Nope,' Lilianne said cheerfully.

'You must be careful going up, and even more careful coming back down,' Sami said. 'Leave your bags here at the bottom. I'll carry water for us. You don't want anything that will unbalance you. There are deaths every year from—'

'Deaths?' Connie all but shrieked. 'No one said anything about dying.'

'*La*, no.' Sami held up his hand. 'Only if you're careless. I won't permit that.'

'Gulp.' Connie pressed up against Lilianne, whose heart was already beating too fast from the guilt of having to betray Sami later that morning after he'd been so kind to both of them. 'We don't have to go all the way up, do we?'

'Of course not. But you will want to.'

'What if we're caught?' Lilianne asked. Her being arrested would not go over well with John Baker.

'This gentleman will pay off any guards that show up. I've taken care of it. Come.' Sami started toward the awesome structure. 'Keep your eyes open, and watch out for loose sand from the storm.'

When it was built, the pyramid's surface had been smooth, its huge blocks covered top to bottom with white limestone. Over the years, that stone had worn away or been pillaged for other construction. What remained were haphazard, often crumbling stones that served as steps. Sort of. Lilianne could see how carelessness could spell serious trouble, and the first hundred feet was a source of some pretty intense anxiety. After that, although

The Jewel of Cairo

their height off the ground was intimidating, the climb took her over, and she and her companions settled into its rhythm as the light around them became more certain, then yellowed into the first rays of the coming dawn. The higher she climbed, up to where the pyramid narrowed and vanished into sky, the more Lilianne felt like she was floating, leaving behind her worries and anxieties. Maybe Connie was right about the pyramid's power.

But probably not.

'Nearly there.' Sami was huffing and puffing, sweat dripping off his forehead. Connie likewise was breathing heavily, but kept up a steady determined pace. 'We should be at the top for sunrise, as I'd hoped.'

The last fifty yards gave them renewed energy to finish the climb. They reached the top just as the sun burst over the horizon, lighting city and desert with a rosy glow, doubly welcome after so many days of the storm's dark-orange threat.

Connie gasped. Lilianne couldn't stop grinning, opening her arms to the sun and sky, breathing deeply, turning to take in the magical views. Desert and the two smaller Giza pyramids on one side, looking like toy versions at this height. On the other, the hazy sprawl of the city and the glittering ribbon of the Nile. She turned again, careful of her footing, taking it all in, chest heaving with emotion.

This. Was. Fantastic.

The three of them stood in awe, watching the light grow and change the scenery. Impossible to have predicted how thrilling it was to be so intimately connected to such an ancient treasure. Her back to the city, looking out at the golden sand fading into the distant haze, Lilianne could have been standing here one, two, three or four thousand years ago. Gilles would love it. He'd see and feel it as she did. She knelt to be closer to the stone, inhaling its ancient scent, and laid her hand on a crumbling corner, imagining the sweat and toil and bodies it had taken to bring just this one piece up so enormously high.

Then she stood again, gazing at the glowing city vista, her throat tightening. Half of Lilianne Maxwell belonged to this place. Something deep in her genes or in her blood was responding to Cairo in a way it hadn't before.

Was she fated to fall in love with the city of her ancestors right as she'd decided to leave?

'Can you imagine the ego that would make someone build a tomb like this for himself?' Connie had settled onto the still chilly stone, skin pink in the morning light. 'Twenty-seven years to finish. Who knows how many poor workers died in the process.'

'This ego-tomb has stood here for over four millennia.' Sami sat next to her, his legs over the edge, and pulled a bottle of water out of his jacket, offering it to Connie. 'What will you leave behind that will last even a fraction that long?'

'That's easy.' She lifted her arms. 'The love I send out into the universe every day will be received and then given again after me in a cycle that will last until time ends. When I die, my spirit will be reborn in another being. That love and that spirit will do the world a lot more good than a heap of look-at-me rocks.'

Sami chuckled. 'Ah, you think so.'

'I know so.' She gulped some water and passed it back.

'And you, Lilianne?' Sami turned to look up at her, offering her the bottle. 'What will you leave behind?'

She took a drink, irritated by the question and the affection in his eyes. 'Dust.'

He laughed uproariously.

'What about you, Sami?' Connie nudged him with her shoulder. 'Are you going to have a boatload of little Samis to bequeath to the world?'

'I will leave my jewelry on the fingers, wrists and necks of people who love it.' His eyes gleamed, reminding Lilianne of his hungry, almost sexual look as he'd gazed down at the diamond necklace brought into his shop. 'Centuries from now – millennia from now – those parts of me will still exist.'

'You'll be practically immortal,' Connie said.

'Speaking of your jewelry . . .' Her beautiful spell thoroughly broken now, Lilianne handed Sami back the water, praying she didn't sound as obvious as she did to herself. 'I hope you'll show Connie the special pieces in your apartment.'

'Of course, of course, for such lovely ladies all things are possible.' Sami tucked the bottle back into his jacket and zipped it up. 'We should climb down soon, before the park opens.'

Lilianne sighed, hating to leave this magic for deception and complications. She wanted to take John Baker's device out of her pocket and hurl it off the edge of the pyramid, for the joy of watching a modern creation smash into a million pieces against one of the world's oldest.

'What was that sigh, Lilianne?' Sami got to his feet, extending a hand to help Connie up.

'Just musing.' Lilianne smiled out at the endless desert, searching for a likely answer. 'I was thinking how strange it is that a place foreign to me in every way can sometimes feel like home. Does that come from my conscious knowledge of my heritage, or is it something deeper?'

'Weighty thoughts for early morning. Perhaps the pyramid's stones are talking to you.'

'I'm sure of it.' Connie dusted herself off. 'I bet I'll feel the same way at the Acropolis.'

'You are Greek?'

'Both grandparents, both parents.' She peeked teasingly at Lilianne. 'Unlike half-breed there.'

'Have you been to Greece?'

'I'll get there one day.' She tied her shawl around her waist, the warmth of the sun already making itself felt. 'Whenever the mood strikes.'

'Ah, that's how I want to live.' Sami gazed at her admiringly. 'Everything at my whim. You must have money.'

'Not a penny.'

His face stretched into astonishment. 'How is this possible?'

On the way down, a cautious process of sitting and sliding rock to rock, keeping their weight low, Sami and Connie argued agreeably about the necessity of wealth for travel, while Lilianne went back to her musing. Did she really want to stay longer in Egypt? Gilles had agreed to leave with her for the US; would he also be amenable to staying longer? Would he heal and thrive here as quickly and as well? How different to be making life decisions with another person's happiness at stake. Lilianne had always enjoyed the luxury of worrying only about herself.

She turned her focus back to her current hit parade of 'ifs'. If she decided to stay, if Gilles agreed and it turned out being in Egypt wouldn't impede or slow his recovery, and if her work at Cairo National Bank was nearly finished, what would Lilianne do next? She'd already been considering taking time off to nurse Gilles back to health in Southport . . . Why not here?

It felt surreal, nearly traitorous, to be thinking about leaving work. For so long, her determined focus and trajectory had been up, to the top of the pyramid, always the top.

She eased herself down another few blocks toward the desert sand, where their guide, waiting with the horses, was still a toy soldier miniature. Most of her life was still ahead of her; taking a few months to tend to Gilles, either here or in Southport, didn't mean a betrayal of her fifteen-year-old promise to achieve great heights. She certainly wouldn't turn into her mother, playing golf and tennis, having lunch at the country club, then retiring to Florida to do more of the same.

A few months...

As they headed down farther, the exhilarating isolation of their former height diminished, the air grew warmer, the horses and guides larger and more real, and with them the task ahead of Lilianne this morning, much more urgent than what move she and Gilles would make next.

By the time they reached the bottom safely, suffering only mild scrapes and tired muscles, she'd gone over her plan until her nerves had settled into calm resolve and she was able to chat normally in the cab to Sami's house. She'd been trained for this – granted, years ago, but she knew what to do – and with Connie sure to be enthralled with the jewelry Sami would show her, Lilianne should be able to get her job done quickly. After that, she was free to treat Sami as a friend, or not, whatever she decided, for as long as she was here.

She hoped he could be a friend.

As expected, Connie loved the shop, peering into the cases and asking endless questions that Sami answered with amused patience until they'd seen practically every piece in the store and Lilianne wanted to muzzle her friend. 'Now, you must come upstairs and we'll have some breakfast.'

'Thank you, Sami.' Lilianne forced a smile, feeling the device against her hip. The sooner she could get this over with...

Upstairs, on their way through the living room, greeted by Sami's white Persian cat, Lilianne subtly scoped out her targeted table next to the chair by the window, still convinced she'd chosen the right spot, near the building's outer wall. An agent outside would be able to pick up a signal fairly easily.

They sat at a dark, heavy dining table set with ornate china, silver and linen, in a room that belonged more to a French castle than an Egyptian apartment. Tapestries woven with medieval scenes lined the walls, and heavy red curtains with gold tassels framed the floor-to-ceiling windows.

Safiya entered with a silver tray on which sat a copper coffee pot and white china cups.

'Hi, I'm Connie.' Connie offered her hand to the housekeeper, who froze, looking in panic to Sami. 'What's your name?'

'Safiya,' Sami said dismissively. 'She speaks no English.'

'You can translate then. Where does she live?'

'She lives here.'

'Here?' Connie looked astonished. 'Doesn't she have family?'

Sami nodded, a single jerk of his head. 'She does.'

'Where?'

Lilianne tried to smile reassuringly at Safiya's anxious face. She must know they were talking about her.

'Small town in southern Egypt.' Sami clearly did not enjoy this topic. 'Why are you so interested in my maid?'

Connie shrugged. 'She's a person too.'

'The lady wants to know about your family, Safiya,' he said in impatient Arabic.

Safiya's eyes darted between him and Connie.

'*Yallah*, tell her.' The sharpness in Sami's voice made Connie jerk around to look at him.

Lilianne ached to speak gently to Safiya in Arabic. The woman's body language spoke of fear. Mistrust.

'I have a father and mother, two brothers and their families, a husband and two sons.' Safiya's voice cracked when she mentioned her children.

'She has a good family,' Sami mistranslated. 'Go get us breakfast, Safiya.'

Safiya practically ran out of the room. Lilianne did not

like this dynamic. Neither, clearly, did Connie, who looked as though she wanted to growl.

'How often does she get to see them? Her family?'

'Often enough. I am very generous with her.' Sami wagged his finger at Connie. 'But my terms as employer are none of your business, young lady.'

Connie forced a grin. 'That is true. Me and my big mouth. I just think it must be hard for her to live so far away from home.'

'Why?' Sami was back to his mischievous self. '*You* do.'

She looked unconvinced. 'Point taken.'

Safiya came back into the room with a nervous glance at Sami, then unloaded an enormous tray onto the table: platters of fresh fruit, decidedly non-Egyptian omelets and British scones, alongside cheeses and warm loaves of fresh *baladi* bread. The silence at the table was electric.

'*Shukran*, thank you, Safiya.' Lilianne smiled, hoping she'd look up and see. 'That looks delicious. *Lazeeza.*'

Safiya made eye contact for a brief second and inclined her head a fraction of an inch before she left the room.

Progress.

'Dig in! Dig in! No formality here. Don't be shy, help yourselves.' Sami pushed dishes of food in front of each of them.

'This looks gorgeous. I'm starving.' Connie piled her plate full.

While they ate, they chatted about Egyptian history and culture, Connie's colorful travels and each other's lives, until they couldn't manage another bite and Lilianne was nearly bursting with the need to get John Baker's odious task over with.

'Safiya, we'll have coffee in the living room.' Sami stood and ushered them to exactly where Lilianne needed to be alone.

They sat, Lilianne trying not to fidget on the couch, Connie across the room, sprawled in a chair, the white cat immediately jumping into her lap and settling down, as if he recognized her from another life.

'Next time I will take you somewhere special.' Sami pulled over one of the chairs near the backgammon set. 'Café Riche, one of the oldest restaurants in Cairo, from 1908. All the intelligentsia would gather there. Like the cafés in Paris, full of writers and artists, but also politicians. It is said the uprising against British rule was planned there in 1919. Nasser went to this café before he overthrew King Farouk. Egypt's greatest writer, Naguib Mahfouz, would write or have meetings there. The singer Umm Kulthum, our most treasured artist, would—'

'Oom Koo-what?' Connie perked up over the idea of a musician.

'Umm Kulthum!' His eyes popped. 'You don't know her?'

'No.' She ducked her head in exaggerated shame. 'Sorry. I'm a hick from the sticks.'

'Ah, such a voice, such passion.' Sami looked transported. 'Her concerts would go on for four or five hours. Each song, an hour.'

'An *hour*?' Connie's mouth dropped. '*One song?*'

'I've heard her,' Lilianne put in. 'Beautiful alto voice.'

'She was constantly on the radio, every Egyptian knows her, every Arab knows her. She toured many countries, but mostly she was here at home, with us, with her people.

'When she died, a year ago in February, four million people came to her funeral. Four million!' He shook his head, voice thickening. 'The whole country grieved. She was a force. Egyptians worshiped her.'

'Like the Beatles.'

'No.' Sami held up an emphatic finger. 'Not like the Beatles. That was young screaming girls whose parents plugged their ears. Everyone, everyone in Egypt was in Umm Kulthum's thrall.

The Jewel of Cairo

The country would stop during her radio programs. Every car played them, every apartment, restaurant and hotel, and every man, woman and child would stop to listen. Half the population knows the songs by heart. You can't imagine it.'

'Almost like she was a prophet,' Lilianne said.

'There has never been and will never be anything like her again.'

'Yes, yes, there will be.' Connie regarded him pityingly. 'That kind of greatness doesn't die. It gets passed along.'

'Did she write her own songs?' Lilianne jumped in to stop another metaphysical argument.

'Ah, no, this is the sadness. Ahmed Rami, an Egyptian poet, fell madly and hopelessly in love with Umm Kulthum from the first time he saw her, when she was quite young. His whole life he saved one day out of every week to spend with her. So many of the songs she sings about unrequited love are his poems, his feelings for her. Imagine this poignancy. His words of love in her mouth, yet with no hope.' He sighed heavily, looking at Lilianne.

'This has been such a great morning. I'm sorry we can't stay long.' Lilianne put her empty cup and its saucer on the couch's end table. 'I know Connie would like to see your special collection, if it's no trouble . . .'

Sami's eyes lit; he got to his feet. 'Absolutely. This way, mademoiselle.'

'Thank you!'

Lilianne followed them to the studio door. As soon as Sami unlocked it, she took a step back. 'Sami, may I use your bathroom?'

'Of course, of course.' He ushered Connie eagerly into his studio.

Perfect.

Pulling the device from her pocket, Lilianne went straight over to the window, applied a couple of drops of the special adhesive John Baker had given her with steady hands she was proud of, and positioned the bug on the underside of the table, pressing it for several endless seconds until it stuck.

Done. All she had to do was get herself silently to the bathroom, noisily back out, and her duty to the US was complete.

She turned and came face to face with Safiya, carrying a silver tray and watching her curiously.

Lilianne managed not to gasp, cursing herself. How had she not anticipated that Safiya would be back out to clear the coffee?

Mind whirling, Lilianne broke into a friendly smile. How much had Safiya seen? There was no safe way to find out. *Just wondering – did you see me plant the bug under the table?*

Would she tell Sami?

Also no safe way to find out.

As usual, Safiya's impassive face gave nothing away. In Lilianne's opinion, the wrong person was doing the spying. This woman was a natural.

She closed the distance between them and in Arabic murmured the first thing that came into her head. 'Are you happy here, Safiya? Is he good to you?'

The surprise question, in Safiya's language, got a fleeting reaction, a slight widening of her eyes, huge in such a thin face. 'Yes, miss, he is very kind.'

The words came out mechanically, as if she'd rehearsed them. She put down the tray and moved past Lilianne to gather up their cups.

Lilianne's skin prickled with dread. 'You can tell me. No harm will come to you for honesty. I might be able to help you.'

Safiya put all the cups onto the tray and straightened. Their gazes clung. Lilianne waited, suspecting she already knew the answer, trying to think what she could do to get Safiya into safer employment.

'He is very good to me.' This time a slight break in her voice, though her face remained impassive.

Sami, you bastard. Lilianne leaned closer to speak urgently. 'If you need help, John Baker at the American Embassy will know where to find me. John Baker. I'm Lilianne Maxwell. John Baker. Lilianne Maxwell. Will you remember?'

The suggestion of a nod, a nearly inaudible *thank you* from lips that barely moved. Then Safiya's face came alive with determination and intelligence. She pointed to the table where Lilianne had put the bug, covered her eyes briefly, then shrugged, the universal gesture of ignorance. *I saw nothing.*

Lilianne nodded in grateful acceptance, offering another smile. Safiya stayed serious, but she didn't turn away from Lilianne's gaze. Apparently they understood each other. Lilianne had offered help. Safiya wouldn't tell. Done.

'Oh my God!' From Sami's studio, Connie's delighted shriek pierced the silence.

Safiya grabbed for her tray. Lilianne leapt to the middle of the room and raised her voice, back in English. 'Oh, Safiya. Thank you for breakfast. It was delicious.'

Safiya inclined her head, expression once again a blank, and headed back toward the kitchen, carrying Lilianne's fate on her thin, proud shoulders.

Chapter 19

Present day

Sophie: *All good here. My ideas for sprucing up the place went well.*
Lilianne: *Excellent! And so much like something Connie would do.*
Sophie: *Really?*
Lilianne: *Would I lie about . . . Oh. Never mind.*
Sophie: *Haha! BTW, I was hired here for a whole month. So I won't be back until mid August.*
Lilianne: *??? What about your clients?*
Sophie: *No worries. We worked it out.*
Lilianne: *Hmm.*
Sophie: *Luuuuuuv yooooou, Mooooom!*
Lilianne: *Haha!* ♥

Sophie finished wiping out the last of the cabinets in Asphalia's kitchen. Surrounding her in the now sparkling decent-sized space, on every available surface, including the floor – she would have used the ceiling, but . . . gravity – sat every pot, pan, baking and serving dish the cabinets had contained. She'd come in super early that morning, examined the chaos and jotted down a few ideas for consolidating and freeing up more surfaces.

Then, after overseeing the bemused residents' breakfasts, she'd gone out again to buy a wall-mounted holder for pot lids and several tiered inserts for cabinets and pull-out drawers, plus a tiny corner shelf unit that would hold items currently unhoused.

Annika obviously had her own method, which must have been either to search through every cabinet for the item she needed or to memorize where everything was, because to Sophie's mind there was no logic or reason to her placement. Baking dishes snuggled up to pots, frying pans cohabitated with serving platters. It was enough to make a good anal-retentive American pull her hair out.

Figurative sleeves rolled up, Sophie set about organizing.

Hours later, all the frying pans played together in their own space, largest on the bottom, smallest on top, ditto the saucepans, Dutch ovens, trays, platters, etc. Drawers that had to be pawed through had their contents organized and visible. A large canister held spatulas, rubber and metal, wooden spoons, whisks and ladles for easy access at the stove. Racks mounted above the sink supported colanders; on hooks beneath them hung mugs that added a practical splash of color. Additional color brightened the sad beige linoleum in the form of grippy easy-clean mats in kaleidoscope patterns. A couple of air ferns added a fresh touch.

All that was left, besides the new appliances to be delivered Thursday, was to hang the rack on the wall so the haphazardly stashed pot lids would enjoy new, luxury accommodation.

'What the hell are you doing?' Lizzie stood in the entrance to the kitchen, wearing a cranky expression and an adorable orange mini-romper that probably should have been a size larger.

'Organizing. What the hell are *you* doing? Aren't you supposed to be in group therapy?'

'Did Annika say you could mess with her kitchen?'

'It's my kitchen this month. She can change it all back.' Except the appliances, but Annika couldn't possibly object to having better quality to work with.

'And what did you do to the dining room? You think a rug, a tablecloth and some fake flowers will trick us all into forgetting we're addicts?'

'You still remember?' Sophie let her jaw drop and her eyes widen in surprise as genuine as she could fake it. 'I was so sure that would work.'

'You think you're Mary Poppins or something, don't you?' Lizzie flung out her arms and high-pitched her voice to a silly sing-song. 'Bringing color and whimsy to the downtrodden.'

Sophie waited a beat, understanding the hostility, not sure how to react. 'How do you know about Mary Poppins? You're way too young. You should read the books, if you like to read. They're different in tone from the movie. Mary Poppins herself is much more cutting in the book, which I think you'd appreciate.'

'Oh really. What makes you—'

'By the way, while you're here, give me a hand with this, will you?' Sophie picked up the pot lid rack and held it out, preferring to have a problem like Ms Lizzie on her side. 'I want to hang it on the wall.'

Lizzie stayed where she was, though her glare softened some.

'No?' Sophie put the rack down. 'That's okay. I can ask someone else to—'

'What do I need to do?'

She pointed to her target, making sure not to show the slightest sign of triumph. 'Hold it up there while I mark where the screw holes are.'

'You don't know where your screw holes are?'

Sophie couldn't help giggling, certain she should be sternly disapproving. 'Tell you what, you take the level and the pencil. I'll hold the rack.'

She showed her how to use the level, pleased when Lizzie got serious about making sure to get the bubble exactly in the center.

'There! There! It's in the middle. What do I do now?'

'Put the pencil in the holes and scribble around.'

Lizzie scribbled. 'Reminds me of the last time I wrote on a wall.'

'Yeah?' Sophie held the rack still while Lizzie scribbled a second time. 'When was that?'

'Right before I left home, I wrote a foot-high "fuck you" in red permanent marker over my parents' bed.' She finished and backed away. 'So they'd have something to remember me by.'

Sophie closed her eyes, letting empathy pain wash through her. My God. The rage in Lizzie's voice . . .

'Well.' She put the lid rack back on the counter and picked up the cordless drill she'd bought from Noble Ace Hardware on North Main Street. 'I bet that worked. But I'm sorry you felt you had to.'

'You have no idea.'

'No.' Sophie met Lizzie's eyes and held them. 'I don't really know what happens here yet, but I do know that your life does not have to suck from now on. I really hope it doesn't.'

Lizzie half turned away. 'Whatever.'

'Have you used one of these before?' Sophie poked her in the shoulder with the drill. 'My dad taught me.'

'No.'

'You're about to.' She showed Lizzie how to choose a bit based on the size of the screw, then made the first hole before she handed the drill over. 'Your turn now.'

'Lizzie.' Lily Anne stood in the doorway, panicked eyes darting around the room before resting on her truant resident. 'You're supposed to be in group therapy.'

Oops. Sophie felt like an idiot. An idiot who should have sent Lizzie straight back where she belonged.

Lizzie turned mutinous. 'I didn't feel like group therapy.'

'I get that, but . . .' Lily Anne glanced around the kitchen again, clearly exasperated. 'What is happening here? And in the dining room?'

'Oh, that.' Lizzie made a la-dee-dah gesture. 'Sophie's trying to make us all a little more *Connecticut*.'

Sophie frowned at her. 'I thought I was Mary Poppins.'

'Lizzie, you need to go to therapy.'

Lizzie set her mouth. 'It's a freaking waste of my time.'

Sophie snorted. 'What else would you do here?'

Lily Anne glared at her. 'I'm not crazy about the way you put that, Sophie, but you have a point. Therapy is part of your agreement with Asphalia House, Lizzie. You're here to do the work, even if you hate it. It's only one hour, and half of it's gone now. Go. Or consequences.'

Lizzie stared mutinously, then stomped out of the room.

Sophie blew out a breath. She could not even begin to fathom how difficult Lily Anne's job was here; so many personalities and so many different forms trauma could take. 'I probably should have—'

'You mind telling me what you're doing here? What all . . .' Lily Anne gestured furiously, '*this* is?'

Another oops. 'I thought it would help if I reorganized the kitchen.' The words sounded lame and squeaky. 'I couldn't find anything, so I thought—'

'It's not your kitchen. Nor is it your dining room. Or living room, or whatever else you'll decide to change without asking.'

Owen: two. Sophie: nothing. She'd been so excited . . . 'I'm sorry. It was supposed to be a surprise.'

'It's definitely that.'

'I mean a good one.' She looked around, still so pleased with how much nicer everything looked. Yes, she should have asked. But what if Lily Anne had said no? It was so healthy and uplifting to have one's everyday spaces made new again.

Still, not a good enough excuse.

'We need to talk about this. Let's go to my office.'

Uh-oh. *Consequences.*

Sophie took her usual seat in Lily Anne's office. Lily Anne took her usual seat in Lily Anne's office. Sophie decided to start the meeting on an unhelpful note, to see if she could get her cousin to smile, at least a little. 'You know, this room could use some color. If you want I could—'

'This isn't a joke, Sophie.'

'I know. Humor is how I cope with ... difficult things. I was hilarious during my divorce.' She put her palms flat on her thighs, bracing herself to go on. 'I was wrong to do all this assuming you'd love it. I should have asked first. But honestly, this place is colorless and depressing. Given that most of the women here are also, if not colorless, then at least depressed, I thought it was a bad match. If I was wrong, I'm sorry. I overreached, but my intentions were good. So maybe purgatory instead of damnation?'

'Yeah ... maybe.' Lily Anne massaged between her eyes.

'Headache?'

'Constant. I'm sorry Lizzie was giving you a hard time.'

'That?' Sophie dismissed Lizzie with a wave, worried about her cousin. 'That was not a hard time. You should go a few rounds with one of the Southport set. Are you the only person supervising this place right now?'

'God, no. There are always at least two of us around, plus counselors and sponsors throughout the day.'

'Do you want to take a walk?' She felt weirdly shy asking. 'With me? A short one?'

'A walk.'

'You know, get outside, fresh air, move your feet one at a time to propel you forward.' Sophie pumped her arms, miming a power walk. 'Give your body and brain a break from all this. I can't imagine how you stay sane.'

'I'm not always sure I am.' Lily Anne's tone was light, but the words had impact. Sophie felt her heart constrict with sympathy and protectiveness, struck by the feeling that she knew her cousin better than she possibly could. Either DNA was powerful, or she was letting her imagination run away with her.

Again.

'Maybe a couple of circuits around the block. Got time?'

Lily Anne looked at her watch. 'I have about twenty-five minutes until the women come out for lunch.'

'I'd like to finish up in the kitchen and be ready in time to help them. Ten minutes? Fifteen?'

'Sure.' Lily Anne got up from her desk eagerly, making Sophie wonder if her cousin needed someone else's permission to take breaks. Sophie was more than happy to provide that permission as many times as she could get away with it.

After Lily Anne had told whoever else was in charge that she'd be away for a short time, the two of them headed out the front door into what had turned into a spectacular summer day, high seventies, breezy and dry.

They turned left and started down the tree-lined street. Small houses with wood-railing front porches and grass lawns, trees and bushes, but not much in the way of flowers or gardens. The air wasn't as fresh as up by Owen's place, and Sophie missed the color and beauty of Southport's gardens, the salty wind and tang of the sea. There was something claustrophobic about being so far inland.

As they walked, she resisted the urge to chatter, letting her cousin adjust to being outside Asphalia House, interested to see if getting away from all her responsibilities, even briefly, would change the tone of their conversation. She didn't have to wait long.

'I'm sorry I reacted so strongly to your redecorating, Sophie. I know you meant well. But it felt like a criticism of how I run the place. I've been in that building so long, I guess I stopped looking at it. I can imagine now what you saw when you came in.'

'I still should have asked.' She walked a few more steps, hoping Lily Anne's slow melt would continue. Because . . . one more bombshell. 'I should maybe tell you about the new appliances being delivered Thursday . . .'

Lily Anne stopped walking. '*What?*'

Sophie turned to face her cousin, struck again by her dark hair and high cheekbones, so much like her own. The similarities gave her energy that made her want to grin and jump around, though inappropriate in the circumstances.

'They're a present. Or a contribution. Or whatever you want to call them. The equipment in that kitchen was practically antique.' It was strange to feel guilty and apologetic over generosity, but she got Lily Anne's point.

'What are we talking about?' Lily Anne had her hands on her hips.

'Oh, not much. A refrigerator, a stove, a—'

'Are you *kidding* me?'

Sophie shrugged. 'You're welcome?'

Lily Anne threw out her arms and let them slap down onto her thighs. 'That's *hundreds* of dollars.'

'All being spent for good.' Sophie met her cousin's eyes, and there was a shock of recognition and connection that made it hard to breathe. Yes, DNA was powerful stuff.

She was disappointed when Lily Anne dropped her gaze. 'You can't just sweep in and change everything like this.'

'So I keep hearing. Maybe someday that will stop me. But I doubt it.' She touched her cousin's arm, wishing Lily Anne wasn't avoiding her eyes. In spite of the serious topic, she was giddy with this new relationship. And there were more cousins-who-looked-like-her still to meet. 'Think of it this way. What if a local donor knocked on the door one day and said they wanted to buy you new appliances. Would you freak out and make them feel like they'd done something wrong?'

Lily Anne took such a deep breath her shoulders nearly reached her ears. 'No. God, no. I'd be thrilled.'

'So be thrilled! Asphalia was started in honor of my mother; why wouldn't I want to help? Plus I'm trying to suck up to the woman who runs it because she's my cousin and I want her to like me.' She was encouraged by Lily Anne's careful smile. 'I just went about it clumsily. No more surprises, I promise. I'll check in about everything. Every time I talk to one of the women, every time I want to buy something, every time I need to use the bathroom . . .'

Lily Anne laughed and resumed walking, much to Sophie's relief. 'You're a piece of work.'

'Apparently I take after my mother.' Lily Anne's silence probably meant Sophie should leave that topic alone, but she couldn't help herself. 'Did your mom ever talk about Connie, besides that she was an addict and a pain in her butt? And don't bother answering carefully. I want to know.'

They reached the end of the block and turned the corner. More porch-y houses, more lawns, more trees.

'Bear in mind that what I heard was my mother's truth, not *the* truth. She had strong feelings about her sister for a lot of reasons. Connie's lack of control mystified her. She felt, like so many people who encounter addicts, that she wasn't trying hard enough to get better, so she didn't deserve any sympathy. She also felt that after Connie died, her parents erased from their minds all the misery she'd caused and made her the martyred saint. Mom felt even more ignored.

'So it's not easy to see Connie outside of Mom's eyes. But to tell the truth . . .' Lily Anne's voice changed, became freer, more melodic, 'I was always fascinated by her, and wished I could have met her. She sounded so full of life and mischief and celebration. I admired the way she threw off everything expected of her and lived as she pleased. To a teenager, that is nothing but romantic. She certainly seemed a lot cooler and more fun than my mother. Of course, I never said so. But Connie always loomed large for me as a fantasy aunt.'

'What about my birth father? Did your mom know anything about him?'

'All she ever said about him were little snippy comments like "that boyfriend of hers". Connie was a drinker, but according to Mom, he got her into more serious drugs and was eventually murdered. Obviously there was more to him if Connie loved him, but I'm no help there.'

'Poor Connie.' Sophie watched a cat stalking a leaf, thinking about her birth mother's sad life, and how she'd managed to spread such joy in spite of it. Like Lily Anne, she was fascinated by this larger-than-life person who'd been her mother for the first five months of her life. When Connie died, she must have experienced terrible loss. Or was she too young to have felt it, at least for long? 'What was Phyllis like?'

'Mom was complicated.' Lily Anne walked steadily, eyes on

the ground, arms swinging. 'Whatever she did, she did devotedly, but I always imagined there was someone in there she was keeping down. Dad came first, us kids came first. When her parents got old, they came first. After they died, Asphalia came first. Every now and then her resentment would pop out in ugly ways. I can see why, but also . . . She defined her whole life by her sister, her children and her parents. If you ask me, none of us erased her, she erased herself.'

Sophie was practically holding her breath, eating up not only the information but her cousin's openness, thrilled with her instinct that getting Lily Anne away from Asphalia, even for this quick walk, would free something in her. 'What was your mother–daughter relationship like?'

'Rocky for a long time. She used to say I had the devil in me. I was a wild child, always wanting to try new things, always wanting to be somewhere I wasn't, always restless, never satisfied.'

'You sound more like Connie than I do. My parents took me all over the world, and while I learned a lot and loved it, I was always relieved to come back to Southport.'

'I'm the opposite. My parents, brothers and sister love everything about Vermont, and don't see the point of looking beyond. I always felt like the freak in my own family.'

Sophie whirled toward her. 'Maybe we were switched at birth! That would explain the big secret my parents can't tell me.'

Lily Anne laughed. 'Pretty tricky to pull that off.'

They turned the next corner. Sophie was already disappointed that their time together would end. She'd have to suggest these walks regularly.

'What are you parents like?' Lily Anne asked. 'I don't even know their names. Are you close to them? You said you felt like the oddball in your family too.'

'We get along great, but yes. My parents are super-achievers, beautiful and handsome, smart, accomplished. My dad, Gilles Aubert, is a photographer, pretty famous, actually. Mom, Lilianne Maxwell, is a retired big-shot lawyer. They're great people, but—'

'Wait . . .' Lily Anne peered at her curiously. 'Your mother's name is Lily Anne?'

'Lilianne, one word. And I know, I already went through the possibilities. My mother was Connie's friend abroad. No connection with your mother, and unlikely that your mom would name you after the friend of a sister she resented, so . . . coincidence.'

They walked on a few more yards. Sophie was fairly sure they were both thinking the same thing: pretty freaky coincidence.

'You were going to say something else about your mom and dad.'

'Yes.' She paused. 'I feel traitorous saying this. In fact I don't think I've said it out loud before.'

'Your secret is safe, cousin.'

She gave Lily Anne a wide grin, and was thrilled to see it returned, along with that strange familiarity, a recognition of their shared genes. So thrilled it took her several more steps to continue with what she'd been about to say.

'I'm an intimacy junkie. Mom and Dad are charming, loving, brilliant, but they're very private. I actually wish I knew them better. They seem to enjoy each other, but their relationship is not quite . . . there.'

'There?'

'They seem happy enough, but it's not a passionate, romantic relationship. They're more like roommates. Which is fine if it works for them, but I'm a passion person. When I'm happy, it's big, when I'm sad, also big. So I've always felt like . . .' she made herself say the awful words, 'like a disappointment to them, though maybe that's too strong a word. An alien, anyway.'

'I understand that feeling. Very much.'

They turned another corner. Only one more. Maybe they could go around again?

'What were you like as a kid?' Lily Anne asked.

'Ha! Docile. House-broken. Good with children.' Sophie grinned at her cousin's laughter. 'Anxious about everything, but determined not to show it to my completely self-assured parents. And I was lonely. My parents were super busy and the house was huge. I always wanted a bigger family to fill it up. I used to bug my mother constantly for more kids. A sister particularly. When that didn't work, I invented one, an imaginary friend named Lulu.'

'No kidding.' Lily Anne looked up from her obsession with the sidewalk. 'I had an imaginary friend too. Her name was Fifi. Mom kept insisting that was a poodle name, but I refused to change it.'

'It is a poodle name. Or a cliché of a French maid.'

'Exactly.' The last corner loomed ahead. 'Where are you staying, by the way? I never asked.'

'I'm renting a cottage from Owen Briggs, master furniture-maker. Which reminds me, I think his workshop would be a fantastic field trip for your ladies on a rainy day. Or any day really. He's very calm and very talented. I was also thinking that if any of the women want to learn to cook, I'm happy to do extra teaching. I can put up a sign-up sheet, or—'

'I thought you weren't trying to take over.'

Sophie glanced at her cousin, alarmed until she saw Lily Anne's smile. 'I *am* trying to take over. Asphalia House, Rutland, Vermont, then *the world*.' She threw up her arms and gave a properly villainous laugh. 'But actually, I thought woodworking would be cool.'

'Woodworking *would* be cool. I'm definitely open to ideas.'
'Oh good! I'll give you his contact information.'
They turned the last corner.
'I spoke to my family last night about you. We had a Zoom call.'

Sophie stopped abruptly, butterflies doing loop-de-loops in her system. 'Three corners' worth of talking and now you mention it?'

'What we were talking about was really interesting. This didn't seem the lead story.'

It was totally the lead story. Lily Anne had grown up in the bosom of her birth family. She couldn't understand how important it was to Sophie that these people accepted her. 'So they know I exist. What did they say? How did they react?'

'About the same way I did. My brothers, Fred and Donny, were freaked out at first, lots of questions. Naomi was more suspicious. There are definite gaps in the logic. But we got through it. They want to meet you.'

'Oh gosh.' Tears invaded Sophie's voice and eyes. She was picturing a Zoom screen full of Greek faces as instantly familiar as Lily Anne's had been. 'I want to meet them too.'

'Dad was . . .' Lily Anne frowned and looked toward the street. 'Dad was weird about it.'

'Weird how?'

'He seemed really shocked. He kept saying, "It can't be." And then he didn't want to talk about it.'

Sophie's joy diminished. She loved the idea of a kind uncle, even though she was way too big to sit on his knee and hear stories. 'My parents didn't want to talk about it either. Makes me feel like toilet paper stuck to someone's shoe. It's there but no one wants to notice or speculate how it got there.'

Her cousin smirked. 'You have quite the imagination. I worry about Dad. He gets confused sometimes. Forgetful. He might not have really understood what I was saying.'

Sophie hoped that was true, then felt guilty for wishing dementia on her uncle. 'Sorry about that. That brain stuff is really hard.'

'It is.' Lily Anne made a move to keep walking; Sophie's mind was so full of all that had been discussed that she forgot to think of a reason to delay and followed.

The last corner was achieved and conquered.

'This was fun, thanks.' Lily Anne's steps slowed; her gaze rose to Asphalia House, the sparkle gone out of it. Her voice had returned to its former near-monotone.

'We should do it again.'

'I'd like that.' She sighed and turned to Sophie. 'Thank you for the appliances and all you did to spruce up the place. I'm sorry again that I wasn't properly appreciative.'

'No apologies needed. I was also in the wrong.' Sophie searched her cousin's eyes, but the connection was gone. 'And the appliances were my pleasure.'

'Okay, then. We're good.' Lily Anne nodded firmly, and the two of them went inside in the silence of casual acquaintances.

Chapter 20

Saturday, May 22, 1976

Braheem showed up at Lilianne's apartment at eleven a.m. sharp. How anyone got anywhere in Cairo exactly on time was still a mystery to her. She and Gilles were waiting outside with a bag of gifts they'd packed the night before, culled from the remarkable assortment of groceries Sami had sent: Iranian pistachios, a jug of Lebanese olive oil, a Viennese chocolate torte and a roll of Syrian *qamardeen* – apricot fruit leather – for the grandkids. In the bottom of the bag, which Lilianne insisted on carrying, padded securely in a towel, was Gilles's loaded camera and a couple of extra rolls of film, snuck in just in case.

'Hello, hello.' Braheem embraced Lilianne, who felt unexpectedly emotional at their reunion given that she'd only met him once. He shook hands with Gilles, who'd been up, dressed and staring morosely out of the window when Lilianne and Connie had returned to the apartment from their pyramid/spy adventure. 'Welcome to Egypt, Gilles. I'm sorry you're having a difficult time.'

Gilles looked surprised, then flashed Lilianne an inscrutable look. 'Thank you.'

'Cairo is no place to rest. We'll take care of you this weekend. Come. *Tfadal*.' He opened the passenger door for Gilles. 'Zahra and Nailah are already at the house. They've probably been cooking since the middle of last night.'

'I hate to have them go to so much trouble.' Lilianne scrambled into the back, tucked the gift bag securely on the floor next to her and relaxed against the plush leather seat, relieved that someone else had taken charge.

'Trouble? How is this trouble?' Braheem got in and started the engine. 'They love every minute.'

Lilianne couldn't imagine, but she certainly wasn't going to argue. Gilles had eaten decently after she and Connie practically forced breakfast on him, but not nearly enough. An Egyptian banquet lunch might tempt him further. He seemed almost normal this morning. Maybe this day would work out. Already as they wound their way out of Maadi, crossing the river on the Al Moneeb Bridge and turning northwest of the city, she could delete one worry from her list: what they'd talk about on the two-and-a-half-hour drive. The men in the front seats seemed to be content without chattering. Braheem pointed out passing sights once in a while, and Gilles made the appropriate murmurs of appreciation, then they both lapsed back into silence.

A relief.

As they left Cairo behind them, sprawl gave way to agriculture, fields interrupted by villages of traditional mud-brick houses with palm fronds sealing their roofs, many with beehive-shaped grain silos settled among the fronds to store the family's food. On the ground, an astonishing network of canals, varying in size according to the need, channeled Nile water throughout the area. Irrigation from these canals still took place using methods Lilianne had learned about in her fourth-grade study of ancient Egypt. Buckets lowered and lifted using a fulcrum, or oxen turning a wheel that was able to bring up multiple buckets at a time. Cotton was the main crop, Braheem said, along with corn, wheat, potatoes, rice and oranges. They saw fig and mango trees, date palms, eucalyptus, cypress and mimosa. The lushness was all the more uplifting and refreshing after the misery of the sandstorm.

Eventually they left the larger roads for a series of smaller dirt ones, passing through yet another village, then through acres of jasmine fields, mounded bushes with waxy leaves shining green in the sun. June was the traditional start of the months-long harvest, Braheem told them. The buds grew during the day and opened at night, releasing their intense perfume over the whole area. The flowers must be carefully picked by hand at their peak to preserve their oils, therefore workers began their day at midnight, often whole families participating, including small children, earning what they could.

He shook his head disapprovingly. 'We pay our workers a fair wage, which means everyone wants to work for us. It's not our main business. We own only a few acres. More was too much to manage. The bushes are not in bloom yet, but you might catch an early blossom or two. The fragrance is exquisite.'

They pulled up to a two-story building standing lonely in a field, its stone freshened with whitewash, windows covered by the lattice woodwork called *mashrabiya*, which scattered the sun, and therefore most of its heat, but still let in light and breezes.

'*Ahlan wa sahlan*, welcome, welcome.' Braheem parked his Peugeot next to two of the boxy Russian cars ubiquitous in Egypt, scattering chickens.

The house's front door flew open, and Zahra emerged wearing an apron, her face pink. '*Marhaba*, welcome.'

Lilianne struggled out of the car into the afternoon heat and was swept into her grandmother's arms. '*Hayati*, Lilianne.'

Zahra smelled of butter and allspice; Lilianne hugged her

back, surprised for the second time at the welling of affection for a grandparent she barely knew.

Zahra crossed to Gilles, standing by the passenger door he'd just closed, looking around as if he'd disembarked onto a new planet. 'Welcome, Gilles, welcome.' She took his hand and held it, continuing in Arabic. 'We are glad to have you in our home. Please treat it as your own. If you need quiet, take quiet. If you need talk, we are here. We want you to be comfortable.'

He inclined his head, looking bemused until Braheem translated.

'Thank you.' Gilles gave his near-smile, and covered her clinging hand with his free one, his color heightening in the heat, making his eyes look clearer, less sunken. 'That's very kind of you.'

Lilianne's heart squeezed at the effort he was making. She pulled out the bag of gifts with Gilles's camera weighing down the bottom, feeling cautiously optimistic.

'Come in, come in.' Zahra waved them inside.

The house was blessedly cool, a corridor leading through a large living room to a shady courtyard with orange and fig trees decorating the interior, the latter laden with reddish brown figs. In the center, a long table nearly covered with platters, bowls and dishes of food. Around the perimeter, seated or standing in small groups, Lilianne's extended family. There seemed to be thousands of them, all strangers.

Beside her, Gilles swore in French.

Uh-oh. Lilianne's optimism faltered. She stood protectively next to Gilles, bracing for a crush of introductions and questions, judgments and teasing neither of them was prepared to handle.

Instead, one young woman, around Lilianne's age, maybe a few years older, detached herself from her group and came toward them, smiling, hand outstretched. 'Hello, Lilianne, I'm your cousin Aida, Khaled's daughter. Welcome, Gilles. How was the drive?'

Her English was accented toward British, her face dark-eyed and lovely, with high cheekbones and a generous mouth.

'Beautiful. It's our first time out of the city.' Lilianne glanced at Gilles, who was staring at his feet.

'My mother, Mounira, over there . . .' Aida pointed to a plump woman in a green dress, whose rounded features looked nothing like her daughter's, 'she was best friends with your mom growing up. You speak Arabic, right? She doesn't speak English.'

'I do, yes.' Lilianne was aware of Gilles's attention wandering, heard him sigh deeply.

'Good. She'll want to hear all about Auntie Dina.'

'I'd love that.' Lilianne was relieved that, at least for now, Aida was the only person they had to deal with. She had to figure out a strategy for getting Gilles settled somewhere he'd be comfortable.

'*Yallah*, everyone.' Zahra stepped into the room, taking off her apron. Voices fell silent. 'We must eat before everything gets cold. Lilianne, Gilles, our guests of honor, please . . .'

'Thank you.' Lilianne glanced at Gilles before taking his hand and practically dragging him to the table of food. He was not going to enjoy helping himself to unfamiliar dishes in a room full of staring people he didn't know.

Except as soon as they started for the feast, the faces surrounding them turned toward each other and conversations resumed, so that they felt almost invisible as they filled their plates, with only Zahra and Aida urging them to try everything, then more of everything, and then more . . .

Hummus, tabouleh, baba ghanouj; *ta'ameya*, the Egyptian

version of falafel; grape leaves stuffed with rice; olives; cheeses, *baladi* bread and *ful medames*, fava beans mashed with spices, garlic, lemon and parsley; chicken stewed with okra and tomatoes; spicy lamb kebabs strewn over a mound of rice; and *koshary*, the dish Lilianne had tried in the street the day she met Sami. Tea was served with the meal, and for those partaking, pint bottles of Stella beer from a company nationalized by Nasser in 1963, which still dominated the Egyptian market.

After they'd loaded their plates as instructed, Aida guided them to seats at an empty corner table, where she sat with them, chatting easily about her schooling in London and her curiosity about the US. One by one, with decent intervals between, other members of the family came up and introduced themselves, talking quietly for a polite amount of time before going back to their seats. The end result was that even though Gilles ate sparingly and was clearly withdrawn, he was never overwhelmed or overcrowded.

Lilianne could not have been more grateful. Obviously the afternoon had been carefully choreographed to avoid overtaxing this man who was a complete stranger to all of them. For his part, though Gilles didn't ask any questions, he answered politely the few directed at him, and except for his increased fidgeting in the chair would have appeared to everyone as a man having a lovely afternoon.

She'd need to get him alone time soon. A languorous walk through jasmine fields would be perfect – except the heat would melt them both.

Dessert, served with coffee, was *umm ali*, Egypt's favorite, similar to bread pudding, made with a combination of puff pastry, raisins, pistachios and coconut, soaked in milk, cream and sugar before baking; and *kunafeh*, consisting of thin pastry strands soaked in butter, layered with sweet cheese and drenched with orange blossom syrup out of the oven. Along with the pastries, platters of dates and watermelon, figs, apricots and mangos.

During dessert, her uncles took their turn. Ramy, the elder, who had a giant mustache and an even larger belly, clearly disapproved of his sister Dina's behavior, and though he was polite, he didn't seem too taken with Lilianne either, especially once he found out what she did for a living. Apparently he'd inherited his parents' traditional take on the family. During their stilted conversation, in French, Gilles started shifting in his seat, then finally burst out, 'Why do you think you can dictate where anyone will be happy?'

Lilianne's stomach sank. Fair question, but . . .

'Dina had everything here.' Ramy gestured around him. 'Family, friends, her own country. What could she want that we couldn't give her?'

'The United States.'

'She didn't need the United States to be happy.'

'Apparently she did. Apparently a lot of people do.'

Lilianne cringed. He meant Helen. 'Gilles, I don't—'

'How can you be happy without your family?' Ramy's voice rose, along with his hand. 'How can you turn your back on the people who love you and who raised you? The people you owe your life to?'

'My mom is happy, Amou Ramy.' She used the Arabic term for paternal uncle, hoping it would underscore the blood they shared. 'I know you miss her, but she has a good life, one she couldn't have lived here.'

Gilles's eyes were hard. 'Yours is not the only way.'

Lilianne glanced around the room and noticed people staring, one table whispering and pointing, a young boy with a mop of dark hair watching them closely. She started to sweat. This couldn't be allowed to escalate.

The little boy raced toward them and tugged hard on Ramy's hand. 'Amou Ramy, you promised to show me how to play marbles.'

'You are right.' Ramy's face softened. 'I did promise.'

Lilianne grinned her grateful relief to the table that had set the child distraction in motion.

Ramy stood. 'Nice to meet you.'

Gilles barely waited until he was out of earshot. 'Not really.'

'Ugh.' Lilianne made a face as if she'd eaten something foul. 'That was a bit of a challenge.'

'There are better words.' He muttered a few colorful French phrases. Lilianne laughed obligingly, thinking it was time to give him a break from the crowd, even such a well-managed one.

'Let's go somewhere—'

'Lilianne.' Her other uncle, Khaled, chose that moment to appear, a handsome graying man with warm eyes and a relaxed air, in sharp contrast to his older brother. 'I adored my sister, your mother. Ignore whatever Ramy said. I love him, but he is old-fashioned and always needs to be right.'

'Thank you.'

A young girl, probably three or four, with a sweet face and a head of dark curls, ran up and hugged Khaled's knees.

He swung her up. 'This is my granddaughter, Dalia. Dalia, this is Lilianne. And this is Gilles. I think he must be a giant, don't you?' He repeated the phrases in Arabic for her.

She smiled and nodded, peeking shyly at Lilianne, then at Gilles through long curling lashes. 'Is he Sa-Nakht?'

Gilles looked curious, the first time Lilianne had seen him show real interest in anything since she'd found him in Paris. 'Sa-Nakht?'

'An Egyptian pharaoh from the third dynasty, somewhere

around 2500 BC. His skeleton was unearthed in the early twentieth century, a very, very tall man.'

'A giant!' Dalia's eyes sparkled. She reached her chubby fist as high as it would go to show the man's extraordinary height.

'They think he had a pituitary disease or gigantism. Dalia loves the story. Don't you, *hayati*?'

She nodded, those dark eyes still on Gilles. 'Are you a pharaoh too?'

He waited for Khaled's translation. 'Would you like me to be one?'

'Yes.' She gave a bounce in her grandfather's arms and pointed. 'You are a pharaoh.'

'I am. For today, anyway.' Gilles smiled broadly, a startling transformation, shedding his misery like a snake's skin. It wouldn't last, couldn't be that easy, but the sight cemented Lilianne's hope and determination.

To her disappointment, Dalia slid out of her grandfather's arms and ran off.

Gilles looked hungrily after her. 'She's adorable.'

Khaled beamed. 'All grandparents think their grandchildren are adorable, but yes, we think she is special.'

The little girl ran back, straight up to Gilles, a pistachio in her outstretched hand. 'For you.'

'Thank you!' He ate the pistachio solemnly and pronounced it delicious. Dalia beamed and dashed off again.

'She is learning about our history. People gave gifts to the pharaohs, hoping they'd intervene with the gods on their behalf.

'What is she hoping for?'

'A bicycle. We're waiting until she's a little older. In the meantime, you might have to eat a lot of pistachios.'

Gilles gave a lopsided grin. 'We pharaohs are pretty good with pistachios.'

The next time Dalia returned, she held out a plump date, which Gilles ate with all the grandeur of a pharaoh, and considerable relish.

The little girl was about to take off again when her grandfather intercepted her. 'Dalia, *hayati*, would you like to show your pharaoh the dance you're learning?'

She turned back, her perfect smooth forehead marred by a frown of indecision.

'I'd love to see it.' Gilles was still, no longer fidgeting, while Lilianne tried to think how to get young children into his daily life, short of having them herself.

'Yes, okay.' Dalia backed into an open space and started to dance, little arms swaying, body turning, taking small skipping steps, all the while singing in a pure soprano the Arabic melodies that sounded so mysterious and evocative to foreign ears.

Around her conversation ebbed, then stopped. A few women started singing along.

As Gilles watched, his hands made an involuntary movement to grab the camera he'd always carried. He rested them in his lap, but his open fingers still held the position they'd occupied so many times before.

Lilianne rose quietly and made a beeline to the bag she'd brought. She dug out his camera, stole back and placed it carefully on his lap.

Gilles stared down at it, up at her, then back at the camera, repulsed, fascinated, wistful.

One by one, then by twos, then in a wave, the Abdallah women and girls got up to join Dalia.

Khaled leaned in to explain that this was a *fellahi*, dance of the *fellahin*, Egyptian farmers. The movements shared similarities with what Westerners thought of as belly dancing, but also incorporated gestures meant to represent daily life – planting and harvesting food, and dipping imaginary jugs into the Nile's waters.

The dance went on, the singing magnified by the chorus of women's voices. Gilles's fingers moved again. Again. Then he picked up his camera, took off the cap, adjusted the settings and started to shoot.

Lilianne clasped her hands in front of her face, forcing her breathing low and slow so she wouldn't cry. Exhaustion was catching up with her. That was part of it. But watching Gilles come back into himself, just that much, for just this moment – she wasn't stupid enough to think he was cured – was wonderful.

'Lilianne! Lilianne! Come!' Zahra beckoned her to join in. Lilianne smiled, but shook her head emphatically no. She didn't know a single step. This was not her country's dance.

'Yes, yes.' Zahra crossed to her, took her arm and dragged her in among the women, who greeted her with exclamations of delight. 'Watch, watch. Like this, then this. This, then this.'

Face burning, Lilianne copied the unfamiliar steps, grateful for the dance classes of her youth, but aware of how sadly she lacked the style, the flavor, the inherent Egyptian-ness of the women's movements.

And yet, as she clumsily wiggled and waved her way through, she saw nothing but enjoyment and welcome on the faces around her. Gradually she relaxed, grew bolder in some of the rhythms, the undulations of her hips and the curve of her arms, and found her body responding.

The singing grew louder, the dancing accelerated. The men watching clapped and shouted exclamations of encouragement, grinning and nodding to the beat. Lilianne found herself laughing, following along as best she could, now circling in a quartet, holding the hands of her relatives, now swaying and tapping her feet, making mistake after mistake, late to this transition, leaving out that step, not caring, nor did anyone else seem to.

She thought of how she felt in nightclubs, always aware that there was a sexual energy in play, men leering, on the prowl, women's bodies flaunted, an energy Lilianne was always faking her way through, pretending that she was part of a game she could never join.

In this room, even struggling through the steps, she began to feel a tight and cold place inside her loosen and warm, an uncoiling that reached outside of her, around the room, and connected her to these women and, through them, to her roots going back centuries, maybe even to one of the men who helped build the pyramids. Her blood. Her family.

Gilles's camera took it all in. The exuberance of the little girl, her steps stilted with youth but perfectly in tune with the older women, who performed so unselfconsciously, with such grace and beauty.

More and more often his lens found Lilianne, focused on her increasing immersion in the joyous communion the dancing brought her.

As he shot, his body seemed to grow stronger, become energized. When he moved the camera aside and she met his gaze, his eyes were lit with a hint of his old fire.

Seeing him transform made Lilianne stronger and more comfortable, less helpless in the face of his pain. Her dancing grew more fluid, more practiced, less self-conscious. She felt more sure of the way forward. Egypt was nothing if not photogenic, so much richer than Southport – the monuments, the history, the remarkable beauty and poverty, the joy and misery, the sere and the lush. Gilles's art would be his salvation, the path to work through his grief and his trauma and recover a life worth living.

In the meantime, she would stand with her family around her, and dance for his camera, dance for his recovery ... and dance for him.

Chapter 21

Two more hours into the party, while Lilianne chatted with her mother's childhood friend, Mounira, giggling over the rebellious daring the two had indulged in together – stealing cooling cookies from a neighbor, sneaking into movies, skipping school to sail down the river – Gilles started showing signs of strain. So far Lilianne's relatives had been champs when dealing with him. Questions were put until he showed signs of discomfort answering, then he was gracefully let out of the conversation to recharge or disappear who knew where in his mind.

But now his camera was down on the floor by his chair and his polite-interest face had drooped into the beginnings of a scowl. The bottles of Stella were piling up beside him, and he'd started impatiently shifting position on his chair every few seconds.

As much as she was admittedly enjoying herself – how much more relaxed and pleasant to get to know these people rather than the parade of embassy wives and business associates foisted on her so far – Lilianne turned and touched his arm. 'Hey, want to take a walk in an Egyptian jasmine field?'

He stood abruptly. 'Yes.'

They left the house without anyone questioning their departure.

The Abdallahs were far from the smothering family her mother had described, though Lilianne had no doubt her grandparents would be formidable opponents in a showdown.

Outside, the air had cooled to a pleasant temperature, skies light enough that they could make their way, but dark enough to feel intimate. They crossed the road and walked to the edge of the jasmine field, where the shiny-leafed bushes grew in neat rows.

'Come.' Gilles took her hand and plowed his way between the bushes into the field. There was a manic purpose to his movements; escaping the party certainly, but he also seemed in search of something she didn't understand and maybe he didn't either.

Then he stopped and began drawing in lungfuls of air. 'A flower must be open early somewhere, or budding. You smell it?'

'Yes.' A fragrant sweetness just this side of cloying, nothing Lilianne would want to wear as perfume. Jasmine grew in profusion as a vine around her mother's development in Florida, so she was familiar with the smell, but in this ancient land, with the sun setting behind them over fields as far as she could see, the scent diluted by the infinite sky dome above them, its fleeting aroma was exotic, entrancing, setting the scene for an Arabian Nights fantasy.

'I hope you didn't mind leaving the party,' Gilles said.

'It was fine.' She didn't sound convincing because she was lying.

'You could have stayed. I don't need babysitting.'

'Of course not.' Lilianne kept her tone light in response to his peevishness, reminding herself it wasn't his fault. 'I was dying to get out here.'

'Here's the thing, Lilianne.' He took her shoulders, making her look up at his extraordinarily handsome face, made haggard and haunted by demons and grief. 'You don't have to lie to pacify me. I know you were having a good time. If we are to make this ... whatever it is ... work, there has to be total honesty. If I'm being a pain in the ass, tell me. It might piss me off, but so what?'

'I don't want to be patronized, I don't want to be treated like a child. I lost ... so much. I ...' He scowled. 'I don't even know what I'm saying.'

She reached up and laid a hand against his jaw. 'You will find yourself again, Gilles, I swear. Maybe not the same man exactly. But enough of him to feel whole.'

'How do you know?

'I don't. I'm making it up. But it sounds good, doesn't it?'

He cracked up, and it was a joy to watch, his dark eyes more alive, smile brightening the awful shadows of his face. 'Right.'

'I believe it, though. Time heals. People go through all kinds of nightmares and come out the other side. I hate to tell you, but you're not that special.'

'No?' He grinned down at her. 'I was so sure.'

She smiled back, surprised to find herself feeling shy. Maybe it was the romantic setting – darkness, crickets singing, jasmine perfuming the air. 'It was nice seeing you taking pictures again.'

'Yes.' He turned to gaze off into the dimming distance. 'Pictures.'

'There are so many amazing places and people to photograph here.'

Gilles turned back, frowning. 'I thought we were going to Southport.'

'Are you in a hurry?'

'I don't know.'

'In Southport, there's also plenty. The whole damn country is photogenic. We can explore together, out west, the Grand Canyon, the California coast, and you can—'

The Jewel of Cairo

'What, take pictures of tourist spots that have been visited by thousands of people with thousands of cameras over the past three quarters of a century? You think I'd have something new to bring to that?'

She didn't know enough about photography or his talent to be able to answer. But she'd seen his drive and his dedication in Paris, where he was constantly summoned, interrupted, pulled away from his life, and jumped in with no complaint. That same admirable quality had been part of what scared Helen back to her dependable, always-around Kansas farm boy. 'You will find something to capture wherever you are. Life is more than politics and war.'

'Flowers and schoolchildren? Weddings and christenings?'

'Stop.' She put a hand to his mouth, taken aback by its smoothness and warmth. 'You're thinking too far ahead. You're too smart and too talented to waste yourself. What you will find, I don't know. It's not up to me to choose it for you. So stop acting like I'm supposed to give you the answers.'

'You think I . . .' He pressed his lips together, closed his eyes, nostrils flaring. Lilianne stood her ground, smelling the jasmine, listening to the crickets, so close to him in this beautiful spot, and waited him out. She couldn't – wouldn't – comfort him through every battle he had to face. 'Yes. You are right. I'm sorry. It's hard to be patient, to feel so . . . unsettled, so outside everything I know.'

'I'm sure.' Southport might suit him better, its comforting familiarity, its easy European-influenced luxury. He'd feel more at home there.

Annoyance burned in her chest. How damaging would it be for Gilles to stay in Egypt? Another month? Two months? Until fall? There was so much here to see, a type of culture and history with so much more depth than the one she could offer him in Connecticut.

Her mother's words came to her, how proud Dina was that Lilianne had put someone else before her own needs, as if she'd never done it before.

Maybe she hadn't. More accurately, maybe she'd never been in a position where she'd been forced to choose.

'All my life things have come so easily to me. I see that now. My family had money, I chose a career and did well. I met Helen . . .' Gilles looked up at the sky fading toward stars, his eyes forced wide to hide tears. 'You too, I think. We haven't known what it is to suffer.'

Lilianne felt her smile grow tight. On paper, yes, her life had been easy. Silver-spoon upbringing, the best schools, professional success at a young age . . . but a personal hell for as long as she could remember. Feeling damaged, with no word for what was wrong with her, no one else she could share her mysterious abnormality with. Not nearly as bad as being bombed on the job, but not easy. 'You're right.'

'In Lebanon . . .' Gilles shook his head. Shook it again.

She put her arms around him as he cried, hoping this was a good sign, a therapeutic sign, letting the grief out instead of holding it in to destroy him. She held him until his body stopped shaking and the quiet sobs eased. Somewhere nearby, a cricket must have stopped chirping, because it started up again, surprisingly loud for such a small creature.

'Lilianne.'

'Yes.' Her voice was husky in the darkness.

'I hope your blouse isn't silk.'

They shared near-silent laughter until it ran out, then walked together through the sweet-smelling jasmine toward a destination neither of them was in a hurry to define.

Chapter 22

Present day

Beezy: *Are you in love with your works-with-his-hands landlord yet?*
Sophie: *Be reasonable. He is awfully nice, though.*
Beezy: *I knew it! I'm going to lose you to him!*
Sophie: *Go play pickleball.*

Two days after the walk with her cousin, Sophie pulled up to Owen's little cottage wondering if she were going to collapse. It was hot for one thing. Second, she didn't think she'd ever been this tired. Starting a new job, coping with Lizzie's continued hostility, starting to get even the tiniest sense of the hill these women were in the process of climbing, trying to learn more about how she fit with a newly discovered cousin who was massively busy – quite the load to be carrying.

Owen was outside his barn, splitting wood with an ax, his back to her, T-shirt drenched with sweat. Her stomach gave a little fizz of excitement. She hadn't bothered him for the last few days, wanting to give the poor guy a break, but she got such a kick out of talking to him.

She parked her Prius and emerged into the muggy air, energy returning, along with her curiosity. He probably wouldn't hear her if she shouted, so she walked toward him, impressed with the strength of his arms and with his aim. Sophie had tried splitting wood once, on a camping trip, after her dad made it seem so easy. That had been plenty. She wasn't a big fan of continuing to look stupid and ineffectual.

Close up, she noticed the change, waited until he was between logs to speak. 'Hey, that looks thrilling.'

He turned, taking off his fogged-up safety glasses and his ball cap to wipe his forehead. Even somewhat prepared, Sophie gasped.

Owen was clean-shaven, and had cut his hair in a style not that different from hers, shorter sides, longer on top. He had a fantastic face, a manly man's chin, and the good cheekbones, now exposed, showed clean hollows underneath. His mouth, cleared of its bushy surroundings, was full and sensual.

He looked like a model. Well, no. Not pretty enough, his features not quite regular, nose a little crooked, one eye slightly larger than the other, which she liked. So okay, he looked like an irregular model.

'Owen! You're gorgeous.'

'Hmm.' He wiped his streaming forehead on his sleeve.

Sophie frowned up at his stunning self, fighting a blush. 'Why are you chopping wood on the hottest day of the month?'

'Busy this morning.' He put a hand to his hip. 'Good way to work out aggression.'

Her eyebrows flew up. 'Are you aggressive?'

'Not generally.'

'But today . . .'

'Aggression, frustration, worries, all of it goes away when you're chopping wood.'

'I'm sorry you're having that kind of day.' She wondered if

his mood had something to do with his phantom wife, but she'd promised to avoid that topic. 'You look . . . totally hot.'

'Yeah.' He tugged on his wet shirt. 'Splitting wood's hard work.'

Sophie giggled stupidly. 'That's not what I meant.'

'I knew what you meant.' He sounded disgusted, which made her want to smile. 'It's too hot for that much hair.'

'I'm delighted.'

He laughed, though unwillingly.

She'd wanted to ask if he'd have a drink with her, but his transformation had made her stupid-shy. *For heaven's sakes, Sophie, you're forty-five, get a—*

'Want to have dinner?'

Sophie nearly swallowed her tongue. 'Sure.'

'Thought I'd grill some ribs. There's plenty to share.'

'I love ribs. I can bring . . .' What could she bring? 'Beer?'

'Got some.'

She went over the contents of her refrigerator. 'Coleslaw?'

'Got that too.'

'Potato salad?'

'Now you're talking.' He gestured to the small stack of unsplit logs lying next to him. 'Let me finish here, clean up and get ready. About forty-five minutes?'

'Sure.' She backed nervously away, undone by the transition from Owen the Mountain Man, for whom she felt great affection, to Owen the Hunk o' Prime.

Unnerving, and . . . sort of disappointing. She'd grown fond of his barbarian persona, was comfortable with that guy.

No, no, he was the same man. Sophie was being shallow judging him by his looks – though usually judging a guy unfairly by his looks worked the other way.

Inside the cottage, she changed into a sundress. Shorts

tempted her, but sundresses were cooler. Right? Nothing to do with worrying about how the Adonis outside would react to her imperfect legs. Speaking of, she should find a time and place to exercise. Busy days at work, but maybe early in the morning? Though at that hour, she'd rather do just about anything else.

Stop.

Why was she worrying about her body and exercise all of a sudden? Because Owen was now handsome?

Defiantly, she pulled off the sundress and dug out her ugliest, comfiest pair of shorts, light blue, puffy and unflattering, and a white tank top that did not hide the danglies she'd acquired on her hitherto sleek arms since she'd stopped being Peter's Perfect Wife.

Downstairs in the cottage's kitchen, she peeled and cubed potatoes and put them on to boil, then whipped up a mayonnaise-yogurt dressing with plenty of mustard, celery, chopped pickle and parsley, wishing she had access to an herb garden. She and Peter had planted a huge bed behind their house, and her balcony in Southport might possibly break off and smash into the parking lot under the weight of the various pots she'd stacked there.

When the potatoes were tender, she drained them and put them in the serving bowl, then doused the steaming cubes with red wine vinegar and salt, flavors they'd absorb as they cooled.

Dessert, something men always wanted but never planned, the most important part of a meal. No time to make cookies, but she had vanilla ice cream in her little freezer, and some fresh raspberries. Plenty of time for her ten-minute chocolate sauce.

Pan on the burner at its lowest setting, she melted unsweetened chocolate in plain water, then added sugar until it melted into lush, dark gorgeousness. Off heat, she added butter, salt and vanilla. Done and never-fail delicious.

A peek outside showed Owen showered, changed and busy at the grill next to his house. He'd already set up a folding table and a couple of chairs.

She mixed the potatoes with the dressing and garnishes, tasted and added more salt, then covered the chocolate sauce pan to sit on the stove until they were ready for it.

Outside, a napping breeze had woken itself up to provide natural cooling. The setting sun would help as well. Owen's ribs – the ones on the grill – looked delicious and smelled better. He must have baked them earlier to finish outside for that all-important smoky-char flavor. Sophie set the potato salad on the table and faced him, determined to behave as normally as possible.

Except he looked so different, she couldn't think of a thing to say. Which never, ever happened to her – except around handsome men.

'How are things going at Asphalia House?'

'Busy. Complicated. Emotional. Exhausting. So far, great.' She found it easier to talk to the grilling ribs instead of him. 'You were right, it was a mistake to change everything the second I walked in. It took a while to talk Cousin Lily down from the ledge.'

'But you did.'

'I did.' She stole a glance at him, then decided the ribs were still safer to talk to. Did he say he had beer?

'So I was wrong and you were right. Again.' She watched him expertly handle a flare-up, sick with disappointment. Their usual easy camaraderie wasn't there, because he was suddenly hot, and she always turned into a self-conscious dork around hot guys. It had taken four dates before she could do more than slobber over Peter.

She resolved to look Owen straight in the eye and forget

all this nonsense about him being a slightly imperfect Greek god come to life. 'Good news. I got the okay for you to be a field trip, even though you might not technically have agreed to the idea.'

'Yeah, I don't think I did.' He didn't look angry, which gave her courage to pursue the idea.

'I take it Lily Anne hasn't contacted you yet? I gave her your number.'

'Not yet. Am I really doing this?'

'Did you really not want to? You absolutely don't have to. Seriously. You know me, rushing off half . . .' She couldn't say 'cocked' in front of him.

'I can come up with something.'

'Really? Thank you. That's really great. Really. Did you say you had beer?'

'There.' He pointed to a small cooler next to the table.

Sophie pounced on it and turned over the cans sitting in ice. Not from any brewery she recognized. 'Want one?'

'I'll take a Rutland Red.'

'Rutland Red.' She extracted a Lake Monster Lager for herself. 'Local?'

'Brewed right here in town.'

'Nice.' She handed the beer to him, staring in the vicinity of his waist, then noticed something she hadn't before. 'You don't wear a wedding ring?'

He popped the top of his beer. 'Because I'm not married.'

Sophie snapped to attention, eyes strained open to their limit. 'You're not married?'

'No.' He looked sheepish. 'I was planning to tell you tonight.'

He wasn't married. Holy moly. It made more sense than a wife who wasn't there and whom he didn't want to talk about, but . . . 'Why didn't you tell me before?'

His turn to contemplate the ribs. 'It's like how you didn't tell your cousin that she was your cousin right away.'

Sophie blinked. Being on this end of that philosophy sucked. She certainly couldn't object, not that she had any grounds to. 'Were you ever married?'

'Yes.'

'To the pediatrician.'

'Yes.'

'With the ill mother.'

'She was ill once.'

Sophie frowned at him, trying to process this new information. 'Do you wish you were still married?'

'Not to her.'

Still not making sense. 'So why the fib?'

He poked the ribs with his spatula, maybe a little viciously. 'A few years after I started renting out the cottage, I had a tenant who . . . became a problem, including breaking into my house and climbing into my bed. From then on, to all renters I was married.'

'I see.' What she'd been about to say, jokingly, was 'So you trust that I won't climb into your bed? You fool!' but just the idea of climbing into his bed was making her blush. 'What went wrong with your marriage?'

He turned and gave her a look. The same I-can't-believe-you-said-that look he'd been giving her all along, but . . . it looked so much hotter now.

'What?' She feigned outrage. 'I was curious. Just tell me it's none of my business. I don't mind. I'm happy to tell you everything that went wrong in my marriage to Peter if you want.'

'Peter was a jerk.'

'I wasn't perfect enough for him.'

They spoke at the same time, then glared suspiciously at each other.

'I was being flip.'

'I was kidding.'

They grinned and chuckled uneasily, and something relaxed inside Sophie that made her more optimistic. He was still Owen, and she could be friends with a gorgeous guy same as a less gorgeous one, it would just take a little more effort. And restraint.

They sat down and heaped their plates with ribs, coleslaw and potato salad. Neither of them had made much progress on their beers, so the same cans stayed on the table. The ribs were moan-inducing, tender and chewy at the same time, flavored with sweet and warm spices and smoke. They ate for a few minutes trying to identify the flavors in each other's food, hitting some, missing others.

'Since you asked, my marriage . . .' Owen put another rib bone on top of the pile on his plate and wiped his hands on a paper towel, 'was a mistake.'

Sophie bit into her third rib, not caring that she was eating heartily and that sauce and grease were coating her lips and cheeks, remembering dates during which she'd cut her food into minuscule pieces to make sure her mouth wasn't too full, that she didn't chew too long and that her lipstick didn't smudge.

Maybe Cathy 'the Catheter' had been right and Sophie had let herself go, but it felt damn good.

'A mistake how?'

'She thought she wanted life in the Vermont hills with an artisan, but actually she wanted life in the big city with a rich husband.'

'How could she get that so wrong? That's like opposite.'

'You've never been wrong about what you wanted?'

'Not that badly.'

The Jewel of Cairo

'Peter?'

She put down her fork. 'No. Up to the last day, if he'd said, "Oh my God, I made a terrible mistake, it's still you now and forever", I would have been thrilled.'

'With a jerk.'

She sighed. 'We had a great life. The only problem was that I couldn't be myself, or what he wanted.'

'Mm, yeah, that's pretty big.' Owen licked his fingers, which delighted her because it gave her permission to do the same.

'So did your wife remarry?'

'Yup.' He spoke curtly. 'My brother.'

'Owen!' She gaped at him, noticing he had sauce on his face, too. Also delightful. 'That's horrible.'

'It was, but not anymore. They're happy. He's a lawyer. He lives in the city. He checked all her boxes.'

'Peter checked all my boxes too.'

'Maybe you had the wrong boxes.'

'How can you have the wrong boxes? They're your boxes.'

'I don't know. Maybe they were the boxes you thought you should have, or maybe they were someone else's boxes. Bottom line, she and I didn't fit, and they do.'

'Peter remarried too. She's high-powered like he is. And also perfect.'

Owen snorted. 'Jerk.'

Sophie giggled. The beer was good and she was probably going to have another. 'You shouldn't call him that.'

'Are you still in love with him?'

'No. No. Not at all. Maybe. I don't know. Or actually . . .' She sat for a while, wanting to get this right. 'I want us to have worked out. I'm sad that I couldn't make him happy. But . . . I do think I realize how impossible that would be. It was just . . . such a beautiful life.'

'Sounds like you miss the life more than him.'

'Maybe I do. Are you still in love with ... Wait, does she have a name?'

'Abby.'

'Abby.' She looked at him speculatively, trying not to be swayed by his recent overabundance of attractiveness. 'No, you don't belong with an Abby.'

He rolled his eyes. 'If you say so.'

'So are you still in love with her?'

'No.'

'How do you know?'

'Because I'm genuinely glad she's happy with someone else.'

Sophie made a face. 'That's way too mature for me.'

He laughed. 'You'll get there. Or maybe not, I don't know. Maybe you'll die with an altar in your room below Peter's picture.'

Sophie nearly choked on her beer. 'If I do, you have permission to split me stem to stern like one of your logs.'

'I'll remember that.'

They didn't eat the ice cream until the light was fading, and didn't break up the party until it became time to find another source of light, which seemed like too much of a commitment to the evening and to each other.

Sophie retrieved her mostly eaten potato salad, her chocolate sauce and the dish and flatware that came from the cottage. Owen did the same, and they called goodnights and went in opposite directions.

In the little house, cool and dry thanks to the air-conditioning, she washed and put away and got ready for bed, humming, feeling content. She got into the beautiful bed Owen had made and settled in.

Little vignettes from her time with Peter spooled through

The Jewel of Cairo

her brain – marriage flashing before her eyes. The beautiful parties they gave, at which she felt like she and Peter were faux-royalty, seeing to their guests' comfort, making sure everyone had something to drink and someone to talk to. The pride in his eyes for what she'd accomplished when the last person stumbled off at some ungodly hour. The way she'd laugh in bed at his parodies of people's behavior until she was crying and gasping, then he'd kiss her and kiss her, tasting of gin and Peter, and they'd make love with passion and excitement the way they had when they first met. Still, after all those years together.

The next day there would be relief that everything had gone off well. The tension leading up to the event, the details, the planning, the adjustments and worrying, the imposter syndrome that made her stress to the point of vomiting – no, she wasn't pregnant that time either; she was *never* pregnant. But it was all worth it! Worth it for that glorious Audrey Hepburn in *My Fair Lady* triumph, and that sense that she and Peter were the beautiful couple that made wonderful things happen.

The dinner parties they hosted, the country club events, the clients and colleagues she'd entertained, the volunteering she'd done. He'd been so proud of her. His wife.

When had all that glitter and glee become not enough for him? When had *Sophie* become not enough for him?

So gradually that she hadn't noticed, or didn't want to notice.

Their lovemaking became less frequent. Sophie thought she'd understood. They'd come to associate sex too strongly with eggs and sperm, the baby-making that wasn't happening. Getting her period had become a source of monthly agony. Coping with friends' news of expecting little ones had become agony. The fertility treatments, the constant disappointment, agony.

But the worst agony was Peter's announcement one evening

that they should stop trying. That it wasn't worth it. That he couldn't be any kind of good father being away from home so much. He knew, because his own father had been away all the time, and it was hard on him.

After all that trying, all that expense and intervention and misery, he hadn't wanted a kid in the first place?

Sophie's world had fallen apart, lost its meaning. Without the fantasy of a baby to hold and care for, all those days by herself in the house became unbearably lonely, unbearably purposeless.

It came to her now, with certainty and a loud gasp that made her bolt upright in bed, that the reason Peter hadn't wanted a baby with her was because he was already involved with Lexy and wanted hers instead. Which he'd gotten. And after his devastating announcement, what had Sophie done? Blamed herself for pushing him away by wanting children too much.

God, she'd been a fool.

Crying didn't help, it would only make her look swollen-eyed and blotchy, but she couldn't stop, and didn't try.

It was a long cry. Many tissues gave their lives over that cry. Surprising after so long. She'd been through therapy, she thought she'd put all this to bed.

Divorce was the gift that kept on giving.

When the crying was over, she got out of bed and drank a glass of water. The light outside the bathroom window was brighter than it should be at this hour. She peered out and drew in an ecstatic breath. Moonlight. Bathing the yard and woods with its pure white reflected light, making long, sharp tree shadows into irregular fence-stripes on the lawn.

The sight was calming, reassuring. Total darkness would have been too oppressive for her mood.

She went back into her room and pulled up the blinds, gently took the Fabergé egg out of her underwear and brought it over to the window. With careful fingers she twisted the shadowy falcon to open the enameled petals. The jewels glittered mysteriously in the color-draining light. The king and queen sat regally as if on display during a parade, the queen eternally cradling her ruby bouquet, now dark gray, the king holding his oddly serrated scepter, turned white.

Such power this exquisite gem represented. Its discovery would be in every paper, its sale would produce millions. People the world over would gnash their teeth at the extraordinary luck of the find, a one-in-a-million lightning bolt of good fortune, and why couldn't it have happened to *them*? She pictured again her fantasy house on the coast in Southport, where she'd rebuild a glamorous life in the place she loved best, totally independent of her parents and of Peter.

Maybe it was her mood, or the grief, maybe it was fatigue, or being so far from her normal circles and routines, but tonight the idea didn't bring her the same stab of joy or the same high-as-a-kite excitement.

Instead, she found herself thinking about Alma Pihl, the artist who'd designed this egg among others, including two for tsar Nicholas II, the only woman given that honor.

Imagine being so young, entirely self-taught, yet so talented. Being able to conceive of such distinctive beauty and ingenuity, not just once, but over and over at the highest level amid the highest stakes. Hired by Fabergé at age twenty as a draftsman, she was given her first major commission at twenty-three, her first Imperial egg commission at twenty-five and her second the following year. Only a few years later, when she must have felt on top of the world, the Russian Revolution forced her out of her job, and eventually out of her country.

Sophie took in a long breath, humbled by the idea of such a remarkable genius overcoming tremendous odds to succeed beyond her dreams, then having to face the abrupt erasure of what she was born to do. An inspiring lesson in survival after a life change, that made what Sophie went through look like a slight headache.

Closing the precious petals, she gently replaced the priceless miracle in the dresser and went back to bed, gazing out at the moonlight until she fell asleep.

Chapter 23

Sunday, May 23th, 1976

Safiya lay in her bed, thinking. John Baker. Lilianne Maxwell. She clung to the names Lilianne had whispered, even while feeling they were keys to a locked room with no doors. What use could either of these people be to her? Yet she made sure she repeated them, the syllables strange and heavy on her tongue. John Ba-ker. Lil-i-anne Max-well.

How Safiya had longed to tell the truth when Lilianne asked if Sami was good to her. The need for someone to be on her side in this hellish loneliness had nearly overwhelmed her. But she knew better than to trust a kind face. Years of suffering and service had taught her to control her emotions.

She wondered how Lilianne had sensed Sami's true nature. Maybe something to do with whatever she'd hidden under the table. Or maybe because in spite of her smiles, Lilianne was sad. Connie, the short, giggly girl, also, though she hid it so well even she might not know it. Each must have lost something precious. If life was different, Safiya and Lilianne might have found more in common than sadness. Maybe they could have been friends.

Useless to wonder. The world wouldn't change by her wanting.

She stretched and turned over, restless tonight, unable to sleep. She tried to imagine Amon and Bebti, asleep in their shared bed. They changed so much between her visits. Yet when they slept, she could still see the babies they used to be. How she wished she could snuggle up next to them.

The apartment door opened. Safiya stiffened. Sami was back early – for him. She prayed he was full enough of liquor that he would go straight to his room and not bother her.

'*Ya*, Sami?'

Safiya shot up in bed, clutching the blankets to her chest. She knew that voice, that thin rasp. Sami kept company with low people – she didn't care how many fine clothes they wore, she could tell when people were low. Sami would sell his own child if it would help him get more money. Too many men were like this, always after more money and more power. Deprived of both, they shriveled into impotence, like their male parts when they finished.

But this man was the worst, the fat one with the eyes of Iblis, the devil. Abraam Al-Kalib.

'Not here. He left the restaurant ten minutes ago. He'll be back soon.' The other voice she also recognized, the voice of Al-Kalib's driver, one of the largest men she'd ever seen. He could kill her with one hand. 'Where's the maid?'

Safiya huddled back under her blanket, praying neither would come looking for her. This job would no longer be worth the money if people like these were involved. The diamond stealing was one thing. She had no doubt these two were part of that, and who knew how much more. But she wouldn't stay around for danger.

John Baker. Lilianne Maxwell.

Behind her she heard her bedroom door opening, inch by creaky inch. She dragged the sheet to cover her hair, nearly choking on her terror, trying to breathe slowly and evenly from stuttering lungs.

'She's in here. In bed.'

Safiya turned toward the massive shape nearly blocking the entire doorway. No point pretending to be asleep.

The giant man smiled. He was as ugly as he was large, blunt features like a baboon, but his eyes were not cruel. 'Sorry to scare you. We're waiting for Sami. You need anything?'

She shook her head, afraid she'd vomit from the fear.

'I'll get you a glass of water.' He disappeared.

Safiya leapt from the bed and grabbed her *hijab* and blouse, covered her hair first, then stuffed both arms into the sleeves and did her best with the buttons, fingers shaking.

Footsteps sounded his return. No time to put on more clothes. Praying to Allah, she jumped back into the bed and covered her lower half.

He came back into her room, carrying a small glass a quarter full. The water looked odd. Cloudy. Not what came out of the tap. 'Here.'

'No. Thank you.' She could barely speak. 'I am not thirsty.'

His smile was gentle. 'Yes. You are.'

She couldn't begin to think of a way out. He was three times her size, many more times her strength. If her cries in this room could bring help, it would have come long ago.

She struggled to remain still, body buzzing with the need to escape, even knowing it would be futile. Her death would be a tragedy for her sons, all she wanted to live for. 'What's in the water?'

'A drug to help you sleep.' The brown eyes were kind, holding none of the lust in Sami's. 'While we talk out there. I crushed the pill so it would work faster. It will be bitter in so little water, but easier to get down.'

Not her death yet, then, though he could be lying. Men like him lied so often it would not even make him blink.

She took the glass. How many times in this house would she have to surrender, how many times would she have to do what the men around her wanted?

Enough. She'd had enough. No money was worth this.

John Baker. Lilianne Maxwell. Repetition could teach even a donkey.

She tipped the liquid into her mouth, grateful there wasn't much.

'Good girl.' He took the glass back, put it on the room's tiny dresser and left, closing the door gently behind him.

Safiya waited five eternal seconds, then scrambled for the glass and spit the drugged water back into it.

A small victory, one she might easily regret.

She dressed the rest of the way quickly, in case they heard her, having no idea how fast the drug was supposed to work, then eased herself back into bed.

There was nothing to hear, no conversation, just two men of evil waiting for Sami.

What if they tortured him? She would have to lie here listening to his screams and pretend to be asleep. What if they killed him? What if they left his body and put the blame on her?

She could not think like this. He who looked for ghosts would find them. She would trust Allah, close her eyes and lose herself in prayer.

What felt like hours later, the apartment door opened again, to Sami's surprised voice. '*Ya Salaam*, how did you get in here? What is it? What's happened?'

'You're a fool, Sami.'

He laughed, a carefree sound. 'I've never denied that. Welcome, welcome, what can I offer you. Whisky? I can wake Safiya if you're hun—'

'I returned to Egypt yesterday from a trip. And I heard

unpleasant news, Sami.' Abraam's voice dripped disdain. 'Your blonde American.'

'What about her?' Sami's voice sharpened. 'What about my blonde American?'

'CIA.'

Safiya gasped. She knew what CIA was from the BBC programs her father listened to on the radio. They could get the stations from Aswan.

'Lilianne? *Lilianne?*' Sami's laughter turned nervous. 'That's impossible.'

'Your dick has put us in danger.' The deep voice of the driver. Safiya gasped again. How could a driver speak such words around his employer?

'Sadly, gentlemen, my dick has nothing to do with Lilianne. To her I am merely the kind Egyptian showing her my beautiful city. And I don't believe she's CIA, or at least not targeting—'

'I saw first-hand.' The driver again.

'First-hand? What does that—'

'None of your business.' The devil spoke this time. 'It's not for you to question his proof. I am satisfied.'

'It's not possible.' Sami was less sure this time, thinking it over. 'I am of no value to—'

'What have you told her? About us? The necklace? The plans?'

'Nothing about the plans.' Footsteps sounded, someone pacing, probably Sami. He was afraid. A meow sounded from Sami's spoiled cat, comical if this wasn't so serious. 'I showed her the necklace, why shouldn't I? It's beautiful. I'm not ashamed of my work.'

'Risky.' The driver said this.

'Why risky? She saw gemstones in a jeweler's shop.' More pacing. 'What do I have that they would want?'

'Me, you piece of garbage, me!' The devil snarled. 'She saw me stop and speak with you on the street. She must have gone running to headquarters with that. What did you tell her about me?'

'That you were the most powerful man in Cairo.' Sami's voice rang with confident truth. 'Nothing more.'

'I'd like to believe you.'

'Abraam, my God, of course you can believe me. I don't lie to you.' Again, total certainty. 'I don't betray my friends. Unlike some.'

He meant Lilianne. Safiya started to pray.

'I don't like CIA around my people, Sami.'

'*You* don't like it? What about me?' Sami's voice thinned, rose higher. Dread gathered in the pit of Safiya's abdomen. His fear was making him angry. She knew what happened when he was angry. 'She betrayed me. Pretending to be my friend. Pretending to enjoy our time together when it was actually her job.'

'She needs to be dealt with.'

Safiya started to shake. The small machine Lilianne had put under the table, was it listening? She'd worried at first that it would explode, until she felt the goodness in Lilianne.

'Done, and soon.' Noises of the men getting up, walking toward the door, heavy steps both of them, one tall, one fat. 'You need to be more careful, Sami. I worry about you.'

The soft voice made Safiya recoil.

Sami didn't respond.

The door closed.

A growl sounded in the living room, followed by a torrent of filthy words, words Safiya wished Allah could clear from her mind.

She heard more pacing, shoes clunking on the floor, swishing on the carpets, another meow. 'She's put me in an impossible position, damn her!'

The Jewel of Cairo

Safiya lay madly calculating what to do, how to protect herself from his rage, how she might help Lilianne, who had been kind to her.

She scoffed at herself. What could *she* do? She had no power, and she had to stay alive for her sons. She couldn't get involved.

Sami's pacing accelerated. He'd come in soon. If he found her awake, he'd know she'd heard everything. Her punishment would be worse.

Quickly.

She stole out of bed and picked up the glass from the little dresser containing the few things she'd brought with her from Nagaa ad Disah. Praising Allah for providing her with an escape, she drained it.

Chapter 24

Monday, May 24, 1976

Lilianne stood outside her grandparents' building, holding herself tightly, trying not to think of that day two weeks earlier when she'd stood here racked with similar nerves but for different reasons. Then she'd been here to say hello. This time, goodbye.

Yesterday afternoon, Braheem and Zahra had driven her and Gilles back into Cairo from their farm. The morning after the party had been a day of talking and coffee, more food and a chance to relax and get to know her grandparents. The bulk of the relatives had cleared out not long after Gilles and Lilianne came back in from their walk Saturday night. While Gilles had gone straight to bed, Lilianne had stayed up with her family, trading stories about their lives on different continents, in different cultures. There was much made of Lilianne's blonde hair and blue eyes, including jokes that she was adopted, though Zahra had sworn there was a blonde back somewhere in their family line. The teasing, well meant, would have been funnier if Lilianne hadn't just fooled herself into feeling she belonged to Egypt and to the Abdallahs. To them she was still the outsider.

Her grandparents had dropped them off at her apartment building with warm hugs, promises of future evenings together and repeated urging to call if she needed anything, anything at all. None of their love and support felt smothering. Perhaps they'd changed since Lilianne's mother had lived here. Or it could be the difference between being a child and a grandchild. Lilianne could remember rolling her eyes plenty of times over parental behavior that seemed utterly inoffensive to her friends.

By the time she and Gilles, exhausted but calm now, had waved her grandparents off, Lilianne had been certain she wanted to stay on in Cairo, though still not quite convinced it would be best for Gilles.

'Lilianne Maxwell?' A suited man had emerged from a black car flashing a State Department ID. 'We've been trying to find you. We have reason to believe you're in danger.'

Having been on the verge of deciding to stay longer, having waited months, *months* to contact her family, Lilianne was now being yanked prematurely home on a flight to New York's JFK airport. A visa had magically appeared for Gilles so he could accompany her. She had come here alone today in spite of the supposed risk, anxious that she not mysteriously disappear from her grandparents' lives as her mother had.

One day she'd come back, assuming no one was after her, or whatever the State Department worried about after her role as an agent had been discovered. She couldn't imagine Sami harming her in any way, but her poking around might have riled up Al-Kalib and his band of merry thugs. She'd bet Al-Kalib's driver had reported back to his boss after seeing her in the CIA offices.

Going home now was a frustrating defeat, leaving the job of exploring this culture and her place in it unfinished. Nor would she be able to help Safiya escape from Sami's abuse into a better situation. Instead, a meek return to the comfortable and the ordinary, letting several people down in the process.

Nailah answered the bell, let out a cry of delight on hearing Lilianne's voice and buzzed her into the building. Lilianne took the stairs two at a time, telling herself to keep this brief, to keep the pain more bearable for everyone.

Zahra was waiting for her at the open apartment door. Just the sight of her plump, beaming grandmother made Lilianne want to cry.

'Hello, Lilianne, *ya hayati*.' Her grandmother grabbed her, kissing both of her cheeks repeatedly, while Nailah beamed in the background, as if neither of them had laid eyes on her in weeks. 'Come in, come in, I'm so glad you are here. I have something to show you. Nailah, coffee.'

'Thank you. Unfortunately, I can't—'

'Come, come. Come inside, welcome, welcome.' Zahra guided her into the living room. 'After I got home yesterday, Braheem and I went hunting, and found picture albums to show you. Here, look.'

The coffee table was laden with enormous albums, some of whose pages of thick black paper indicated they'd been filled generations ago. There was no way Lilianne would be able to stay and see them all.

'Sit, sit. Are you hungry?'

'No, no. You fed me so much over the weekend. I can't—'

'You're much too thin, you should eat. Nailah!'

'I'm here, I'm here.' The older woman shuffled in carrying an enormous tray with coffee, a bowl of *ful medames* – the ubiquitous and addictive Egyptian dish of mashed fava beans – along with a platter of dates, dried apricots and figs and a plate of miniature pistachio baklavas that looked like bird nests.

Lilianne groaned silently. Not only would it be difficult to extract herself as quickly as she wanted, it would be even harder now to go back to the country of Doritos and Devil Dogs.

'First,' Zahra sat beside Lilianne and opened an album over their laps, 'I thought you might like to see pictures of your mother as a child.'

Lilianne opened her mouth to protest, but she couldn't resist, so she watched and listened, eating when prompted – frequently! – her need to depart weighing on her chest.

The pictures were wonderful, page after page of Dina Abdallah, alone or with her brothers, evolving from a black-haired infant to a chubby toddler, then from a wiry child to a curvaceous teenager. Only a few photos showed her familiar smile – when the camera had caught her playing with her brothers or one of the family's cats. In pose after pose, she stared stonily at the camera, curious in babyhood, suspicious in childhood, defiant on the cusp of adulthood.

Zahra stopped at a picture of Dina standing next to a stylish woman whose hair was twisted in a gravity-defying bun and who carried a cigarette in a holder. Around Dina's shoulders, a fox fur, which she clutched possessively under her chin with both hands.

'This is Sabra, my sister, after her marriage and after she moved to Jordan, visiting us after a trip to Paris.' Zahra made a cluck of disapproval. 'Look at this fur! In Egypt! She was unbearable, lording it over all of us, boasting of Parisian palaces and New York theaters and caviar and champagne and freedom. As if freedom was there for the taking for every woman, no matter her circumstances, as long as she didn't live in Egypt.

'Your mother found her own god that day.' Zahra's face creased in dismay. 'I'd never seen such shining eyes. On my own daughter. After that, she was lost to me, to all of us.'

Lilianne stared at the picture, Dina's face so young, so smooth, hair pulled back in a simple ponytail, unpainted lips parted in a joyous smile not seen in any of the other pictures. The day that gave the rest of her life focus, caught in this snapshot.

What would her mother say if she saw it now? Dina Maxwell did not seem like a woman with regrets. Would she have made the same choices at the same points if she could do it all again? Would *she* be happy with what she'd leave behind after her death?

'Braheem and I thought she was too young to make such a decision for herself. We came down hard.' Zahra drew a plump finger over the figure of her fur-trimmed daughter in Sabra's embrace. 'But in forbidding her from thinking about leaving, or talking about leaving, we created our own tragedy.'

Lilianne was torn between sympathy for her mother's need to live the way she saw fit and her grandmother's grief for a mistake she now saw clearly.

'Did you ever try to contact her? After she left?' Lilianne kept her voice neutral, not wanting to imply any blame, knowing Mom had never tried to mend the breach either.

Zahra closed the album. 'All we knew was that she moved to the US. What state? What city? Your country is infinite and we had no idea where to look. When she married, of course she'd have changed her name. She was lost to us.'

'I'm sorry.' Lilianne pressed her lips together. A lump grew in her throat.

'Tell me about Dina.' Zahra's voice was low, full of pain. 'Tell me about your mother.'

Lilianne took a sip of coffee, conjuring up a slideshow in her head. Mom playing tennis in white culottes with white terry sweatbands on her head and wrists. Mom presiding over parties at their house. Mom consulting with decorators, surrounded by paint samples and fabric swatches. Mom sitting in tight-lipped denial in the car on the way to yet another doctor or psychiatrist appointment for her less than perfect daughter. The top of her head behind the newspaper in the mornings.

'She loves her life in the US. She's very happy there. My father is well off and she's been financially secure. She has plenty of friends and enjoys throwing big parties. She does a lot of volunteering around Southport, our town. She gardens, plays tennis, goes sailing. She and my father travel a great deal . . .'

'Ah yes.' Her grandmother looked pained. 'The life of a royal lady. This is what she wanted. This is what we couldn't give her. My sister was the same, ignoring nice boys from our village, always on the lookout for older, successful men. When does money become more important than everyone you love? More important than your country, more important even than your family? Certainly nothing we taught her. I don't understand.'

'Maybe it was always in her. Something in her basic wiring.'

'Maybe.' Zahra clasped Lilianne's hand in hers. 'Tell me, *habibti*. What did she say about us? What did she tell you?'

Lilianne sighed, wishing she could answer this differently. 'Not much, Teta. She just said she'd left Egypt young and that she no longer kept in touch with you and Braheem. She mentioned her brothers and Nailah, and when I asked, she showed pictures she must have brought with her. You and Braheem cutting the cake at your wedding, and one of the whole family, including your parents.'

'Is that where those went? I searched for years!' Zahra managed to look both incensed and delighted. 'And when she knew you were coming to Cairo? What then?'

Lilianne hesitated, thinking of the letter Mom had sent warning her. Why had she taken her mother's word over something she could find out for herself?

Connie's voice spoke in her ear. *Because you were chicken.*

'Mom didn't object to me contacting you. Not at all. I don't know if her attitudes have changed, though, as yours have.' Lilianne checked herself. Why didn't she know? 'I'll ask her. I'll ask her a lot of things.'

'Good.' Zahra patted her hand. 'Even attitudes about ourselves can change. You would make a great wife and mother, Lilianne. I've seen you with Gilles. Very patient, very sweet, anyone can see how much you love him.'

Lilianne bristled. 'He's a friend.'

'So?' Zahra shrugged. 'Can we not love our friends?'

This was forbidden territory. Even for family. Lilianne put her empty cup back on its saucer. 'Zahra, I'm afraid I have to go back to the US much sooner than I expected.'

'How sooner?'

'This afternoon.'

'*Yih!*' Her grandmother's dark eyes opened wide. 'An emergency? What has happened?'

'A combination of things. I'll be able to help Gilles better in my own town. It's quieter, and I know the doctors.' She rushed on, seeing Zahra about to object. 'Cairo is too much like Beirut. He needs to feel he's starting over. Then a work issue came up, and my father needs my help. He's moving and . . . very busy.'

She stopped talking. The reasons had sounded much more convincing in her head.

'Ah, no, *hayati*.' Zahra put her hand to her heart, eyes filling with tears. 'We just found you.'

'I know, I know.' Lilianne touched her shoulder. 'It's not my choice. I was planning to stay.'

'Yes. Yes. I understand.' Her grandmother patted her chest, looking stricken. 'I feel I'm losing my daughter all over again. Braheem will be devastated.'

'I'm sorry.' Lilianne looked down, unable to bear the distress in Zahra's eyes. 'I want you to come to the US. You and Braheem and Nailah. If money is an issue, I will pay. Gilles will need time to be calm in one place, but when he's feeling better, I want to show you my home. And I want you to be able to see Mom again.'

Zahra's surprise turned into a hesitant smile that bloomed into certainty. 'Yes. Yes, *hayati*, we must do this. We know where our daughter is now, we must see her. If the mountain won't come to Muhammad, then Muhammad must go to the mountain.'

'Settled.' Lilianne moved to stand up.

'One more thing before you go.' Zahra leaned forward and slid the stack of albums aside to reveal a large manila envelope. 'I thought you might like this. It's for you to keep. I have more copies.'

Lilianne picked up the envelope, unwound the red string anchoring the flap closed and drew out a stiff piece of folded white cardboard that opened to reveal a sheet of onion skin covering a studio photograph of . . . herself. Except not. 'My God.'

'The resemblance is even more striking than I remembered. I told you there was a blonde in our family. This is your great-great-great-grandmother, who makes possible your hair and eyes. She and my great-grandfather, Mostafa, met on one of his trips to London. Her name was Josephine.'

Lilianne couldn't take her eyes off the photograph. Josephine wore a gown with an embroidered bodice and a multi-strand necklace of pearls with matching earrings, her hair swept up in a complicated chignon. Elegant. Regal. With features so much like Lilianne's own.

'My grandmother said she was very British. She kept the house in line, everything proper and in its place, everything on strict schedule. She drove her Egyptian servants crazy.'

Lilianne stared into the blue eyes so much like hers, wishing there was a way to bring them to life, to answer all the questions spinning through her mind. What had made Josephine brave enough to defy social convention in her new country? How did it feel to be an English woman in Cairo in the nineteenth century, here for the building of the Suez Canal and the takeover of Egypt by the British? How did she feel about giving up her life and home for a foreign husband? How did Egypt shape her?

'It was not a love match. My *teta* said Josephine – her mother – came from a large family outside London, and was not well off. Her choices were to be a teacher, governess, maid or nun, and she was dying to get out of England, with its rain and fogs. She wanted a husband and family, not a life of drudgery. She caught the eye of my great-grandfather, who was quite a bit older, and she jumped at the chance.'

Another person leaving a home that couldn't give them what they wanted. Lilianne thought of her own mother and of her great-aunt Sabra, both rejecting Egypt in the pursuit of different lives. Of Gilles, rejecting Paris.

What did Lilianne want now? For so long she'd thought she knew, but factors kept changing. No longer a safe home for her at Maxwell with Dad gone and Kane all but sure to take over. No longer a safe home in Egypt.

'According to my *teta*, Josephine and Mostafa were not passionately in love, but they were happy together.' Zahra turned from looking nostalgic to piercing Lilianne with her gaze. 'That can work for you too, Lilianne. You and Gilles. I've seen how you look at each other. Not with passion. But with real love. That can be enough. Life is too hard to live on your own. Too hard.'

Lilianne laid the picture of Josephine in her lap. 'Teta, I can't—'

'Gilles is a good man, Lilianne. He needs you, you see that.' Zahra took Lilianne's chin in a firm grip and made her turn toward her. 'But I don't think you see how much you need him as well.'

Chapter 25

Present day

Sophie: *After all that, not going to meet the rest of the family this weekend! Excuses, excuses!*
Lilianne: *Sorry.*
Sophie: *It'll happen. I'm determined.*
Lilianne: *That I know.*
Sophie: *Helen still there?*
Lilianne: *Yes.*
Sophie: *And . . . that's okay?*
Lilianne: *It's wonderful.*
Sophie: *Good. Gotta go cook. Love you.*
Lilianne: ♥

Sophie checked on the day's sign-up list. Her offer to teach cooking to the Asphalia residents had proved popular and fun for everyone involved. Lizzie was on the list for today. She'd come once before, had obviously enjoyed it, and when she wasn't trying to skewer Sophie, she was not bad company.

If Sophie did say so herself, the kitchen looked fantastic. The floor was still awful, though the colorful rugs relieved the beige tedium, and a new paint job wasn't going to happen soon, but the new appliances had been delivered as promised two weeks earlier, and the room had become warmer and more welcoming as well as more practical. The residents were clearly happy with the changes Sophie had made to their menu, introducing new flavors into old standards in the food bible whenever she could. Maybe it was her imagination, but the dining room chatter seemed brighter and more inclusive, and the women were slowly beginning to incorporate more ingredients and flavors into their own breakfast and lunch menus as well.

Sophie was settling into the routines of Asphalia House and enjoying getting to know her cousin, who seemed to feel the same. Lily Anne was smiling more often, and they found they had more in common than just their childhood invisible friends, like similar tastes in movies and books, in music and in food. They didn't sunburn, they'd both had crazed teenage crushes on John Cusack, preferred cookies to cakes or pies and, given the choice, salty to sweet. Both had childhood allergies they grew out of and were prone to strep throat in college. They'd both done fine in school but were never turned on academically, and they'd both kicked a nail-biting habit in their twenties.

All of which was probably about as much as any two people could find in common, but to Sophie the discoveries had been intoxicating.

The one disappointment was that the trip the previous Saturday to meet the rest of the family had been postponed a week by Lily Anne's father, Uncle Clyde, for reasons no one understood. However, Lily Anne had insisted that she and Sophie and her siblings would show up to his house this coming Saturday whether her dad was ready to host them or not.

If he didn't want to see them, so be it, but Sophie's weeks here were going quickly, and she'd want the chance to see her family more than once. She hoped.

From the sparkling new refrigerator she pulled out ingredients for the evening's dinner, one she was excited about. Since she'd have a helper in the kitchen, she'd decided to rebel and go completely off-book for the first time to make potsticker dumplings with a side of butter-braised bok choy. The dumplings weren't difficult, but time-consuming in the quantity they'd need. If these women were anything like Sophie, after the first bite they'd have trouble finding their appetite's off-switch.

Lunch had come and gone, and the women should be just finished with their exercise period. Lizzie would show up soon, which always put Sophie on her guard. Time spent with her could be spirited fun or challenging, depending on her mood.

Fifteen minutes later, Lizzie stomped in wearing sunshine-yellow shorts with a sunflower-strewn top.

'Hello, summer day.' Sophie held up a hand in front of her eyes. 'Where are my sunglasses? You look great. Cheerful.'

That was in reference to her clothes. Her face looked anything but cheerful – red-rimmed eyes and the beginnings of a scowl.

One of *those* days. Poor Lizzie. 'We're making potstickers. Know what those are?'

'Yes, I do inhabit this planet.'

'Good to know.' She got out a large bowl. 'Hands washed?'

'I just showered. Haven't picked my nose, so still clean.'

'Good enough.' Sophie would choose her battles. 'We're mixing pork, ginger, spinach, scallions, soy sauce and rice wine, then pulling a lazy one and stuffing wonton wrappers because making that many dumpling wrappers by hand is too fiddly.' She plunked a bunch of scallions on the cutting board in front of Lizzie and handed over a chef's knife, handle-first. 'Finely chopped. Have at it.'

While Lizzie sullenly minced scallions, sniffing now and then, Sophie peeled a large knob of ginger with the edge of a teaspoon.

'What was your exercise of choice today, Lizzie?'

The Jewel of Cairo

'Swam at White's pool. They drive us out if we want to go.'
'Were you a swimmer in high school?'
'Yup.'
'Any good?'
Lizzie shrugged. 'Okay, I guess.'
'Crap day today, huh? Want to tell me about it?'
'If I wanted to tell you about it, I'd tell you about it.'
Sophie tried to look both puzzled and pissed. 'Wait, really? That's how it works?'
Lizzie rolled her eyes. 'You wouldn't understand.'
'Why not?'
'Because you're not an addict. Because—'
'My mother was an addict.'
Lizzie looked startled. And interested. 'Really?'
Sophie's turn to roll her eyes. 'What, that makes me human all of a sudden? Worth speaking to?'
'I can't picture it. You can't have grown up with that.'
'My birth mother was an addict. My adoptive mother is not.'
'Oh. Okay then.' Lizzie went back to chopping. 'Is your birth mom sober now?'
'She died when I was five months old. So probably, unless there's a fantastic bar in heaven.'
Lizzie tried to hide a grin. 'How much of this should I chop?'
'All of it.' Sophie rubbed the ginger up and down the grater, trying to figure out how to unlock this woman's misery, not sure it was possible. If her cousin, with her years of experience, and the staff of therapists hadn't made a dent yet, what made Sophie think she could? 'When you're done, you can choose chopping spinach or adding the seasonings. We'll mix it all up with the pork, then I'll show you how to fold the dumplings.'
'Your mother might have been an addict, but you weren't around her.'

'Ah. So I don't get to be in the club after all.' Sophie glanced over to see how Lizzie would take that. Not well, apparently. 'Here's how I see it. Everyone on earth has the same set of feelings. We all go through things, and we all feel those feelings, good, bad and in the middle. I can never know exactly what your life is like, and you can never know what mine is like, but we can—'

'Oh, don't give me that crap. You grew up in privilege with parents who wanted you and gave you everything.'

Sophie put down the grater. 'Is this a suffering contest? Because you win. I can't compete, Lizzie. I did not suffer as much as you did. Congratulations, okay? My question is, why do you feel like you need to prove that victory over and over again? If you think your life was, is and always will be shit, why the hell are you here?'

'Screw you.' Lizzie threw down her knife and faced Sophie furiously. 'You think you can—'

'No.' Sophie held up a strong hand. *Stop.* 'Screaming at me is keeping me at a distance. It's the easy way. Coward stuff. What is your problem that you refuse to let this place help you? What do you gain by that?'

Lizzie released breath, wilting in the process. 'There's no point. This place can't help me.'

'Not if you don't let it, no. And if you're not going to let it, why are you here?'

She held Sophie's gaze, stony-faced, trembling. 'I don't have to tell you, Connecticut.'

'No, you don't. You can stay in your cage. But I bet it's lonely in there, and the zookeeper probably doesn't clean it very often.'

Lizzie stayed silent, wrestling with her breathing, face wanting to crumple.

'What happened today that set you off like this?' Sophie

gentled her voice. 'I'm not a therapist. I'm not on staff here. I will not report back to teacher.'

'Why do you want to know?'

'Because, Lizzie ...' She paused, worried about the risk she'd be taking, then decided what the hell. She leaned across the kitchen island and changed her voice to a syrupy purr. 'Whatever you say will make my wonderful life feel even *more* magical.'

It worked. Amazingly, it worked. Lizzie cracked up and threw a piece of scallion that landed in Sophie's hair.

Whew.

'The serious answer?' Sophie looked intently into the sullen brown eyes. 'Because I give a shit, Lizzie. I have no idea why, because you've been nothing but rude and hostile from the moment you saw me, but I do. Now ... spinach or sauce?'

Lizzie swallowed. Shifted her weight. 'Sauce.'

'We'll need about a quarter-cup of soy sauce, same of the rice wine, and a tablespoon of sesame oil.' Sophie pushed the bottles toward Lizzie, then added the ginger and scallions to the ground pork she'd dumped into a bowl big enough to bathe a small child. 'You can pour it all straight in.'

'What do you think it's like to be an addict?'

Sophie took her time positioning a large handful of spinach on her cutting board. This was her test. She could feel it. Screw this up and she was Connecticut now and forever.

'I picture it like being a member of a cult. At first it's great, you're part of something that makes you feel good, accepted, and like the rest of the messed-up world not only can't hurt you anymore but no longer matters. The past doesn't matter, or the future either. All that matters is that the pain of being alive is gone, and you have power you can rely on to keep it away.

'Then after a while you realize you're stuck in something you only partly realized you signed on for. Out of control, helpless, terrified, unable to change yourself or your circumstances. Like trying to swim to the surface of a deep pool after you've been fitted with cement shoes you thought were Manolo Blahniks.'

Lizzie poured carefully measured soy sauce over the pork. 'Poetic.'

'Thanks.' Sophie went back to her spinach. 'I worked hard on it.'

'So . . .' Lizzie scowled, picked up the rice wine and put it down again. 'They want my parents to come for family therapy.'

'And that's bad because . . . ?' Sophie held up a hand when she saw Lizzie's face. 'I'm asking you, not challenging.'

'Because my parents don't care.'

'And you know this how? Again, asking. You know these people. I don't.'

Mouth set in a firm line, Lizzie poured rice wine over the pork like it was gasoline over her enemies. 'I would know if they cared.'

'That makes sense. But it doesn't answer the question.'

'I guess not.' The words were low and shaky.

Sophie made herself keep chopping, even though the spinach was fine enough, wanting to enfold Lizzie in a long, magical hug that would fix everything for her, certain this was a taste of why Lily Anne looked perpetually torn apart.

'My sister Olivia died. Drunk driver. She was perfect, like you. Smart and funny and pretty.'

'God, I'm sorry, Lizzie.' Sophie put her knife down. 'And thank you for the compliments.'

'Don't get used to them.'

'Absolutely not.' She swept the chopped spinach into the bowl, hoping that was the right next step for the recipe. 'I wouldn't dare.'

'My parents lost their shit. I mean, of course.' Lizzie spoke quietly, eyes on the counter top. 'Their child was gone, the perfect one, and they were stuck with me.'

Sophie reached for the wonton wrappers, trying to act as if they were discussing the weather, heart breaking, throat thick. She understood more than Lizzie knew.

'I heard Mom saying one night that she wished it had been me. Dad didn't argue.'

Sophie inhaled sharply. 'Oh Lizzie.'

'Yeah, well, sorry if I don't love the idea of those people showing up to . . .' Lizzie glanced up and did a double take. 'Are you *crying*?'

'No. God, no.' Sophie wiped hurriedly at her tears. 'Chopping spinach makes my eyes water. Noxious stuff.'

'Well, shit.' Lizzie stared back down at the jar of sesame oil in her hand. 'You probably need a hug or some crap, huh?'

Hope rose. 'It might make me feel better.' *It might make you feel better.*

'Yeah. Good.' She glanced toward the hallway. 'I'll see if I can find someone to help you.'

Sophie burst into giggles. Lizzie joined her, and their laughter caught fire, lasting longer than the joke merited, because it was a lot better than crying and didn't puff up their eyes.

Then, having decided what the hell, Sophie walked around the island and hauled Lizzie into her arms for a long, rocking hug that made them both cry, puffy eyes be damned.

'So it's all good now, right?' Sophie spoke against Lizzie's cheek. 'This was your big cinematic breakthrough scene. From now on you're cured, and you'll be a model participant and go on to be the first female president of the United States.'

Lizzie stepped away, wiping her eyes. 'Give me a break, Connecticut.'

'You know what?' Sophie rubbed her hands together gleefully, inspired by the perfect plan. 'I know exactly what you need.'

'Yeah?' Lizzie gave her the look of a fourteen-year-old facing her *so*-clueless parent. 'What?'

'To chop wood.' She grinned as if she were announcing that Lizzie had won the lottery. 'I can set you up.

'Gee whiz. That's so neato, Aunt Sophie!'

'In the meantime, talk to Lily Anne if you can't get your therapist to understand. Tell her why you're not ready to see your parents. I guarantee she'll listen, but you have to tell her.'

Lizzie's face closed down. 'Maybe.'

'I'll take maybe. Want to make some dumplings?'

'Yeah.' Lizzie sniffled and accepted the tissue Sophie held out to her. 'Yeah, I do.'

∽ Chapter 26 ❧

Sophie buckled her seatbelt in Lily Anne's passenger seat, ready as she could be for the drive to meet her extended family. She'd slept like crap for the past two nights, and had spent the morning agonizing over what to wear. If her uncle and siblings showed up in jeans and she wore linen . . . Ugh. She was determined to be herself, but not *too* much, in case her new family found herself off-putting.

Another Sophie superpower: her ability to tie herself in knots over the simplest things.

In the end she'd chosen a blue and teal paisley skirt paired with a blue sleeveless cotton top, over the moon when Lily Anne showed up in a peasanty teal sundress that made them practically a matched set. No matter what the rest of the family wore, she and her cousin would be equals.

'So, Cousin Lily Anne, I had an excellent idea.'

'Uh-oh.'

'I'm asking first, as promised. How would you feel about handing Lizzie Borden an ax?'

'An ax!' Lily Anne put her bright red Hyundai sedan into gear. 'Are you speaking figuratively? I hope . . .'

'Nope. Owen Briggs, the guy I'm staying with? The woodworker?

He swears by splitting logs for working out stress and hostility. He said it's something you don't know you need until you do it.'

Lily Anne pulled out onto Route 4. She'd come half an hour out of her way on this hot, humid Saturday morning, which Sophie let her do only because she was too nervous to arrive at Uncle Clyde's house alone. 'That's what our exercise and meditation classes are for.'

'Right. And those are great, but they're both missing what Lizzie needs.'

'I'm afraid to ask.'

'Violence!' Sophie announced happily. 'Annihilation. The power to destroy. Lovely, delicious wreckage in her wake.'

Lily Anne chuckled drily. 'You want to hand the least cooperative and most disturbed member of the house an ax.'

'And point her to a pile of logs, yes. With Owen dancing attendance. I think it would do her good. Maybe all of them. Maybe after his woodworking demonstration he can give lessons to all the residents.'

'This is a completely wacky and dangerous idea, you realize that, right?'

Sophie feigned confusion. 'Is that a problem?'

'My liability for accidents would be through the roof.'

'Oh. I forgot. You have to live in reality. Maybe they could sign something?' She thought it over. 'How about "I understand that I will probably cut off my own foot, and that's okay with me"?'

'How about no?' Lily Anne turned to peer at her passenger. 'You anxious about today?'

'What gave me away?'

'The buzzing noise in the car. I assume it's your nerves.'

'Must be.' Sophie indulged in a smug grin. It had been a joy watching her cousin loosen over the past two weeks, letting out a funny whimsical side she must have buried under so much responsibility for so many years. 'I dreamed that mid conversation your siblings grew fangs and claws and shredded me into strips that your dad sautéed for dinner.'

'Ooh, good one. Mine was that we couldn't get to Dad's house. The road kept undulating up and down, and we finally got swallowed by a sinkhole that spit us out in Las Vegas.'

'Oh, very nice.' Over the past week, Sophie and Lily Anne had taken more walks and hung out when they could, but this would be a whole day of togetherness, and it already felt comfortable and energizing, like hanging out with Beezy, only . . . family.

'I've noticed you've developed a really good rapport with the residents in a short time. It's impressive. You stay yourself, but you're also really present for them.'

'Oh. Thanks.' Sophie was never quite sure what that phrase meant, but it was obviously a compliment. 'I'm enjoying getting to know them.'

'Have you ever thought about this kind of work permanently?'

The suggestion startled her. 'No. Not because I'm against it. I just . . . haven't.'

'Well, you're good. The way you've gotten as far as you have with Lizzie is huge. She said you'd told her to talk to me.'

'About her parents visiting?'

'Yes. They're definitely not invited. Not this soon. We didn't realize.'

'Oh good.' Sophie's heart swelled. 'Good for her. I'm proud of her. That was hard.'

'You've made a real difference.'

'Thanks.' Sophie sat still, taken aback that someone as efficient and remarkable as Lily Anne would be admiring *her*, with zero experience and a tendency to run off in a million directions without thinking any of them through.

She'd certainly never imagined spending her life around women in various states of turmoil and misery, though there was also plenty of hope, determination and remarkably intimate female camaraderie. Watching the growing self-esteem and power of those who did the necessary work was remarkable and inspiring.

Something to think about.

'Thanks for your nice words, Lily Anne. The job thing . . . not really on my radar.'

'Yeah, it wasn't on mine either, but here I am. Anyway, just want to say I'm grateful for what you've brought to the place. The food in particular. I'd gotten so used to eating without giving it any thought. I'm going to have you teach Annika your secrets.'

'It's nice to feel appreciated.' She meant it. She'd always felt pressured and apologetic for her work in Southport. People there had access to fine restaurants, grocery stores stuffed with exotic ingredients, and phone apps that brought them recipes from around the world. What could she add to make her special? Granted, Asphalia's food bible was an astonishingly low bar, but . . .

Something else to think about.

They drove on through Vermont's beautiful tree-frosted hills, passing small towns that Sophie found herself wondering about, having glimpsed some of the darker side of living in near-poverty and isolation.

'I never asked you. Are you seeing anyone? Dating?'

Lily Anne's question cut short her musing. 'No, not me. My divorce traumatized me and my self-esteem is down around my ankles. How about you?'

'Not me either. I don't have time.'

'Aw, c'mon. That's an excuse, not a reason.'

'See? You're doing it to *me* now. Cutting through the nice comforting lies I tell myself, jeez.' Lily Anne rolled her eyes. 'Truth? My reasons are about the same as yours.'

'Relationship trauma? Was there ever a Mr Lily Anne?'

'I had a serious boyfriend, from high school until I was in my mid twenties. We were both planning to work abroad, for the government. I got stuck here and he went. Since then, I've had a few relationships, but nothing was that good, and ... well, weeks go by. Years go by. I'm busy, and reasonably content alone.'

Sophie could easily see how that would happen, and decided Lily Anne should give herself a break and look for love again. Advice Sophie could also give herself.

'I don't know.' Lily Anne slowed behind a turning car. 'How many people end up living the life they thought they would when they were younger? I bet not many, and a lot of those that do find out it's not what they expected when it's too late to change. Maybe I'm just trying to make myself feel better, but that's how it seems.'

Sophie thought immediately of Alma Pihl, and the dramatic change in her circumstances. 'I was living the life I wanted when I was married to Peter. Then he got tired of me. That screwed it all up. My best friend, Beezy, however, does have the perfect life. She's gorgeous, has a fantastic marriage to a guy she adores and who adores her, two smart, well-adjusted kids, a sailboat, a beautiful house and a successful career as an interior designer, which she loves and is incredibly good at. She had a great relationship with her parents and both of her brothers. I mean, it's sickening.'

'There must be something she isn't telling you. Irritable bowel syndrome or something.'

Sophie giggled. 'Nope.'

'Wires? Internal gears? I'm pretty sure she's a robot.' Lily Anne threw her a grin. 'So do you still want that kind of life?'

'Absolutely.' The response was automatic, then her stomach kicked her, the way it did when she was lying to herself. After some digging, she found herself considering Alma's self-reinvention in a new light. No longer a brilliant designer creating baubles for the ultra-rich, no. But a brilliant teacher, inspiring a new generation of artists, bringing to many lives a different type of riches. By all accounts she was adored and appreciated by her students. 'Or, maybe, I don't know. This is going to take some soul-searching.'

'So search. You have about forty-five minutes.'

Sophie cracked up. 'What's your perfect life?'

Lily Anne sighed. 'Having money and time to travel. To see things outside Rutland, outside the US. To hear life stories from people who aren't from Vermont and who aren't addicts. To sit on a sunny beach with soft sand, strong sun, turquoise water, a fantastic novel and move only when I want to.'

'The fantasy of the chronically overworked. Don't you get vacation?'

'Yes. But I can't afford to go far, and I keep in touch in case Asphalia needs me.' Lily Anne gazed at the road ahead as if it were an invitation. 'My boyfriend and I were all set to take the foreign service exam after college, but my Yeya Eleni – my grandmother – wasn't well, so Mom asked me to delay a year and help out. Tom agreed to wait with me. Then during that year Mom was diagnosed with breast cancer. My siblings were all settled into their lives, and I was the only one who could take over Asphalia while she was in treatment. She died four years later, and by that time Tom had long gone, and those early dreams seemed self-indulgent beside the work I was doing. So I never followed them.'

'You put family and Asphalia first. Like your mom.'

'Ouch.' Lily Anne hunched her shoulders. 'It sounds less saintly when you put it like that.'

'Anyone who can run that place is part saint. No doubt in my mind.'

Her cousin shook her head. 'The residents are doing the hard part. They work to get off their drugs in rehab. At Asphalia they work to make sobriety stick. After they get out, the work continues, but with much less structure and support. When they leave, most will have to change their lives completely. Address, friends, habits, jobs, everything. Some will have good family support, some will essentially have to find a new family. It's brutal, and inspiring and humbling to be part of.'

Sophie thought of Lizzie, soon to be cut loose into the world, estranged from her parents, having to avoid the friends she'd used with, hiding her pain, fear and vulnerability behind all the bluster. The danger of it made Sophie a bit panic-breathless, in awe of the courage forging a new self required.

Humbling indeed.

She looked down at her fingers, clenched in her lap, thinking of the Fabergé egg tucked into Owen's dresser, its azure petals and the graceful king and queen surprise inside, the genius of Alma Pihl and the miraculous circumstances that had brought the jewel into Sophie's life.

Such perfection was never going to be hers to keep. But for the first time, she could imagine herself being at peace letting it go.

Chapter 27

Monday, May 24, 1976

'You understand?' Sami stared at Safiya with eyes that usually made her cower.

Not today. Today she felt only hatred, and disgust. Did she understand? *Yes*, she'd understood. He'd only explained his plan twenty times.

She'd played her part as the stupid peasant girl too well. He had an important errand for her, he'd said. He wanted to play a little joke on Lilianne. He'd make sure her apartment was empty, then Safiya was to sneak in and hide a little surprise, the Fabergé egg and its carriage, somewhere not too obvious, but where Lilianne would stumble over them before too long. A closet, or a dresser drawer. Could she do that, please?

Safiya knew it was nonsense. That jeweled egg was Sami's ticket to a life of riches and leisure. He would never do something so frivolous with it, or so risky. It had taken her all of ten seconds to see through him. After she planted the egg, Sami would call the police, or what passed for police in his circles, say he'd been robbed of his greatest treasure and accuse Lilianne of theft. The egg would be found in her apartment. She'd be arrested. He'd have his payback. Al-Kalib would be satisfied.

But Sami was a fool to trust Safiya. She'd need time to figure out how she could sabotage this plan. Lilianne would not suffer in an Egyptian jail because of her.

Last night after the thugs had left, Sami had come to her as she'd known he would, to dump his humiliation. Her drugged state hadn't put him off. She'd been only dimly aware of the hideous act, unable to move or fight. She was still sore today, with new bruises.

Enough. She had reached her limit. No amount of money was worth another night in this house. Instinct told her that this errand would provide her with a way to get her own revenge for the past three years. Fury and outrage had made her brave. But she needed more than courage.

If only she could have an hour to think. Sami had explained that a 'colleague' – no doubt another of Al-Kalib's criminals – would be driving her to Lilianne's apartment and would know how to get her in.

Then what? She couldn't leave the egg in the apartment. Nor could she get it to John Baker with the driver watching her, and even if she could, there was nothing illegal about Sami owning a family heirloom. More likely suspicion would fall on her. It would come down to her word against Sami's about what he'd planned to do. Women from tiny villages were no match for rich gentlemen with powerful connections.

Neither could she keep the egg. There would be no way to sell such a famous thing, if Sami's words about its fame were to be believed. She'd borne endless lectures about the valuable items Sami owned, pretending to be bored and uncomprehending, filing every detail away. He thought her too stupid to understand, but she knew more about the world than he thought.

'I don't need to tell you to be careful.' Sami was breathing heavily, sweating, holding the purple satin bag containing the egg and carriage close to his side, reluctant, even in his eagerness, to hand the precious item over. Safiya had never seen him like this, tie crooked, hair sticking up on one side. Fear had made him careless. Careless people made mistakes, which could make them more vulnerable. Or more dangerous.

'I will be very careful.' She kept her head down, not wanting to look at him, afraid her hatred and contempt were becoming too big to contain. Hatred, contempt and a low-burning excitement. Her heart was beating quickly. Allah willing, there would be a way today to get her revenge.

If only she could think.

'Excellent.' He cradled the bag under his arm and picked up the phone, misdialing, having to start over. 'She's ready. Yes. Good.'

Safiya wasn't ready. She needed more time to plan. How to save Lilianne. How to bring Sami down.

How to escape.

The words came to her naturally and inevitably, freezing her with such a thrill she was afraid she'd faint. And yet that would have to be part of the day. She'd known when she woke up this morning that she couldn't stay. Staying would only invite more of the same treatment she'd put up with for far too long.

Allah hadn't yet shown her the way, but she knew that today all would be possible.

'He'll ring the bell when he's downstairs. You go down and he'll take you to Lilianne's building. There's no one there, I've checked. The driver will warn you if either of them comes back early. But you must be quick.'

'Yes.'

He forced a jovial smile and carefully, painfully handed over the bag with the egg in its gold carriage. 'She'll enjoy this little game. Quite funny.'

Safiya could only bring herself to nod, too afraid to speak in case some of her true thoughts and feelings spilled out.

'I'll be back this afternoon.' He gave the silk bag one more longing look, then rushed out, nearly tripping over an untied shoelace, cursing furiously, slamming the door behind him.

Safiya stared after him until his footsteps no longer sounded, then turned as if a spring had been released, giving her a view into his studio, where she saw the most beautiful present Allah had given her since the birth of her sons. Even more beautiful than the egg Sami had handed her, swaddled in its padded bag.

He'd given her the gift of Sami's carelessness. In his studio, the cabinet that had contained the egg and its carriage was not quite closed. Open just a crack.

She nearly laughed, awed by Allah's power. Sami always locked the cabinet. Always. Locked it, put the key in his pocket, the gesture as natural to him as breathing.

As she got closer, Safiya realized what had happened. In his rush, he'd turned the key, yes, but without making sure the door was closed. The bolt protruded ineffectively past the frame, resting on the dark wood.

Inside this cabinet lay the unfinished diamond necklace and the list of where the stones had come from. Lilianne's John Baker could make use of those. Maybe they'd be enough to put Sami in jail. Maybe they'd be enough to hurt Al-Kalib and his driver too, or at least slow them down.

Maybe John Baker could even help Safiya get back to Nagaa ad Disah to be with her sons. She could find a job in Aswan. It might not pay as much, but money had lost its allure. She'd seen how Sami could live among the most remarkable riches and still be lonely and miserable, plagued by demons that drove him to take and take without thought of anything but his own pleasure.

She tried to picture herself at the American Embassy, showing up in her *hijab* and her shabby clothes with a bag full of diamonds and a piece of paper. Lilianne had said John Baker would help. But he could just as easily have her arrested before she could explain herself. Even then he might not believe her.

She needed time to think. The driver would come soon.

If the necklace and paper disappeared with her, she'd be the only suspect. Sami and Al-Kalib would hunt her down. They knew where she lived. She was arrogant, imagining herself powerful enough to take on her employer and his seedy friends. For all their sophistication, they weren't worth half of most people in her village.

She begged Allah to show her a way, eyes closed, lips moving in silent prayer. As she stood, a great peaceful calm fell over her.

Allah had answered. Sami deserved to suffer. If she died in the attempt, He would care for her, and allow her to keep watch over her sons, who would thrive in her parents' care.

This was her chance. Somehow she'd find a way.

She went into her tiny room to retrieve the meager stash of cash she'd saved after sending money home every month. It would be enough for a train ticket, all she needed. She bent to slide out her battered suitcase from where she'd shoved it under the bed, then stopped. If her possessions disappeared with her, there would be no doubt in Sami's mind who was responsible for the theft.

Slowly straightening, she picked up the drawings her sons had made for her: the one Amon had done years ago, when she'd first left to work for Sami, a picture of himself to bring with her, a giant circle face with arms coming out where ears should be; and from Bebti, a page of scribble. She would miss these, but if she had the boys to hold in her arms, she wouldn't need them so badly. She replaced them on the table by her bed and left the room.

Back in Sami's studio, she calmly extracted the diamond necklace from its velvet box, and the list of clients from whom Sami had stolen the stones. Men and their egos. Why else would he keep such a careful record of his deception? She could practically smell his pride on the paper, listing line after line of Egypt's wealthiest, and the pieces they'd brought to him, trusting his skill and reputation. She scanned the list, noting with satisfaction that Al-Kalib's name was atop a column showing his share of each transaction.

All diamonds were traceable, Sami had once told her. She'd made sure to look at him blankly. Traceable? What did that mean? Her poor female brain was unable to understand anything of the kind. But she knew this was valuable evidence, the proof not only in the list, but in the diamonds themselves.

Traceable, Sami.

The necklace, wrapped in one of Sami's handkerchiefs, fit easily in the bag with the egg and carriage.

Was punishing a sinner also a sin? Certainly it must be a lesser one.

Allah forgive her.

In the living room, she methodically went around making it look as if someone had come in to rob the apartment. Door to his studio open, safe open, cabinet open, a few chairs overturned for good measure, a couple of drawers emptied as if they'd been searched. He'd never think Safiya capable of such a ruse. It would throw him off at least for a while. He'd probably accuse Al-Kalib of the theft, and Al-Kalib would accuse him back. They could peck each other to death like fighting roosters.

Finished with her crime scene, she couldn't resist a peek under the table where Lilianne had put her little machine. It was gone, the wood showing damage where it had been removed. Who had found it? Who had removed it? This meant Lilianne's CIA would not have heard Sami's plan just now.

None of this was her concern.

She went to stand near the front door, breathing hard, mind spinning. What had she missed? What should she have done differently?

No answers, just a feeling that none of this was really happening, yet it was too late to take it back. She'd made her decision.

Instead she would trust in Allah, and rejoice that she had finally refused to be treated like garbage. When she walked out this morning, she wouldn't be coming back.

That thought was so cheering that when the apartment buzzer rang, Safiya was able to walk downstairs as naturally if she were going marketing.

Outside, a dented brown Russian car, unremarkable compared to any other in the city, with a weaselly-looking driver who jerked his thumb toward the back seat. Safiya sat silently for the drive, trying to breathe calmly, looking around as they went through neighborhoods she hadn't seen before, still not sure how to accomplish all she had set out to do.

Allah would let her know what to do when the time came. She had only to trust Him.

The city was endless, choking, noisy, crowded with buildings and bodies. How she longed for space, the low houses, fields and peaceful animals of her village, the flow of the Nile and the cheerful chatter of her sons. Allah willing, she would see them all soon. Though she was well aware of the danger of cheating Iblis, the devil. If you cooked with poison, you must eat it.

After what seemed like forever, the car pulled up in front of a building that looked like most of the others around it.

The driver walked her to the entrance and pressed buzzers for various apartments until a voice answered. Half laughing, charming, remarkably convincing, he identified himself using a last name from one of the upper floors, explaining that he'd gone out for one second and forgotten his key too late to catch the door before it closed.

They were buzzed inside.

Up on the second floor, outside Apartment 4, he produced a set of funny-looking keys and had the door open only slightly slower than if he'd had the real key.

Allah would deal with Sami's friends too.

'Go.' He jerked his head toward the open door. 'I'll wait downstairs.'

She worked not to show her relief that he wouldn't come in with her. 'It might take me some time.'

'I have nothing else to do.'

She nodded and stepped inside, taking a moment to marvel at the modern furniture in such dull colors. Gold and earth, beige and brown, and everything excessively padded, like the couch and chairs were made from mattresses. Was this what Western houses were like? So bland and lifeless. No rugs, no tapestries, no bright cushions.

She took a quick tour, searching for something that might get her out of this misery. The first bedroom she looked in was a mess of colorful clothing piled and draped over every surface. That would be Connie's.

The second bedroom had to be Lilianne's, completely empty except for packed bags that gave Safiya a thrill of relief. She was leaving. Sami wouldn't be able to touch her.

Two bags on the bed, one large, zipped and closed, a smaller one next to it, still open, on which was laid a doll that took

Safiya's breath away. She was large, as big as Safiya's arm was long, dressed in clothing finer than anything Safiya had ever encountered except in books. Silk and leather, ribbons and furs. Jewelry that sparkled like real diamonds.

A princess, with a captivating face – wise and a little sad, lashes and brows painted over brown eyes that stared at Safiya.

Safiya stared back, feeling new energy coursing through her. This was her answer, she knew it. Sami had told her he'd wanted to give the egg to Lilianne as a present.

If Safiya hid it in Lilianne's suitcase, Lilianne would take it to the US. But when she found it, she'd feel the need to return it. This egg wasn't something a person like Lilianne would keep.

What if Safiya hid it where even Lilianne wouldn't find it?

A squeeze to the doll's middle was disappointingly unyielding. No way to hide the egg inside her body. Maybe between the legs, under her skirt? It would certainly disappear there. Unlikely anyone would be peering up the doll's dress.

Safiya gazed again at the sweet, wistful face, not quite satisfied.

Then a thought, so perfect it could only come from Allah.

If the princess's head was hollow, the egg would fit inside. The carriage wouldn't, but that, though gold, was of lesser value. Losing the egg would hurt Sami the most.

Safiya lifted the dark curls. Their strands were attached to a cap that fit over the doll's head. If she could work the cap free, she could glue it back in place with flour and water.

If.

She worked carefully, sweat trickling down her back, prying up the hair as gently as possible. The glue was old and cracked, gave easily, only one small tear that she'd be able to patch.

Underneath, exactly what she'd hoped for. A hollow shell, a nest perfect for an egg.

From the padded bag she retrieved the egg and the handkerchief used to protect the necklace. She rolled the egg into the soft cotton and eased the bundle into the hollow head.

A miracle. It fit snugly enough that it wouldn't rattle or be damaged by the doll's motion. Lilianne would take Sami's prized possession back to the US without knowing it was there. The egg would simply disappear.

Safiya laughed and moved silently to the kitchen to find flour and water for a paste that she smeared sparingly onto the edges of the doll's skull, then carefully replaced the hair.

Hurrying now, she rested the beautiful doll back onto the bag, worrying she'd feel heavier to those accustomed to holding her, worrying the hair might slip before the glue dried and look crooked.

Nothing she could do about either.

Fifteen minutes had passed. She prayed the weaselly driver would be napping or smoking, happy to have nothing to do, not caring how long she took.

There was still the problem of the carriage, too big to hide the way she had the egg. But at least it wasn't as recognizable nor as precious.

She might be able to sell this one. The money would enable her sons to live well, eat well, be educated and have better lives than she or her parents or certainly her sick husband could ever give them.

How wrong would it be? How low was she willing to stoop for their sakes?

She was running out of time to decide, and she still had to clean the bowl she'd used for the paste. Back in the kitchen, it rinsed easily except for one stubborn spot that had to be scratched off with her—

'Safiya?'

Safiya whirled around, nearly dropping the bowl, heart pounding with fear.

Connie, yawning, bleary-eyed from sleep, standing in the kitchen, the door to the balcony open behind her.

Sami had made a mistake. Connie was here.

It was impossible not to look guilty. Impossible to explain that she'd broken into their apartment to help. That she was on their side.

'I'm sorry.' She put out both hands in appeal. 'Sami sent me here to . . . Lilianne is in trouble.'

Connie shook her head, shrugging helplessly.

'Lilianne is in trouble.' Safiya heard herself speaking slowly, as if that would make a difference. 'I'm trying to help her.'

Connie shook her head again, then brightened, held up a finger and went for the phone.

'*La*, no.' Safiya reached her elbow just as she picked up the receiver. *Yes* and *no* were English words she knew. 'No Sami.'

Connie looked confused, then her face cleared. 'No, not Sami. Sean. My friend.'

Safiya knew the word 'friend'. Her terror abated some. '*Arrabiyya?*'

'Yes, Arabic.' Connie smiled warmly while dialing, as if waking up to find a stranger in her apartment happened all the time.

Safiya watched her making funny English sounds into the phone, hoping the driver didn't come to check on her, wondering what she was going to tell this Sean man to relay to Connie. The egg was safe from Sami. There was no reason to include anyone else. The less Connie and Lilianne knew, the better and safer they'd be too.

'Okay.' Connie handed the receiver over.

Safiya took it, staring at Connie's friendly face, in awe of her easy trust and acceptance. It was nearly impossible not to trust and accept her in return.

In another flash, Allah, the most merciful and compassionate, showed Safiya the way yet again. John Baker might be suspicious if Safiya brought him a diamond necklace and the paper, but Connie, with her white skin and guileless eyes, could dance in and be believed by everyone, no matter what she said. Safiya would entrust those to her.

That left only the carriage and a long wrestle with her conscience.

Confidence returning, Safiya took the receiver. She kept the story as plain and simple as she could. Her family, Sami's treatment of her, the men who'd come in and drugged her, and their plot to frame Lilianne, thinking she was a spy.

She left out that Lilianne *was* a spy. That was not her business to spread around.

Then she told Sean how he and Connie could help her put Sami and the others in jail, and how much she needed to get back to her children.

When she'd finished, she passed the phone back to Connie, and watched her eyes widen then narrow as she listened to Sean's translation. Every emotion on her face. Connie couldn't have survived in Safiya's shoes. The thought gave Safiya some pride, which she banished quickly with a prayer of apology. It was not her place to feel superior to anyone.

With Sean as interpreter, she and Connie worked out the rest of the plan. Safiya would be driven back to Sami's so the Weasel Man didn't sound an alarm. Connie and Sean would take the stolen stones and the damning list to John Baker at the embassy. He could notify local police, who would take him more seriously than either Safiya or Connie.

The next part of the plan was Connie's idea, one she insisted on. She and Sean would meet Safiya at the train station the next morning to hand back the carriage and make sure Safiya got on board safely.

'Yes?' Connie stood waiting, her face lit with excitement.

'Yes.' Safiya spoke in English, nearly faint with joy. 'Yes, yes, yes.'

It was hard not to think she was nearly free.

Free! After three long years. Free!

She prayed Allah would forgive her for lying and for stealing. Maybe it would help that she would use the gold for her children's benefit. Maybe too there would be better medicine for Menes if she could afford to pay.

Downstairs, she found Weasel Man smoking in his car, radio blaring, unconcerned with Safiya or the time she'd taken. She got into the back seat, hoping if he sensed her satisfaction, he'd mistake it for pleasure at having done her master's bidding.

On the way back to Sami's apartment, Safiya sat quietly, staring down at her hands, trying not to think of all that could go right and all that could go wrong. If the plan worked, she'd be home soon, her son's warm bodies pulled close. If not, she could end up at the bottom of the Nile.

They pulled to a stop at Sami's shop. Safiya thanked the Weasel and got out of the car, walked into the building she'd first walked into three years earlier, a younger and more innocent woman, and waited until she was sure the car must be gone. Then she slipped out the back entrance and disappeared into the city.

Chapter 28

Present day

Beezy: *Haven't heard from you in forever, what's up? Bitch neighbor complained today that my cucumber plants were infiltrating her side of the fence. Imagine this woman in a real crisis. Now c'mon, wiggle out from under your hot landlord long enough to text your friend who misses you.*

Sophie: *Miss you too! Landlord still a friend. Not likely to change. Going to meet the family today! I'm excited and terrified and excited and terrified and . . .*

Beezy: *Understandable. They will love you, because you are wonderful. Let me know how it goes!*

Sophie: *Like I wouldn't?*

Lily Anne's childhood home in Strafford was set off the main road just beyond the small town center. The house was a good size, painted dark gray with white trim and the narrow wooden siding of homes built in the late 1800s. A generous lawn and gardens that looked as if they'd seen better days surrounded it, and the sound of rushing water indicated a stream nearby. A pretty, welcoming house that Sophie immediately liked the look of. 'You were born here?'

'Born and raised.' Lily Anne looked around the property with obvious affection. 'My grandparents' house is outside Rutland, but Dad was from Strafford, so he and Mom bought here. She wasn't thrilled about being so far away from her parents, but we still got to know our *yeya* and *pappou*.'

'I'd love to see your . . . *our* grandparents' house.'

'I'll take you. Let's go in.' She started toward the steps, then turned back. 'You ready?'

Sophie grinned. 'As I'll ever be.'

'All right.' Lily Anne bounded up, Sophie close behind her, and rang the doorbell. They waited a tense half-minute until the door swung open to a lanky balding man with a fringe of stringy hair that reached his shoulders. 'Hey, Donny. I brought your cousin to meet you. This is Sophie Aubert.'

He inspected Sophie with dark eyes similar in shape to Lily Anne and Sophie's, though his features were blunter, and his skin was the type that would sunburn easily. '*Oh-bear*? What kind of name is that?'

Sophie was taken aback – but then they were all nervous, and what had she expected, a hug and kiss? 'It's French. My father is French. My adoptive father, that is, Gilles Aubert. He's—'

'Okay. Come on in.' He disappeared, leaving the door open.

Strange beginning.

'You aren't going to get courtly manners in this house,' Lily Anne whispered. 'But they're good people.'

'I don't need courtly manners.' Sophie stepped over the threshold, excitement mounting.

Inside was a bit of a mess. Empty cups, magazines and newspapers were stacked haphazardly in the living room, and a glance into the kitchen showed dishes strewn over the counter. The dining room, in full view, was neat as a pin. Possibly no one ate there.

The Jewel of Cairo

Her cousins were gathered in the living room. Donny had sprawled onto an enormous black vinyl couch next to a woman who must be Naomi. Which meant Fred was the one in the black recliner, a can of Budweiser nestled in the chair arm's cup holder. The TV was on, showing a movie in which countless people were being annihilated with bombs and bullets.

'Hey, turn that off,' Lily Anne ordered. 'We have company.'

Fred, stockier than his brother, and with a full head of dark curls, found the remote and turned down the sound, leaving the picture going. 'Hey. Sophie, right? I'm Fred.'

'Hi, Fred.' She stood awkwardly, wearing her so-great-to-be-here face while her newly found cousins stared. 'Hi, Naomi.'

'Nice to meet you.' Naomi looked younger than her brothers, heavily made-up, with slightly more olive skin, a dead ringer for Phyllis.

'So you're Connie's kid, huh.' Donny folded his hands behind his head, watching the soundless movie. 'Cra-a-zy Aunt Connie.'

Naomi's eyes wandered from the TV to Sophie. 'Do you remember her?'

'No, I was adopted at five months.'

'Mom told us stories.' Fred gave a whistle. 'Probably good she didn't raise you.'

'You don't know that.' Lily Anne came to Connie's defense. 'She was sober during her pregnancy.'

Fred looked skeptical. 'How do you know that?'

'She and my adoptive mother corresponded.' Sophie's cheeks were starting to hurt from making the pleasant face. 'They were close friends.'

'Where's Dad?' Lily Anne asked.

'Upstairs.' Donny yawned loudly. 'Not feeling well.'

'What's wrong with him?'

'How should I know? He just said he wasn't up to meeting Sophie and to tell her sorry.'

Lily Anne huffed. 'I'll check on him.'

She headed for the stairs, leaving Sophie with the difficult job of keeping her optimism propped up. In her fantasy, her cousins were eager to meet her, had a lovely meal planned and kept her busy answering question after question.

'So.' Fred picked up his beer and took a swig. 'Connie's kid.'

'We've *established* that.' Naomi gave her brother a scornful look.

'Yes I am.' Sophie would keep trying. 'I know you home-school your kids, Naomi, and that you guys have pot farms. That's about it. I'm dying to know more.'

'Like what?' Fred asked.

'I'm married with two sons,' Donny offered. 'I bowl on Saturdays, and I like to hunt deer, fish for trout. Live close to the land.'

'Oh, listen to you, Mr Back-to-Nature.'

'Shut up, Fred. You don't do anything but drink and play video games.'

More of Sophie's optimism slumped off. 'I'm sure your farm keeps you busy.'

'Yeah. See?' Fred sneered. 'My farm keeps me busy.'

Sophie decided no one was going to invite her to sit down, so she chose a chair and sat.

'Honestly, I wasn't sure I believed you were our cousin,' Naomi said. 'Lil seems convinced, but . . .'

'It is a pretty weird story.' Sophie glanced around to include the men. 'Do any of you remember your mom talking about Connie's good side? Or anything about my birth father?'

'All she told me was that they weren't close.' Natalie inspected a fingernail. 'That Connie was super needy, sucked the air out of whatever room she came into, never took anything seriously, yadda yadda. If you ask me, that last part is just Mom's opinion, because she took *everything* seriously.'

'Hey.' Donny smacked her with a couch pillow. 'That's not true.'

'I was wondering.' Fred tore his eyes from the movie. 'Did you get any of your mom's alcoholism genes?'

'Jesus, Donny.' Naomi rolled her eyes.

'What? Jeffrey died of alcohol poisoning, and we worried about Lil after that guy Tom left the country. She lost it for like a year.'

Sophie's heart contracted with sympathy.

'Man, did she ever.' Donny chuckled. 'Partying like—'

'Oh, I love this part.' Fred turned the sound back on. A car chased by a cop soared through the air, on fire, and crashed into a gas pump, which, predictably, exploded.

Footsteps made Sophie turn, in anticipation both of meeting her uncle and of being rescued. She was sure over time there would be much to love about her cousins, but nothing was obvious yet.

'Dad's not coming down.' Lily Anne appeared calm, but Sophie could feel her anger. 'I don't know what's wrong with him. He's being really weird.'

Naomi snorted. 'What else is new?'

'C'mon, guys.' Lily Anne crossed to Fred, grabbed the remote from his hand and turned the set off. 'Sophie's only here for a while. Try to get to know her.'

'She's right. Sorry about all the testosterone,' Naomi said. 'So . . . we heard you were adopted to Connecticut. Where were you born? Seems like Connie lived all over the map.'

'I was born on Crete.'

Lily Anne whipped her head around, eyes wide with astonishment. 'On Crete? You were born on Crete?'

Sophie nodded.

'But . . .' Her cousin looked hopelessly confused. 'So was I.'

Fred sputtered into his beer. 'You were not.'

'Yes.' Lily Anne was obviously shaken. 'I was.'

'You weren't born on Crete.' Donny spoke more gently. 'Mom never went anywhere.'

'I asked her about it once. She said she was visiting Connie and had me early.'

'What are you smoking, Lil?' Fred said. 'Can you imagine Mom going abroad? Or anywhere?'

'Especially in her third trimester.' Naomi laughed at the idea. 'Ms Super Worrywart going all the way to *Greece* to visit a sister she didn't even *like*? No way. She wouldn't even have traveled to New Hampshire. That's like ten minutes.'

Lily Anne opened her mouth, shut it. Tried again. 'I was born on Crete. It says so on my birth certificate. Non-negotiable.'

During the sibling exchange, an idea had occurred to Sophie, an unimaginable, impossible idea that would make total sense of all this confusion, and also blow her and Lily Anne's worlds apart.

'When is your birthday, Lily Anne?' She already knew the answer. All the secrets, the promises not to tell. It made sense. Except it made no sense whatsoever, given what she knew – or thought she knew – about her parents.

'September fifteenth.'

Sophie's throat started closing in on her. So did the living room walls. 'What year?'

'Nineteen seventy-eight.' Lily Anne was watching her in alarm. 'At five-oh-two p.m.'

Sophie stood, struggling to speak. 'I have the same birthday. The same day, the same year, the same place. You're three minutes older. Connie was—'

'No.' Lily Anne grew pale. 'That's not possible. My birth certificate names my parents, Phyllis and Clyde Corson.'

Sophie walked over to her sister's stiff figure. 'They change your parents' names on your birth certificate when you're adopted. Mine says Lilianne and Gilles. But they don't change where and when you were born.'

'What the hell?' Fred's voice. 'What's going on?'

Fred was ignored.

Lily Anne stared back at Sophie, dark eyes wide, then narrowed in disbelief. Sophie waited, knowing she'd need time.

Slowly into those dark eyes came realization. Clarity. Warmth. 'Oh my God. Oh my God, Sophie. I think you're right.'

'About *what*?'

Fred was ignored again.

'Lulu,' Lily Anne whispered. 'Fifi. It's so *obvious*.'

Sophie clutched her arm, needing to touch and to hold on to her sister. 'You're named after my mother. Connie's best friend.'

'I *said*, what the hell is going on?' Fred demanded.

'Think about it, Fred,' Donny snapped. 'Same birthday, same year, same island.'

'They're twins,' Naomi said in awe. 'Lil is Connie's kid. Mom and Dad totally lied to us.'

'Wait, she's not my sister?'

'Fred!' Naomi groaned, her trance broken. 'Of course she's your sister, moron. Adopted sister.'

'No, she's my cousin.'

Naomi turned on him. 'Stop talking.'

'It's true.' Fred held up both hands in protest. 'I'm not saying it's bad. It's . . . I don't know what it is.'

'It's weird.' Donny stared at Sophie as if she'd just this second showed up at their house. 'It's messed up. Really messed up. You guys need to talk to Dad.'

'You're not kidding. Come on, Sophie.' Lily Anne emerged from her shock and grabbed Sophie's arm, eyes bright with exhilaration and fear. 'We're going upstairs.'

She stomped up, breathing hard, Sophie behind her matching her breath for breath. Her twin. Her twin sister. Denied to her for forty-five years by parents she'd trusted. It was unthinkable, and yet, as Lily Anne had said, it was so obvious. Their immediate bond. The sister-shaped hole in her life she'd tried to fill with Lulu and Beezy. Lily Anne had done the same with Fifi, each attempting to recapture the twin she'd shared life with from conception until five months after birth.

The only thing the truth did not explain was why they'd been separated, and why that had been kept such a secret.

'*Dad.*' Lily Anne knocked and opened the door simultaneously. 'I'm coming in with Sophie to find out what the hell is going on.'

Sophie's Uncle Clyde was a slight man with a mop of uncut gray hair, wearing jeans and a sweater that probably fit him when he was considerably more robust, but now hung on his thin frame in sad beige folds. The material was pilled and stained. His sharp chin bristled with unshaven hairs. His eyes were hazel, red-rimmed, as if he hadn't been sleeping for about a decade.

'Who is this?' Lily Anne pulled Sophie in front of her father. He looked up unwillingly, eyes full of such grief and shame Sophie could barely stand to look at him. At the same time, if he'd been part of this, he deserved all that shame and more. 'No idea? I'll tell you. She's my sister. My twin sister. I'm Connie's child. Connie and some guy we don't even know. Not yours. Not Phyllis's. Isn't that right?'

'Yes.'

The confirmation made Sophie wince, and her sister explode. 'Why didn't you *tell me*? I look different from the rest of you, I act different. My brothers teased me mercilessly that I was adopted, and I always felt that way. You and Mom let me go on feeling that way. Like a . . . like a . . .'

'Red grape in the green bunch?' Sophie blurted out.

'Yes.' Lily Anne squeezed Sophie's forearm, speaking more calmly. 'The red grape in the green bunch. What the hell, Dad?'

Her father regarded her steadily. 'Your mother decided this. It made sense at the time. I wasn't around. I was out working to keep you all fed. So you could have better lives.'

The look of impatience on Lily Anne's face told Sophie she'd heard this anthem before. 'You should have told me I was adopted starting the second I could understand words. That's how you handle adoptions.'

'You weren't supposed to find out.'

'What kind of answer is—'

'You were never supposed to find out. It was impossible that you would find out. That's why we didn't tell you. So you'd never feel that you were anything but our child. So you'd never feel that someone didn't want you.'

Sophie couldn't stay quiet. 'Our mother wanted us. She was thrilled to be pregnant. She died, she did not give us up.'

Clyde took in a hunched breath that thrust the sharp points of his shoulders against the worn wool of his sweater. 'There was to be no contact between the families. We told no one. The other parents swore they'd tell no one. Your mother was adamant about that. This was her idea, and it should have worked.'

Lily Anne scoffed. 'Don't lay all this at Mom's feet. You were in on it. You could have—'

'I was traveling constantly. Your mother was taking care of four children already. Naomi was barely two, Fred and Donny were three and five, Jeffrey seven. She was supposed to add two more babies to that?'

'We are *sisters! Twins!*' Lily was practically panting. 'Why didn't you give both of us to Sophie's parents so we could have been raised together?'

Sophie's stomach roiled. Maybe Mom and Dad hadn't wanted both of them. Maybe *they'd* caused this mess.

'They would have taken both of you.' Clyde thrust a hand through his hair and clutched a handful. 'Your mother insisted we take one because you were her sister's and she shared your blood.'

Lily Anne looked apoplectic.

Sophie jumped in. 'We both shared her blood.'

Clyde's stare turned fiery. 'It was a damn fine thing for Phyllis to do. This was one more mess of Connie's she was stuck cleaning up.'

'Oh nice, Dad. We were *babies*, not messes.'

'You have no idea what she did for that woman, that sister of hers.' Clyde's face was red now. He was shaking. Sophie was terrified he'd have some kind of attack. 'How much she sacrificed. It was too much for her to take on two more babies. You don't have children, you have no idea. Your mother was a saint for taking one of you.'

That logic was so screwed up, Sophie didn't know how to tackle it. Phyllis could not have been any kind of saint if she thought nothing of tearing siblings apart for her convenience. Why hadn't Mom and Dad stopped her? Why hadn't *anyone* stopped her? Sophie and her sister had been irrevocably and infinitely let down by the people they should have been able to trust the most.

'Oh, I see, Mom was a saint for splitting us up so that by five months we'd lost everyone we knew and loved. Our mother, our father and each other.' Lily Anne's face was the same shade as Clyde's. 'At least you should have told me after Mom died. That's on you.'

'No.' He rose from his chair. 'I could not do that. Even for you. I lost Phyllis after four years of agony. I was not going to betray her trust after that.'

'Oh, good to know. Thanks, Dad.' Lily Anne's sarcasm was undercut by her trembling voice. 'I'm going to drive my sister back to Rutland now. You can go on thinking of your silence as honoring your late wife if it makes you feel better, but if you ask me, you're just a massive coward.'

She turned and bolted for the door. Sophie, caught by surprise, had one unpleasant second to view the shock on her uncle's face before she followed her sister downstairs, not sure she'd ever felt this unmoored, even when she found out Peter was boinking another woman.

'I don't need to ask how that went.' Downstairs, Donny was looking grimly at Lily Anne's face. 'I'm sorry this is so . . . whatever it is. I was telling Fred and Naomi that I remembered something. Something that's been bugging me forever but I ignored because I couldn't explain it. Jeffrey came to me one day – Jeffrey's our older brother who died, Sophie.'

Sophie nodded, heart pounding, face hot, a surreal ringing in her ears. It was an effort to concentrate on what Donny was saying.

'He said that for years Mom kept telling him about Lil coming home from the hospital, all the details of her birth, the same ones she told all of us, but that she kept saying to him, "You remember that, don't you, Jeffrey?" And he didn't. Not a bit of it. That bothered him. He couldn't remember anything about you, Lil, until you were a few months old. He felt like he should have. He would have been about seven when you came, old enough to remember. Not like the rest of us.'

Tears rose in Lily Anne's eyes and spilled over. She began to sob. 'My God, the lies. The silence and the lies. I can't believe this is my life.'

Sophie looked around at the trio of siblings, who were gazing at their adopted sister with combinations of fear and compassion. None of them moved to comfort her.

She moved herself, putting an arm around Lily Anne's shoulders until she got control of herself. 'Want me to drive back?'

'No. No. I'm okay.' Lily Anne sniffed and wiped at her eyes. 'Great to see you, guys.'

'Lil . . .' Naomi came over and awkwardly touched her arm. 'This makes no difference to us, you know. Mom and Dad made a huge mistake not telling you, but as far as we're concerned, you're . . . I mean you're still our li'l Lil.'

'Thanks, Naomi.' Lily Anne hugged her sister, then her brothers, who'd wandered over sheepishly. At least the hugs were long and sincere.

Points for that.

Back in the car, Sophie and Lily Anne sat for a long minute, stunned, both undoubtedly feeling alone in a world that had conspired against and betrayed them.

As if on cue, they turned and looked at one another. Then burst out laugh-crying at the over-the-top absurdity of what they'd just learned. They were sisters. Twins, who'd shared a womb for nine months and a house for five, inseparable for every moment of that time, then forced to soldier on through forty-five more years without each other.

Lulu and Fifi, no longer imaginary, finally back together, where they belonged.

Chapter 29

By the time Lily Anne and Sophie arrived back at Owen's house in Bridgewater Corners, after a stop for lunch – Greek salads – they were both exhausted.

'See you Monday.' Sophie held out her arms and they embraced awkwardly in the small car.

'Monday.' Lily Anne's eyes filled. 'Maybe we'll be halfway back to normal by then? A quarter?'

'There's always hope.' Sophie unbuckled her seatbelt and got out, bending toward the window to wave one more time. 'Monday.'

Still half numb, she stood watching her sister drive away, wanting only to . . . something. She'd never been this full of so many conflicting emotions, and had no idea what to do next, how to untangle and in what order to deal with them.

'Whatcha looking at?'

She whirled around at Owen's voice. He'd come out of his workshop and was walking toward her, tall, solid and still so unexpectedly handsome. Sophie hadn't seen such a welcome sight in her whole life.

'Uh oh.' He must have noticed her blotchy mess of a face. 'Things didn't go so well.'

'Owen.' Her chest heaved with a new avalanche of emotions. 'I need to . . . I need to chop wood.'

'Right. Okay.' He pointed to his official chopping stump. 'Wait there. I'll get the ax.'

Sophie watched him stride back to the workshop, deeply grateful. No questions, no consideration, just 'Okay.'

She would miss him.

He reappeared carrying a small ax and a spear-like implement. 'Here's your ax. If you don't like that, this gizmo you use by putting the sharp end on the log, lifting this weight on top and letting it drop down. The force drives the point in until the wood splits.'

She looked carefully at both tools. 'Gimme the ax.'

One corner of Owen's mouth turned up. He held out the blade, a pair of safety glasses he'd unhooked from his back pocket and a pair of work gloves small enough for her hands – they must have belonged to his wife. 'Need a lesson?'

'Please.'

He put a log on its end in the middle of the enormous stump and mimed holding an ax. 'Stand solidly, feet apart, knees unlocked. Measure where you want to hit and make sure you're comfortable with the distance. Lift the ax up. Bring the ax down. Bam. If you miss, try again. I still miss plenty.'

'Thanks.' She'd never seen him miss, but was grateful for the pep talk. She put the glasses on, and the gloves, and took hold of the ax.

Legs apart. Knees unlocked. She hovered the ax over the center of the log and adjusted her stance. Lifted her arms. Brought them down with all her might.

Hit the very edge of the log and toppled it off the stump.

Oops.

'Good. You were close. Try again.'

She balanced the log back, measured her stance, lifted her arms ...

Missed again.

She gave a huff of frustration.

'Try not swinging so hard. Keep your eye on the log and visualize the ax hitting it.'

Rebalanced. Remeasured. Relifted.

Thunk. The blade bit into the top inch or so of the log. Sophie grinned in triumph and lifted the ax to keep chopping. The log came up with it. 'Argh!'

Owen's quiet voice. 'Either keep bashing down or pull out the ax to try again. You'll get it.'

Pulling out the ax took some wrestling, but she managed.

Getting the log to split took a few more tries, but she managed that too. And when the wood did finally split, cleanly if not evenly, Sophie was so astonished, she stared for a second as if expecting it to put itself back together just to piss her off.

She gave a victorious whoop. 'Got it!'

'You did great.' Owen set up another log for her. 'Go again.'

The cuts became more even, her stroke surer. Her arms hurt, sweat was pouring off every part of her body, but she kept going, channeling her anger and pain and frustration into firewood she wouldn't be around to see burning. Over and over, striking harder and harder, grunting like a demented pig, until her shoulders burned and her arms started shaking.

'I better stop.' She lowered the ax, amazed at how much more peaceful she felt, though not a single problem had been solved. 'I might not be able to lift my arms tomorrow.'

'Feel better?'

'Much. Thank you.' She frowned up at him. 'I'm sorry. I was such a mess I wasn't thinking. You just had to interrupt whatever you were doing to tend to my insanity.'

He grinned. 'You're fun when you're insane.'

'Thanks.' She wiped her dripping forehead with the hem of her top, not caring if he saw her poochy belly underneath. 'I think I should shower.'

'And drink about a gallon of water.'

She nodded, still breathing hard.

'And plan to have dinner at my place.'

Sophie made a face. 'I may not be fit company, Owen.'

'That's why I invited you. Come by whenever you want.' He picked up the ax and the other splitter thing and walked back to the shed, whistling.

In the cottage, Sophie drank her body weight in water, ignoring text messages from Beezy and her parents. She waited until she'd cooled down, then showered and dressed, forgoing makeup and hair-drying. Her body was pleasantly exhausted – she would definitely not be able to move her arms the next day – and her brain was pleasantly numb.

Wood-chopping ruled.

Downstairs, she paused in her kitchen, searching for something to contribute to the meal, and settled on crêpes, because they were easy, and because . . . guys and dessert. She could make the batter in the blender in five minutes, and cook them at Owen's house.

Fifteen minutes later, she was on her way across the yard with a blender jar of batter, raspberry jam for spreading and folding, and some leftover chocolate sauce, because raspberries and chocolate belonged together.

She knocked with an arm that was still trembling, smelling oregano and roasting chicken, hungry because she and Lily Anne hadn't managed to do more than pick at their lunch.

The door opened to Owen walking away. 'Come in. Chicken's just done. I gotta take it out to rest.'

'Smells fantastic.' She followed him to his kitchen, both elegant and rustic, with cabinets he'd made himself from local red maple.

'Easy recipe.' He took the chicken out, burnished to a gorgeous brown, sitting on a pile of vegetables in a roasting pan. 'What do you have there?'

'Batter for crêpes. You have a pan that will work?'

'Basic non-stick.'

'Perfect.' She put the blender jar on the counter and set the chocolate sauce at the back of the stove, where it would warm from the residual oven heat.

'I have wine to go with the chicken. Want some now? Have a seat.' He pointed to the table set for two at the end of the room, by windows overlooking the forest.

'Wine would be great. Just half a glass.' She sat and watched him open the bottle and pour. And then the words came out of her, no planning, no forethought. 'I found out today that Lily Anne isn't my cousin.'

He glanced over, then went back to pouring the wine. 'No?'

'She's my sister. Fraternal twin.'

'Whoa.' Owen brought the glasses over and sat opposite her. 'That's pretty heavy stuff.'

'No kidding. They separated us.' Her voice cracked. 'At five months.'

'Good God. Reason?'

Sophie shrugged, trying not to cry again. 'My aunt and uncle had too many kids already and could only take one of us. My mom was my birth mother's best friend, so she took me. Why anyone thought this was a good idea I have not yet figured out.'

'Sophie. I'm sorry. That should not have happened.'

'I don't know how to deal with it. I'm furious, and I'm sad, and I'm . . .' She put down her wine, reminding herself to keep breathing. 'I'm barfing my personal problems all over you, when you only signed up to be my landlord.'

'As long as it's figurative barfing, I'm okay with it.'

She laughed like a slightly crazy person, which she was. 'Owen, you are a good, good man.'

'Maybe. What's next? Do you know yet?'

'I know what I want to do. Drive back to Southport tomorrow and tell my parents they are horrible unfeeling people who made the stupidest mistake ever, followed by the stupider mistake of trying to hide the first stupid mistake.'

Owen took a sip of wine and contemplated the rest in his glass. 'I'm going to tell you about one of the smartest decisions I ever made.'

'Okay.' She waited. He didn't move. 'What?'

'Not loading my shotgun and hunting down my brother and wife after I realized they had helped themselves to being a couple.'

Her chest ached with empathy. So much pain. 'What did you do instead? I mean, how much wood can a person chop?'

'Or a woodchuck.' He grinned at her kindly. Such a good man. 'Instead, I waited. I sat on my rage and pain until it calmed down enough for me to talk to it sensibly.'

'What did you tell it?'

'That my brother and my wife loved each other and I loved both of them, and what happened happened.'

'No way.' She made sure she looked good and disgusted. 'That is ridiculously big of you.'

Owen shrugged. 'The alternative was cutting off my brother and wallowing in bitterness that would eat at me for the rest of my life.'

'Oh.' Dramatic sigh. 'I guess that wouldn't be too pleasant.'

The Jewel of Cairo

'Don't get me wrong. There was plenty of bitterness for a long while. Shitty things I said and shitty things I did. But I knew that wasn't who I wanted to be. So I invested in a goddamn halo.' He put his glass down and got up to retrieve the chicken. 'There were times I hated that halo more than anything I've ever hated. But I never regretted putting it on.'

'I'm sure it looked cute on you.' She deserved the look he gave her. 'Is there anything you do regret?'

He thought about that while he moved chicken and vegetables from the roasting pan to a platter and spooned broth over both. 'Sometimes I worry I'm missing out on a bigger life. But this one suits me pretty well. What about you?'

Sophie bent her head, fighting the restarting of her tear machine. 'I regret wasted time. Being married to the wrong person for the wrong reasons. Not knowing my sister. Not understanding myself well enough to figure out what I want to do. Not having enough courage or faith in myself.'

'That's quite a list.' He set the platter on the table. 'But I don't see that you're out of time to do those things. How old are you?'

'Forty-five.'

Owen looked startled. 'Really?'

'What?'

He rolled his eyes and picked up a carving knife and fork. 'If I tell you, you'll think I'm sweet-talking.'

'Oh, go ahead, Owen. Sweet-talk me. It's been a crap day.'

He laughed and started carving. 'I thought you were in your late thirties.'

'Oh Owen.' She clasped her hands to her heart. 'I am suddenly and deeply in love with you.'

'Yeah?' He put a slice of breast meat on her plate. 'Wait till you taste this chicken.'

He wasn't kidding. The meat was juicy and the skin crisp, but the best part was the oregano, lemon, garlic and olive oil he'd poured all over. Every bite, chicken or vegetable, was a garlicky, lemony, herby schmaltz-fest, and Sophie was surprised to find herself eating ravenously. She no longer felt as if she were going to implode and explode at the same time. More importantly, she no longer felt she had to decide what to do right away.

The crêpes were delicious, though it took a while to figure out Owen's stove, so the first was burned and the second gummy. By the third, she'd found the sweet spot, and they ate the delicate pancakes spread with the jam, rolled into tubes and drizzled with chocolate sauce.

Not too shabby.

After the last dish was washed and put away, the wine bottle half empty, Sophie was ready to collapse from fatigue. Owen insisted on walking her across the yard, claiming he had to get something from his shed. At the cottage's little door, Sophie turned to him, feeling shy and awkward.

'Thanks for dinner, and for talking out this whole pigsty of a mess my family created for Lily Anne and me to wallow in.'

'Nice image.'

'I guess.' She blew out a breath, looking down at her sandals. 'Twice I haven't taken your advice to look before I leap. Twice I've regretted it. I'd really love to call my parents right now and bitch and moan and cry, but you convinced me it would be smarter and more peaceful to go to bed after this really nice evening with you.'

Maybe it would also be smarter to stay out the rest of her month and confront Lilianne and Gilles in person after she got back. As calmly as she could.

'That sounds like halo material to me.'

'You're fabulous.' Sophie hugged him hard and let go before the desire to cling put any weirdness between them. She was in no shape to involve him further in her messes, and, well, there wasn't any point starting something they'd have to stop in two weeks. 'Goodnight.'

'Goodnight, Sophie. Sweet dreams.' He turned and ambled away. Sophie made herself go into the cottage, because it would have been really tempting to stand and watch his tall masculine form crossing the yard in the moonlight.

Chapter 30

Sunday, June 20, 1976

There had been days since Lilianne and Gilles had been living in Southport that were everything Lilianne had hoped for in bringing him to her hometown. Beautiful spring days, the world around them fully green and blooming. Azaleas, dogwood, magnolias and crabapple had breached the bleak winter landscape; rhododendrons and their mates of summer were on the verge of exploding. The wind coming off Long Island Sound no longer held the faintest hint of a bite. Days of exploring and wandering that finished with long conversations over dinner they cooked together in the Willow Street kitchen and ate in the house's cozy dining room by candlelight. Days that filled Lilianne with peace and purpose of a nature more satisfying than any she'd known, giving lie to her emphatic assertions that she preferred to live alone. Days when she had to force herself to remember this was not her life, nor Gilles's, but borrowed temporary happiness.

Today was not one of those days. Nor had the past several even come close. As May had turned into June and June rolled along, the good days became fewer. But Gilles seemed to like the therapist he chose after trying out a few, and though he came back from the sessions exhausted and close-lipped, he kept going back, which had to be a good sign.

Today, though, he'd come back furious.

Tonight, as he picked morosely at their supper of mustard-maple-glazed salmon from a recipe Lilianne had found in Dina's wooden recipe box, she was on edge, discouraged, and perilously close to losing patience, which it seemed Gilles needed from her in an almost inexhaustible supply.

She'd finished the Cairo bank project, and was casting around trying to figure out her next move, between horrified calls from her father, who couldn't imagine Maxwell Investments continuing without a Maxwell in it, and calls from her mother about how to run the house, as if Lilianne hadn't lived here for the first twenty years of her life.

She'd heard from Connie a few times, once in a phone call not long after they'd arrived back in the US. Her friend had been terribly upset, the line hadn't been good, and it had been hard to piece together the story, but somehow Lilianne understood that Safiya had not shown up at the train station to take possession of the gold carriage, and that Sami had been shot. Lilianne was spooked enough to urge her to leave Cairo as soon as possible, and had given her the name of a contact on Crete, Spencer Oakes, a good friend from her CIA training days, who'd been assigned there and who'd be able to pull all kinds of strings if Connie needed help.

Then she'd hung up, absolutely sick at the idea that something might have happened to Safiya, that Al-Kalib had gotten word of her betrayal and taken revenge.

For days since Connie's call, Lilianne had been thinking about the housekeeper's stony, dark face, and how it had come to life in their moment sharing secrets in Sami's living room. She'd contacted John Baker, hoping he could help, but he clearly wasn't willing to waste time and resources looking for a woman from a tiny village who'd probably just gone home.

How grossly unfair the world could be.

She watched Gilles pick at his food and felt a surge of illogical annoyance, not for the first time, that he'd chosen to cover the war in Lebanon when he was already in such bad shape over Helen. And that he continued to act as if his suffering was so much worse than anyone else's.

Slow breath. A weak moment, unworthy of her and unfair to him. He was trying to get better.

'Gilles.' She waited until he looked up. 'I thought tomorrow we could go for a sail. My friends the Deckers have launched their boat for the season. A sunset sail with cocktails? How does that sound?'

'Yeah, maybe.'

Another surge of irritation. He needed her compassion, but she was running low. He'd take his camera sometimes and leave the house for hours with no word on where he was going or when he'd be back, leaving her frantic with worry. 'Sounds like a fun evening to me.'

Silence.

She ate more of her salmon, cooling and just overcooked enough that the edges were chalky. Her fault. She'd been distracted watching the kids across the street try out their new pogo sticks. It made her itch to be a child again. A different child.

'We should also try a trip to New York. If you're ready. I haven't been in such a long—'

'Yeah, maybe.'

Yeah, maybe. Yeah, maybe. Yeah, maybe she'd take his salmon and dump it in his lap. He'd let his hair grow despite her hints that it needed a cut, and hadn't shaved in days, possibly not showered either.

What now? What did Lilianne need to do? Show him a

mirror? Hold his head under the kitchen tap and scrub him like a baby?

He poured himself another glass of wine. She'd only sipped from her glass and the bottle was more than half empty. How could she stop this slide? What if he ended up no better off than the way she'd found him?

The idea made her panicky and sick. She took another sip of her wine, a nice Sauvignon Blanc that her mood had turned sour and off. 'I bumped into a high school friend yesterday. She wants to have us over for—'

Slam. His fist on the table, making their plates jump.

'What the *hell*, Gilles?'

'I don't care about your friends.'

'Oh, that's nice, thank you.' She whipped her napkin off her lap and hurled it onto the table. 'Fine. Then you talk. For a start, why don't you tell me what the hell is the matter with you? Are you bored here with me? Want to go back to Paris? To Cairo? To Leb—'

'It was yesterday.' He nearly shouted the words over her tirade, his face reddening. 'Yesterday!'

'*What* was?'

'The wedding. I called to find out.' His voice was anguished. 'I couldn't stand it anymore.'

She squinted at him. Had he lost his marbles? '*What* wedding?'

'Helen's! *Helen's!* To her farmer boy!' His dark eyes were wide, glittering with rage. It was such a relief after his recent catatonic state, Lilianne almost cheered, except that much pain was nothing to celebrate.

'Gilles. I'm sorry. I hadn't been keeping track.'

He slumped forward, elbows on the table, hair tumbling over his contorted face. 'I was sure. I was so sure she wouldn't be able to go through with it. That she'd realize, somehow she would realize that she didn't love him. That she couldn't bear to commit to this . . . this person, knowing how much she loved me. That everything we meant to each other would win. Because true love is always supposed to *win*.'

He burst into sobs.

Lilianne sat stunned, blinking at him. All this time she'd spent in the fantasy of playing house with this man, everything for him was still Helen.

Of course. Of course it was. Not even six months since she'd left him.

'Gilles.' She broke through her shock, went over to him, put her hand on his shoulder, her frustration and judgment leaking away, replaced by compassion . . . and something close to envy.

This emotion of his, this all-consuming passion, this physical need for another human being was nothing Lilianne would ever know. Watching his agony now, she could feel some relief. How exhausting to live amid such a dazzling array of highs and lows. And yet . . .

How extraordinary to matter to someone that much.

Gilles shoved back his chair, grabbed her and hauled her almost violently into his lap. She fell sideways against him, fitting tight against his chest.

His kisses weren't for her, she understood that; the passion in them was anger, also not for her. She submitted, knowing he needed this, suppressing her own need to get away.

As quickly as he'd started, he pulled back. 'Lilianne. My God. I'm sorry. I was out of my mind. Forgive me.'

She forced herself to face his humility, finding that intimacy more invasive and harder to stand than the kisses. 'It's okay. I understand.'

Why didn't he release her? Why didn't he let her get up? Why did he go on staring as if he were trying to climb inside her? As if he were seeing something that held him there? The way he'd moved his camera aside to stare at her in Paris, and stared again sitting on the couch together in the Cairo apartment, and again while she was dancing at the Abdallah farm.

What was he seeing?

He lowered his face again, slowly, and this time the kiss was for her. She felt it from the moment his lips touched hers. No passion, no possessiveness. Deep sweetness, unlike any kisses she'd ever had.

Her tense body made no response, nothing in the places that normal biology dictated were supposed to react, but his mouth on hers gave her pleasure, and her heart became fuller than she thought possible, and more vulnerable. She felt like a child in his arms, innocent, fragile, at risk of being shattered by the wrong word or thought.

'Marry me, Lilianne.' He was grinning now, into her eyes, repeating the ridiculous proposal. 'Marry me.'

She laughed, she couldn't help it, giddy with emotions she couldn't understand. 'Ask me in six months, when your visa runs out and when you'd have some chance of meaning it.'

He laughed too, a coarse, painful sound, but without bitterness. 'Then let me take you upstairs, Lilianne. Let's lose ourselves, forget all the pain and the past and be together tonight.'

Tears came to her eyes. How she wanted this. How right it would be, to help ease his pain for a little while, something she'd clumsily been trying to do for weeks, in every way but this. 'I can't.'

'C'mon, Lilianne. Let go. Do something stupid and senseless and ridiculous. For once in your perfectly controlled life, give over. Let me make love to you.'

Her laughter died. She touched his beautiful, anguished face, reveled in the new connection they'd formed tonight, felt the need to keep that, to hold it, cement it forever, knowing she was reaching beyond anything possible. 'You don't understand. I can't.'

He gazed, uncomprehending.

Maybe it was the wine, the kisses, the vulnerable beauty in his face, or the eyes he opened to her, eyes she could see into without end, that made her want to open herself in return, to be equally vulnerable to this man who had become so important to her. Maybe who always had been. A soul as damaged as hers.

Tears spilled down her cheeks. She pushed back memories of the confession to her mother and forced herself past crippling fear. 'I physically can't. I show no passion because I was born without any. This thing you feel for Helen, with your body, I . . . can't. I can't feel anything like that. I'm abnormal. Broken.'

Slowly, Gilles's face cleared, as if all the tiny shards of Lilianne had finally come together in his mind.

'Ah, Lilianne.' His voice was deep with grief for her. 'I'm sorry you—'

'You don't need to be sorry.' Hostile, defensive, everything she'd decided not to be. 'I'm—'

'No, no.' He put a gentle finger to her lips. 'I'm not sorry you are like this. I'm sorry you think it makes you less. Because that isn't true, Lilianne. It's not true.'

She stared at him in astonishment for one, two, three seconds, then she dissolved.

He gathered her close, rocking her as she cried out her relief and her fear and her longing, as if she were the more damaged of the two of them. As if she were the one needing strength and patience, and he the one with plenty of both to give.

Chapter 31

Thursday, September 23, 1976

'Want to take a walk?'

Lilianne looked up at Gilles in surprise. She'd been going through a stack of reports to appease her father, who was still in freak-out mode over the idea that her leave of absence from Maxwell Investments might become permanent. So far the jury was still out. She enjoyed many things about her relative life of leisure, except the lack of purpose. Law school had been on her mind more and more often, something new to pursue after Gilles no longer needed her.

'Sure.' She pushed the papers aside and got up from the desk in her upstairs office, her parents' bedroom while she was growing up. Early-fall light was coming through the tall windows, tree leaves making dancing patterns on the floor and walls. Still mostly green, their season was coming to an end, glory time in New England, when woods became a blaze of color. A walk would be a delicious break from numbers and formulas. Yet she couldn't shake a sense of dread.

'Any destination in mind, or just feel like walking?' She tried to take in Gilles's mood without staring too obviously. His color was high, eyes alert and clear. Watching his slow, painful return toward his old self had been a deeply satisfying pleasure over the past five months. The night he'd broken down over Helen's wedding had been a turning point. Once he'd accepted that she'd married Kevin, Gilles seemed better equipped to put that piece of his grief behind him and focus on healing the war trauma. He still disappeared for long hours with his camera, but Lilianne no longer worried about having to go search for his body.

Not coincidentally, after breaking her childhood vow by unearthing her secret, Lilianne had felt herself relaxing into her life here in Southport and with Gilles, and relaxing into herself, despite understanding it was temporary. She even got a secret thrill when they were out in public and people assumed they were a normal couple. Why wouldn't they?

'I thought we could walk down to the beach.'

'Sure. Let me get a sweater.' She abandoned her paperwork and went down the hall to her childhood bedroom, redone by her mother as a 'surprise' after Lilianne left for Wellesley. Not much of a surprise that the room had become exactly what her mother would want, curtains and bedspread in a delicate floral pattern, perfectly complemented by the rug, wallpaper and throw pillows on the bed and window seat. Lilianne still hadn't gotten used to the feel of it. Like walking into a furniture showroom. At least Sarah made a familiar splash, wistful and elegant on the window seat, greeting Lilianne at the start and finish of each day.

Gilles was waiting at the bottom of the stairs with an expression that had become familiar over the past week or so, maybe longer. He'd been ... not moody necessarily, but distracted, thoughtful, somewhere else. The weeks his tourist visa would allow him to remain in the US were dwindling. Something was on his mind, and she'd been preparing herself to hear that he'd decided to return to Paris. His country. His family. His friends. His career.

The Jewel of Cairo

Why would he stay here? He deserved to love again, to have a rich and rewarding life with a French Helen who wouldn't desert him for the Kansas cornfields. Lilianne would miss him something fierce but would be forever grateful for the grace, acceptance and humility he'd not only practiced, but taught.

Outside, they walked the length of Willow Street, then turned right onto Old South Road, typical of Southport: narrow, lined with green trees, opulent houses – most white with black shutters – white picket fences, perfect lawns and sumptuous landscaping.

Founded in the seventeenth century, the town had escaped the canned feel of subdivisions and other planned communities, and was unselfconsciously peaceful and beautiful. Lilianne had felt more at home here and more content than she'd expected after so many exotic travel adventures. The world still beckoned to be explored now and then, but she'd fallen under Southport's spell in a way she never had as a rebellious teenager. Seeing it through older eyes, while still aware of its foibles, she felt new appreciation for its strengths.

'Walking for me in France was always on Parisian sidewalks, unless we were on vacation in some mountain or ocean tourist town. This has been very nice.'

Has been. The tense did not bode well. 'I've turned you into a 'burb lover.'

"Burb?'

'Short for suburb. Not city, not country.' She gestured around her. 'In between.'

'Yes, I see.' He lapsed back into quiet that lasted most of the way down Pequot Avenue.

Lilianne had grown used to his silences, and had stopped feeling the need to fill them.

A Mercedes slowed next to them; the window rolled down. 'Hi, you two.'

'Hi, Margie.' Lilianne smiled, wanting to roll her eyes. Margie had never given Lilianne the time of day either in high school or after, until she caught sight of Gilles. Suddenly, she couldn't get enough of her 'old friend'.

'Glad I bumped into you. Chesney and I are having a casual do tomorrow. Drinks and snacks, starting around six.' She directed the invitation to Gilles, pushing her sunglasses on top of her hair, tipping her head to one side. 'Are you in?'

Gilles glanced at Lilianne, who shrugged and nodded. 'That sounds very nice, thank you.'

Margie couldn't have been more delighted. She cooed, in fact.

Lilianne checked herself. She was acting like a jealous wife. It was important to continue reconnecting with people here in town, especially if Gilles was going to return to Paris. Margie was kindly offering an opportunity.

They waved the Mercedes off, Lilianne still annoyed by her reaction. Margie had always been an incorrigible flirt – more about needing reassurance that she was attractive than actual pursuit. Gilles was gorgeous and charming, and his foreigner status made him all the more exotic and attractive. Even Lilianne melted a little every time he said her name, his accent so delicate on the Ls, making the American pronunciation sound like an assault.

Margie wasn't a threat. This was about Lilianne. And Gilles. She was becoming dangerously attached, dangerously vulnerable. Everything she'd thought she couldn't be. How ironic that such a remarkable discovery about her ability to be with someone had come on the verge of losing it.

They reached their destination, Southport Beach, a curving strip of sand forming one side of the semicircular cove at the mouth of the harbor. Two steps onto the packed sand and

The Jewel of Cairo

Lilianne's patience ran out. 'Something's been on your mind, Gilles.'

'Yes.' A pause that seemed to go on forever. 'I need to go back to Paris.'

Even though Lilianne had expected the words, they were still a punch to her gut. 'Okay.'

He gave her an odd look. 'That's it?'

'Wrong answer? What am I supposed to say?'

'I don't know. I expected more. You seem full of something you're not saying.'

Damn his perceptiveness, but she'd stand firm. Once before she'd made herself supremely vulnerable to him. If he was leaving, there was no point laying herself open again.

'I'll miss you.' She meant the words to come out playfully.

They didn't.

'I'll miss you too. But I still have my apartment there, and all my things.'

'Yes.' Her throat cramped. She would not cry. She wouldn't.

Gilles turned to give her another searching look. She kept her eyes on the sand, noting carefully the indentations of other footprints, making herself think about the tide that would come in and erase them all, leaving the sand new and untouched, a twice-daily re-virginization.

'Do you want to come with me?'

Her heart leapt. For three or four steps she considered, until reality set in. 'My life is here now, Gilles. In the US.'

She wouldn't mention law school. Her plans would no longer be his concern.

'I need to see my family and let them know something of what's been going on.'

'Of course. That's important.' Lilianne sounded as sincere

as possible, not sincere enough to fool him, but trying made her feel better.

The breeze picked up, bringing a hint of its coming bite. Waves swished in and out on the shore. A seagull let out a guttural call then fell silent, as if defeated by the emptiness around it.

'I think two weeks should be enough. Maybe a month.'

Lilianne stopped walking. 'Two weeks.'

It took Gilles a moment to realize she wasn't next to him and turn back. 'What? Not long enough?'

She laughed, feeling her cheeks flush as relief flooded her, as all her bravado was exposed for the bull-poop it was. 'Good God, Gilles. You said you were going back to Paris. I thought you meant forever.'

He looked at her as if she were speaking gibberish. 'No, no, I'm not going back. My life is here with you.'

My life is here with you. Her laughter turned into tears that horrified her. 'For God's sake, Gilles. Look at me. I cry around you and no one else.'

He gave a lopsided grin that made her heart tilt. 'Maybe because you love me?'

She met his eyes, knowing that whether he felt the same or not, her words would reach a place of safety. 'Maybe. I mean, in the way that I can.'

Gilles drew his hand down her cheek in a tender caress that made her briefly capture his fingers to keep them there. 'I love you, Lilianne. In the way that I can.'

'Helen.' She felt no jealousy, only pity for her friend's mistake, and guilt that her pain had turned into Lilianne's happiness.

'Yes. Helen. But bearable now.' He took back his hand, looked out to sea, a gust ruffling his curling bangs. 'My tourist

The Jewel of Cairo

visa is coming to the end. I need to work again. To work here, I will need a green card.'

'Yes. Sure. I can help you apply for one through—'

'I think we should get married, Lilianne.' He turned back, dark, expressive eyes clear and calm. 'For practical reasons, yes, the visa, but also because we have empty spaces we fill for one another. We are good together. The past months have proved that.'

Lilianne took in a long breath, sorting through emotions of joy, caution and fear. As much as she loved the idea of grabbing hold of this life with him, marriage could be a mistake for both of them. 'I'm not everything you need, Gilles. You might meet someone else, another Helen, and fall truly in love.'

'There is only one Helen for me.'

She wouldn't insult him with a contradiction. Statistically, he was undoubtedly wrong, but life wasn't about statistics. 'What if she gets a divorce and is free someday?'

'Helen will never divorce.' His eyes narrowed, though his voice stayed gentle. 'She made her choice. She will do anything to make it work. This is her nature.'

He was probably right about that. Lilianne made a face. 'She's a fool.'

'Maybe.' He looked forlornly out at the water, hands shoved in his pockets. 'Or maybe she knew something I didn't.'

Lilianne touched his shoulder. 'We can visit her someday, out in Kansas. We'll invite Connie, bring Sarah and show up, maybe as a birthday surprise.'

'Maybe. But that's someday. I want to talk about now and us.' He took her hands, pulled them together in his, his gaze intense. 'I think I can make you happy, Lilianne.'

'Gilles.' She was whispering through threatening tears,

exactly like the love-struck idiots she'd made fun of so many times. 'You already make me happy.'

'I do? Oh, okay.' He nodded enthusiastically. 'In that case, I don't need to do anything.'

Lilianne rolled her eyes.

'What do you think, *chérie?*' He was looking at her as if she were the answer to his prayers. 'Honest reaction.'

Complicated reaction. They'd certainly been happy over the past months, but that wasn't enough. 'I want to make sure you understand that if you marry me, you'd be giving up the chance for a normal relationship with a normal woman.'

'Lilianne.' He was clearly exasperated.

'I'm serious, Gilles. You've been through a nightmare that you've only recently emerged from. I want you to be sure that it's not just because you feel better and I'm around.'

'I know what I'm getting.' He lowered his forehead to hers. 'A woman who has stood by me at my absolute lowest without quaking, and who—'

'Oh, no. I quaked.' She refused to let him make her some kind of saint. 'I nearly broke china over your head several times.'

'Okay, then, I'll be getting a woman who never broke anything over my head in spite of wanting to.' His forehead was warm. Their breath mingled. Around them, the breeze carried ocean scents and a preview of fall's crisp air. 'Together you and I have gone through more than anything Helen and I were tested with. We can make this work.'

She needed to be very sure he understood. 'What about sex, Gilles? You need that. You're human.'

'Oh, *I'm* human? What does that make you, a unicorn?' He pulled back. 'I'm going to need to spend a lot of time erasing this stupid idea of yours that you're somehow not a whole person.'

'I *meant* . . .' breath for patience, 'that you might need to go elsewhere for—'

He made a very French sound of dismissal. 'Stop trying different ways to warn me off the same thing, Lilianne. I have thought this through. You are not afraid of being close to me. We'll find what works for both of us. There are all kinds of pleasure. What's good between us matters more.'

Lilianne stood battling her fear, her insecurity, her long-held convictions, only to realize in a light-bulb moment that her uncertainty over this marriage stemmed not from her own feelings, but from insecurity about his.

That was something she'd never be able to control. No one who promised marriage could control that, and there was no point trying.

She'd spent too much of her life denying what she truly wanted.

Even so, it took three attempts before the words emerged. 'I'm willing to try. If you're sure.'

'I am sure, Lilianne. You? I think not so sure.'

She moved a curl off his forehead, absurdly delighted when it sprang obstinately back. 'Helen was convinced I was in love with you back in Paris. Did she ever tell you that?'

'No.'

'So it's possible I am sure, and have been for a long time, I just haven't allowed myself to believe it.'

Gilles's smile was quick and glowing, and it occurred to Lilianne, with a jolt of joy, that he'd been feeling almost as nervous and insecure about her answer as she was.

'I had nothing to look forward to when you came to rescue me in Paris, Lilianne. So many times I thought about ending my life. Now another chance, a new beginning. For this, we need a proper proposal.' He fumbled in his pocket, then knelt in the sand, eyes twinkling, arm outstretched holding a black velvet ring box. 'Lilianne Maxwell, my tower of strength and my wounded, vulnerable warrior, will you do me the honor of becoming my wife?'

She laughed, she couldn't help it, he looked so deliciously comical and serious. 'My God. A proper proposal, from Sir Lancelot.'

'Your knight in shining denim. Getting cold and wet at the knee.'

'Well, Lance, I'll make this quick.' She took the box and opened it, feeling like she was starring in some other woman's romantic fantasy. The ring was a simple diamond solitaire flanked by bar-cut emeralds that glittered in the fall light. She loved it at first sight. 'Gilles, this is stunning.'

'Yes?' He stood and helped slide it onto her finger. 'I stole one of your rings and copied the size.'

'It's perfect.' She looked up at him, feeling ridiculously shy in the face of so much emotion. 'I accept your wet-kneed proposal, and will marry you as soon as possible for immigration purposes, and because I love being with you. And because you've made possible a life I never allowed myself to believe I could have.'

He bent down carefully; their lips were chilly until they met and warmed. Chaste kisses, sealing a promise. Kisses Gilles drew back from with the lively eyes Lilianne remembered from before his trauma. There would be more backsliding in the months to come, more hard times for both of them, she knew that. But now and then, more and more as time put distance between him and all he'd suffered, he'd be back to the man she'd known and loved in Paris. Because of her? She could only hope so.

'Let's go home, *ma fiancée.*'

'Yes.' Humbled and on top of the world, Lilianne moved to his side and tucked her arm through his, still trying to grasp that for so many strange and remarkable reasons, she'd be living such a very normal life. 'Let's go home.'

Chapter 32

Present day

Lilianne: *Haven't heard from you in a while, sweetie. Not answering calls either! Everything okay? How did the family meeting go?*
Sophie: *Fine, Mom. All good. Super busy. I'll be home next week.*
Lilianne: ♥

Goodbyes always sucked. Awkward, messy, tearful, never the right words – Sophie hated them.

Working at Asphalia had been gratifying in a way her previous jobs hadn't come close to. Every resident was a puzzle, to be worked on until enough pieces fell into place that she could get the total picture. How to treat them, how they responded, what set them off, what soothed them.

She loved interacting with the women. They were remarkable people, and there was a mother-hen bittersweet satisfaction in graduating a chick out into the world, knowing there were predators out there but that at least the fledgling was leaving with as many resources as possible.

Sophie also wouldn't be leaving Asphalia as the same person. The residents had opened up such a poignant yet inspiring window onto their courage and determination in battling demons and pain. She had so much appreciation for the tough work involved. Humbling, as Lily Anne had described it. Sophie would always carry that humility with her, and was grateful for it.

The next awful goodbye – Owen. The woodworking event he'd hosted for the residents had been a smash. He'd been informative, skilled and adorable, managing to produce enough words along with his demonstration that everyone learned a lot. In fact, Betsy and Dee had both asked about coming back for lessons, and he'd seemed enthusiastic – for Owen. Which meant he'd said, 'That'd be okay.'

However, the wood-chopping lessons were not to be, nixed by Lily Anne as too risky. Sophie's clueless suggestion to visit a place in Rutland for ax-throwing was also vetoed because the place served alcohol. Lily Anne *had* agreed, though, to look into boxing and various martial arts as exercise options, for rage release and to build self-confidence.

The third goodbye – to her twin sister. Sophie couldn't even think about that one without wanting to bawl, but that too would have to happen.

She'd initially been planning a blowout last dinner for the Asphalia House residents, but it occurred to her that would be unnecessary showing-off, and likely to get her a particularly vicious teasing from Lizzie. So she'd save the caviar and blinis for her return to Southport. Instead, she'd bought frozen tilapia from the supermarket and breaded it herself, grinding crumbs from a stale baguette and infusing them with grated Parmesan, lemon zest, garlic and fresh thyme. She'd also prepared a brown rice and parsley salad, dressed with a garlicky lemon vinaigrette and studded with cut-up grapes and pecans.

For dessert, an old favorite of her mother's: peach cobbler

swirl, a bottom layer of baked peaches and pecans topped with biscuit dough rolled up around butter and crystallized ginger, then sliced into thin circles. Plus ice cream, of course.

At six p.m. sharp, the fish and salad were on the table, served with a smile to the chatting women, who thanked her as usual but otherwise acted as they normally did. That was fine. They had plenty to worry about, and Sophie was proud of the now colorful dining room and her other changes to Asphalia. They might not make a measurable difference in anyone's recovery, but they couldn't have hurt either.

Annika would be back Sunday evening, but only until Lily Anne could hire a replacement. Being in Norway with her family had made Annika realize how much she missed her home, and she was moving there permanently. Lily Anne had immediately offered the post to Sophie, but Sophie also missed being with her family in her home town.

At six thirty, Sophie retrieved the empty plates – empty was always a good sign – that the residents had stacked for her, and brought out the warm cobbler and ice cream to oohs and aahs that made her glow.

More appreciation than she'd ever gotten from her Southport clients.

She was back in the kitchen, trying to stay so busy she didn't remember how sad she was, when Betsy strutted in wearing one of her usual look-at-my-boobs outfits. 'We need you at tonight's meeting.'

'Oh. Well, sure.' Sophie propped the sponge against the dish drainer so it would dry. This was a first. She had no experience with twelve-step meetings and no idea what they'd need her for. 'Why?'

Betsy smiled oh-so-mysteriously. 'Come see.'

Sophie took off her apron and followed, hoping there wasn't

going to be a big fuss, because anyone being nice to her would set off another boo-hoo fest. She was annoyed to be grieving this hard. Southport was all of a three-and-a-half-hour drive away. She could easily come back to spend weekends here several times a year, depending on the life she crafted for herself back home.

But it did feel like she was leaving forever.

The residents were in their usual circle of chairs. In the middle, instead of one of the longer-term residents or a counselor, who usually led these meetings, stood Lily Anne, hands behind her back.

It looked as if they were planning to be nice to her.

The back of Sophie's throat started cramping. This was going to get soggy.

'Sophie. We knew you were only going to be here for a month, but it's gone much too quickly, and we will miss you.' Lily Anne's voice went suspiciously husky. She stopped to clear her throat. 'You have brought so much color to Asphalia, not only the decor and the wonderful food, but yourself – your cheerfulness, your humor, your patience and your friendship.'

Nodding and smiles around the circle.

'Thank you.' Sophie tried to hold back tears by opening her eyes wide and not blinking. Didn't work. The first slid down, making her blink, which started a lemming-like stream.

Her tears set Lily Anne's off, and whatever else she was going to say was lost. She mutely passed over a rectangular box wrapped in bright tulip-strewn paper.

Sophie was about to unwrap it when Lizzie got to her feet. 'I want to say thank you for getting me into the kitchen. I'm thinking of taking classes, maybe going to culinary school. And . . . thanks for yelling at me when I needed it.'

Sophie looked guiltily to Lily Anne. 'I yelled very quietly and with deep compassion.'

'Oh yeah.' Lily Anne rolled her eyes. 'I'm sure.'

'Thank you, Lizzie.' Sophie patted her heart, sending affection with her eyes. 'It's been a pleasure. I'll want to keep in touch to hear how you're doing.'

'Open your present!' Betsy yelled.

'Okay.' She tore off the paper and opened the box to find a white toque with black script embroidery around the brim: *Chef Sophie.*

'Oh my gosh, thank you so much.' The lemming tears leapt one after another off the cliff of her lower lids. 'Working here was good for me. I learned a lot from all of you. I hope Lily Anne will find you a new chef who isn't afraid of spices. I will visit, and I'll be thinking about all of you often and wishing you good, healthy, positive things.'

Applause and smiles all around. Sophie drank it in, tears back under control, feeling full to the brim, with sadness, but also joy, deep satisfaction and gratitude.

When the applause died down, Lily Anne clapped her hands. 'Okay, ladies. Back to reality here. Time to start your meeting. I'll see you all tomorrow.'

She and Sophie went down the hall together – still dingy and gray, but cheered greatly by the colorful prints, both classic and modern, lining the walls – toward the front door where Sophie had first set eyes on her sister.

'Drive safely. Promise you'll visit soon. And think about my offer?'

'I promise I'll do all three things.' Sophie hugged Lily Anne close, wishing Asphalia House could be magically transported to Southport so she could see her sister more often. They'd spent the last weeks together as much as possible, which wasn't much given how busy they were. They'd also called Uncle Clyde one evening when they were feeling reasonably calm, and had gotten the story all over again, with more detail, which they'd hashed and rehashed until they felt they could almost understand, if not condone, what had happened. No true villains, just impossible choices.

Sophie couldn't be more grateful – again – to Owen for keeping her from hate-bombing her parents without trying to understand more of the situation. She was still angry – both sisters were – but at least when she went home, she would no longer need to chop wood quite as badly.

'I'll show up so often you'll get sick of me.'

'That'll take some doing.' Lily Anne's eyes shone with affection. 'You've done a lot for me, Sophie, just by being here. I'd become so set in my routines and worries that I'd forgotten to enjoy life.'

Sophie cringed comically. 'No, no, don't do that. You need to promise you'll find ways to travel more. Maybe we can go somewhere together?'

'I'd love that.'

'Me too.' She hovered awkwardly, delaying the inevitable. 'So . . . I'll see you soon.'

'Yes! Soon.' Lily Anne wiped a tear off her cheek. 'Jeez, you'd think you were moving to Transylvania.'

'I know, we're ridiculous.'

They hugged one more time, then Sophie made herself step back, turn, and walk down the front path to her waiting car, clutching her new toque to her heart, along with a lot of good memories. It would be impossible to make up for so many lost years, but the two of them would undoubtedly have a lot of fun trying.

In the car, chin wobbling, lip trembling, Sophie waved one more time to her sister, who stood in the doorway waving madly back.

Her twin!

The drive to Bridgewater Corners was familiar and all too brief. She pulled up to the cottage for the last time, wrung out, hoping Owen would be around, and at the same time hoping he wouldn't be. Part of her wanted one more evening to hang out with him, the exhausted rest of her wanted to finish packing for the trip home, crawl into bed, have a little cry and get some sleep.

No sign of him, not even his truck. Disappointed and relieved, she brought her toque inside and placed it lovingly into her open suitcase. Then she finished packing until the only things left out were her clothes and toiletries for the next day, and the Fabergé egg, which she put next to her bed. Their time together was also drawing to a close.

That finished, she went outside and sat breathing in the cooling mountain air, watching the light fading, thinking of August in Southport, the beach, the country club, the shopping, the parties . . .

So familiar and so far away from this quiet purity of air and countryside.

When it started getting dark, she went inside. A few minutes later, she heard Owen's truck pull in. For a moment, she was tempted, and even turned back toward the front door. But she'd been through too many emotional scenes already that day. This one, in the soft darkness of a summer evening, would be her undoing. She'd wait for the sunshiny energy of morning.

Nothing on TV interested her, her phone was annoying, nothing in the cottage she wanted to read, so she started back upstairs

A knock.

Oh dear.

Back downstairs, heart thumping, she opened the door. 'Hi, Owen.'

The Jewel of Cairo

'Hi.' He stood gazing at her.

'Do you want to come in?' She hoped not.

'No. I'm leaving early tomorrow. Thought I'd say goodbye now.'

'Oh.' Her tear ducts heard the word 'goodbye' and started cranking up machinery she put a stop to as best as she could. 'Well, okay. Thank you for being such a great host. And dinner companion. And friend.'

Owen nodded.

Sophie managed a smile. 'And all-around chatter-buddy.'

'Yeah.' He coughed nervously. 'So . . . thanks for . . . So your . . . I felt like I was . . .'

She waited, a bit breathlessly, but he seemed to have stopped functioning. 'You're very welcome for all of that. Whatever it was.'

Owen did a face-plant on his palm. 'Lemme try again. Using my brain this time.'

She giggled, amazed that she was able to. He was so adorable.

'Before you came, I was stagnating. Didn't realize it. But having someone to talk to again, and now the chance to work with Asphalia House . . . they're the kicks I needed. Well, you were the kick I needed.'

'That's . . . that's fantastic. I'm so glad. You have so much to give, Owen.' Sophie met his eyes as she'd met them dozens and dozens of times, but this time, out of nowhere, she wanted to kiss him so badly she had to fold her arms and step away. 'I'll be back, to see Lily Anne. We can hang out.'

'Okay.' He looked like he was sure that would never happen. 'That would be good.'

Then he stood there. And she stood there.

Worst, most awkward pause ever.

'Well, goodbye.' He started to turn away, then checked himself, turned back and gave her a brief hug. 'Safe travels.'

'Thanks, Owen. You too.' It wasn't until she took one more peek at his tall figure striding away and closed the door that she realized she'd just wished him safe travels and he wasn't going anywhere.

She'd miss him. Terribly. But the feeling would fade. This wasn't her place. He'd find some rugged Vermont woman, and the two of them would sit out on his front porch every evening, smoking pipes and not talking.

After several minutes wandering around the cottage feeling unmoored and bereft, she remembered she'd been about to go back upstairs when Owen had knocked, so she climbed up to the beautiful flying-ducks bed and picked up the precious falcon-topped Fabergé egg to make herself stop thinking about Owen.

She cupped the egg affectionately, admiring the noble falcon, the gleaming blue lotus petals outlined with tiny flawless pearls. Tomorrow she'd be back in Southport, back in the embrace of its familiar seaside charm and summer bustle. Her parents would need to be told she'd discovered their secrets, then, with Helen, they'd figure out how the precious jewel might have gotten into Sarah's head, and who could claim it now.

Sophie had already relinquished her fantasy of the multi-million-dollar house in Southport. Other people had always taken care of her. The egg wouldn't be any kind of rescue, just one more way to keep from taking responsibility for her own life.

Back home, she'd do the necessary work. She'd need to figure out her next career move, maybe find a job at a place similar to Asphalia. Hiding here had been a wonderful respite, and a chance to regroup, but she didn't want to hide any more. It was long past time for her to bloom on her own.

The Jewel of Cairo

Speaking of which . . .
One more time, only for her.
She turned the glittering falcon and with a satisfied smile watched the delicate flower open.

Chapter 33

Friday, February 18, 1978

Lilianne parted the curtains in their hotel room in Chania to look out at the town's charming harbor, a Cretan cove calmed by a long stone breakwater on whose end a small lighthouse stood like an exclamation point, ready to guide boats into the safety of protected waters. On the shore, age-old buildings stood cheek by jowl above a line of shaded cafés and restaurants.

Beyond the barrier, the Sea of Crete, at the Aegean's southern end, was a restless, mesmerizing blue. As she watched, a fishing boat chugged out of the harbor, leaving for the day's work. It seemed impossible that anyone was going about their day, engaging in normal routines and activities.

Connie was dead. Lilianne had taken the call from Spencer Oakes, the friend from CIA training she'd put Connie in touch with. Spencer worked at the US naval base a few hours away from Chania.

The news still hadn't sunk in. Lilianne had last heard from Connie late this past summer in a long letter saying she'd never been happier. She loved Crete, had found her ancestors' village, had a regular job and had fallen in love – *I know, I know, but for real this time.* She was also pregnant and thrilled about it. The letter had been written in a steady hand, coming out of an obviously clear head, unlike the previous ones, which had been so worrying that Lilianne had asked Spencer to check on her.

Happy, in love, pregnant, a mother to twin girls, and now gone, hit by a car while walking to work. If she'd only left the house one minute sooner or one minute later . . .

Agony.

The devastating call had come on February 15. The night before, Valentine's Day, she and Gilles had been up late, drinking champagne and looking through their wedding album, remembering the glorious day and all that had occurred. Lilianne felt almost guilty now, as if such joy shouldn't be permitted with her friend's chance for happiness gone.

She and Gilles had married at Pequot Church in Southport the previous June. Braheem, Zahra and Nailah had flown out from Cairo to be part of the festivities. Lilianne had decided not to tell her parents they were coming, worried her mother might balk at the reunion. When the doorbell had rung on Willow Street two days before the wedding, Dina had been helping tie handfuls of Jordanian almonds into net bags to give out as guest favors. Lilianne had faked being too busy to answer and sent her mom, then followed silently to peek, praying she hadn't made a terrible mistake.

As she watched, Dina had gasped with surprise and launched herself into her father's arms, then her mother's, and finally those of a weeping Nailah, for long hugs that had Lilianne beaming and tearing up herself.

Such different tears from those she shed today. Connie, badly injured, had been rushed to the hospital. Spencer had been with her at the end, when she whispered that she wanted her twin daughters raised in Vermont by her sister, Phyllis.

According to Spencer, the father, Nico, was a disaster and had met some ungodly end of his own shortly before the girls were born. Disaster maybe, but Connie had loved him, and his death had left her alone.

Lilianne shoved the thoughts away. She couldn't afford to break down now. She and Gilles were in town to collect the girls and bring them to Vermont. Spencer had told them that Phyllis already had four children of her own and a husband who traveled, therefore she couldn't make the trip herself. Lilianne and Gilles had volunteered in a flash, though the idea of coping with two unfamiliar babies on the eleven-hour flight to JFK from Athens . . .

What else could they do? The sooner the twins were in their permanent home, the better.

A fresh wave of grief hit. Lilianne had cried so much her tear ducts should have run dry by now.

Behind her the door opened to Gilles, who took one look at her face and came over to envelop her in his arms, laying his cheek on top of her head, rocking her tenderly.

When she could control her tears, she pulled away, wiping her eyes. 'Gorgeous out there?'

'Yes. The light is remarkable.' He held up his camera, now constantly back over his shoulder where it belonged. 'But it was hard to enjoy. I kept thinking of how much Connie loved it here. How she could have brought her girls to the ocean to play every day, how they would have loved her energy and her imagination. What a cheat life can be.'

'Yes.' Lilianne's voice wobbled. 'Yes to all of that.'

Gilles exhaled grief, rubbing his forehead wearily. 'I guess we should go.'

'I'm ready.' She half laughed. 'I lied, I'm not ready. I'm never going to be ready.'

'There is no way to be ready for this. We'll just do it.' He held out his hand.

They made their way to the meeting place Spencer had set up, an address in Nerokouros, a small village at the foot of the island's interior mountains. The babies were being cared for by the same nurse Spencer had hired for Connie when she'd been flattened by her anguish over Nico's death and struggled to cope with the girls alone.

The house was an unremarkable two-floor concrete structure with balconies, like most of the buildings they'd seen on the island. Spencer, a man in his mid thirties with thinning brown hair and an appealing face now lined with sadness, was at the door to greet them. Lilianne had liked him immediately when they'd trained together for the CIA, and her reaction hadn't changed. Intuition also told her he'd had more than friendly feelings for Connie. Spencer would have been so good for her.

The nurse, Irida, was a cheerful middle-aged woman whose English was stilted but whose smile and sympathy were comforting. The twins were napping in another room when they arrived, so, using Spencer as translator, Lilianne and Gilles were able to ask Irida about their care in as much detail as they wanted. How to change a diaper. How to heat milk for their bottles. What to do when they cried. What to do when they screamed. For six hours. On the plane. The diaper they'd have to wait to practice once the little ones were awake, but they did heat up a couple of bottles, testing the milk's temperature on the inside of their wrists, where the skin was sensitive enough to mimic how the liquid would feel in a baby's mouth.

'Good babies. Good babies.' Irida grinned widely. 'Sweet babies.'

As if to prove her wrong, an angry wail sounded from the other room.

'Awake babies,' Gilles said.

'Hungry.' Irida beckoned them toward the back of the house. 'Come. I show.'

Gilles and Lilianne exchanged glances and grim smiles. From now until they handed the bundles of joy over to Connie's sister, these would be their children.

Irida led them through the sparsely furnished home to a bedroom with a mountain view, where the babies shared a large, ancient-looking cradle next to what was undoubtedly Irida's bed.

Lilianne hung back as the nurse approached the twins, cooing in Greek, Gilles right beside her. He was all in on this trip, making Lilianne wonder if he'd been honest when he'd said he didn't need children in order to be happy. She flashed back to Dalia, the little girl at her grandparents' farm who'd charmed out of Gilles his first genuine post-trauma smile.

'Oh *look*.' Gilles's somber expression lifted. Lilianne had heard that reverent tone before, when he encountered something of staggering beauty he wanted to capture on film. But instead of reaching for his camera, he reached into the cradle for the unhappy girl. 'Hello, mini Connie.'

'Sophie.' Irida pointed to the child in Gilles's arms.

'Hello, Sophie.' Gilles held her effortlessly. Sophie looked surprised, but not unhappy, gazing up at him as if he was one of the wonders of the world.

She was beautiful. Gilles was entranced. Lilianne took a step forward and peered into the cradle, where the second baby girl lay kicking and waving jerkily, as if she hadn't quite mastered the use of her own limbs. She had features similar to her sister's, but not identical. And where Sophie had a sweet single whorl of dark hair, this little one would need a haircut soon.

'Hello,' Lilianne said doubtfully. 'How are you?'

The child began crying. Lilianne felt panic growing in her

belly. She'd been trained to handle just about any complicated situation, but felt utterly helpless around this little person.

Irida leaned over, scooped up the baby with practiced ease and handed her to Lilianne, who cradled her awkwardly, terrified she'd drop her. 'Lily Anne.'

'Yes. Lilianne.' Lilianne jerked her head toward her husband. 'And he's Gilles.'

'No, no.' Irida giggled and pointed to the baby in her arms. 'This Lily Anne.'

Lilianne's mouth dropped open at the same time her namesake's did, but for different reasons.

'Lilianne.' Gilles's voice broke.

Lilianne did her absolute best not to cry all over the baby, who stared up at her with fascination, even when a tear splashed onto her cheek.

'Connie named her after you.' Spencer had followed them into the room. 'She wanted you to know that.'

'And . . . Sophie?' Gilles asked.

'After a woman named Safiya whom Connie met in Cairo.'

'Safiya!' Lilianne gaped at him. 'She named her daughter after Safiya?'

Spencer nodded wearily. 'There was a story there, one that affected Connie deeply. She asked me to try to find Safiya, but I was never able to locate her. Connie was afraid something had happened to her.'

'Yes, she told me.' Lilianne's stomach roiled. She'd wanted to hear that Safiya had been discovered happily back with her sons and family. 'I'm sick about it. Any idea what happened?'

'We don't know.' Spencer said. 'A friend of mine went down to her village to try to find her and her family, with no luck. Apparently they'd left suddenly. I'd like to think she's doing fine somewhere. Connie so admired her courage.'

'I did too.' Lilianne thought back to her last view of Safiya, the straight, proud shoulders and thin body, her promise not to say anything about seeing Lilianne plant the bug. Safiya had long ago learned to take care of herself. She could well be enjoying life with her children and family somewhere safe.

In her arms, Lily Anne made adorable coos and random vocalizations, kicking and reaching with an intense, wide-eyed gaze of concentration, not seeming to mind Lilianne's beginner clumsiness. Lilianne drank her in, becoming entranced by the remarkable fact of this miniature human. Like watching the ocean, or a fire, essentially unchanging yet infinitely variable. And so sweet.

Until Lily Anne's little face screwed up and she let out a lusty howl of outrage, which started Sophie off as well, though more quietly.

Lilianne looked to Irida, wondering what the hell she and Gilles would do when this started and there wasn't anyone around to tell them how to fix it.

'Food. Food. You sit.' Irida pointed to a rustically carved rocking chair for Lilianne and the bed for Gilles, then handed them each a bottle.

Gilles got it right immediately, or maybe Sophie did. It took Lilianne a few tries to find the best position, infuriating Lily Anne, but eventually she and the baby settled, Lily Anne sucking greedily at the rubber nipple.

'Look at her. How . . . precious.' Lilianne was not given to using words like 'precious'. She was not used to feeling gooey and sweet like this either, or responsible for something so remarkable and so fragile.

Gilles was bent over Sophie, watching her suckle, looking happier and more relaxed than she'd seen him since before his trauma. Maybe even happier than on their wedding day, though that had been joyous for them both.

He must have felt her stare, because he met her eyes and smiled, an unspoken longing in his own that set Lilianne's nerves on alert.

He wanted this. Fatherhood, parenthood, a complete family. Dear God.

They'd talked about it and agreed that children were not in the cards for them as a couple. Had he been humoring her? Had he changed his mind? Suppressed those feelings until now, when they were unavoidable with a baby in his arms?

She returned his smile briefly and turned back to Lily Anne. During the many sleepless hours leading up to this trip, she'd tried hard to anticipate all the complicated emotions their extraordinary errand would produce.

This one was unexpected.

They spent the day at the house with the babies, with a break for lunch and a nap – jet lag was very much with them – then dinner and a comfortable if erratic sleep at the hotel. Over the next three days, they repeated that pattern. It wasn't long before Lilianne felt less anxious around the little ones – though she would never take to this temporary parenthood as naturally as Gilles had. She could understand a little more why her very independent mom had relied on nannies. Caring for kids didn't demand much intellect, but it did demand an astonishing amount of stamina, anxiety, uncertainty, and more responsibility than she'd ever come close to bearing.

And she and Gilles weren't the ones getting up with the twins at night.

The flights from Crete to Athens to New York's JFK airport, and the subsequent long car ride to Connecticut, were an exhausting nightmare of tension. Lilianne felt as if she were traveling with twin bombs, fuses set to go off anytime, anywhere. The babies – and Gilles and Lilianne – did about as well as could be expected, but Lilianne didn't think she'd ever been so glad to see the house on Willow Street, even though there was so much still to do. Though she and Gilles were home, the girls weren't.

Practically zombies from exhaustion, they still had to make doubly sure all they'd bought before they left for Greece was packed and ready for the trip to Vermont. They'd show up with everything they thought Lily Anne and Sophie might need, for both the next few weeks and the next several months. Clothes, diapers, formula, toys, books . . .

Before they fell into bed that night, they called Connie's sister to let her know they'd be arriving around lunchtime the following day. Both of them had been tempted to settle into Willow Street for several days to get over jet lag and make sure the girls were healthy and okay after their latest ordeal. But the twins needed to be home with their permanent caregivers as soon as possible.

Neither of them had been charmed by Phyllis. Instead of deep sadness over Connie's death, and a yearning to give the twins a good life, she'd reacted as if Lilianne and Gilles were planning to drive up and empty bags of cement onto her front lawn.

A little gratitude wouldn't have hurt.

The drive to Vermont was glum as a result. Lilianne was torn in half. She couldn't wait to give the babies up to someone who would take better care of them than she could, and so she could *sleep* again, but she wasn't convinced that person was Phyllis, and being around Sophie and Lily Anne for the past several days had sneakily endeared them to her, producing Mama Bear feelings she hadn't thought she was capable of. She'd never be a 'baby person' the way Gilles was, but the twins were so heartbreakingly vulnerable, Lilianne would have to be made of stone not to fall for them.

She really hoped Connie's sister wasn't made of stone.

Phyllis, her husband, Clyde Corson, and their three sons and two-year-old daughter lived in Strafford, a small town in east Vermont, not far from the New Hampshire border, surrounded by thickly forested hills currently blanketed with snow. The large gray wooden house, most likely built in the nineteenth century, was set amid gardens awaiting spring under a thick white covering. Off to one side, a swing set and child's clubhouse sat near a brook that provided a gurgling, rushing soundtrack.

Kid paradise.

'Okay. Well.' Gilles had been silent most of the drive up, his apprehension over their errand matching Lilianne's. Just looking at Sophie in the rear-view mirror, sleeping soundly, her cheeks flushed, made Lilianne's throat tighten. She wouldn't get to watch these girls grow up to be women, would miss seeing how much of Connie cropped up in either of them, how much of their unknown father, how much all themselves.

'Here we are.' She opened the car door to much colder temperatures than coastal Connecticut. They'd bought warm outfits for the girls, sunshine-yellow and leaf-green onesie parkas, bright spots against all the white and gray. The cold woke both babies quickly. Sophie blinked in surprise as Lilianne picked her up out of her seat. Lily Anne scowled and let out a screech, then settled in Gilles's arms.

The front door opened and an unsmiling woman they assumed was Phyllis came down the long set of front stairs bundled in a gray parka, carrying her daughter, who looked enormous in comparison to the twins, a chubby-cheeked child hastily swaddled in a blanket. Phyllis nodded briefly to each of them, dark eyes dull. 'You made it.'

Wonderful to meet you as well. Lilianne checked herself, trying to imagine what she'd say and look like if she had four children and a husband who traveled, and was being handed twins right after she'd lost her sister. She'd cut Phyllis some slack. A lot of slack. 'We come bearing precious gifts.'

Phyllis nodded grimly, eyeing the twins. 'Yes, well, we'll need to talk about that.'

Gilles and Lilianne froze on opposite sides of the car. Their eyes met across the black metal, round with dread.

'What's there to talk about?' Gilles had survived the stress of the trip to Greece without backsliding into one of his now rare moods, but she could sense his tension was at snapping point, and hers wasn't far behind.

So many emotions were already involved in the circumstances and in this surrender, Lilianne was not in the mood for complications. 'We brought everything the girls will need, including clothes and diapers and—'

'Come inside. We can talk over lunch.' Phyllis turned and walked up the steps, her daughter twisting to stare over her shoulder.

Lilianne and Gilles followed, Lilianne holding Sophie protectively. The way Gilles's arms encircled Lily Anne, she'd bet he was ready to get back in the car with both kids and return to Connecticut.

Understandable. But no.

Inside the house, they dug the babies out of their snow suits, which would probably fit them for all of another two weeks. Lily Anne kicked madly, thrilled to be free of the bindings. Sophie frowned up at Lilianne, as if asking why she would be removed from such gorgeous soft surroundings to cope with a drafty open room.

They warmed bottles for both girls and fed them on the living room couch while Phyllis puttered in the kitchen and her toddler daughter ran urgently back and forth until her brother, older by about a year, came out to investigate and tripped her. The screaming was remarkable.

The twins startled. Sophie began crying. Phyllis yelled at her children, which startled the girls all over again.

Finally Phyllis turned on the TV, which got both kids to sit and stare so Lilianne and Gilles could finish, Lilianne trying to relax her body as much as possible so her tension didn't filter through to Sophie.

Was this the last time she'd get to feed her? The hungry, intent way Gilles was watching Lily Anne made it clear he was thinking the same thing. They burped the twins, not even smiling at the unladylike eruptions that usually made them giggle.

'Lunch is ready.' Phyllis cut off her son's objections by plunking sandwiches and milk in front of him and his sister. 'We grown-ups need to talk. You can eat in front of the TV *just this once.*'

Sleepy Sophie snuggled her head into the curve of Lilianne's shoulder. The idea of leaving this sweet-smelling bundle with growly somber Phyllis felt like handing her to a hungry mountain lion.

Growly, somber Phyllis served lunch in the drab brown kitchen, which was at least brightened by a dried flower arrangement, a bowl of bright apples, crayon drawings stuck to the refrigerator with alphabet magnets, and Lego pieces scattered over a kid-sized table and chairs in one corner. Lilianne breathed a bit easier. If the house had been austere, with no signs of kid stuff, she would have run right after Gilles to the car.

Maybe.

Tuna sandwiches, carrot sticks and potato chips were ready for them on the square wooden table.

'Nothing fancy. I don't have time for fancy.'

As if they'd showed up demanding beef bourguignon.

'That's fine. We don't need fancy.' Gilles spoke curtly, sitting at the table with Lily Anne asleep on his shoulder, her Cupid's bow mouth making occasional sucking motions. He looked as wary as Lilianne felt. 'Your house is beautiful. And a great location, especially for kids. All those woods to play in. I would have loved that.'

Phyllis sat opposite Gilles, looking miserably down at the table. She was thinner than Connie, and taller, with shorter hair, though she had the same wide mouth and chin. It was not surprising, at least on first impressions, that the two of them weren't close.

'Dig in.' Phyllis picked up a sandwich and took a minuscule bite.

Lilianne kept one hand across Sophie's back, supporting her adorable diapered butt in the crook of her elbow, and picked up her own sandwich. 'What are your kids' names?'

'Youngest there is Naomi. Her brother is Fred. Donny and Jeffrey are in school.'

'That will be nice, for them all to grow up together.' Lilianne smiled pleasure she didn't feel. There was tension in the room, and she couldn't tell if it was emanating from her, Gilles, Phyllis or the walls of the house.

Phyllis's grim expression grew grimmer. 'Look. I've been thinking about this a lot since I heard about Connie. I know she wanted me to take both of her kids, but that's not going to be possible.'

Lilianne stopped with her sandwich on the way to her mouth. Gilles put his back on the plate. 'You're not taking the twins?'

'I'll take one. I can't handle more. Naomi wasn't even supposed to happen. I thought I was done with Fred. It's too much. Six children is too much. We were planning on three.'

Lilianne gaped, forcing herself to loosen her reflexively

tightened grip on Sophie, which had produced a sleepy grunt of protest.

'You can't separate them,' Gilles said savagely. 'You can't split up twins.'

'They're non-identical. Same as any siblings.' Phyllis held his gaze, non-blinking. Her dark eyes were cold, lifeless. How could they have come from the same genes as Connie's, which had invited everyone to share her joy in life? 'My pediatrician said as much. I called to make sure separation wouldn't harm them. He said they'll adjust and be fine.'

Everything in Lilianne rejected that idea. How could these girls not have a special bond after sharing a uterus for nine months and then a world that had been beautiful for such a short time before they lost the center of their universe? Nico, Connie, Irida, now Lilianne and Gilles – they would have depended on each other for their only sense of constancy.

'I can't believe that's true.' Gilles was calmly furious.

'My pediatrician should know.' Phyllis picked up her sandwich, then put it down again. 'I'll take one of them. My parents will have my head if I don't, and I owe Connie that much. The girls are our blood. But no one can make me take two. There's no law says I have to.'

Gilles stood, a sure sign he was near the end of his rope. 'It's unethical. Immoral. They need to grow up together. You must respect that.'

'You don't understand. I've spent my entire life coping with Connie's disasters.' Phyllis lowered her voice when Lily Anne whimpered. 'I took the rap for half the bad stuff she did so she wouldn't be punished or expelled. I hid her alcohol and her drugs and her boyfriends, and cleaned up her vomit. I sent her money after she went abroad, to keep her alive, and because that life seemed to be good for her. She thrived in a way you wouldn't understand unless you'd seen her here. This state, our parents, their expectations, their lack of understanding, they suffocated her until the only path left was self-destruction.

'I was the one person who understood her nature, her inability to control her impulses, her tendency toward addiction. I loved her and wanted to protect her. I wanted her to kick her awful habits and get well. But eventually I realized I was throwing my love and hope and money onto an inevitably sinking ship, and I couldn't take the disappointment anymore. Now my parents are devastated once again, and once again I'm the one who has to pay the price for her carelessness and amorality.'

'No. She loved Nico. The girls' father.' Lilianne's voice came out tight and harsh. 'She was clean and sober. She'd changed. Motherhood changed her.'

'Too late, apparently. I will do my duty, but I won't fray myself to the bone for her even if she is my sister.' The clear, hard voice softened. 'Was . . . my sister.'

'This was your *sister's* last request.' Gilles said. 'That you care for her children.'

'I know.' Phyllis's face crumpled into a more human form. 'But she was never here, she had no idea what my life is like. Please understand, I'm not only doing this for myself, but for those babies too. I can't be a good mother to that many kids. It's not fair to me or to them.'

Lilianne and Gilles exchanged anguished looks. This had been much easier when the issue seemed black and white. When they could assign Phyllis as evil and themselves as good. When it was crystal clear that keeping the twins together was simply the right thing to do.

'I know it's not ideal. I've . . . I've agonized over this as well. There may be a sense of loss for the girls at first. But not lifelong suffering.' Phyllis sniffed and stared down at her lap. 'Truly. I would not do this if I thought it would ruin their lives.'

The idea was too horrible, and yet . . .

'We'll take them,' Gilles said. 'Both.'

'Gilles . . .' Lilianne wanted to shriek with panic. Twins! She couldn't. It was too much.

Immediately she recognized the irony, which brought on more empathy for Connie's sister. Easy for Lilianne to think that adding twins to Phyllis's crowded household was the right thing to do. But when it came to her own enormous, empty house? The thought of taking on two children made her want to run screaming.

Sophie turned her head, giving a soft sigh, her breath warm against Lilianne's neck.

'I'm sorry.' Phyllis pressed her lips together. 'I know this is incredibly difficult. It is for me too. Connie wanted me to raise her children. No matter how I felt about my sister, I still can't turn my back on that. But I can't take both.'

One of the kids over by the television punctuated the tense silence with a belch worthy of a frat boy.

Phyllis giggled nervously, making Lilianne stare in wonder. It was as if Connie had flown into the room and inhabited her sister's body. Same smile, same funny giggle; the resemblance was striking, and strangely endearing.

'I know this wasn't what either of you wanted to hear. I've contacted an adoption agency and they've agreed to find a local family for whichever one I don't take. I'll make sure she goes to a good home.'

'Without her sister.' Gilles sat back down, looking defeated.

'She might gain a sister, but no, it won't be this one. And the child I take? She won't ever know she's adopted. I don't want any child of mine to have to wrestle with the feeling that she belongs somewhere else. She'll know only total love and acceptance right here in this house.'

Lilianne swallowed hard. Everything Phyllis said made sense on some level, but none of it sat well.

'We'll need time to think about this,' Gilles said. 'Time to adjust.'

Phyllis turned newly lifeless eyes on him, and it occurred to Lilianne that her face became wooden out of shyness and pain rather than cruelty or unfeelingness.

'I'm grateful that you and Lilianne went all the way to Crete for my nieces. But . . .' she looked away from his piercing stare, 'you don't have a say in this. My sister's children. Her wishes. My wishes. I'm sorry. I can see how much you care.'

As much as she hated every word that exited Phyllis's mouth, Lilianne had to admire her strength in saying them, and she had to stomach their truth. They had no right to these children. No ground to stand on except their own gut feeling that the twins belonged together. If, as Phyllis claimed, there was no law against separating them, and if she had a doctor's word that Sophie and Lily Anne would be fine raised apart, what did Lilianne and Gilles's objections matter? Even if they were right?

Phyllis was blood. Phyllis was family.

'Gilles.' She could see her husband winding up to escalate the discussion. 'She's right. We need to accept that. We need to bring the girls' things in and go home.'

'No.' He stood abruptly, making Lily Anne's eyes shoot open. Her little features crumpled, working up to a good scream. 'Is there a place where my wife and I can have a private conversation?'

'A place with a changing table, preferably.' Lilianne wanted to curl up and sob. Lily Anne was yowling, Sophie was getting restless, both girls needed fresh diapers and Gilles was about to be hostile and unreasonable.

'You can use Naomi's room.' Phyllis stepped out from the table. 'Come with me.'

Lilianne picked up the diaper bag and followed. Which child would grow up here? Which child would go home to strangers? How would Phyllis ever choose?

The thought made her sick.

Naomi's room was adorable, walls covered with cheerful floral wallpaper, a mobile hanging over her white crib, little farm animals spinning and tangling above her while she slept. A small bookshelf overflowed with books: *Goodnight Moon*, and *Where the Wild Things Are*, *The Little Engine That Could*, and *Tuggy the Tugboat*, *The Snowy Day* and practically everything Dr Seuss ever wrote.

Lilianne swallowed the lump in her throat. Books were a good sign.

Gilles put Lily Anne on the bed and got her into a new diaper like a pro, while Lilianne did the same – less like a pro – for Sophie at the changing table, marveling, as she always did, at the perfection of her wriggling body.

'Lilianne.'

Something in the careful gentleness of Gilles's tone made Lilianne wary. She turned slowly, delaying the moment when he'd speak again. This was going to be big. He wasn't sure she'd like it. She wasn't either, and even less sure that she was in the mood to handle anything but going home to bed. 'Yes?'

'There's only one way I will accept what Phyllis offers.'

'Gilles, we don't have grounds to demand—'

'Let me finish.' He held up his hand, proud, handsome, and perfectly at home holding Lily Anne against his broad shoulder.

This man was born to be a father. He and Helen should have been together, making a crowd of children.

'I will accept Phyllis's solution on the condition that we take the other child home with us. I want to adopt Sophie.'

Lilianne had no idea what to say, how to field that, whether to laugh or cry. A child! An adoption. They'd be parents. She'd be a mother.

This was so far from anything they'd agreed to, so far from anything she'd anticipated for her life.

And yet . . . so was the man standing in front of her.

Her heart started pounding. She had no answer for him, could only come up with a question. 'Why Sophie?'

'There's no way to choose rationally. Sophie because having a wife and daughter with the same name would be confusing. I don't know any other criteria that would make sense.'

Lilianne found herself shaking. She should have seen this coming. She should have been considering it herself, so that she'd be able to respond to him now with something other than fear and objections and a deep-down certainty that it was the right solution. The only one either of them could live with.

'Gilles . . .'

'I know what you're going to say. That you'd be a bad mother, that you didn't sign up for this. But you didn't think you could marry either. I'm not even sure you thought you could love. Because of some chemical imbalance in your body? That has nothing to do with your heart.'

She nodded. He'd been saying some version of this since they got engaged, and she loved him for his faith in her, though she wasn't always convinced she deserved it. 'But if it turned out I didn't like being married, we could divorce. I can't give a child back, Gilles.'

'It won't all be on you. I'll be here for you, and for Sophie.'

The Jewel of Cairo

He put an arm around Lilianne, held her close, Lily Anne's small body included in their embrace, Lilianne's hand resting lightly on Sophie's belly to keep her safely on the changing table. 'You're not your mother. You have so much more love in you than you know. And if *we* don't take her . . .'

Lilianne closed her eyes against his warm chest. Was there any other solution? She had a visceral reaction against handing either child over to a stranger, would feel as if she and Gilles had tossed Connie's baby out into a wilderness to fend for herself. There were wonderful adoptive parents everywhere, but there were also awful ones. There was no way to know.

A soft syllable from Sophie on the changing table made them turn and bend over her, their heads close together.

'I'd have to give up law school,' Lilianne said.

'Don't be ridiculous. There's no reason you can't go to school. We can have help in the house, a nanny or au—'

'No.' She was sure about that. 'No nannies.'

Gilles grinned, sensing Lilianne was on the edge of giving in, his eyes warm with pride. 'I'll be working from home at least until I find a studio, and even then my hours will be my own. I won't be like your father, constantly at the office. This will be our baby, not just yours. We'll be a family, Lilianne. Whole and happy.'

A family.

They watched Sophie's arms reaching up, then out, her legs kicking. Her lips pursing, opening. Such a small being with such enormous impact. How could Lilianne ever be sure? Her heart wavered. Her head was filled with objections and complications and consequences and a list of what-ifs that could circle the planet.

She let out a groan of frustration. Sophie turned toward the sound and met Lilianne's eyes, her own widening. The child was so intent on growing, on developing, so serious about all of it. Lilianne could imagine neurons firing in that tiny brain at several times the speed of hers, making connections, trying to make sense of everything. It was miraculous.

Lilianne leaned down farther and grinned, unable to resist. Sophie gave a grand wave of her hand along with several hefty kicks of both legs, and then, her first miracle. She caught Lilianne's face with both hands and gave a wide and unmistakable grin.

Lilianne was lost. For all her fear, she couldn't bear not being there to see every milestone, every bit of what this child could and would become. She owed it to Gilles, she owed it to Connie . . . and she owed it to herself.

Chapter 34

Present day

Beezy: *Why have you been so hard to get talking? I'm worried you're already mountain-man-married. Thank God you're coming back today. Party tonight at the Jacobsons', you're invited and you must come. Tomorrow you and I are sitting down for a looong catch-up. Country club at noon? Safe travels! Can't wait to see you. Lots to tell you! Big smooches.*
Sophie: ♥

Sophie parked at the Stop & Shop, bleary-eyed from the drive from Vermont but knowing that once she got home to her condo she would not want to get into the car again. One foot out, then two, stiff from sitting too long, and she pushed herself to standing. People thronged the parking lot, mostly women wearing expensive outfits – even the rattiest jeans and the simplest sundresses were probably designer. The pavement reflected the heat and humidity of a typical summer afternoon, shopping carts rattling across its bumpy surface.

Well. She was back home.

The supermarket felt about forty degrees cooler than outside, making Sophie grateful for the thin cotton sweater that

Vermont's fresh morning air had made necessary. Her drive had been uneventful, one pee break and here she was, noon on a Saturday, when everyone in the entire state was doing grocery shopping.

Nicely timed.

She snagged a cart from the dwindling supply and tried to get her road-joggled brain to concentrate on what she might need. Produce. Fruit, vegetables . . . She paused by the avocados, and picked one up to check whether it was ready.

'Feel ripe?'

She didn't have to look up to know who it was. Her heart sped and her cheeks heated. 'Hi, Peter. Feels pretty good, yes.'

'What are you making?' His eyes were warm, along with his smile.

'I was thinking about guacamole, to go with vegetable quesadillas.' She hadn't been, but why not?

'Sounds delicious.' He was pink from sun, summer-lightened blond hair attractively tousled. He wore a blue polo shirt that matched his eyes, and white shorts that showed off his muscled legs.

He was still hot enough to make her go weak-kneed and blushy. 'How are you doing? How's impending fatherhood?'

'Oh.' His smile dimmed. 'Lexy's doing great. It's going really fast.'

She frowned at his flat tone. Hadn't Lexy said he was thrilled? 'You sound apprehensive.'

'Yeah.' He looked around, then pinned her with that blue stare that made her go all shivery. 'It was kind of a surprise.'

Sophie tried very hard not to gape at him. A *surprise*? She'd done everything possible to conceive Peter's child, and his new wife, oops, just couldn't help herself? 'Well, wow, but the very best kind, right?'

The Jewel of Cairo

'Yeah. Yeah.' His eyes darted around again. 'Lot of changes coming up.'

The flutters in Sophie's stomach stilled into dismay. He didn't want this child. He hadn't wanted hers either, he'd just gone along with it for a while, then put on the brakes. Thank God Sophie had never conceived.

She felt suddenly deeply and agonizingly sorry, not only for Lexy, but for their baby.

'It's great to see you, Soph. I've been thinking about you lately. You look really good.' His eyes skittered over her body. 'Did you lose weight?'

Did she . . . Sophie wanted to punch him harder than she'd ever wanted to punch anyone. Why didn't he just say, *Thank God you're not as fat as you got to be?* 'Not on purpose.'

'Anyway, yeah, I've been . . . remembering the good times we had. Nice memories. Really nice.'

She could not believe this. Whenever they'd met after the divorce, he'd always sidled away as soon as he could possibly escape from her. 'Well that's good. I'd hate to think every time my name was mentioned you wanted to hurl.'

He laughed nervously. Peter did not get nervous.

'You know, we should get together sometime. Have a drink. Be friends again.' His voice dropped and grew husky. Sophie knew what that meant. Knew it like she knew herself. That was his I-want-you voice.

Like Pavlov's dog, she felt herself responding, body warming, heartbeat accelerating, flashing memories of the incredible athletic sex they used to have all over the house.

Luckily, she was not Pavlov's dog.

'A drink with you and Lexy, you mean?' she asked sweetly.

'Sure, if you wanted.' He took a small step closer. 'Or just us, maybe at that bar you liked so much up the coast.'

'Oh?' She cocked her head. 'You mean where we conveniently wouldn't run into anyone we know?'

His grin spread. 'That's the one. You know Southport, people would be all over seeing us together.'

She touched his arm gently. 'No. Sorry, Peter, but no.'

'Oh. Yeah, okay.' He tried to look unconcerned. He was not used to rejection, certainly not from her. 'Just thought I'd ask. I miss you, Sophie. That's not bullshit.'

She believed him. She really did. Poor guy. Lexy must have turned out to be one of those horrible selfish people who sometimes thought of herself instead of Peter all the time, the way Sophie had. And with a baby in the house, he'd be demoted even further.

'Are you seeing someone?'

Sophie wanted to laugh. As if another man was the only possible reason she wouldn't jump at his generous offer. Suddenly he didn't look hot at all, or like a leader among men, or the answer to her prayers, but like a vain lost soul, unable to like himself unless someone else adored him unconditionally.

And it hit her right there next to the avocados that their marriage hadn't failed because Sophie wasn't good enough. It had failed because, as Owen had pointed out several times, Peter was a jerk. The worst part was that it had taken her over twenty-five years of her life to realize it.

'Peter, it was good to see you. Say hello to Lexy. I need to get my shopping done.' She gave him a brief hug and turned away, the first time since their divorce that she'd been the one to end a chance meeting. Every other time she'd stood too long basking in his Peterness, wondering what she could do or say to fix what had happened.

No more.

She finished her shopping and drove home, in better spirits than she'd been in since leaving Vermont that morning.

Her little apartment welcomed her back, looking plain after so much beautiful furniture in Owen's cottage. The sound of I-95 wasn't really like the soughing of the winds in the trees either.

But Southport was home, to her and her family going back generations. It had the ocean, with its smells and breezes, beautiful houses everywhere she looked, a vibrant community, and her condo had a really nice refrigerator and an excellent range. All very good reasons to settle back in.

She texted Lily Anne, her parents and Beezy that she was home safely, thought of texting Owen, then thought better of it. Clean break was best. She needed to shift gears to the reality of filling the currently empty life stretching out ahead of her. After putting away groceries, she made herself lunch, had a short nap, then texted her parents that she was free for the rest of the day, and what time did they want her?

Her mother texted back immediately.

Now! Miss you!

Now. Sophie inhaled, exhaled and decided now was as good a time as any.

See you in fifteen.

Fifteen minutes later, Sophie walked up the driveway to the side door of 14 Willow Street, past the place Lulu used to wait for her to come home from school. In her bag were the gifts she'd bought from Woodstock early in her Vermont month. Deeper in the same bag rested the Fabergé egg. She'd decided to tackle the twin sister situation first, to get the roughage out of the way, and leave the egg for a delicious dessert.

'Knock knock.' She opened the door and stepped inside.

Her father appeared seconds later, grinning like a fool, and swept her into his arms. 'Welcome home, Sophilu.'

Her mother appeared over his shoulder a few seconds later, looking beautifully serene as usual, but beaming, and the hug she gave Sophie was one for the ages.

That was not usual. They must have been worried she'd discover their terrible secret, and were euphoric now that she'd gone and come back without any signs of a freak-out.

Little did they know.

'I come bearing gifts.' She hoisted the packages, following her parents toward the back of the house. 'Is Helen here?'

'Yes, I am.' She was standing in the living room, wearing a blue dress and a wide smile, looking ten times younger and stronger than when Sophie had last been there.

'I have a gift for you too. Nothing big, little Vermont-y things.'

'Thank you.' Helen gave her a hug and a kiss on her cheek. 'That is very sweet of you.'

'Come on into the sun room.' Her mother led the way.

The table was set with a sweating pitcher of iced tea, a bowl of fresh plums and a plate of Sophie's favorite, Linzer sandwich cookies, which usually only appeared at holiday times.

'Tea?' Lilianne was already pouring a glass, adding a sprig of mint before she handed it to her daughter.

'Thank you.' Sophie sat in the familiar room she'd sat in so many hundreds of times with her parents. It felt different today, more as if she were visiting, less like coming home.

Helen accepted a glass of tea from Lilianne and sat on the love seat next to Gilles, who put his arm along its back behind her.

Oh. Right. That. With everything else on her mind, Sophie had forgotten about Dad and Helen's strange chemistry.

She looked at her mother at the same time her mother looked

The Jewel of Cairo

at her. Fighting her instinct to duck away, Sophie widened her eyes in a question. Lilianne narrowed hers and shook her head, the barest of shakes, only once.

Was that *Don't worry, nothing is going on*, or *Don't make a scene, it's all good*?

Either way, Sophie was glad Mom was okay, but Sophie wasn't, and wished Dad would cut it out.

She handed out the Christmas ornament for her parents and the honey and beeswax salve for Helen, plus Darn Tough wool socks and maple and cheese products, realizing she'd overdone it. Three of them in the same house, with three blocks of Cheddar, three boxes of maple candy and three jars of syrup.

'Lovely.' Helen held up the salve. 'My hands are destroyed by Kansas winters around the ranch. I'll enjoy this.'

'Speaking of the ranch, we're going back out there next week to meet Helen's son and his family, and to see her granddaughter, Teresa.' Gilles looked fondly at Helen, who smiled up at him as if they were about to announce it was their honeymoon. Sophie's body tensed.

'Mom's not going?' She couldn't keep the acid out of her tone.

Helen looked surprised. 'Of course she is.'

An uncomfortable silence followed, during which Sophie decided that if they were uncomfortable already, she'd ruin nothing by diving right into her news.

'I want you to know that while I was up in Vermont, I found out that Lily Anne is my twin sister.' She was not at all surprised by the shock and dismay on her parents' faces. Nor was she finished. 'We were both stunned, of course, but we talked to her father a couple of times, and it sounds like Phyllis was behind most of it, though I guess she had her reasons.'

Despite Sophie's most valiant efforts, bitterness crept into her tone. She thought of Owen and the halo he hated wearing but never regretted. 'So obviously I've been through some things. Upset, anger, grief. I feel cheated out of the years I could have spent with my sister. That part of it is still beyond me to understand, but I accept that at the time it felt like what you had to do, and I . . . grudgingly accept, though it's hard to agree, that you felt keeping your promise to Phyllis and not rocking the boat was more important than allowing me to know Lily Anne.

'There's only one thing I want to know that Clyde couldn't tell me.' She looked down into her lap because she was angry again, and it was easier than looking at her miserable father and her stony mother. 'Did you and Mom plan to have children before I showed up?'

Her parents moved abruptly, as if avoiding fists aimed at their faces, which, along with their hesitation, answered the question pretty handily.

'No.' Her mother spoke in a low voice, sounding more defeated and sad than Sophie had ever heard her.

In Sophie's lap, the iced tea shimmered from the trembling in her legs.

No. They hadn't wanted kids. And when they were forced to adopt one, they got undirected, low-achieving Sophie instead of ambitious, strong, practical Lily Anne.

She thought back to Lizzie, whose parents wished she'd died instead of their other daughter.

Lilianne got to her feet, looking grave. 'There's a good reason we weren't planning on kids, Sophie.'

'Lilianne.' Gilles stood and put out his hand as if to stop her. 'Are you sure?'

'Yes.' She drew herself up resolutely. 'There's been too much hiding.'

Gilles looked worried.

Helen looked worried.

Neither of them looked as worried as Sophie.

But she got up, and her worried self followed her mother out the screen door into the damp, heavy air of the backyard, where Sophie and Lulu had spent many childhood hours playing make-believe. 'Let's walk.'

'Where?'

'Aimlessly around our lawn.'

'Okay. But Mom ...' She fell into step beside Lilianne, dreading every word of this conversation. 'Before we do this, what's going on with Dad and Helen? And don't say nothing, because it's really obvious.'

'I won't say nothing. I've been thinking hard about a lot of things while you were gone. We've kept too much from you, Sophie. At first it was because you were too young, but as you got older ... I guess it became a habit. Silence is easier than bringing up difficult topics.' Lilianne stopped to prop up a drooping stem of a peach dahlia. 'That was a mistake, one we've made more than once. We should have treated you more as an adult instead of our child who needed protecting.'

Sophie drank the words in breathlessly, feeling she'd been given a gift as precious as the Fabergé egg. 'Thanks for that.'

'As for the rest.' Her mother straightened briskly. 'I'll be blunt.'

No surprise there. They kept walking, at a slower pace than Lilianne's usual purposeful stride, along the wooden fence that defined their property and provided privacy from neighbors.

'Back in Paris in the mid 1970s, your Dad and Helen fell in love.'

'Dad and *Helen*?' Sophie couldn't believe what she was hearing. When did her parents' Parisian romance happen if not then? 'Not you?'

'No. Helen was engaged to a man she eventually went back to, in Kansas. Your father took it hard. Hard enough that he volunteered for an assignment in Lebanon during their civil war.'

Sophie tried to picture her gentle father, creator of so much beauty, signing up for such destruction and violence. 'I had no idea.'

'You didn't, I know. Gilles called me from Paris a few months later, when I was living in Cairo working for your Grandpa Maxwell's bank. He was in terrible shape. PTSD they call it now. To us it was shell shock, and barely understood. I brought him back to Cairo to help him recover. I had no idea what I was doing, but I had faith, a totally naïve faith, that I could fix everything.'

Sophie pictured her mother's no-nonsense nurturing softening under her father's spell. Now *that* was romantic. 'But it worked.'

'He was never completely the same, but yes, it worked.' Lilianne shooed away a mosquito investigating her hair.

Never completely the same. Sophie's heart contracted. What had her father been like before Lebanon, and how much of his somewhat distant nature stemmed from that trauma? She would have loved to have known about this decades earlier, so she could have understood his detachment better, had more compassion and been able to disentangle his behavior and reactions from their relationship.

'Your dad and I moved back here and eventually married so he could more easily apply for US citizenship.'

'For citizenship?' Sophie stopped walking. 'Not for love?'

'We did and do love each other, sweetie.' Her mom turned with a peaceful smile. 'But not the way he and Helen do.'

Sophie closed her eyes for a long second, trying to process that. Wasn't *anything* in this family the way it appeared? It was so hard to imagine that her powerful, remarkable mother, who'd fought and won countless court battles, risen up the ranks to partner, volunteered in town, cooked delicious meals, kept her house and herself in impeccable shape, was all the while martyring herself to a passionless marriage.

And yet it explained so much of what Sophie had felt growing up. Separate bedrooms, only gentle, brother-sisterly affection between them. And it explained why Dad had come to life with Helen home, perhaps a glimpse of who he'd been so long ago in Paris.

'How did you stand it? Did you have affairs?'

'No.' Her mother spoke brusquely, then busied herself with a rose bush. 'Which leads to why we weren't planning children.'

Sophie waited, watched her mom turning over yellowing leaves on one of the plants, then nearly jumped when Lilianne lifted her head resolutely to meet her daughter's eyes.

'This is hard for me to say, even now. In all my long life, I've only told two people besides doctors and psychiatrists: my mother and Gilles.'

Sophie broke out in a cold sweat, stomach turning acid. She wanted to put her fingers in her ears and run far, far away. This was going to be bad news.

'I'm asexual.' Her mother dropped her eyes. 'I don't have sexual feelings for . . . anyone. I never have.'

Sophie had been so primed to hear about a dreadful, incurable disease that she nearly crumpled from relief. And then . . . from relief to confusion. 'Mom. Wow. That must be . . .'

She didn't have any idea how it must be. She thought of her and Peter. Every room in the house. Even the garage.

'I love your father and he loves me. That's all I needed. But he . . .' Her mother's voice quavered for a split second before she rallied. 'He needs Helen. Those vacations we took together . . .'

Sophie's relief turned to ice. A picture rose of her father and Helen frolicking on a beach, giggling and splashing each other, while her mother sat nearby under a shade umbrella reading Plato.

'My God. Mom.' Tears filled her eyes. She was remembering all those nights Peter had stayed out late, being so sure what he was doing and so full of denial at the same time. That pain . . .

She couldn't imagine anything more horrifying.

'I don't apologize for not telling you about this sooner. It was my business.'

'Of course.'

'Plus it's hard to pick the right time to tell a child her father is in love with someone else, her parents live an alternate lifestyle, and her mother is queer.'

'Mom!' Sophie half laughed. 'You're *not* qu—'

Oh. Yes, she was. This would take getting used to. A lot of getting used to.

They turned at the pear trees espaliered against the side of the garage, Sophie trying to rewind her mother's life and play it again with this new information. 'That must have been awful, especially when you were a kid. No one talked about this stuff back then.'

'No kidding. I was completely alone with this. I knew about gay, I knew about what we then called "cross-dressers". But this, nothing. I assumed I was a mutant. I *am*, I suppose, in a strictly biological sense, but at least I've known for many years now that I'm far from the only one.'

Sophie struggled to connect that vulnerable, suffering child with her image of Lilianne Maxwell, Attorney at Law. 'I'm so sorry. All this time I thought you were perfect, and that your life was perfect.'

'Ha! Not remotely. But my life *is* perfect. For me.'

The Jewel of Cairo

'Even with Helen . . .'

'Yes, Sophie, truly.' Lilianne turned and put a hand on Sophie's shoulder, her blue eyes clear and untroubled. 'I love Helen. She and your father are my best friends. I am happy that they are happy together. Having her in his life again . . . it's wonderful to see.'

Sophie flashed back to Owen talking approvingly about his brother and his ex-wife's happiness. The halo he'd decided to wear was the same one her mother had on, generosity beyond anything Sophie felt capable of. She'd only wanted Peter and Lexy's agonizingly slow deaths. 'I thought my life with Peter was perfect.'

'Huh?' Lilianne turned with an appalled expression. 'Peter stifled you. You were like his little pet dog. I wanted to hit him with my car.'

'Mom!' Sophie cracked up. 'Why didn't you say anything?'

Lilianne's steps slowed further. 'I guess because my mother said everything, and everything she said hurt. When we adopted you, I swore I would let you live your own life, make your own choices. I failed often, given how I was raised, but I did my best.'

'No perfection.'

'No.'

'Except Beezy.'

'Beezy *is* perfect.' Her mother flung up her arms and let them slap down on her thighs. 'Which makes her more of a freak than either of us could ever be.'

Sophie laughed so hard tears came to her eyes. 'Mom. I love you.'

Lilianne beamed. 'I love you too.'

The moment was so huge, Sophie didn't know what to do with it. First time for those words from her mother's lips. She wanted to frisk and gambol around the beautifully landscaped yard.

'And Sophie, I want to make clear what a joy you have been to both of us. Our lives would have been empty without you. I only wish we could have raised Lily Anne here too. I thought about her all the time. That was one of the most difficult things your father and I have ever been through.'

'She'd love to meet you. She's remarkable. You'll really take to her. She's more . . . practical than I am. More organized and—'

'Sophie.' Her mother clamped a hand down on her shoulder, gazing at her earnestly. 'Stop comparing. Stop putting yourself down. You are a remarkable human being, one who made our lives complete. We're both so proud of you.'

Sophie snorted. 'Of what, my failed marriage and my failed career?'

Her mother looked astonished. 'Of you, Sophilu. We're proud as hell of *you*.'

Sophie made it through dinner and dessert without shrieking that she had a Fabergé egg in her bag, partly because dinner and dessert were the best time she'd had with her parents ever. Helen . . . okay, she would have to get used to that. Not Helen herself, but what she represented. Recalculations. Readjustments. What was one more upheaval among a family that excelled at keeping secrets?

As long as there weren't any others, which Lilianne had sworn up and down there weren't. But for the first time at that table, Sophie felt like the fourth grown-up instead of the child. Her parents had both gone through hell, as she had. They were in this stewy mess of the world together.

Dinner was cold poached chicken called *tonnato* in Italian, which sounded much more appetizing than 'with tuna sauce', because who wanted to eat that? It was garlicky and vinegary and umami-fully delicious. Sophie didn't know anyone who made it except Lilianne, out of a recipe in an ancient *New York Times* cookbook that had belonged to her own mother.

Sophie should have made this for the Asphalia residents, just so she could watch their turned-up noses morph into grins of appreciation at the rich flavor. The thought gave her a wistful homesick feeling, which was surprising, since that wasn't her home. Not the way Southport had always been.

Alongside the chicken, a salad of sliced tomatoes, olive oil and fresh basil, and to finish the meal, lemon sherbet with more of the Linzer cookies people had been too tense to eat earlier.

Sophie scooped up her last sweet-tangy spoonful of sherbet and pushed back her chair, brimming with anticipation.

She put her hand into her bag, pulled out the Fabergé egg and set it on the table next to the plate of cookies. 'Look what I found in Sarah's head.'

Best line ever.

Lilianne gasped and put her hands to her mouth.

Gilles looked startled.

Helen peered at the egg. 'How pretty.'

'Where did you get that?' Lilianne looked as if she'd seen a ghost. 'How did that get here?'

'I told you. It was inside Sarah's head.'

Three faces turned to her.

She wanted to giggle. This was fantastic.

'Inside Sarah's *head*?' Lilianne was on her feet now, napkin dangling from her belt buckle, clearly freaked out, which was not a state Lilianne was ever in. '*That* was inside Sarah's *head*?'

'I found it when I straightened her hair.'

'That was weeks ago,' Gilles said. 'Where has it been?'

'With me.' Sophie was prepared for that question. 'I wasn't ready to share it. I am now.'

Which two sentences said more than anyone at the table would ever understand.

'So that's why Sarah's hair went crooked.' Helen leaned in to look more closely. 'Where do you think the egg came from?'

'I know.' Lilianne sat down again. 'It belonged to a man I met in Cairo.'

Sophie's skin prickled. 'You knew Sami Sayed?'

'Yes. There was a gold carriage the egg sat in. The set was one of Sami's prized possessions. He had no family, and was planning the rest of his life around selling it. I have no idea how this could have happened.'

'Wait.' Gilles stiffened and reached out to his wife. 'Remember at the airport when we left Egypt? You were pulled out of the line and searched. Back then, being singled out like that was really unusual.'

'That's right.' Lilianne's hands were at her temples, face tense with concentration. 'I remember the officer was apologetic, but said he'd had some kind of tip. I had no idea what was going on; he never said what they were looking for. Do you think it's connected to this?'

'Could be. But who would have . . .' Gilles shook his head. 'It makes no sense.'

'Good Lord.' Lilianne had gone pale. 'I smuggled a Fabergé egg out of Egypt!'

'But it's . . .' Helen looked doubtful. 'I mean, is it a *real* one?'

'Yes! *Yes!*' Lilianne rose from her chair again. 'It was made, I don't know, sometime before the revolution in Russia. Sami's grandfather commissioned it.'

'I found the description online. The egg is listed as lost, not stolen. There's no mention of the carriage.' Sophie reached out and twisted the falcon, causing the petals to fall open, revealing the king and queen. 'It was an anniversary present from Sami's grandfather to his wife.'

Gasps from Gilles and Helen. Lilianne nodded. She'd seen this before.

'What do we *do* with it?' Helen asked.

Lilianne's face and body reordered themselves into take-charge mode. 'We'll have to . . . We'll contact the . . . I have no idea.'

The four of them stared at the egg as if it could answer all their questions, which it undoubtedly could except for not being able to speak.

Sophie picked it up and passed it to Helen, the first person to touch it, besides her, in half a century.

'It's so beautiful.' Helen cradled the egg carefully, eyes wide behind her lenses. 'Whose do you think it is now? Is Sami still alive?'

'He was killed not long after I left Cairo. He had ties to organized crime and got on the wrong side of Mr Big.' Lilianne looked stricken. 'No one apart from me would have had access to Sarah, except for Connie and Gilles.'

Sophie had thought this through about a hundred times. 'Someone must have broken into your apartment and planted it.'

'Oh my God.' Lilianne put a hand to her throat. 'I think I know who. Just before your father and I left Cairo, Connie told me she'd woken from a nap to find Safiya in our apartment with the carriage. Safiya must have just hidden the egg before Connie caught her. Safiya was Sami's maid, by the way, Sophie. You were named after her.'

'I was?' Sophie put a hand to her chest, loving the idea of being named after a woman of such courage.

'What a story.' Helen handed the Fabergé egg to Gilles with appropriate reverence. 'But if Safiya stole it from her employer, why would she hide it?'

'I'm just guessing here, but ... Sami was horrible to her. Prosecutably horrible. Safiya must have known how much he counted on the sale of the egg to finance the rest of his life.' Lilianne let out uncomfortable laughter. 'Rest in peace, Sami, but my God, if I'm right, she had the most triumphant last word I've ever heard of.'

Helen marveled. 'I hope she got away with it.'

'That we don't know.' Lilianne's expression dimmed. 'But I certainly hope so. She was very lovely and very brave.'

Sophie stared at the egg in her father's hands, thinking of what her namesake had risked. So many hopes and joys and sorrows associated with this precious bit of metal and rock.

'We'll need to do some discreet inquiring. Except I doubt you can keep anything discreet about a Fabergé egg.' Gilles passed the egg to his wife. 'How much do you think it's worth?'

'Many millions,' Lilianne said. 'Many, many.'

Sophie took in a sharp breath. Suddenly the idea of making her discovery public, bringing on the inevitable storm surrounding the Fabergé egg's history and value, felt like a terrible mistake.

'It belongs in a museum,' Helen said.

'Absolutely.' Gilles nodded firmly. 'I'll call my dealer in the morning.'

Defiance rose inside Sophie, urgent and strong. 'I think we should wait.'

Three pairs of eyes looked at her in surprise.

'For what, honey?' Gilles asked.

Sophie got up to take the egg back from her mother, groping for the right words. 'When I first uncovered this, all I could do was fantasize about cashing it in to buy myself the largest house possible. As if money was all I needed to be independent, to finally grow into myself, to feel worthwhile. Of course I never would have taken it, it doesn't belong to me, but that was why I brought the Fabergé egg with me to Vermont instead of letting you know right away what I'd found.

'This last month . . . well, I don't feel that way anymore. So much has changed for me. But I do feel there's something we need to figure out before we let this go, something about why this miracle appeared just now. Maybe it has to do with Safiya, or Connie, or Sami, or with the designer, Alma Pihl . . . I don't know what it is, but I don't want us to end up doing the wrong thing by deciding too quickly.' Sophie shrugged helplessly. 'I can't explain it any better than that.'

She sat back down, bracing herself to hear all the reasons her idea was stupid, based on nothing more than emotion, without taking into account things like insurance and liability and—

'My goodness.' Helen's eyes were misty. 'It's like Connie just entered your body.'

'Yes.' Lilianne was smiling with admiration. 'Okay, daughter of Connie, we can wait. Not long – the egg deserves its place in history. But it's been sitting in Sarah's head for the past fifty years. A little more time won't hurt.'

Sophie had been so primed to be overruled as ridiculous that she nearly fought against her mother's agreement.

Well.

She found herself grinning through the rest of the evening, grinning all the way home. As she walked into her apartment, a text from Beezy.

You back yet from dinner? Great party at the Jacobsons', come on over!

Sophie put the phone down. Kicked off her shoes, got herself a glass of water.

The Jacobsons were a delightful couple with a gorgeous house not far from the harbor; Sophie enjoyed them and their friends. It was only nine o'clock. She didn't have to get up and go anywhere the next day.

Or the next.

Or the next.

She tried to imagine what Owen was doing just then. What Lily Anne was doing. How Lizzie was coping, and Betsy, and Dee, Lori and the rest.

And it hit her that it didn't make any difference if she went to the party tonight or not. It hadn't made a difference to her Southport clients when she left. Beezy missed her, but Beezy's perfect life went on. Lilianne and Gilles missed her, but they had their perfect lives too.

At the Jacobsons' party there would be a lot of alcohol and a lot of food, and people would stand around having the same conversations people in Southport always had. About people and politics, pickleball and portfolios, all their beefs and boats and babies.

Sophie didn't make a difference here. She'd left for one month – she could leave for two or twenty. But in Vermont, during that same short month, for a wonderful institution and several equally wonderful people, Sophie had made a real difference.

She picked up her phone again, but instead of replying to Beezy, she texted her sister.

Found a replacement for me yet? I'm thinking I might need a job.

Three minutes later: *OMG! There is no replacement for you! Come back, come back! Everyone misses you! I'm not kidding.*

Sophie couldn't stop smiling.

She'd miss the hell out of Southport. She'd miss her friends and the ocean, the charm that made the place so easy on the eyes, the luxury that made life here so comfortable. But the town had changed since her childhood, money had become less something people had and didn't talk about and more something they competed to display and gloat over.

Sophie loved the town. It was her home. But it was not where she was needed, therefore no longer where she belonged.

She texted Owen. *I'm thinking of coming back up in a couple of weeks or so. Will your place be available?*

The answer came immediately. *Yup.*

Sophie giggled. Her man of many words. *I'll have details soon. Need to extract from here. Sell my condo, etc.*

Wait, you're moving here?

Thought I might. What do you think?

Good. Very, very good. I forgot to kiss you before you left.

She inhaled sharply, lightning zinging through her system, warming it deliciously. She was crazy about this guy, why hadn't she admitted it to herself?

I forgot to ask you to.

Think I could fix that when you get back?

Sophie laughed in sheer joy, full of purpose, sure of herself and her place – and worth – in the perfect life that lay ahead.

Yeah, Owen. That'd be good.

Follow Connie's story in *The Temptations of Crete* . . .

Tuesday, May 25, 1967

'I'm sorry, I really have to get back to work.' Sean looked down at Connie with genuine regret. They were standing in the spectacularly beautiful and ornate main room of Cairo's Ramses station, where they'd agreed to hand over the gold carriage to Safiya before she caught a morning train back home.

'Of course you do.' Connie put a hand to his cheek; his fair skin was flushed from the heat. 'You've been totally amazing.'

He'd been indispensable. After they'd learned from Safiya of Sami's scheme to plant the miniature carriage on Lilianne, and his equally devious plan to create a necklace from stolen diamonds, Sean had immediately left work to drive Connie to the US Embassy.

Even stone-faced John Baker hadn't been able to hide his excitement at seeing the necklace and the tell-all list of cheated clients, with Abraam Al-Kalib so blatantly incriminated. John had been frustratingly close-mouthed about next steps, but Sean later told Connie he was confident the evidence would be enough for Al-Kalib to be arrested. Before they'd left his office, John had patted Connie on the shoulder and told her she should be very proud of what she'd done.

What *she'd* done? Connie hadn't done anything. Safiya had

been the hero in this story, the one who'd taken all the risks, who'd borne up under Sami's mistreatment until she found a way to win. It was for her sake that Connie hadn't said anything about the carriage now in her bag. That omission would be Connie's shot at Sami for how he'd treated his servant.

Except Safiya hadn't showed for the agreed-on train. Or for the next one.

'I'll see you later.' Connie kissed Sean and smiled into his blue eyes, dismayed to feel herself shut down, though she took care not to react visibly. Sean had been so wonderful while she was here, showing her the sights, offering his home for as long as she liked now that Lilianne's apartment would need to be readied for new tenants.

Nothing had changed, but Connie knew. When that signal came, she always knew. It was over. He wasn't the one who'd last.

'I'll stay for one more train.' She pulled back from his embrace. 'It's just another half-hour.'

Sean glanced around. 'I hate leaving you here by yourself.'

'I'll be fine. Connie Pappas is a tough old broad.'

'Connie Pappas is a sweet young lass.' He kissed her again. 'You be careful.'

'I will be.' She waved cheerfully when he turned back to smile, heart heavy with disappointment. She'd miss him, his upbeat energy, his sexy English accent and his kindness. What more did she want?

She'd know when she found it.

With Sean out of sight, Connie put on her sunglasses and tried to make herself invisible, not her usual groove. That morning, knowing she'd be engaged in subterfuge, she'd pawed through her suitcase for her most conservative outfit, but in brown paisley harem pants and a brown and yellow daisy top, she still stuck out like a sore thumb. The more men commented or asked if she needed help, the more she had to remind herself that all people were beautiful inside, or she'd shriek at them.

The minutes ticked by; her anxiety for Safiya grew. The next train was due to leave in fifteen minutes.

Ten minutes.

Five minutes.

No sign. Had a crisis of conscience made Safiya leave earlier, without the carriage? Or had Sami found her? Or Al-Kalib's thugs?

Connie couldn't bear those thoughts. Evil could not win. Evil could never win.

Another long wait, another Aswan train. Still nothing. Connie could come back tomorrow and wait again, but instinct told her the gesture would be useless.

Safiya wasn't coming.

She moved reluctantly toward the exit, the small weight in her bag banging against her hip. What was she going to do with the carriage? She couldn't keep it.

Sami had told her the piece was designed by a brilliant young Cretan artist his grandfather had discovered, which had made Connie fall even harder for its graceful simplicity, more her style than the flashy egg.

But Safiya had earned rights to the carriage for what she'd endured and what she'd accomplished. Connie laying claim would be simple theft.

There was only one solution. The carriage had been made for the Fabergé egg. They deserved to be reunited. Though Connie couldn't stand the idea of going back to Sami's apartment and making nicey-nice with such a jerk.

How freaky-strange that the carriage ended up in our apartment! How on earth did that go down?

Maybe Sami would claim it had been a joke. *Haha*, they'd have a good laugh, each hating the other for what they knew.

Half an hour later, a mess of adrenaline and anxiety, Connie emerged from a cab several doors down from Sami's shop. The driver had been unable to get closer. Police cars, an ambulance and a crowd blocked the street and sidewalk.

Heart pounding with dread, Connie joined the spectators, casually working her way toward the front.

'What happened?' She spoke English to the woman next to her, hoping she'd understand.

'Him.' She pointed to a shaken young man, whom Connie recognized as Sami's assistant, sitting next to a policeman. 'He came early to work and heard shouting upstairs. Then shots.'

No. Oh no.

'I live next door.' A tear ran down the woman's cheek. 'Shooting here in Zamalek! God have mercy.'

The gilt-inscribed door of the store opened. The crowd shifted in anticipation. A stretcher emerged.

Sami.

Gray skin, eyes closed, a medic administering oxygen. Gasps around her, then murmurs in Arabic. A few people crossed themselves.

Connie forgot to breathe.

The stretcher was loaded into the ambulance. The doors closed. The vehicle pulled slowly away. No siren, no rush to the hospital.

A bad sign.

Connie turned and pushed through the bodies until she could find space, except there didn't seem to be enough air anywhere. No air in all of Cairo, no air in the entire country.

'You okay?'

She looked up at the largest man she'd ever seen. He could

be an offensive lineman for any US football team. Among Egyptians, he was truly terrifying. 'A shock.'

'It's tragic.' He spoke mildly, as if to him this was just another day's murder.

Familiar certainty flooded Connie. She had to get out. Out of Cairo, out of Egypt, away from any association with people who invited such bad karma, who spat on everything right and good about being human.

She walked quickly away, feeling the giant man's eyes on her back like gun sights on a target.

Crete.

Something of vital importance waited for Connie on Crete. She'd known that for years. Something so huge and life-defining it had terrified her, making her delay the trip over and over.

Whatever it was, she'd face it now, taking courage from a beautiful Egyptian woman who had confronted mighty forces all alone, far from her family and friends, and had beaten the bastards at their own game.

Today's events added up to a sign that Connie needed to go, taking the carriage with her. What she'd do with the precious item remained to be seen. Maybe the universe would reunite her with Safiya; maybe Connie would come back to Egypt and find her.

But tomorrow she'd embark on her life's next chapter. Connie Pappas and a precious bit of gold, traveling to the land of their creators and the inevitability of their destiny.

Acknowledgments

Many heartfelt thank-yous to Kashmini Shah and Sherise Hobbs at Headline Publishing for patiently taking over the editing of this book on top of their already heavy workloads. An extra huge thank you to Jane Selley, who has patiently and skillfully smoothed my language and corrected my mistakes.

I am deeply indebted to Kathleen Sutherland and to Michelle Johnson, aka Las Vegas's First Lady of Jazz, for their generous time and willingness to share their rich experiences and impressions of Cairo in the 1970s. Much gratitude also to Sarah Coupe, founder and director of Grace House in Portland, Maine, for taking time from her incredibly busy schedule to answer my questions about running a safe house for women. A smile and a wave to Will Notte at Phoenix Books in Rutland, Vermont, for information on where to buy posters and art in that town. And special thanks are reserved for my lifelong friend Katie 'Monster' Baker for being a huge help in matters of which I had little to no understanding.

As always, mushy thanks to my husband, Mark Stodder, for being a wonderful reader, sounding board, patient listener and occasional shoulder. Special for him in this book is the reference to a car chase on TV – his joke solution for every problem I've complained about in every book I've written since we met. This one's for you, Mark.

The Women of Consequence series will return . . .

Coming soon!

The Fortune's Daughters trilogy

A compelling and enthralling series of family secrets, romance and self-discovery...

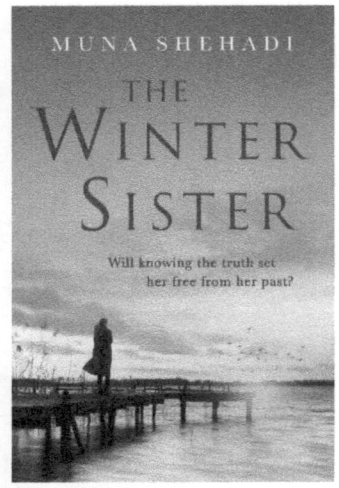
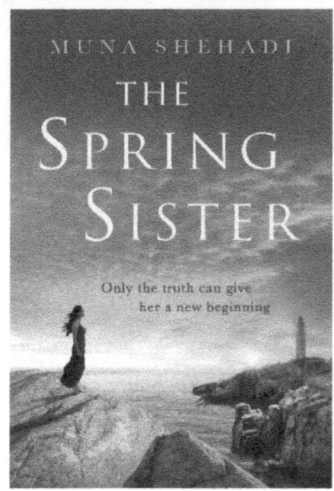

Available now from

At the heart of a great love lies a devastating secret . . .

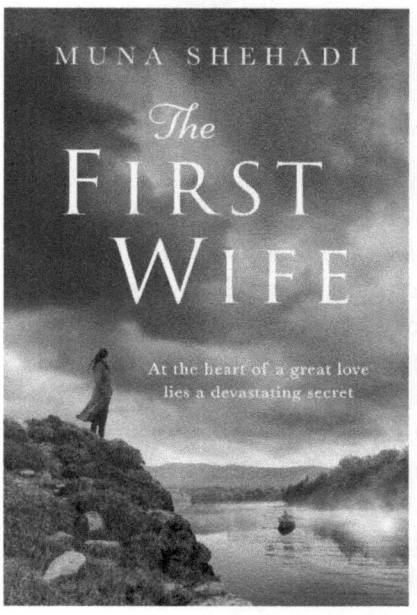

'Clear your schedule and dive into Muna Shehadi's latest triumph, *The First Wife*! Her vivid characters walk right off the page and into your heart . . . I love this book!'

VICKI LEWIS THOMPSON,
New York Times bestselling author

Available now from

RAISING READERS
Books Build Bright Futures

Dear Reader,

We'd love your attention for one more page to tell you about the crisis in children's reading, and what we can all do.

Studies have shown that reading for fun is the **single biggest predictor of a child's future life chances** – more than family circumstance, parents' educational background or income. It improves academic results, mental health, wealth, communication skills, ambition and happiness.[1]

The number of children reading for fun is in rapid decline. Young people have a lot of competition for their time. In 2024, 1 in 10 children and young people in the UK aged 5 to 18 did not own a single book at home.[2]

Hachette works extensively with schools, libraries and literacy charities, but here are some ways we can all raise more readers:

- Reading to children for just 10 minutes a day makes a difference
- Don't give up if children aren't regular readers – there will be books for them!
- Visit bookshops and libraries to get recommendations
- Encourage them to listen to audiobooks
- Support school libraries
- Give books as gifts

There's a lot more information about how to encourage children to read on our website: **www.RaisingReaders.co.uk**

Thank you for reading.

---

[1] OECD, '21st-Century Readers: Developing Literacy Skills in a Digital World', 2021, https://www.oecd.org/en/publications/21st-century-readers_a83d84cb-en.html

[2] National Literacy Trust, 'Book Ownership in 2024', November 2024, https://literacytrust.org.uk/research-services/research-reports/book-ownership-in-2024